BAD INTENT

Other books by Wendy Hornsby

Half a Mind
No Harm

The Maggie MacGowen series:

Telling Lies
Midnight Baby

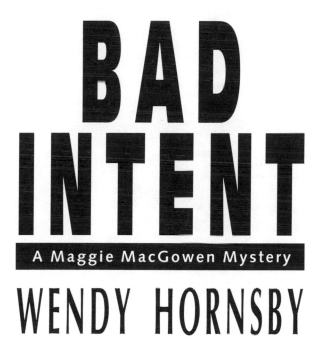

BAD INTENT

A Maggie MacGowen Mystery

WENDY HORNSBY

A DUTTON BOOK

DUTTON
Published by the Penguin Group
Penguin Books USA Inc., 375 Hudson Street,
New York, New York 10014, U.S.A.
Penguin Books Ltd, 27 Wrights Lane,
London W8 5TZ, England
Penguin Books Australia Ltd, Ringwood,
Victoria, Australia
Penguin Books Canada Ltd, 10 Alcorn Avenue,
Toronto, Ontario, Canada M4V 3B2
Penguin Books (N.Z.) Ltd, 182–190 Wairau Road,
Auckland 10, New Zealand

Penguin Books Ltd, Registered Offices:
Harmondsworth, Middlesex, England

First published by Dutton, an imprint of Dutton Signet,
a division of Penguin Books USA Inc.
Distributed in Canada by McClelland & Stewart Inc.

First Printing, August, 1994
10 9 8 7 6 5 4 3 2 1

REGISTERED TRADEMARK—MARCA REGISTRADA

Hornsby, Wendy.
    Bad intent : a Maggie MacGowen mystery / by Wendy Hornsby.
        p.   cm.
    ISBN 0-525-93817-6
    1. MacGowen, Maggie (Fictitious character)—Fiction. 2. Women
motion picture producers and directors—California—Los Angeles—
Fiction. 3. Women detectives—California—Los Angeles—Fiction.
4. Los Angeles (Calif.)—Fiction. I. Title.
PS3558.0689B33 1994
813'.54—dc20   93–42405
                                                                                    CIP

Printed in the United States of America
Set in Century Book
Designed by Leonard Telesca

For Alyson and Christopher Hornsby, fellow oarsmen on the long voyage.

I am indebted to so many people. To begin: Terry Baker, who offers succor and shares room service. Beth Caswell, the Frick to my Frack time and again on the rubber chicken circuit. Jan Burke, for whom there will always be a duck on my bike and Myers at my house (Sedona. Sedona.). And my editor, Jennifer Enderlin, who is both patient and wise. I can't forget Officer Doug Senecal, Metro Division, LAPD, who lent his handsome mug and impressive pecs to the Cause, as well as the ever ready Dragnet. Thank you.

A truth that's told with bad intent
Beats all the lies you can invent.

—William Blake (1757–1827)
"Auguries of Innocence"

CHAPTER

1

It ain't none of my grandbaby's fault. He's a good, Jesus-lovin'
boy. Like I say, it ain't his fault Kenny Jackson got hisself
killed. You ax me, I say it's the lying police should hang they
heads for takin' away the baby daddy, puttin' him in that jail
for his child's whole damn life. What's he suppose' to do?
Fourteen years my grandbaby daddy been in that jail, four-
teen years for something he ain't even done. You lock up an
innocent man that way, who's gonna see to it his boy come up
right? He ain't got no mother. He ain't got no one but me. I tell
you this, for damn sure I ain't got no help from the lying
mothuhfuckin' poh-lice.

Etta Harkness looked directly into the lens of my video camera, but she was playing to the crowd we drew, changing her
answer to my question to please them, to feed their anger; the
signs they carried said things like "No More Police Brutality"
and "Justice for the Brother."

LAPD had the intersection beyond the courthouse cordoned
off so that a few busloads of protestors couldn't get to the
demonstration that was massing in front of Parker Center, the
city's police administration building. Because of my camera,
we drew the frustrated overflow unable to get past the corner.
I didn't know what the issue was, but the mood was easy to
read and, I confess, had me worried about getting away intact.
The weather didn't help—it was over a hundred degrees and
not yet noon.

What Etta was saying was of no use to me, or to my documentary project: the question had been about how her grandson Tyrone, age fifteen, had managed to get himself charged with murder. But I let her run on, kept recording as she slipped into heavily accented ghetto-speak for the crowd, didn't comment when she changed the story, transferred blame from her own broad shoulders to the police, because I wasn't sure what the mob would do if I put my camera down.

Just about the time the light flashed on, warning me my battery charge was low, the police let six or eight news vans through their barricade. The vans parked at the curb in front of the courthouse and began disgorging jeans-clad video crews and fully made-up on-camera talent. Our spectators were drawn away, magnetized by prime-time news possibilities.

When they were gone, I turned off my camera and faced Etta without the lens as intermediary. "What was all that about?" I asked. "What happened to 'the boy's dad was a con and his mother was a junkie'?"

"They was." Etta had the grace to blush, a deep rose that glowed under her mocha-colored makeup. "But the police never helped me none."

"What about Officer Flint? You told me Officer Flint bailed out little Tyrone all the time."

"I didn't mean him." She touched a tissue to her sweaty upper lip. "It was them others."

"Right," I said. If truth is beauty, and beauty is in the eye of the beholder, then I guess that, by extension, truth must also be a matter of personal preference. At any rate, a variable. "You want to go somewhere cool and have a soda before I walk you to the bus stop?"

Etta dabbed at her temples. "I thought I might go on by the police station and see what's happening. I don't get downtown much."

"Suit yourself." I handed her all the change I had in my pocket, for the bus. "I'll be in touch."

Before she walked away toward the line of police in riot gear, she said, "Say hey to Officer Flint for me."

"Sure," I said, but I thought it was about time for me to do more than say hey to the man.

I had turned my life, and my fourteen-year-old daughter Casey's life, upside down to be with Mike Flint. We had agreed, we would spend two and a half years together in L.A. while Mike finished his twenty-five years on the LAPD and pensioned out. I could do that time standing on my head, as long as it meant breakfast every morning with Mike. But Casey and I had been in town for almost a week, and the one person in this city of three million I had not seen much of was Mike Flint.

I walked into the courthouse, stopped at the first pay phone, and dialed Mike's office.

"Homicide Specials." A familiar voice. "Detective Merritt. Can I help you?"

"Depends," I said. "Can you sing all three verses of 'You Are My Sunshine'?"

Merritt laughed. "Hi, Maggie. Let me get Mike."

A pause, then, "Flint here."

"MacGowen here," I said. "What did you do this time?"

"Give me some choices."

"Look out your window. There are a few hundred demonstrators on your lawn. I thought you might be in trouble again."

"No more than usual. Do you have any clothes on?"

"None."

"Damn, I wish I could walk out of this place right now."

"That's why I called. I'm still downtown. Meet me for lunch."

"Sorry." Mike's baritone was deep, cranky. "I'm waiting for a warrant to come down."

"Anything interesting?"

"Could get ugly. The witness I've been looking for? Neighbors saw her at her mother's house this morning. The old lady won't talk to me, but if she doesn't decide to get helpful real soon, I'm gonna take my tire iron, rip the bars off her front door, and ramshack de' place. As soon as I get the warrant."

"Give me an address, I'll bring my cameras."

"Not a chance."

"You okay, big guy?"

"Yeah." He sighed. "I'm just real tired of the way this goes down. No one wants to talk to me. The daughter saw a murder, for chrissake. All I want to do is bring her in, get her statement before the killer gets to her. I explained this to her mother, but do you think she'll help me even if it means saving her own daughter? No way."

"Perspiration is coursing down between my pert breasts," I said. "Forget the old lady."

Finally, he laughed. "Don't tempt me."

"I will if I want to. Come out for an hour. The old lady will wait."

"Sorry, baby," he said. "Listen, I located the people you need to talk to for your film. LaShonda DeBevis works for the L.A. County Library, the Lennox Branch. The last known address for Hanna Rhodes is her grandmother's." He gave me a number on Grape Street in Watts.

"Forget Hanna," I said. "I don't have time to track her down."

"Trust me, she's worth the effort," he said. When Mike is sure about something, he can be very pushy about it. "If you want to talk to people who grew up in the projects, you can't do better than LaShonda and Hanna. Just don't tell anyone where you got the information. I can draw a two-day suspension for unauthorized use of the DMV files."

"Good. Take the two days and we'll go lie on the beach."

"Can't do it."

"I tried," I said, feeling let down. It was no big deal, I told myself. I really didn't have an hour to spare, either. "Don't hurt the old lady when you boot her door."

"Not if she gets out of the way."

I smiled at the image. "You sure talk tough for a guy with dimples."

"I don't have dimples."

"Take a look in a rearview mirror."

He laughed. "I love you," he said.

"Sure," I groused. "Sure."

"Maggie . . ." His voice trailed off, followed by a short thinking silence. "Screw it. Give me ten minutes. I'll meet you by the coffee place down in the civic center mall."

The camera I held was heavy. Ten minutes didn't give me time to put it away in my car. But I said, "I'll be there waiting."

"Hold on. Merritt wants to talk to you."

Merritt came back on the line. "Maggie?"

"What's the word?"

"I think I've got it." He began to sing, "You are my sunshine . . ."

CHAPTER

2

Mike ran in an easy but determined lope. Past the line of speakers on the Parker Center lawn—"It's time, Los Angeles, to demand justice, to demand accountability from those who abuse it"—down a gauntlet of picket signs and then through the cordon of riot-ready police, his marathoner legs pumping, silk tie flapping against his shoulder. People in his path, even the visibly angry ones, made way for him, stepped aside when they saw the big detective shield on his belt, the holstered automatic he held flat to his side. He wasn't even breathing hard, but I was fairly gasping just watching him.

I cannot explain the effect Mike Flint has on me, I only know its power. Way back when my parents still thought they should try to influence my choice of men, they would have warned me off Mike. I wouldn't have listened to them any more than I listen to my friends who warn I should be more cautious.

Mike was certainly nice to watch when he was in motion, a visual I wanted to keep. From my perch above the mall, next to the city's official monstrosity, the Triforium, I taped his progress through the demonstrators.

Mike has a long, slender, runner's body, a craggy Bogart face, and prematurely snow-white hair. I would describe his looks as striking rather than gorgeous, unless we're talking about Mike naked, in which case the latter definitely applies.

Among all the detectives working homicide with the Los Angeles Police Department, Mike has the highest rate of spontaneous criminal confessions. I think the reason the bad guys spill it is because Mike can look and talk like everyone's favorite Uncle Ned. When he wants to.

Mike crossed First Street against the light and headed into the teeming human mass pouring into the underground mall, looking among them for me. I blew a modest ballpark earsplitter to get his attention, kept the camera on him until he came close enough to reach up and cover the lens with his hand.

"You're late," I said as he aimed a damp kiss at my face. "I'd just about given up on you."

"Something came up. Let's get out of this crowd." He took my heavy camera under one arm and me under the other and, still in a hurry, impelled me upstairs against the downstream of foot traffic; the usual early lunch hour crush was made heavier by demonstrators seeking relief from the relentless, pounding heat.

Without breaking stride, we went straight into the relative quiet of the Children's Museum, through the gift shop and into a side exhibit area, stopped finally in front of a tall tinted window that overlooked the street and Parker Center below. Next to us there was a six-foot robot made entirely of plastic Lego blocks. Its recorded voice repeated at twenty-second intervals, "I contain eighty thousand Legos. You can build me at home."

I took Mike's arm and watched him watch the demonstration. I recognized some of the speakers, the incumbent district attorney candidate and a ghetto preacher with political ambitions of his own among assorted movers and shakers.

"What's it all about?" I asked.

"Bullshit variation on the usual. D.A.'s pulled up an old case, wants to ride it into the hearts and minds of the voters. Let's just hope he doesn't start another riot."

Two grubby-faced tots stepped on my toes so they could get up close to Mike.

"Is that a real gun, mister?" piped a little towhead about five years old with a big-eyed stare. "Are you going to rob us?"

"No." Mike drew back in mock offense. "I'm a cop."

"No you're not, big fibber. Real cops wear a cop suit."

"This is my cop suit. See the badge?"

I had to turn my head to cover my laughter. I didn't want to embarrass the kid. His friend did the honors for me. He punched the towhead and whispered loud enough for the entire room to hear, "He's a grandpa cop. That's a grandpa cop suit. Ask him if he hits people."

"Only when I have to," Mike said, laughing.

An adult, properly chagrined, came and fetched her charges. "Sorry," she said to Mike, and scooped the boys away, scolding them about speaking to strangers.

I leaned against Mike's hard shoulder. "Grandpa cop suit? I need to buy you a new tie, cupcake."

"Don't bother. I have all the ties I need to get me through the next two years and five months."

Outside, a line of black and white cars with lights flashing drove up onto the Parker Center lawn and scattered the crowd that surged toward the building's glass entrance. People ran like ants under a garden hose. I could see they were yelling and screaming, but I couldn't hear anything except the happy little voices inside the museum. I was glad we were in out of the noise this time, away from the forward, panic-driven rush.

"Tell me about this old case," I said. "Seems to have struck a chord. You boys get caught beating someone again?"

"Not even close." Mike gave me his narrow, tough-guy gaze. "Just doing our job, putting a bad guy in jail. Anyway, it doesn't matter what we did or didn't do. The people want bread and circuses, and the D.A. is delivering. It's as simple as that."

I said, "Uh huh."

I must have sounded more skeptical than supportive, because Mike sighed from some deep and angry place. He turned away from me to check the growing fracas outside. Mike, always so assertive, so know-it-all, seemed uncharacteristically burdened.

"Tell me the truth," I said. "It's not simple this time, is it?"

"No." He tried to smile, but couldn't make it stick. "Boss came to talk to me—that's why I was so late getting out of the office. Looks like it might be my turn to take a shot."

"What did you do?" The words came out okay, though my chest felt too tight to breathe. Mike had told me enough war stories about the good old days on the force that I had some idea what the range of possibilities for getting in trouble was, and knowing that didn't make me feel any better. I gripped his hand, felt him grip back. "Mike?"

"I told you," he said. "We were just doing our job: a clean collar, a good conviction. One more con off the street."

"There's more to it than that or the D.A. wouldn't be making an issue of it. Tell me about the case."

"I don't remember all the details—first murder I worked when I made detective. Off-duty cop got shot during a routine robbery. We made a clean collar, got a good conviction. The D.A. can say anything he wants to about it, but he can't change the facts."

"When was this?"

"Michael was still in preschool." He frowned while he calculated. "Fourteen, fifteen years ago."

"Police usually turn it on to find a cop killer," I said. "So, what happened? You go overboard?"

"It was nothing like that. Wyatt Johnson wasn't killed because he was a cop. He was killed because he was in the wrong place at the wrong time."

"That makes a difference?"

"Big difference. It was a routine street crime, and that's how we handled it."

The question I didn't ask was how they handled routine street crime fifteen years ago. I had heard plenty of stories about brawls and wild chases and had seen the old scars on Mike's body. I knew fists and flashlight blows came under standard operating procedure in the days before the rhetoric of kinder and gentler was enforced. I could see Mike was worried. The big question I asked was, "What can happen to you?"

"Nothing. The statute's run out on anything actionable. All they can do is give some grief to everyone who worked the case. Won't hurt anyone, but who needs it?" He looked down at me. "They can't take my pension. Anything else? Who gives a fuck?"

"Indeed," I said.

"Indeed," he mocked. His pager beeped. "I have to get back. See you at home around five."

"You'll be home?" I asked. "Should we be baking a cake with a file in it?"

He backed up. "No. Jesus. I told you twice—it's a piece-of-shit case. By tomorrow it will be a nonissue again."

Between waves of kids, we were alone for a moment,

me, Mike, and the Lego robot. I took advantage of the pause in chaos to put my arms around Mike. I said, "I'm worried."

"Trust me, baby." He kissed the back of my neck. "It's not a big deal."

"I trust you, Mike. About as far as I can throw you."

CHAPTER

3

*It ain't none of my grandbaby's fault. He's a good, Jesus-lovin'
boy. Like I say, it ain't his fault Kenny Jackson got hisself
killed.*

"Meet Miz Etta Harkness," I said. "Age forty-five, grandmother of one, great-grandmother of two."

"She gives good sound bite, Maggie." Ralph Faust, from the
Los Angeles bureau of Satellite Network News, reached over
and shut off my video player. We were in my newly rented office, the remains of lunch bagged and stashed under an end table. "Pathos, bathos, and a bleeped obscenity to hook the
viewers as we segue into a commercial. I'll give you a thousand
for that half-minute of videotape."

I thought about the offer, low-ball, but within the standard
range. Money wasn't the issue here. As an independent filmmaker, I share film goodies all the time, now and then for no
payment other than lunch or a favor I might want to redeem
later. I hesitated because Ralph Faust was a shark and I had to
think about the possibilities.

I let him wait without an answer while I sliced through the
sealing tape on one of the cartons the movers had left in the
middle of my office floor. Then I let him wait some more while
I transferred the junk in the carton into the drawers of my
rented desk.

The desk was a good, big, well-scarred wooden thing. I liked
it very much, and wouldn't have minded claiming it as my own.

But, under the circumstances, renting seemed like a good idea. I wasn't at all sure Los Angeles and I were going to take to each other. The rented status of the desk bothered Mike. He had said, "Make the leap, Maggie. If nothing else, you can commit enough to buy a desk."

If the desk was going to be an issue, I was glad it had some character, a history even. No one at the furniture rental agency had bothered to clean it out before sending it over, so it came with a full supply of someone else's dead pens and a two-year-old appointment calendar.

Under the calendar I had found a folder of snapshots, pictures of a bunch of old guys at a Sigma Pi fraternity reunion picnic. They looked to be working hard at having fun, their expensive my-wife-bought-me-this sports togs stretched over fully ripened, middle-aged beer guts. Pretty cute, actually. I was especially fond of the moon picture, half-a-dozen round, naked white asses on display for the cameraman. One of the old boys held a card above his peachlike butt with "Moon Pi's" written on it in bold letters. I thought I might use the picture for my Christmas cards.

"So, Maggie." Ralph's grin was stretched thin. "We have a deal?"

"Why do you want Etta?" I asked.

"I'm covering the Police Commission hearings and what I have is too flat. I think Miz Etta would give my coverage some power."

"Etta wasn't at the Commission hearings."

"What she says pertains. You know, cops and the ghetto."

"Uh huh," I said, watching him closely. "It's a big stretch, though. Muddies the line between straight news and manufactured stories. Doesn't that bother you?"

"Not at all."

"How did you know I had the tape?"

"One of my stringers was covering the demonstration downtown this morning. He saw you outside the courthouse, heard some of the interview. He told me it was good. He was right. So, you selling?"

"Sure." I dropped the empty carton onto the pile of empty cartons behind me. "Except, Casey's orthodontia bill is past due. Etta will cost you fifteen hundred."

He nodded. "Sold."

The tooth-sucking smugness that crossed Ralph's face just then told me that he had been prepared to pay something more for Miz Etta Harkness on the courthouse steps, told me that maybe he had neglected to tell me something significant. I was bothered a hell of a lot more about missing the point than I was in missing out on a few more dollars.

As I said, Ralph was a shark. I should have been sharper. But I had things other than Etta on my mind.

I turned on the computer and loaded the standard release form off my hard drive, made a few changes to give Ralph nonexclusive, one-shot broadcast rights, typed in the dollar figure, set the printer for two copies, and ran it.

"Just one restriction," I said, groping in the desk drawer for a pen that worked. "I'm not finished with Etta yet. I'll be real cranky if you edit my tape to make her look less than dignified. I don't want her to quit talking to me."

"Trust me." Ralph glanced at the release I handed him and signed it. "What's your project?"

"A documentary on growing up in the federal housing projects. Bullshit variation on my usual," I said. "Any time the subject is mothers and kids, I seem to get the job. I'm doing this one for commercial TV—the next anniversary of the L.A. riots comes during sweeps week—so the money is good for a change. But honest to God, Ralph, I'd give it up in a heartbeat for a filthy hard news story."

"That's the MacGowen I know." He laughed malevolently. "The rest of us are real glad you've gone independent, Maggie. You made it tough on the competition."

"Liar."

"I miss you in the trenches."

"I didn't say I wasn't in the trenches, Ralph. Just different trenches from you network types."

He passed me the signed release. "Give me some background on Etta."

"I only met her last night. This is all I know: She took over raising her grandson when her daughter O.D.'ed. The kid was ten when she got him. By then, he was already in a gang and running on the streets. Now he's fifteen. This morning he was arraigned for murder. It's a family tradition. His daddy had a hearing this morning, too—a parole hearing on a murder conviction. Poor Etta couldn't be in both places."

"Poor Etta, indeed. San Luis Obispo is a good four-hour drive from L.A."

I was ready to sign the release until he said that. I put down the pen. "How'd you know his dad was in San Luis?"

"You told me."

"No, I didn't."

He shrugged, smiled his shark smile. "My stringer must have mentioned it."

I would have argued, but among the dead pens in the top drawer, right there beside the orthodontist's bill, was the second notice for payment of Casey's tuition. So, okay, maybe it was partly a money thing. I signed the release, crammed my copy into the drawer, and pushed Ralph's copy toward him.

He broke the silence that had settled over the room with a smooth conversational gambit: "Your project sounds like an interesting one."

I took a couple of deep breaths. "Anything else I can do for you, Ralph?"

"Not professionally."

When I stood, my standard dismissal gambit, he rose too, unfolding six and a half feet of worn-out skeleton. He was a skinny, aging preppie, his expensive clothes rumpled as if he were forever stuck in rebellion against a too-strict mother. Going about life looking like an unmade bed was perhaps the most endearing quality about Ralph.

"Can I buy you a drink?" he asked, ejecting his thirty seconds of Etta from the machine and slipping it under his arm. "Want to swap some lies about the old days in prime-time news?"

"Another time. I'm trying to get out of here early. You see the unpacked piles around this office? You should see what Casey and I have to deal with at home."

"You girls are going to like L.A., Maggie."

"Maybe it has to grow on you," I said. I looked out the window, across the dense-packed freeway and toward the hills beyond.

We were in day four of the September Santa Anas, hot, wild winds that blast down through the canyons north of the city. According to the bank across the street, the air temp outside was one hundred and two, again, and the humidity a crackling zero percent. The winds had died down somewhat, enough to let in a puke-yellow layer of smog. I was not enchanted by any of what I saw.

I got up and walked Ralph to the door. I made my cheek available for the obligatory air kiss. This was L.A., after all, and I was trying to fit in. But he grabbed my shoulder in a quick, just-us-jocks squeeze instead.

"Maggie," he said, grinning again. "A little advice. For anything to grow on you, you have to stand still and let it take root."

"I'll remember that."

Ralph's a big shit, but he's far from stupid. I opened the door and listened to him walk away down the linoleum-covered passageway. I was tired of Ralph, but his leaving left me feeling oddly alone.

I made some calls. My second-string shooter, a free-lance cameraman named Thieu, had some scheduling conflicts so I had to set new appointments with a Catholic Social Services counselor for Thursday and a county case worker for Friday to accommodate him. I called Central Juvenile Hall to make sure that everything had been approved for me to come in on Wednesday to talk with Tyrone Harkness.

Finding LaShonda DeBevis was my next priority. I wanted to interview LaShonda DeBevis on tape because she would give symmetry to my documentary. Like Tyrone, she had been raised in the Jordan Downs projects. What made her different was that she had finished school and gotten out. A rare success story.

Mike had told me LaShonda was a librarian in Lennox, a neighborhood down by the L.A. airport. I got the library's number from information and placed the call.

"LaShonda transferred out," I was told. "She's gone up to the Hacienda Heights branch."

I asked for the number there, and called Hacienda Heights. After some telephone tag, I got to the head librarian, Chuck Kaufmann.

"Sorry to keep you waiting," Kaufmann said, talking fast. "We're in the middle of a remodel. It's pretty chaotic. Anyway, Miss DeBevis isn't here."

"When will she be in?"

"Can't answer that. When her paperwork came down Friday, it was a surprise to me. With these budget cuts, I was told I had to lay off some staff. Out of nowhere, here was a transfer with less seniority than any of my people. I called downtown and raised some Cain. They backed off and somehow in the fuss they decided to release the funds for the carpet I requested three years ago. That's what all the noise is you hear. I want to get the new rug nailed down before someone in the head shed changes his mind."

"So, where is Miss DeBevis?" I asked.

"All I know is my carpet is blue," he said. "But try Valencia."

I gave him my number in case he heard from LaShonda, then I tried Valencia. No LaShonda DeBevis. I didn't have time to call county personnel and go through their procedures. I looked at my schedule and decided I could squeeze in a trip down to Lennox to talk to her former co-workers within the next few days.

There are a lot of Hanna Rhodes stories in the ghetto—drugs, teen pregnancy, prison time—but Mike knew her and insisted she was worth some effort to find. The number he had given me for her grandmother was no longer in service and there was no new listing in the city. I put her name aside. If I had time at the end of the week, I would get back to the search.

There were a lot of other details I could have tended to, but I needed to get out, move around a little.

I gathered up some unedited tapes and a ream of notes, stuck a reminder on the door for the custodian *not* to clean my office—I would clean, if I wanted clean, myself—and locked my new deadbolt.

There is nothing quite like stepping from an air-conditioned building out into the full force of a true Santa Ana condition. At first there is an instant of chill as every bit of moisture on your body suddenly evaporates. Then comes a wave of heat like a solid white light that envelops you, blinds you, pours into your lungs, and steals your breath. By the time I had crossed fifty feet of shimmering asphalt and made it to my car, I felt thoroughly desiccated. Like bleached bones in the desert.

The free-lancers from the offices across the hall from mine were off in a corner of the lot filming face shots for a political spot; the elections were six weeks away. I recognized the incumbent district attorney, Baron Marovich, scowling his God-am-I-earnest scowl for the camera. He had made it from the brouhaha downtown unscathed, his perfect graying hair unmolested. He didn't seem to perspire.

I knew the city was in for a nasty campaign siege when I saw who his campaign manager was, a rotund little gnome watching the filming from the driveway. In the world of political whores, Roddy O'Leary was a high-dollar, big-breasted, all-night-whips-and-chains fuck. He had a genius for creating Willie Horton-like nightmares for the opposition, fingering with amazing accuracy exactly what scared the shit out of the largest number of registered voters, and playing on it.

It seemed to me impossible that Roddy O'Leary could have been spawned by woman. More likely, he was the residue left when the air of some smoke-filled room cleared.

O'Leary was watching his candidate with exquisite concentration. I rolled up alongside him, letting my front fender all but kiss his ass. He turned around in shocked surprise and recognized me before he could let off his usual stream of expletives. He backed up and leaned in my window. Sweat poured down his red face, plastered his short-sleeved shirt to his round belly.

"Move it, O'Leary," I said. "You're blocking the driveway."

He laughed too hard, showing a lot of tobacco-stained teeth. "What brings you to town, MacGee?"

"The name's MacGowen," I said. "I'm not sure what I'm doing here. I thought I came down to work, but I'm beginning to think that somewhere along the way I must have sold my soul to the devil, because it feels like I'm in hell."

"It's hot," he confirmed, wiping his face. "But like Truman said . . ."

"It was good advice," I said. "Problem is, there's no way to get out of this kitchen."

He laughed some more. I said, "How come you're stooping to a district attorney race? Last I heard, you were humping for a big-time governor somewhere in the East."

His smile grew hard at the edges. "In my game, you're only as good as your last campaign. You can't always pick a winner."

"Excuse me." I cupped my hand behind my ear. "Did you say can't always *pimp* a winner?"

He threw back his head and laughed until his cheeks glowed from tears as well as sweat. Trust me, I'm not that funny. When he was finished, he snuffled and snorted and caught his breath.

"God, I've missed ya, MacGee."

"MacGowen," I repeated. "And I've been around. You just have to know where to look. I saw your candidate making a jackass of himself in front of Parker Center this morning. What was that all about?"

"Case of police harassment, wrongful imprisonment. It's a good issue."

"May be a good issue, but do you have a good case?"

"Does it matter?" Roddy belched a little puff of whiskey-laden air. In politics, his kind was going the way of the dinosaur, pushed out by Bright Young Men, and now and then, by women. I wondered how desperate he might be for this win, how many campaigns he might have in his future if he lost another one.

"Better be careful, Roddy," I said, nudging his elbow out of my open window. "Tug on Superman's cape, you'll find out if it matters."

CHAPTER

4

November 6, 1979. Los Angeles (UPI).

Police Officer Wyatt Johnson, age 25, was shot and killed by a thug just after midnight this morning in a Southeast Los Angeles gas station.

Authorities said the off-duty officer, a four-year veteran with the department, was shot five or six times in the head and chest in the station's restroom.

A witness told authorities that Johnson, who was not in uniform at the time, made a telephone call just before going into the restroom. Moments later, shots were heard and one or two gunmen quickly ran from the station, disappearing into the darkness. Johnson's wallet was not missing and authorities say they have no motive for the killing.

That was very nearly all the papers had to say about the killing that was at the center of Mike's new problems. For all the fuss it had stirred, I confess I was disappointed it had been such a low-wattage caper.

I scanned the microfilm and found one follow-up story printed two days later recapping the first story, adding more details about the six wounds Officer Johnson had received, some family background, funeral arrangements, and a reward offer of five thousand dollars from the L.A. County Professional Peace Officers Association for the arrest and conviction of the killer or killers. The police had no leads. The obituary appeared on the third day after the death, listing his wife, Beth, one child, Wyatt, Jr., his mother, and a sister as survivors. And that was all.

I went through the *Times* microfilm index again, searching through the end of 1979, all of 1980 and 1981. I found no arrest reported, no summation of the trial or announcement of the verdict. Not a single further listing for the dead cop. Nothing.

I had looked up Johnson only because I am nosy and because I was in the microfilm files anyway. My original goal had been finding background information on the father of Etta's grandson, a convicted murderer named Charles Conklin. It would have been nice if point A, the killing that had set a particular course for the child's life, had been a recognizable case, something for the viewer to hang his time perspective to, as in, the day Kennedy was shot, where were you? I knew the date he was sentenced, February 1982, but there had been no news stories about Conklin, either. Because I didn't have Kennedy, or anything even close, I would have to provide the narrative framework myself.

I was in the Encino branch of the county library, alone except for a few old men reading newspapers or dozing by the front windows. The quiet made me feel sleepy.

I went out to the circulation desk to buy a roll of quarters and went back to my microfilm reader and ran copies of the Johnson items. Then I blew the rest of the change on background stories for my project: the Three Mile Island nuclear disaster, American hostages seized in Iran, Soviet invasion of Afghanistan, double-digit inflation.

Globally, the late seventies had been one disaster after another. As always. Locally, there was a comforting consistency: Bradley was mayor, Gates was police chief, Baron Marovich was running for office.

Because I had seen Marovich twice already that very day, I turned back to the November 6, 1979, Metro section story about developments in the primary for city attorney. Marovich had been the third man in the race, the play maker. His opponents were charging him with improper fund-raising and condemning him for turning a traditionally gentlemanly political exercise into a vile brawl.

Plus ça change my French grandfather would have said: the more things change, the more they stay the same.

Marovich's current campaign had been tagged by the morn-

ing paper as a record-breaker in character assassination. His
opponent challenged his financial disclosure statements. Same
old stuff. Marovich even looked about the same now as he had
in the old news photo accompanying the 1979 story, except
that his helmet of hair had grown gray and a few new lines
marked the corners of his eyes.

I made some notes on the margins of the slick photocopies
and filed them away in my bag. I returned the spools of microfilm, stopped for a drink of water, and went back out into the
heat.

I was at least two weeks behind on my filming schedule, and
with the workload I faced, I knew I was going to fall back another week or two before I finished. I needed help. My knight,
as far as work goes, is Guido Patrini, associate professor of
film, UCLA.

It was just past three o'clock when I finally found Guido on
campus—in a computer lab, begging time from a techno-nerd
who had a plastic pocket protector pinned to his tee shirt.

"You're early," Guido said to me.

"I was supposed to be here yesterday," I said.

"So." He pointed an accusing finger at me. "You did remember."

I sighed and Guido put his arm around me. It felt so good to
have someone hold me up that I let my head rest on his bony
shoulder. Guido is about my height, maybe five-seven, a spare
frame of a man strung together with sinew. Even his curly
black hair seems to have muscle. I think he may be my best
friend in the world.

"I'm sorry," I said. "I'm feeling overwhelmed."

"Not working out with Mike?" I heard some eagerness in his
tone.

"We're fine, Guido. There is just too much going on in my
life right now to keep track of everything."

"Bet he's a handful."

"So are you. Show me what you have."

We shambled arm in arm across the quiet, shady campus
back to his trailer behind the fine arts building where special
film projects had been relegated after the last earthquake.

As he opened the trailer door, he said, "It's a good thing you
didn't come yesterday, because I didn't have anything for you

except a lame excuse. I recut Mrs. Ruiz this morning, dumped all that footage from the visitor room at the jail. I like it now."

The trailer was cool inside. The fall quarter had not yet begun so the usual mass of puppy-eager film students Guido normally has *en train* were blessedly absent. It was nice to have Guido all to myself for a change.

I took a bottle of mineral water from the film refrigerator and sat down next to him on a saggy reject of a sofa. He punched a TV monitor remote and Serafina Ruiz's profile filled the screen: broad nose, high cheekbones, straight black hair pulled into a ponytail.

"He is a good boy," she was saying, tears filling her dark eyes before she looked down at the beads in her hand.

Guido had pulled the camera back for a two-shot to include my filmed reaction in the frame. Visually, the scene was good. Behind us the windows of the Lincoln Heights jail, just out of focus, were a fuzzy, pale checkerboard of barricaded windows. It was good neutral, angular contrast to Mrs. Ruiz's round contours, my blue shirt.

Below camera I held the sheaf of booking slips she had given me to look over, a collection that chronicled her son's activities from the time he was twelve. She kept the booking slips in a kitchen drawer with her market coupons.

"Mrs. Ruiz," I said, "when did your son Arnulfo join the Eighteenth Street gang set?"

"He don't belong to no gang. I made Arnulfo promise me he would stay away from those boys. Gangbangers killed his brother."

I fast-forwarded through the tape, all the stuff about how Arnulfo the altar boy had just refound Jesus and turned his life around and was planning to go back to school. The kid was holy all right. A holy terror. I heard the same story of impending redemption from every delinquent's mother I talked to.

Close in on the booking slips, my voice reading through them chronologically:

"Age twelve, arrested for curfew violation, out after ten P.M. unsupervised. Malicious mischief, vandalizing public property. Auto theft—joy riding. Possession of a concealed weapon—a knife. Minor in possession of a firearm. Age thirteen, truancy, assault, armed robbery."

I turned off the tape.

"What?" Guido sat up. "You don't like it? I think it plays tight."

"Yeah. It's tight. It's great." I pulled my knees up under my chin and looked at the blank screen as if it might hold some answers to questions that eluded me. It hurt even to think what I was thinking.

"I know how you feel." Guido put his hot hand on my knee and looked soulfully into my face. "It is awesome, Maggie. Deep. You've made a beautiful, sympathetic portrait of this woman. My God, what she has lived through will make every heart bleed."

I put my hand over his. "If that's what you're getting, then I've lied to you."

"Lied?"

"Lied. I have tried, Guido, really tried, but I can't find a lot of sympathy for Serafina Ruiz. She has one kid in jail, another one's dead. Her thirteen-year-old daughter is pregnant for the second time. Her youngest is a paraplegic because he ran into the street and got hit by a car—at eleven o'clock at night. Tell me what a toddler was doing out, unsupervised, so late."

"Hard times," Guido said, black eyes narrowed at me, warning me there was a correctitude barrier I was about to cross. "Serafina shoulders a heavy load all by herself. It's a rough neighborhood. Give her credit; she does her best."

"Really?" I said, challenging him. "Serafina can't take care of what she already has, but she's pregnant again. I think her kids should sue her."

"Maggie?" He was aghast. "Are you in there? Have aliens taken over your mind? Have they done something evil to my hero?"

"I feel taken over. I have listened to so many horror stories." I got up to pace around the cluttered trailer, tripping over cords and equipment, miscellaneous battered, black-painted stuff. It was all so familiar, my work milieu. The sort of place that had helped me create the big video lie.

I stopped in front of Guido and narrowed my eyes in imitation of him. "Guido, my friend, I offer you a profundity, a cliché: There is nothing easier than bringing a child into the world, and nothing more difficult than raising it well. Trust me. I have one child, and it's all I can do to keep her safe, keep her on the straight and narrow, because that straight and narrow line is as treacherous and as slender as the edge of a razor. Every day we get through safely I say a little thank you to the fates. And believe me, if it weren't for all my efforts, and Mike's, and ballet giving her structure and direction and keeping her occupied, I know we would be in one hell of a mess."

"You think Serafina should have had one child, like you? Should have had nice middle-class parents and a white-bread education, like you?"

"I think Serafina should have figured out what turned her kids into thieves and murderers, and fixed it. She sheds good tears, Guido. And she breaks my heart. But it takes a hell of a lot more than tears to take care of her children and herself. We are not powerless."

"I see," he said.

"Do you?"

"Yeah. I see that my old friend needs some time off. The last two, three years you've been working too hard, Mag. Why don't you put this one aside for a while? Take a break, give yourself a couple of months to settle in, get your perspective tuned up. You're beginning to sound like that cop you're living with."

"I'm on deadline, Guido. No film, no check. No check, no groceries."

"So?" He looked at me, exasperation giving his olive cheeks color. "Now what?"

"Define the fine line." I found my bag on the floor and took out Etta's tape, traded it for Serafina's in the player, and sat down on the edge of the sofa beside Guido.

"It is my perception," I said, "that in postapocalypse Los Angeles, gangs are used as a symbol for everything that has gone to shit. Let's be careful not to hang the gang rap on their mothers. We'll tone down Serafina—she is so passive—get more from Etta Harkness and women like her. You'll see why when you meet Etta."

"*Good Housekeeping* mother of the year, huh?"

"No. Just one ballsy lady. You'll like her."

CHAPTER
5

The freeway was a shimmering, blazing hot nightmare. The heat seemed to have endowed everyone on the freeway with a hair trigger and, worst of all, my car air conditioner was out. I hadn't had it serviced for three years.

In Northern California where I live—rather, used to live—fluorocarbon coolants are sufficiently environmentally incorrect to make using air-conditioning on the rare hot day a matter for public scorn. Truth is, I never remembered to get the damn thing fixed.

I drove up the 405 and over the Sepulveda Pass into the Valley in bumper-to-bumper spurts of speed and fast stops. A trip that should have taken no more than fifteen minutes stretched well beyond an hour. I hadn't yet learned how to gear my life's schedules around rush hour, the way the natives do; everyone who doesn't have to be on the road hides out until the worst is over.

By the time I pulled in under the branches of the eucalyptus sheltering Mike's condo complex, I was desperate for quiet, a cool bath, a place to lay my head.

Mike had bought the condo with wife number two, Charlene, the decorator. She had turned it into something worthy of a magazine layout before the reality of being a cop's wife got to her. The carpet was dull silver gray and there were only two bedrooms to accommodate four of us.

Though the condo was on the good side, the south side, of

Ventura Boulevard, it wasn't far enough on the good side to be up in the hills where there might be a consistent ocean breeze, some view. There were other reasons I didn't like living there, beyond location, smog, and dull gray carpet. I'm not a jealous person by nature, but I felt there was entirely too much of Charlene in that condo.

Our newly combined households had three cars but only a two-car garage. I was last one in for the day, so I had to go find a slot in guest parking and hike back through the landscaping. I didn't mind, because once I had parked I was more or less home. Santa Ana wind whipping through the trees was nice, the pool filter gurgled pleasantly. I could count the steps until I was inside, count off the seconds before I was running a tub and washing the outside world away.

Already feeling better, I opened the front door. A blast of noise as wild as the heat outside hit me full face. Headbanger music cranked up on the living room CD, an electric drill somewhere, and Bowser, our dog, all competed for air space. For a second I couldn't decide whether to go in or not. In the end, I steeled myself and walked out of the frying pan and into the fray.

The music was so loud I could feel the bass through the soles of my Reeboks and the treble in my fillings. Michael, Mike's college-freshman son, sat sprawled on the living room floor surrounded by his new textbooks and a litter of schedules and course syllabi he was organizing into notebooks. When he looked up at me the smile he gave was absolutely beatific he seemed so happy.

"How was the first day?" I screamed.

"Hot," he yelled back. "Effin' hot."

"Got all your classes?"

"All but one. Had to petition it."

He was on a new threshold and eager to leap through. I loved his enthusiasm as much as I hated his music. I fairly itched to smash the CD with my heavy bag, but I gave Michael the best smile I could muster—he was someone else's son— covered my ears with both hands, and fled toward the far reaches of the condo.

I found no relief when I opened the door into the long hall that runs between the bedrooms. The dog was shut away behind a bedroom door, howling to cover the noise of the drill in Mike the Elder's hand. I nearly tripped over the drill cord.

Mike and my daughter, Casey, were affixing an eight-foot-long hardwood ballet exercise barre to the hall wall. I believe Casey was supposed to be holding up her end of the barre so Mike could see where to drill holes into the wall studs for the heavy support bolts. But Casey was using the barre as she held it, stretching out one spidery-long ballerina leg, then the other. Mike, with a pencil in his mouth, was trying to yell something at her that she couldn't hear over the combined din of CD, drill, and dog. Maybe that was safer—for him, she was someone else's child.

On my way past, I gave her rock-hard rump a sharp tap.

"Hi, Ma," she shouted. "Don't you love this?"

"Are you helping?" I asked.

Casey looked over at Mike, saw the grimace he tried to transmogrify into a smile, and straightened right up. "Sorry," she said, chagrined, and planted both skinny feet on the floor again so she could hold the barre firmly on its marks.

Mike had full hands, barre in one, drill in the other. My captive, at last. I had to mess with him because there was nothing he could do about it. I gave his rump some attention, too—more like the squeeze test I give melons at the market than the tap I had given Casey. Mike rolled his eyes to let me know he liked it. I pressed up behind him and kissed the soft, short hairs at the back of his neck until he broke out in goose bumps. He turned off the drill, lost the pencil between his teeth, and gave me his face to kiss. I obliged.

"Hi, baby. Almost finished here," he said, turning the drill back on. I gave him another pat and went to tend to Bowser before his anguish did some real damage to the far side of the bedroom door.

I opened the door slowly to keep Bowser from bounding out and getting involved with the drill or romping through Michael's books. He let me know he was happy to see me, but Old Bowse weighs over fifty pounds and he made it difficult to get in through the door. When I managed to squeeze into the room, in his glee, he nearly knocked me over.

I thought his eyes still looked a little glassy from the tranquilizers he had taken for his flight down from San Francisco the day before, but his energy had returned sufficiently for him to have thoroughly trashed the room. Shoes, clothes, pillows, freshly laundered bath towels covered the floor. Maybe he didn't like the gray carpet, either.

Seeing me made him stop barking. In appreciation, I got down on the floor and let him nuzzle me, rolled him over and rubbed the long fur on his belly. He smelled like the Giorgio bubble bath I had left beside the tub. I didn't want to go into the adjoining bathroom to confirm what I suspected.

Suddenly, the drilling stopped. Mike shouted something and, miraculously, the music disappeared, too. It took a moment for the last reverberations to ripple through the air before blessed silence was restored. But it came.

Bowser growled once, looked around as if he had lost something, then he sighed big time for both of us. He hardly looked up when Mike and Casey came into the room.

"All finished?" I asked.

"All finished," Mike said.

"It's perfect, Mike." Casey made a slow pirouette. "Thanks."

"No problem. Just stop growing, will you? I don't want to have to raise the sucker."

"I wish," she said. At five-eleven, she was only three inches shorter than Mike. "Can we take it with us when we move?"

Mike groaned.

Bowser got up, routed through the rubble on the floor until he found his leash, which he dragged over to Casey.

"Want a walk, old man?" she asked him. "Want to go see if that little schnauzer is down by the pool?"

Walk was the dog's operative word. Bowser danced around Casey until she managed to hook the leash to his collar. They left the room in a flurry of expectant yelps and slobbery glee and long-legged *jetés*.

Mike closed the door behind them.

"What a day," he said, lying down on the floor beside me. "You look pale."

"I feel a little pale. It's the heat."

"You're just worn out," he said. "Moving is a lot of work."

I yawned. "Thanks for introducing me to Etta. I made a little extra pocket change off her interview. I sold a piece of it to Satellite Network News."

"You gave Etta a split, of course."

"That's not the way it works, Mike. I own all rights to Etta's video image."

"Doesn't seem fair."

"If I gave her any money she'd have to report it, then the Department of Social Services would screw around with her welfare benefits for months. I'll find another way to compensate her. Okay?"

"See that you do." He had a wry grin. "Etta and I go back a long way. Did you talk to LaShonda and Hanna?"

"I haven't a clue where to find Hanna, and LaShonda is lost somewhere in the county library system."

"But you're pursuing them?"

"Uh huh." I yawned. "Still have your job?"

"For another two years."

"I saw Marovich's campaign manager this afternoon. He says this case is a good *issue*. What is it exactly the D.A. says you did?"

"Says we coerced some witnesses to identify a murderer, tainted the conviction."

"Did you do it? Little rubber hose action on the witnesses?"

"The witnesses were ten- or eleven-year-old kids. And I told you this morning, it was a good case."

"That's what you said." I yawned again.

"Better put you to bed early tonight."

"Good. A bath. Food. To bed." I rolled over on my side and stroked his cheek. "But what if I have other things in mind than sleeping?"

"You usually do."

It was just getting interesting there on the floor when the telephone rang, the beige one, the separate line Mike keeps for calls from Parker Center. Nine times out of ten, when that phone rings Mike has to put on his tie and go off to work. I hate that phone.

When the ringing started, Mike tried not to react too quickly, and I didn't let him go. We were at home, finally. Alone, finally. Whatever it was could wait, I was sure.

By the third ring I had lost him—I could feel him growing more tense—so I rolled away, grabbed the phone, and passed it to him. He had the grace to mutter, "Damn," before he accepted the call.

The call was just one more aggravation at the end of an altogether annoying day. I wanted a long walk on the beach until I figured that would mean another hour on the freeway. So, I went in to start the tub.

Bowser had trashed the bathroom, too. I left the rubble to be cleaned up later, except for wadding up great lengths of toilet paper streamers because they tangled underfoot.

I turned on the water, scooped up a handful of spilled bubble bath from the floor, and dumped it under the running tap. Just about the time the bubbles crested the top of the tub, Mike came in, looking grim. As he stood there watching me undress, his expression only grew blacker.

"Do you have to go in?" I asked.

"No."

"What's up?"

"I retire in two years and five months."

"Really?" I said. "You haven't reminded me for three minutes."

He slouched against the doorjamb, taut muscles working along his jaw as he pulled off his sweaty polo shirt.

"Who was on the phone?" I asked.

"The lieutenant. He had some questions."

I straightened up and faced him. "How much trouble are you in, Mike?"

"None. It's just a big pain in the butt."

"So?"

"So, I don't want to go through it." He kicked off his sneakers as he fumbled with his belt. "In the wrong circumstances, two years and five months can be one hell of a long time."

"Uh huh. What are you thinking?"

He had his jeans down around his knees, but he stopped to look at me. A long, hard look. When he reached for my hands, his gray eyes were dark with some powerful feelings I couldn't read.

"I'll tell you what I'm thinking," he said, at last. "I've had it. If I retire right now, I can draw almost half of my pension. By Christmas, we could be living in the woods a thousand miles from the city."

"Dream on."

"I'm serious."

"Then go ahead and quit. But first tell me how you're going to pay Michael's tuition at Occidental for the next four years on a partial pension. Don't forget to add rent for him, because he won't be able to live at home with you if home is a thousand miles away."

"You mean, live with *us.*"

"No. I'll still be here, chauffeuring Casey to performing arts school and working. You're the only one retiring. I don't have a pension to retire on."

"You sound mad."

"I'm getting there," I said. The bubble bath suddenly looked ridiculous. "If you are serious, then you should have had this revelation before last week. We made a deal, you and me. Two years and five months in L.A., then we talk about going back to civilization. Tell me about pain in the butt: I jumped through hoops to get work down here, find office space, rent out my house, enroll Casey in a new school, move all our shit. We haven't even found our way to the closest dry cleaner yet, so you damn well better not start talking about bugging out for another two fucking years and five months."

"Whoa," he said. "Sorry."

"Exactly. Whoa." I was steaming by the time I got to that point, but he had the beginnings of a smile for some reason.

"Now what?" I demanded.

"Did you know your nipples get hard when you're mad?"

"Did you know your dick gets hard when I'm mad?"

He looked down at the front of his boxer shorts, at the single eye peeking out through the fly. I reached into the fly, brought out that spying eye and kissed it.

"Either get into the tub," I said, gently squeezing, "or lie down here on the floor. But do it right now."

Mike threw back his head and laughed. "I thought you were tired."

"Which will it be?" I stroked him.

"The tub." He took me by the hand. "We just have time for a quick scrub-a-dub, though. My father's coming over to meet you."

CHAPTER

6

"You two get yourselves married yet?" Oscar Flint, Mike's dad, winked at me over the top of his beer bottle, his first drink since he'd arrived, but certainly not his first of the day. "Or you just shackin' up?"

"Give it a rest, Pop," Mike said.

"We're just shackin' up, Oscar." I was standing in front of the open refrigerator. I handed Mike a head of lettuce and a big, ripe tomato. "Anyone ready for another beer?"

"Not yet." Oscar persisted: "I don't know what's holdin' you two back. Hell, Mike's already talcon the long walk two times. He knows it don't hurt none."

"We don't want to talk about it, Pop." Mike was supposed to be making a green salad. He began chopping lettuce into tiny little bits with a very large knife. Wisely, Oscar moved toward the far side of the kitchen counter.

Oscar was a sturdy block of a man, not nearly as tall as Mike and Michael—they're both six-two. He had heavy, square, working-man's hands. His face was deeply lined, a road map of hard living and power drinking. He still had a full head of kinky red hair. I couldn't see much of him in Mike except for a certain cast to his posture and the furrow between his eyebrows. And a few rough edges; sometimes rough edges give you something to hold on to.

I held my breath while I turned the chicken under the

broiler. Then I picked up the bag of fresh corn on the cob and carried it over next to Oscar. He didn't offer to help shuck it.

"It's wonderful to meet you at last, Oscar," I said, stripping an ear. "Mike has told me a lot about you."

"I just bet he has," Oscar chuckled. "We did okay, though, didn't we Mikey? He tell you I had me a little body and fender shop over in Glendale?"

"It was a chop shop," Mike said. "He was always getting raided by the DMV."

"Worked a lot of hours," Oscar went on, "but we scraped by, the two of us. 'Course, with all the government regulation nowadays, you can't hardly support a family with a small business like that. Deduct this, insure that, pay out to Social Security and unemployment and all that crap for your employees, pretty soon you got nothin' left to buy groceries with. It don't pay to run a business no more. Had to close the place down."

"Pop, you never made a Social Security payment in your life." Mike looked up at me from his lettuce pile. "He used to hire illegals, Maggie, and always paid them in cash so there were no books."

"I don't apologize for it," Oscar said, cocksure. "Them Mexes was real good workers. Learned fast, put in a full day's work. You can't find hard workers like that no more. Everyone nowadays wants a free ride."

Mike chuckled. "Nothing stays the same."

"Now that's the truth." Oscar emphasized the point by putting down his empty beer bottle with a clunk. He looked over at me. "What line of work's your folks in, honey?"

"My father teaches physics at UC Berkeley," I said. "My mother was a concert pianist until her arthritis became too bothersome. Now she directs a musical conservatory in the Bay Area."

"Well, la-di-da." Oscar raised a pinkie and waved it at Mike. "Last wife's a looker, this one's a brain. At least, when you two get around to having kids, they'll be musical."

Mike glanced up. "We aren't married and we're not having any kids."

"Mikey's mom played the piano, too." Oscar rattled on as if he hadn't heard Mike. "He ever tell you? Big lounge out on Pico. Nice place, pretty good money, too. She did that till she lost her figure after the third kid. Then she went to slinging burgers at a drive-in down in Montebello. Almost in East L.A. What a dump. Biker hangout. That's where she met the asshole she run away with. Moved her and Mikey's sisters up to Merced. Guess she's still there."

"She died three years ago, Pop. Remember? We went up for the funeral."

"Oh, yeah." Oscar deepened the furrow between his eyebrows and thought it over. Seeming confused, he looked up at Mike. "Got another beer in that icebox, Mikey?"

"Sorry, Pop," Mike said. "We're all out."

There were two six-packs behind the watermelon.

Mike seemed to be embarrassed by his father or something his father had said. That surprised me, because I thought I knew him better. With me, Mike had always been open about his hardscrabble upbringing, the scrapes his alcoholic parents got into, a few narrow misses with the law of his own. I wondered what nerve Oscar had touched.

All of us carry wounds from childhood that neither time nor accomplishment can heal. Now and then those old wounds get hit just right and they start to bleed, no matter how hard we try to keep them covered up. As I watched Oscar standing there, weaving a little in the middle of Mike's shiny kitchen, I began to wonder if maybe he had brought with him the scary specter of the kid who used to bail his dad out of the drunk tank every Monday morning, the kid who signed his own report cards when he didn't know where to find his mother.

I have made it a point to forget everything I learned in Dr. Hauser's Modern European philosophy. But what came to mind out of somewhere was Nietzsche: "That which doesn't kill us makes us stronger." Fine. But we can be strong and still hurt like hell.

I picked cornsilk from my fingers and went over to my tall, white-haired Mike. He was lost in thought, reducing the fat tomato to runny pulp. I touched his hand above the knife and he looked over at me, expectant, waiting for a question.

I stretched up and whispered into his ear. "I love you, Mike."

He smiled, oddly shy. I guessed because Oscar was there. Maybe not.

"How'd I get so lucky?" he said. He looked down at the pulverized tomatoes. "We're making tacos, right?"

"Broiled chicken and salad."

He laughed then, and started to say something I'm sure would have been pithy. But, like so many epiphanal moments in my life, the telephone interrupted. Mike wiped his hands and reached for it. "Flint," he said into the receiver, and then, "No shit," a couple of times. As he hung up, he was reaching for the small television that sits on the counter next to the sink.

"What is it?" I asked.

"That was Merritt. Says to turn on the news."

The Parker Center demonstration was headline news—rocks and bottles thrown, a case of heat prostration—but "in-depth analysis" of the issue behind the fuss was promised after the weather report. We were waiting for the anchor to get to it when Casey and Michael burst in from the ice cream store, optimists in that miserable weather, carrying an insulated bag that was already leaking.

"Hi, Pop," Michael said, clapping his grandfather on the shoulder in passing as he dashed to the freezer. "How's it going?"

"Just fine, son. Just fine," Oscar grinned. "Who's your tall friend?"

It was Casey's turn to blush.

"Oscar," I said, "this is my daughter, Casey."

Oscar made a show of looking all the way from her toes to the top of her head. "Your daddy play basketball?"

"No," Casey sighed. "He's a litigator. And the weather up here is hot."

Borderline smart-alecky, I thought, but I didn't say anything.

On the screen, the weatherman predicted hundred-degree weather through the week.

"Come on, Casey," Michael said, taking her elbow and leading her toward the living room. "Let's dub those CD's. If you're going to ride the bus, you'll need lots of tapes for your Walkman."

"Pretty cute couple," Oscar said when the kids were gone.

Mike said, "Ssh," and leaned toward the television.

A background roll showed the front of the county Criminal Courts building downtown L.A. Howard Mansell, a veteran local-news reporter, read from notes ruffled by the hot wind. "In an extraordinary, perhaps unprecedented move, the Los Angeles County district attorney's office has joined with defense attorneys representing a convicted murderer in asking the Superior Court not only to free a man the D.A. worked to convict a number of years ago, but also in asking the judge to wipe his conviction from the records.

"Fourteen years ago, Charles Pinkerton Conklin was convicted of first-degree murder and sentenced to life in prison for shooting a police officer inside a Southeast Los Angeles service station restroom. The preponderance of evidence was supplied by two juvenile eyewitnesses who testified they saw Conklin at the murder scene. In affidavits presented to the district attorney by Reverend Leroy Burgess, those eyewitnesses now say that undue and unrelenting pressure from the investigating detectives frightened them sufficiently to cause them to lie when they identified Charles Conklin.

"The district attorney stopped short of pronouncing Conklin innocent of the crime, saying instead that the actions of the police so tainted the trial that the verdict must be set aside. A hearing has been set for Monday, one week from today.

"The police department's only comment has been to say that they are conducting their own inquiries."

I turned to Mike, furious. "You lied to me."

"I did not." Mike was watching Oscar get his own beer from the refrigerator, apparently more worried about another beer than about defending himself. "It's political bullshit. Cops make good targets."

"I know who Conklin is," I said. "Mike, you set me up with Etta."

"Yeah. So?"

"You just plain set me up."

"It isn't that way."

On screen, Mansell went to comments from friends and family of the imprisoned man. Mike reached to turn off the television, but I stopped him when I saw a too-familiar face filling the screen. I yanked up the volume, the better to hear my own fifteen-hundred-dollar piece of tape roll. The copy wasn't very good, washed Etta's mocha makeup with a reddish cast. But then, Ralph had run copies in a hurry, probably on the cheap.

Mike watched Etta on the screen, horrified.

"You ax me," Etta was saying, looking into the lens I had

held that morning, "I say it's the lying police should hang they heads for takin' away the baby daddy, puttin' him in that jail for his child's whole damn life. What's he suppose' to do? . . . Fourteen years for somethin' he ain't even done. You lock up an innocent man that way, who's gonna see to it his boy come up right?"

CHAPTER

7

Let me just clear up one misconception here, I'm not a priest or an ordained minister of any kind. I never said I was. Sure, I wear a clerical collar. That collar opens a lot of doors for me that wouldn't normally open for a private detective.

I'm not a flimflam man. Leroy Burgess is not getting rich off the misfortunes of others. My organization, Pastoral Crusade, is completely nonprofit.

The show was taped, but my rage was live. Leroy Burgess, the man in the backward collar I had seen at the demonstration. A beefy, balding, dock-worker type, he had created the issue that was eating a hole through my midsection, had put in motion forces that were beginning to make me think I was a jerk for persuading myself I could find domestic bliss with a maverick like Mike Flint. I had never met Leroy Burgess, but I was nursing an unhealthy hatred for the man.

Leroy Burgess sat in the middle of a too-blue Satellite Network News set surrounded by district attorney Baron Marovich, my old pal Ralph Faust, and a gorgeous, pin-stripe-suited young woman I had never seen before. I thought it looked like an unholy sort of alliance, and leaned forward from my seat in the middle of the bed to hear every word without turning up the volume.

I wanted to be able to hear what was happening in the rest of the house. Someone was washing dishes in the kitchen, MTV was on the living room TV. I was being left alone to cool off, but it wasn't working. Because of Leroy Burgess.

Burgess dominated the slot:

Every year Pastoral Crusade gets hundreds of requests for help from men in prison who say they are innocent. Most of their cases have no merit. Now and then we find one that does, like Charles Conklin. We won't even look into a case unless every avenue of appeal has been exhausted and there is no one else who can help.

Take Charles Conklin. Here's a poor, barely literate individual, with no resources, no connections whatsoever. How is he going to get the ear of the courts? When Charles wrote to me, I did some checking. From the beginning I saw that the conviction was seriously flawed.

I gave in and turned up the volume. I needed to know about the beginning.

We dug into the case record. We found conflicting testimony, a tainted confession, the word of a jailhouse snitch who got conjugal visitation rights in payment. We went back into the neighborhood and found the witnesses who had testified against Mr. Conklin at his original trial. Every one of them told us that they were pressured, threatened, and even bribed by the detectives assigned to the case, Detectives Mike Flint and Jerry Kelsey.

That's when we took the files over to D.A. Marovich. I fully expected to be thrown out of his office. But I should have had more faith that our Lord, who loves justice, would be in our corner. Mr. Marovich listened to us, understood the implications of our findings right away. He has such confidence that the original investigation was tainted that he persuaded one of the city's big-dollar law firms to represent Charles Conklin on a pro bono *basis. Without charging a retainer, Jennifer Miller will lead the appeal team.* Here Burgess leered at the young woman sitting erect beside him.

I picked up the telephone and dialed Ralph's direct number at SNN.

"Faust," he said.

"I'm going to sue your ass, Ralph," I said, seething.

"Maggie!" He seemed pleased. "You're watching the broadcast. I'm flattered."

"You're fucked. I'm going to drag up every despicable shard

I have on you and sell it to *Hard Copy* and the *Enquirer.*
'Scumbag reporter sodomizes chickens in the jungles of El Sal-
vador while colleague lies wounded at his feet.' I have film,
Ralph. You know I do."

"Calm down, Maggie." Ralph seemed to find my anger funny.
"Jesus Christ."

"I sold you single broadcast rights to that piece of tape and
you sold it all over town."

"So? What's the big deal?"

"The big deal is, you lied to me about why you wanted Etta
Harkness."

"What, you never lied to a colleague?" Ralph laughed, a
smug bark. "You're an old industry pro, Maggie. You know I
would never give away a breaking story."

"Who tipped you about Etta's relationship to Charles
Conklin?"

"I have sources, just like you have sources. I don't give them
away, either. You're acting like a baby, Maggie. What's the big
deal?"

"I expected a higher professional standard from you."

"Professional standard? Look who's talking. For you this
whole thing is personal. Personal in the person of Detective
Mike Flint. I've heard about what the affidavits in the D.A.'s office say about your boy's interrogation techniques, kiddo.
Makes me think you have unplumbed potential. I just wish
you'd told me a long time ago that you like it rough. We missed
out on a whole lot of fun, you and me."

I had to take a couple of deep breaths before I could say
anything. In that small space of time, my mind cleared considerably.

Ralph kept talking. "You should know better than to sleep
with your story, Maggie. It's your objectivity that gets fucked."

"Keep in mind, Ralph," I said with new calm, "you breached
my copyright when you resold the tape. Now, your ass, your
firstborn, the deed to the miserable hovel you call home are
mine to broker. My attorneys will call you."

I slammed down the receiver and turned off the television. I
hadn't seen Mike standing at the far side of the bed.

"Feel better?" he asked. Without the television, the room
was dark. All I could see of him was his starchy white shirt and
the dark line of his tie.

"I'm all right," I said. Actually, I did feel better. So much better to scream at Ralph than at Mike. "Where's your father?"

"Michael drove him home. Dad likes you."

"I don't know why. Sorry I abandoned you with the dishes. I didn't want everyone to hear what I had to say to Ralph and I couldn't wait any longer." I sat up, decided I might as well go on living. Mike started to turn away. I reached for him, hooked my fingers inside his belt to hold him.

"Talk to me," I said.

"I didn't lie to you. I told you in the beginning that I put Tyrone's papa in the slam."

"When were you going to tell me Tyrone's papa was Charles Conklin?"

He smiled, the beginnings of a teasing smile. "I have to let you find out some things all by yourself. Besides, when I introduced you to Etta, Charles Conklin was still nothing but LAPD prisoner number 1475533-C. Who knew Star Search would come looking for him?"

"Tell me how you came to set me up with Etta."

"Etta," he repeated. "You were asking me about the projects, about the kids who grow up there, right? I thought of Etta right off because she had just called me. The D.A.'s investigator and this Burgess guy came around her place asking questions about Conklin, what she remembered about the old case. She thought it had to do with Conklin's parole hearing, but all they wanted her to talk about was me. She called me, thought I should know about it. I told you, me and Etta go way back. I used to help her out now and then."

"Tell me exactly how you helped her out." Etta and Mike were about the same age. She was not unattractive and I was sure that in ordinary circumstances she was a lot of fun.

"I told you Etta's daughter was a junkie," he said. "When I was still working Southeast, my partner and I were all the time picking up the girl for dealing and solicitation. Every time she was arrested one of us would always go to her house, fetch Tyrone, and take him over to Etta's, make sure she had enough for extra groceries until her daughter made bail. No big deal. A couple of times, when the little snot got bigger, Etta asked us to come straighten him out. You know, put a little healthy fear into him. That's all."

"Etta told me, and I quote, 'for damn sure I got no help from the lyin' mothuhfuckin' poh-lice.' If you helped her, why would she say that?"

"Because she was upset and she didn't have anyone else to blame. We take shit like that all the time. She didn't mean me."

"That's what she said. Was your partner Jerry Kelsey?"

He frowned, shook his head. "I only worked that one case with Kelsey. By choice."

"Why?"

"Because he was a boozer."

If I were a suspect and Mike was grilling me, I would cave, confess anything to him. He always seemed to know everything. I sighed, relaxed a little. "I'm sorry," I said.

"Sorry for what?"

"For helping them. Now you've been identified by name it can get very uncomfortable. All I can do is say I'm sorry I played into their hands in any way. But it's your own damn fault for trying to end-run me."

"Did it ever occur to you that there are just some things you don't need to know?"

"Never."

Mike took the telephone off the bed and set it on the night stand, fussed with the cord, straightened the lamp shade. Changed the subject. "Do you really have film?"

"Of Ralph and the chickens? Sure. He was just fooling around, but the pictures look bad."

"Hang on to them." He bent down to kiss my cheek, a good-bye sort of kiss. "We might need them."

"Where are you going?" I asked.

"The lieutenant wants to go over some things with me. The department is putting out its own reinvestigation of the case, looking to see if we did anything wrong the first time." His voice was even, but his hands were clenched into tight fists. I knew he was angry. Offended. "Police commission's all hot, calling for my midnight-blue blood. I tell you this, if I get offered up for the sacrifice, I'm taking out more than a few with me. I've been with the city long enough to know how this game is played."

"Ralph called me a baby," I said, still hanging on to his belt. "Ralph was right. I should have cooled off before I phoned him."

Mike pried my hand away. "I have to go."

"Count to ten, Mike." I turned on the bedside light and got up to my knees on the bed to be more on a level with him. "Stay here a little while longer. Count to ten a few more times."

"I can't. It won't hurt to have an edge when I talk to certain people. I'll call you."

I listened to him walk away, his footsteps muffled by the dull gray carpet. He wasn't going to tell me anything he didn't have to. That's the way he is. I hate being kept in the dark. That's the way I am, and the reason I've done okay in my work. There was no way I wasn't going to go snoop around, not when I had resources, Etta prime among them. When I heard the back door close, I got up, found my shoes, and went down the hall.

Casey and Michael were in the living room with MTV blaring. They were an attractive pair, Casey on the floor with her long auburn hair swaying as she did her stretches, Michael on the couch with a biology book open in front of him. It occurred to me that if Mike had gone out the front way he would have had to stop and speak with them. Maybe seeing them would have put things back into perspective a bit, settled him down in the way they always ground me.

Michael is a more handsome version of Mike, just as Mike is better looking than Oscar. A refinement by generations. Michael's Italian mother gave him thick, dark hair that he wore shoulder length, to the chagrin of his traditional father. When Michael pierced his left earlobe, Mike stopped mentioning the length of his hair.

My bag was on the end table where I had dropped it. I picked it up and fished for my keys. "I have to go out for a few hours. Will you two lock up? Casey, you need to be up by seven for school orientation tomorrow. What time are you going to bed?"

"Ten, I guess." She stretched backward so far that she was looking at me upside down. "Who's driving me?"

"I am," I said. "I'm staying for the parents' meeting. Maybe we can find someone you'll be able to carpool with. I'm really leery about sending you so far on the bus."

"I'll be okay." Like a swan, she rolled her torso up straight again. "Jeez, Mom, I've been taking buses since I was a kid. You let me take the BART to Berkeley all by myself before I was ten."

"Sure," I said. "I put you on the train at one end and your grandfather was waiting for you at the other end with a stop watch in one hand and a telephone in the other. This is different. For one thing, this is Los Angeles, not San Francisco. For another, a city bus ride is hardly the same as a BART trip or a Saturday movie outing with a bunch friends. You'll be going all the way to Pasadena and back every day. You may have to transfer. The afternoons you have body conditioning, it will be dark before you get home. I don't like the bus, Casey."

She gave me a very wise, teenagery eye roll. "Like, you're going to drive back and forth to Pasadena twice a day? I'm sure."

"I miss Lyle," I said, feeling overwhelmed.

"Me, too. But where would we put him?"

"Good question." I did miss Lyle. He had been our neighbor until the big earthquake a few years back leveled his house. We had taken him in because it seemed the sensible thing to do until he could rebuild. But Lyle had stuck. I don't know exactly how it had happened; it just seemed so natural. He became indispensable, the housewife who took care of the domestic details like meals and carpools in exchange for a room and our utter devotion. Lyle was still in our house, watching over the tenants. I wondered whether he might reconsider moving to Southern California.

I went over and kissed the top of Casey's head. Without much confidence, I said, "We'll work it out. Don't stay up too late."

On my way past Michael I gave his shoulder a pat that felt awkward to me.

"Maggie?" Michael caught my hand. When he closed his book and set it aside, I sat down on the arm of the sofa next to him. "I can help out. Casey's school is just down the freeway from mine. Most of my classes are in the morning, but I'll be spending a lot of time in the library. I won't mind staying around late to pick her up."

"Thank you," I said. "In other circumstances I would give you the speech about how this is the best time of your life and you should take advantage of your new freedom, be your own gatekeeper. As it is, I appreciate the offer. Sometime this week we'll sit down and try to work out a schedule we can all live with."

"No problem." He smiled his father's wry smile. "I'm looking forward to it. I've never had a sister to torture before."

Casey turned to him. "Sister? Since when?"

"You may be as close as I ever get. Have to make the most of it."

I could see she was flattered by the attention, though she tried to cover her pleasure with an air of disdain.

"I already have a brother," she said. "A half-brother. He isn't potty trained, either."

I left them happily swapping insults.

When Mike and I decided to move in together, I ran through dozens of possible scenarios for the way Casey and Michael would get along. The range began with Bambi meets Thumper and ended with Godzilla meets King Kong, the colorized version. We were less than a week into this experiment and everyone was still on company behavior. Once the rigors of our daily routines had worn the veneer away, I knew things would change. Could be for better, or for worse. In the meantime there was peace, for which I was grateful.

The night air was soft and warm, scented with dry eucalyptus and freshly watered lawn. It was oddly quiet, only the mechanical hum of air conditioners, the pool filter, traffic on Ventura Boulevard in the distance for company. All the neighbors seemed to have shut themselves up inside, staying cool.

Below the moonless sky, the lighted pool looked like a beautiful shimmering blue window. There would be no one to see me, I thought, if I just dove through the glassy surface of the water and swam myself to utter exhaustion. I was sorely tempted.

Instead, I got back into my car and drove down to the big Ralph's market on the boulevard. I bought a coconut cake and a six-pack of Dr. Pepper. I figured that a drop-in guest at Etta's who came bearing dessert was more likely to be let inside than a mere intruder. If Etta Harkness had a telephone, this entire excursion would have been unnecessary.

I had to talk to Etta. In the first place, she needed to be warned that there could be a media melee coming to her doorstep. In the second, I had to know what she knew about Mike and Charles Conklin, because Mike wouldn't tell me any more than he had to.

When a wife finds out about a mistress, she has an overwhelming need to go take a look at the bitch. That's how I felt. Mike was keeping secrets, and I needed to go feel the bedsheets, check for wet spots.

I had the freeway system more or less figured out. To get to Southeast L.A. from Encino, I took the Ventura to the Hollywood to the Harbor. Traffic was light, nothing to it. Until I exited at Century Boulevard and left the lights of the freeway behind. As I looked around at the crowded scene, Mike's cautioning voice was in my ear—I had no business being there, alone.

I was in the riot zone. Pick your riot. Both 1965 and 1992 had left a legacy of boarded-up, burned-out shells of buildings. For Sale, For Rent, Available Now signs were overgrown with weeds and covered with graffiti. The battered survivors were liquor stores, check cashers, walk-up bar-b-ques. Barred doors. No such thing as a display window. Gang tags on everything that stood still for even a moment. Down side streets I saw whole blocks laid bare and abandoned.

I was fascinated to see it at night. And I was frightened about being there alone. I could not move anonymously through this scene, could not easily just slip away. When I glanced at my face in my rearview mirror, what I saw were my blue eyes, as obvious and bright against the dark as the blue swimming pool had been. I felt like the ten ring on a target.

Century Boulevard runs directly beneath the final approach for jets landing at the Los Angeles airport. The big planes, only a thousand feet overhead, couldn't drown out the street mix of busted mufflers and motorcycles in first gear, boom boxes, people in a confrontational mode.

Making the jog from Century down Central to 103rd Street, I got caught at a long signal. As half a dozen kids surged into the street to panhandle among the cars, I pushed the automatic door locks, made sure all windows were up, knocked my bag off the seat into the dark space under the dashboard. A scrawny little guy, maybe all of twelve, with a massive overbite, started smearing my windshield with a grubby rag while he held out his other hand to me.

"Fifty cen'," he demanded through the closed window. What he lacked in height he made up for in hostility.

Cars front and back wedged me in. I looked away from the

kid, watched for the opposing traffic light to turn yellow because forward was my only way away from him.

"Fifty cen', bitch." He pounded my window with his fist. "I wash your window. Pay up."

The light turned green and I started to move with the car in front, but the kid held on to the door, still demanding money from me. He scared me. Halfway through the intersection I found a slot to the right, changed lanes, and accelerated through. I dusted the kid. I dusted a share of beloved liberal sensibilities as well as I watched the boy dodge moving traffic. It hurt that I didn't care whether he made it back to the sidewalk intact or not.

I turned down Lou Dillon Street into the Jordan Downs projects. Sinking feeling didn't go far enough to describe how I felt. Profound doom came closer. I had been to Etta's apartment twice before, both times during the day, both times with Guido. Even then it was scary. At night, alone, with half the street lights out, it was insanity.

The air was maybe fifteen degrees hotter in the projects than it had been in the landscaped grounds of the Valley condo. Young people here were hanging outside looking for air, looking for diversion. A lot of yelling, chasing around, empties on the curb.

All the buildings looked alike, popped from the same crude mold: stark two-story cinder-block rectangles laid in ranks, with saggy clotheslines crisscrossing the patchy lawns between them. It looked institutional, like a prison without gates or bars.

The address Mike had given me for Hanna Rhodes's grandmother was on Grape Street, in the same block as Etta's apartment. On Grape Street some of the units had been painted purple, the color of the Grape Street Crips set. The color helped me get my bearings. I passed the grandmother's apartment first, and thought about stopping by, but there were no lights showing. I drove on.

I found Etta's ancient Bonneville parked in front of her place. Parked on the lawn next to it were a dozen or more teenagers in black Raider shirts and wrap-around sunglasses. They watched me without much interest. I scoped them, measured the ten or fifteen feet between my car and Etta's front door, and decided it was a possible mission.

I didn't have the sort of car anyone would want to steal—there were better ones parked all around. But it was my only means of exit so I did not want anyone to mess with it. If I kept my talk with Etta real short, I thought I would be okay.

I wanted to have my hands free, in case, so I left the cake and the Dr. Pepper in the car. I shouldered my bag, locked up, and set off on a rapid jog toward Etta's with my keys in my hand.

I drew kids like a magnet; I don't know where they all came from. They started in on me right away:

"You from the County?"

"Hey, give me some money."

A little pudge came up close behind me, breathing booze in my face. I glanced at him as I switched my bag to the other shoulder, out of his reach.

"Don't I hear your mother calling?" I said.

"Don't get smart with me, bitch. What the fuck you doin' here?"

A bigger boy ran up beside him. "Grab the bitch, take her purse."

I was maybe two yards from Etta's when her screen door popped open and a mass of man stepped out.

"Get your ugly nigger asses the hell away," he boomed. Amid a chorus of obscene back talk, the kids slithered off.

"Thanks," I said, slipping into Etta's living room past the man. It was hot inside and sweat poured off his round black face. The name embroidered on his soiled oil company overalls was Baby Boy. He was at least six and a half feet tall, maybe three quarters that big around the middle. He reeked of beer and sex.

Etta lounged on the sofa nursing a forty-ounce bottle of malt liquor. While Baby Boy looked as if he had come directly from work, Etta had dressed for an occasion: silver satin stretch pants, a silky blouse tied in a knot above her midriff roll. Whatever the occasion she had dressed for, I clearly had not been considered in her plans.

"What you doin' here?" she asked, the way you address a cockroach in your sugar bowl. Her eyes had a glaze.

I stayed by the door, keeping an eye on the car. "I got permission to take a videocamera into Juvenile Hall Wednesday morning when I talk to Tyrone. Thought you might want to ride along. I can pick you up around eight."

"Wednesday?" She looked over Baby Boy as if measuring him, deciding how much of him would be left by Wednesday morning. Her gaze turned back to me. "What else you want, honey?"

"Did you watch the news tonight?" I asked.

"The news?" Etta's head bobbled. "I didn' watch no news. We was busy, wasn' we Baby Boy?"

"Yes we was." Baby Boy laughed, a deep rumble like rolling boulders.

"I'm sorry you missed it," I said. "A few seconds of the interview you did for me got picked up and attached to a piece on Charles Conklin. You were on the six o'clock news, Etta, calling the police motherfuckers."

"Hey, baby," Baby Boy grinned. "You was on the TV."

Etta raised a hand for him to slap. She was bombed but not too anesthetized to drag up a reaction.

"Thought I should warn you," I said. "The district attorney has attached his star to Charles Conklin's grievance. If reporters want more of your story, it won't take them long to find you. They can swarm over you like angry bees. Trust me, it could get intense."

"Like how?" she asked.

"Relentless questions, film crews dogging you, people looking in your windows, going through your trash, snooping into your personal business. You won't have any secrets left to tell."

"As long as Pinkie gets out the jail, I don' care what they do."

"Pinkie is Charles Conklin?" I asked.

She nodded. "What I say?"

"Do you believe he's innocent?" I asked.

"Don't care about that, neither." She slurred her words less as her apparent interest level rose. "Where he is now, he don't pay no child support. He don't do nothin' to help bring up the boy. I want his ass out here where he be some use to me."

"Tell me about Mr. Conklin," I said.

"Got nothin' to say about him." With the bottle, she was waving me away. But she kept talking. "He is scandalous. I told my girl to stay outta his way. He was dealin', runnin' my baby on the street, stealin' cars. He was sent up for messin' with his own little girl."

"Roll that by me again," I said. "The little girl part."

"He went to jail for messin' with this little girl," she said, her pitch rising at the end. "Left my girl with a baby when he got arrested. She was only fourteen herself."

"Besides Tyrone, he has a daughter?"

"He has a lotsa kids. An' he don't take care of none of them."

"Nice guy, this Charles Conklin." I began to relax for Mike a little. Even the most egregious sob sister or opportunist, Roddy O'Leary included, couldn't make a media hero and martyr out of a child-abusing pimp.

Etta refortified herself with a long pull from her bottle. When she put the bottle down again, she seemed surprised to see me still there. "Was there somethin' else?"

"That's about it," I said. "Except, maybe you should get yourself a lawyer."

"Me?"

"You may need to protect yourself, Etta, if the sleaze TV people come asking you to sign exclusive interview agreements with them. They can be tricky."

"What did you call that?"

"An exclusive agreement."

"Is that like the paper you had me sign?"

"No. You signed a release form giving me the right to commercial use of the interview we taped. It doesn't keep you from giving interviews to other people."

"If I sign a' exclusion thing with you, will those reporters you told me about stay away from me?"

"Not necessarily. Anyway, I can't pay you for an exclusive. The best I can offer is to put you up in a hotel for a while if things get hinky," I said, hoping I had a credit card that wasn't maxed out if it came to that. "You could take a little vacation until the press loses interest and moves on."

She smiled at the idea. "I ain't had no vacation in a long time."

Baby Boy had a gleam in his eye.

I was ready to go pack her a bag, even though hiding her away was a risky idea that could backfire on all of us if the story got hot. I kept talking. "Go to legal aid tomorrow and get a lawyer before you do anything."

"Hold on one minute." Baby Boy took a step toward me. "You say you don't have money. But those TV people do. A lot of money."

"How much?" Etta demanded.

"Depends on what you have to say and how badly they want it," I said. "Anywhere from a few hundred dollars to tens of thousands."

"They gonna ax me about Tyrone, the way you done?"

"Probably not," I said. "They'll want to talk about Charles Conklin and the police who sent him to prison. The district attorney is saying the police threatened the witnesses to make them identify Charles. Do you know who those officers were?"

"Yes I do. Officer Flint and Officer Kelsey. I know them for a long time."

"They must have questioned you and your daughter, maybe some of your neighbors. Did you ever hear anyone say Officer Flint threatened them? Mistreated anyone? Forced them to change their testimony?"

"He's the police," she said, shrugging. "You know how they are."

"No, I don't know," I said. "Suppose you tell me."

"Uh huh." Etta, who had been very serious and very blasé through the entire conversation, finally gave me her beautiful, big, toothy smile. "Now let me ax you a question. Did Officer Flint ever mistreat you?"

"Excuse me?" I said.

"I'm beginnin' to understand what you doin' here. He told me you was his lady now. I think I better take your advice and get me a lawyer before I talk to anyone. Includin' you."

"You catch on fast," I said. "Just one more question, and it has nothing to do with the other business. I've been looking for a woman named Hanna Rhodes. She grew up in the projects. She would be twenty-four or twenty-five years old now. Do you know her or her family? The last address for her grandmother is on Grape Street."

"Hanna?" Etta looked up at Baby Boy before she answered. "Go look in Sybil Brand or Frontera. She in the joint more than she out."

"Thanks," I said. "What about Wednesday morning? Do you want to come to Juvenile Hall with me?"

"We'll see," she said, flirting at Baby Boy. "We'll see."

Smooth dismissal gambit: Baby Boy opened the screen door and held it for me. "Thanks for comin' by."

"Bye, Etta," I said, walking out past Baby Boy. "I'll be in touch."

No one bothered me on the walk back to my car, not with Baby Boy standing in the doorway watching. I was grateful to him, and grateful that the car was intact. I wasted not a step, not a movement getting to the car and inside with the doors locked behind me. The engine started, the lights came on, reverse worked, so did drive. I sighed; none of my doomsday scenarios had happened.

I had a moment's pause, however, when I noticed that the boys who had harassed me going in were sitting on the grass eating coconut cake and drinking Dr. Pepper.

CHAPTER
8

At eleven, when I got back to Encino, the night was still warm and the condo grounds were still deserted. I had expected people to be outside when the air had cooled off, to walk or swim, or get blasted *al fresco*. If they had come out, they had gone back inside early. The quiet was beautiful. I walked straight to the pool.

Again, no one. For a change, there were no splashing toddlers, no cocktail-hour schmoozers and oglers, no senior watercisers. Simply, no one. Such a rare circumstance left me with no alternative: I stripped to bra and bikini panties, black ones, and dove into the cool still water.

The first lap was heavy going. My arms seemed weighted and I couldn't find my rhythm. By the third lap, I was moving easily, loose and strong. I didn't bother to count turns, I just swam like a machine until my thighs were full of fire and my shoulder muscles froze up from fatigue.

At the point where I could not swim another stroke, I stopped in the middle of the pool, rolled onto my back, and looked up into the black and starless night. I floated while I caught my breath, my heaving chest sending ripples around me.

The pool was a delicious luxury. So was the solitude. I thought about the kids at Jordan Downs who had access to neither. I suffered a flash of guilt for the pleasure I was having, a pang akin to the stab I felt when Oscar said "la-di-da" when I told him what my parents do. He had meant it as a put-down.

I wasn't born poor, nor was I born rich. We were hard-working comfortable, somewhere in that range where children might have ponies but weren't taken skiing in St. Moritz. I was never coddled or spoiled. I never went hungry. In my heart I knew I had nothing to be ashamed of. But, as Guido had pointed out, my heart still bled for everyone else.

Relaxed to the point of sleepiness, I hauled myself out of the water, slipped into my shirt, gathered my things, and stumbled home.

Michael was asleep on the living room sofa. He had ceded his bedroom to Casey, how willingly I wasn't sure. I suspect that it had been Mike's idea, born out of a notion that girls need more privacy than boys, some stubborn remnant of chivalry. Whatever, it was a noble gesture, a big help in the short run. I felt very strongly that we had to find Michael a space of his own, and soon.

We were looking for a bigger house.

From habit, I checked on Casey, saw her sleeping in the usual tangle with Bowser. I yawned, wiped away the water running down my neck, and opened my own bedroom door. The elves had cleaned up Bowser's mess, refolded the bath towels and stacked them on the floor.

Mike, wearing only boxer shorts, was stretched out on the bed, propped up on pillows and surrounded by street maps, the newspaper classifieds, and a couple of rental guides. He had reading glasses perched low on his nose. When I leaned over to kiss his bare shoulder I dripped water onto his reading matter.

"Is it raining?" he asked.

"I went for a swim."

"Naked?"

"Almost. You should have been there."

"If you'd whistled, I would have been."

"There was no time," I said, beginning to shiver. "It was an emergency sort of thing."

"I can understand that," he said. "Feel better?"

"Much." I peeled off my soggy shirt and underwear and started for the bathroom.

"Where've you been?" he called after me.

"Out."

Mike's big terry robe was on a hook in the bathroom. I put it on, wrapped a towel around my hair, and went back to the bed. Still shivering, I slipped under the covers and snuggled up against Mike, stealing his body warmth.

When I had quit squirming and had my cold feet wedged under him, he said, "Out?"

"I went to Etta's."

"Guido go?"

"No. I went alone."

I might as well have hit him across the face. "You went to Etta's alone?" he exploded.

"Etta does it all the time."

"Jesus Christ, Maggie. Promise me you won't ever go there alone again."

"Okay."

"I used to work that neighborhood. You have no idea what can happen."

"I said, okay. I won't go there alone again."

"Okay."

He was still breathing hard when he enveloped me in his arms. He muttered, "Jesus," a couple of times, most unprayerfully. He needn't have fussed; I would never go back there alone. I had been scared from the moment I got off the freeway until I got back on it. With reason. I could add up at least four incidents that occurred during the space of an hour that might easily have gone deadly wrong. That's four possibilities before I gave any thought to car problems or drive-bys. Mike was right: Etta's neighborhood was no place to wander through alone, at night. I should have known better.

All my moving around under the covers scattered his maps and classifieds. I retrieved a section of ads sliding off my hip: houses and apartments to rent, three bedrooms. He had starred a few.

"Find anything?" I asked.

He shook his head. "The geography's the tricky part. You want a canyon or ocean view out of the smog belt. Michael has to be within easy commuting distance of Occidental in Eagle Rock. Casey needs access to Pasadena. I don't want to spend my life on the freeway. The neighborhood has to be reasonably safe. We need at least three bedrooms, but we can't spend much more than we'll get in rent for this place, assuming we find a renter. Any ideas?"

"One thought," I said. "If we find something big enough, I won't have to rent an office. I miss working from home. When I have to work late, it's so much easier to keep track of Casey if I'm in the next room instead of down the freeway. God, I'm beginning to hate the freeway."

With a corner of the towel he dabbed at water on my cheek. "Sounds like regrets."

"What sort of regrets?" I asked.

"Moving down. You miss your own house."

"I miss order." I played with the little patch of hair at the base of his throat. "I wish the elves would come in and move us to a cottage in the woods somewhere, do the laundry, drive Casey around while they're at it, because the details are beginning to overwhelm me. That's a long way from regret. Remember what I told you when we decided to live in sin?"

"Let me think." He rested his chin on my wrapped head. "You said that you wouldn't care if we had to sleep on army cots in an abandoned airplane hangar, as long as we could wake up together every morning."

"Something like that," I said.

"An airplane hangar would give us more space than we have here."

"Look into it, will you?"

"Yeah." He gathered the ads and maps and dropped them off the side of the bed.

"How was your meeting with the lieutenant?" I asked as he slid between the sheets and snuggled into me.

He found my breast inside the robe and covered it with his warm hand. "You don't really want to talk about all that now, do you?"

"Actually, I do," I said. "What did the lieutenant say?"

Mike frowned and rolled onto his back. "We didn't get very far. He wanted to go over the case with me, check our procedures. Then he told me to take some time off. I can come with you to Casey's orientation tomorrow. Maybe we can spend the rest of the day house hunting."

"Time off? Like a suspension?"

"Not at all like a suspension. Just until things cool off, I'm going to be invisible. One thing you have to understand: As far as the department is concerned, I'm not in any trouble. They're taking good care of me, because they believe me."

"That's okay," I said. "But if you disappear, won't it look like the department is hiding something, keeping you under wraps?"

"You know, we did some things differently in the old days when our job was keeping the peace instead of holding teat-to-teats with the bad guys to keep their feelings from getting hurt."

"That's a new one." I laughed, getting a strong visual. Teat to teat was a definite improvement on head to head.

"You know what I mean," he groused, but not serious about it.

"I know what you mean. You used to kick butt and take names later, or something."

"Kick ass," he corrected. "Kick ass."

I had to ask: "Did you kick Charles Conklin's ass?"

"I just helped him decide it was time to move out of the neighborhood. The witnesses were little kids and he kept them terrorized. Soon as he was gone, they couldn't talk fast enough. They saw Conklin at the scene with a gun in his hand. They saw him run away. We had a jail-house snitch to corroborate them and, boom, we nailed Conklin, dead bang."

"The D.A. says you intimidated the kids."

"Didn't have to. The girls came clean, that's all."

The girls. Hearing that made something click. Two girls, ages ten or eleven, about fourteen years ago. So, okay, I was a philosophy major, but I can still add about ten and about fourteen. Comes to about twenty-four.

Feeling something between befuddlement and anger, I scooted out of bed to get my bag. I pulled out the newspaper copies and, sitting with my back against Mike's raised knees, I sorted through them.

"It's weird, Mike," I said, hearing sarcasm. I passed him the three short news items about the shooting of Officer Johnson. "I thought that when a police officer was shot everyone made a big fuss about it. Big funeral with thousands of officers in uniform, a eulogy by the chief, grieving family on TV, a motorcade, bagpipes—the whole twenty-dollar package. Johnson got none of that. Why not?"

"A few things." Mike put his glasses back on and began reading through the articles. "Like I told you, Johnson was off duty and out of uniform when he got it. Second, we thought he might have been up to something dirty."

"Dirty with Charles Conklin?"

"Don't know. We didn't pursue it once we had an arrest. You have any idea what our caseloads are like?"

"But a fellow officer was shot. Surely that meant something. Another thing, there was nothing in the paper about Conklin's arrest. When did you get him?"

"About a year after the fact. Jail-house snitch came looking for a deal, spilled for us."

"I'm so disappointed," I said, nudging him to make room in the bed; he seemed to have spread out. "Where were you great big detectives all that time? Out eating doughnuts?"

"If it had been my case from the beginning, we would have gotten Conklin on day one." Mike sounded defensive. "The original investigators screwed up on it, got lazy I think, didn't follow up on leads. They talked to Conklin, but they let him go. The department did a six-month follow-up, then filed the case away for another six months. It probably would have stayed in limbo, except Chuckie Conklin got himself sent to jail on an unrelated charge—crimes against a child—and couldn't keep his mouth shut. To keep from getting poop-chuted all day like the other pedophiles, he started bragging that he had taken out a cop."

"Poop-chuted?" I said.

"Think about it." He set the clippings aside.

"Oh," I said when I got it. Mike should have come with a glossary of cop-speak. "Was he in jail when you arrested him?"

"No. He was out terrorizing the neighborhood again by the time we bagged him. It was a tough case to make; no one would ID him when he was out loose. Everyone was afraid of him, of his whole damn family—especially the kids. I told you, we helped him decide to move on."

"You want to explain how you helped him decide?"

Mike yawned. "Aren't you tired yet?"

"No," I said. "I just love to listen to you talk. I could stay up all night."

He looked down at me. "What is this? You have a recorder hidden somewhere?"

"Sho', you right," I said in my best imitation of Mike.

"Let me see." He yanked off the covers and grabbed the front of my robe—his robe—and started to peel it off me. "I know you've got a bug in here somewhere. Give it up before this gets ugly."

"Sometimes I like it ugly," I said, laughing, trying to hang on to the robe.

"You called it." His stiff little mustache tickled the inside of my thighs as he searched. And probed. I just threw off the robe and gave him access.

Mike is a genius with his hands and his tongue—expertise that comes from vast experience. After all of the wild and crazy things we have done with and to each other, he can still amaze me, make my eyes roll back in my head. But that night, though Mike was in peak form, I couldn't clear my mind enough to be of much help. After a few minutes he figured something was wrong and raised himself. He looked at me, his face framed between my knees.

"Where did I lose you?" he asked.

"I'm confused." I reached out for a handful of his hair. "I'm trying to put things together. I have two piles of information that should flow together, but they simply do not seem to exist on the same plane of truth. They will not merge."

"Someone lie to you?"

"You." I sat up to look him square on, feeling angry and confused. "I know you lie to me all the time about things you've done on the job—you pretty things up so I won't judge you."

"That isn't lying. If you haven't been on the streets, there's no way you can understand what goes down."

"Maybe," I said. I had backed up from him, out of his zone of magnetism. I tried to, anyway. As mad as I was, I still wanted to hold him. Realizing that made me even angrier. "Maybe not. Right now I need you to tell me the truth. The names of the little girl witnesses? They wouldn't be LaShonda DeBevis and Hanna Rhodes, would they?"

He sighed.

"You're using me again, Mike. I don't like the way that feels."

"Me, too."

"You better explain."

He sat naked in front of me, looking shamed. And gorgeous. I think that if he hadn't been naked I would have been a whole lot angrier. Mike doesn't leave himself vulnerable, ever. If he could sit there completely exposed, then he felt safe with me. That is, whatever he'd done wasn't so bad it would make me turn on him.

"Just spill it, Mike," I said, sitting cross-legged in front of him, our knees touching.

"I'm under orders," he said. "I can't talk to anyone who was involved in the case."

I nodded. "The department is reinvestigating for you, but you can't play."

"Not exactly reinvestigating. The department is going over procedure, making sure we did things right the first time. That's all. But I want more. The D.A. and this asshole evangelical private eye, Leroy Burgess, are trying to get a convicted murderer out of prison on a technicality. The city doesn't give a shit if he gets out, as long as we don't come off looking too bad. Doesn't anyone but me care that he's guilty?"

"You want me to talk to the witnesses?"

"In the course of this project you have going, if you were to talk to them, that would be good."

"What is it you want me to find out from them?"

"Just if the girls are okay. If you can find them and they're okay, that's enough for me."

"No message?"

"No. Except maybe watch out. The D.A. said he has new affidavits from them saying they were coerced all those years ago. If they were ever coerced, it was when they signed those new affidavits. This whole thing really stinks, Mag. I worry that LaShonda and Hanna might be in some trouble."

"I'll do what I can. Just don't lie to me anymore."

"I'm sorry."

"You already said that."

"I don't know what else to say. Problem is, I'm used to taking care of my own problems. I'm not good at asking for help, but I can't get inside alone this time. Since you were in the neighborhood, I hoped maybe you'd knock on a few doors for me."

"You have to say, please Maggie, give me a hand."

"I just did."

"You're some tough guy, Flint," I said, softened by his anguish. "You've got skin like a baby, but you're some tough guy."

He tried to get up an attitude. "I don't have skin like a baby."

"Yes you do," I said, nuzzling his abdomen. "And dimples on your vanilla ice cream butt."

"Ass," he said, breaking into a smile, getting hard again. "And no, I don't."

But he does.

CHAPTER
9

The telephone rang deep in the small hours of the night. Startled out of my sleep, I made a quick accounting of my near and dear as I rose to the surface of wakefulness: Michael and Casey were both safely tucked into bed, Mike was wrapped around me. Panic abated.

Mike reached through the dark and picked up the phone, muttered something, then tapped me with the receiver.

"It's for you," he said, and fell face down into his pillow.

I managed, "Hello?" expecting to hear my mother or father with dire news.

"Miss MacGowen? It's me, Etta Harkness. You ax me to tell you if I know anything about Hanna Rhodes?"

"What time is it?" I asked.

"Hanna just got herself shot. Up on Hunnerd-twelve. Baby Boy say she still lyin' up there on the sidewalk. The ambulance only just got there."

"Where is this?"

"Hunnerd-twelve and Wilmington."

"Is she badly hurt?"

Etta coughed. "She dead."

I was awake, but I felt disoriented, still unaccustomed to waking up in Mike's bedroom. I reached over and gave his shoulder a nudge. "Etta says Hanna Rhodes is dead."

Mike took the phone from me and grilled Etta for a few minutes. He said good-bye and turned on the light to dial Southeast

Division. He asked for the sergeant on duty and grilled him, too. When he finally hung up, he sat on the edge of the bed, staring at the wall.

"What happened?" I asked.

He shook his head. "Don't know. Southeast only got the shooting call twenty minutes ago."

I slipped out of the warm bed and shuffled, yawning, toward the closet.

"Going somewhere?" Mike asked.

"Down to 112th Street and Wilmington. I never got a chance to interview Hanna. Now it's too late."

He had that deep crease between his brows. "Is Guido going with you?"

"You aren't coming?" I stopped and looked up at him dumbly.

"I can't go. I want to, but I can't. Department orders."

"And you aren't going to argue about me going?"

"Would it do any good?"

The answer was no, but I still wanted some argument. Even with Guido, I doubted I would feel safe about going back into Southeast. I was going, but I wanted Mike with me. I said, "What does this mean, you're tired of me and sending me down there is easier than hiring a hit man?"

"I'll never get tired of you, baby." He hugged me as a matter of punctuation. "I'm hiring Guido to go with you. And don't worry, I'll have Southeast Division watching for you."

"You call Guido. He loves to roll out in the middle of the night."

When I came back from the bathroom, more or less dressed and alert, Mike was lifting a hard leather gun case from the top shelf of the closet. He unlocked it and took out a little .38 with a two-inch barrel and the hammer filed off. He inspected it, loaded five rounds into the cylinder, and offered it to me.

I wouldn't accept it. "I'm not licensed to carry, and that filed-off hammer is strictly illegal."

"If you get into a position where you have to use this baby, the legality of it will be the last thing we worry about. It's powerful, and you know how to use it. I filed off the hammer when I was working undercover so I could conceal it and still pull it out without snagging on everything. It's the best thing for you to carry." He pulled up the back of my shirt and tucked the little revolver into my belt, with the barrel lying along my spine.

He kept talking as if I was embarking on some expedition into the war zone. "Guido's on his way over. You're going to take my car because it has a phone. When you get to the scene, pull in among the black and whites as close as you can. And don't go anywhere on your own. Don't stop for coffee, don't walk off looking for a bathroom. Stay in tight at all times. Got it? Stay tight."

"My God, you're bossy," I said, adjusting the revolver in my belt. "I can take care of myself."

"And another thing," he said.

"Shut up, Mike."

"Get me a camera shot of everyone there. Try to get cars, too."

I smiled, looking at the misery on his face. "I know you're being so agreeable about me going only because it's next best to you going yourself. Right now, though, cupcake, it's time for you to back off. You have to trust me. I'll try not to get blown away. I'll find out everything I can. In the meantime, don't work yourself into a coronary."

He pulled me against him. "You're such a smartass."

"Half right," I said. "The part about smart."

I went out by the garage to wait for Guido because I didn't want him to knock on the door and awaken Michael. I did a lot of yawning; in police parlance it was 0300—as they say it, oh-three-hundred hours. Or, as they say in civilian parlance, too fucking early.

A light breeze stirred the early morning air, but it was still warm. The driveway and the stucco walls radiated heat, so I stepped onto a patch of lawn where it was cooler.

Mike came outside with a Thermos of coffee just as Guido pulled up. We helped Guido transfer equipment from his car to Mike's Blazer.

"One thing you need to keep in mind, Guido," Mike said, handing over his car keys. "If anything happens to Maggie, I'll have to kill you."

"Fair enough." Guido palmed the keys. "Save me the effort of doing it myself. Be too dull to live without her."

"My heroes," I said, and climbed into the passenger seat. First thing, Guido handed me a loaded 9mm Smith and Wesson automatic. Feeling like Annie Oakley, or maybe Che Guevara, I took out the clip, zipped it inside my bag, and stowed the pistol under my seat. Then I did something essential for survival: I poured us both some coffee.

Wilmington Avenue is one block west of Grape Street, nine blocks south of the Jordan Downs projects. All of the police activity was on 112th, halfway between Wilmington and Grape. We followed the coroner's van around the corner and parked close beside it among the police cars.

The crime scene was defined by portable floodlights and yellow police tape: an irregular Z beginning on the porch of a small woodframe house, stretching diagonally across the street, encompassing some sidewalk on the other side, and ending at the fence around an elementary school playground. Roughly down the center of this no-entry zone, in a jagged, drunken trajectory, was a trail of bloody footprints on the pavement, punctuated here and there by full hand prints and circles I suspected showed where the victim had fallen to her knees a few times. The trail ended on the porch of the house, where Hanna Rhodes lay under a pink flowered sheet.

Guido, always hyper when he sees a cinematic scene, hopped out with a videocamera at the ready, and began taping Hanna's route from the school to the house. There were enough people in uniform around that I decided he was sufficiently chaperoned to go off without me. I had my own agenda.

It was nearly four when we got there, but we beat the two detectives in suits—a man-woman team that had come to take over. Right away, they went to the sergeant in charge of the crime scene to get the first report. I wanted to hear it. With my little tape recorder running in my pocket, and a 35mm camera in my hand, I sidled up beside the detectives.

The sergeant's nameplate said Chan.

"We got the call at 0215 hours," Sergeant Chan said. "The resident, Mrs. Kennedy, heard two shots fired, heard a car drive off, then a few minutes later heard someone on her porch calling for help. She looked out and saw Hanna Rhodes collapsed where she is now. Mrs. Kennedy called 911 before venturing outside. The victim expired prior to the arrival of officers or paramedics at 0221 hours. Paramedics applied CPR, but there was no victim response. They ceased efforts and declared the victim dead at approximately 0230 hours. Paramedics observed a through and through gunshot wound to the chest area of the victim, and a superficial, defensive-type wound to her right forearm."

"Uh huh." The woman detective had been taking notes. "Mrs. Kennedy see the shooter, see the car?"

Sergeant Chan shook his head. He glanced at me, but didn't question why I was there. No one did.

The neighbors, in various forms of nightclothes, clustered around the edges of the scene, knowing to stay back. There was some curious chatter among them, now and then some laughter. My race, or my attire—boots instead of bunny slippers—maybe the fact I had come by car and moved about with a purpose and a camera, I don't what it was, but I was set apart from the neighbors. Without challenge, I had free access to the crime scene.

I walked up to the porch, leaned over the police tape, and took a few frames of Hanna's covered body, the pool of blood seeping from under her sheet and the pile of clothes the paramedics had left in the coagulating mess: yellow stretch pants, a striped tube top with a black hole through it, a cheap white cotton jacket.

Guido followed the coroner's people up the porch steps, recording their movements as they photographed Hanna. Any fragile evidence that might have been on her person or on the porch would have been destroyed by the paramedics. So, while they were meticulous, they were not delicate. Hanna's shrouded corpse lay in the middle of their activity, no more honored than the pile of clothes beside her.

When I zoomed in on Guido's face and snapped a few frames, the woman detective decided to notice me.

"You with the coroner?" she asked. She had a pen poised over a metal clipboard.

Before I had figured out what to say, I felt a firm hand grip my elbow. I turned to find one of Mike's former partners, Hector Melendez, with his detective shield showing over his jacket pocket.

"Hey, good-lookin'," he said to me, and winked. The woman detective still had her pen poised. To her he said, "Excuse us," and walked me back toward the sidewalk.

Mike often talked about Melendez and their adventures together on uniform patrol as rookie cops, and in bars after hours, then, later, when they had families, working part-time security jobs to earn enough to cover their first mortgage payments. I knew all I needed to know about Melendez: Mike trusted him.

Melendez had a tall, spare frame that carried no excess; a distance runner, like Mike. I thought he looked awfully sharp for a middle-of-the-night roll-out, loafers with a spit polish, crisp shirt, silk tie carefully knotted, a professorial tweed jacket. Certainly a few cuts above the generic cheap suits favored by most of his colleagues.

He took me around to the far side of his plain city car.

"What are you doing here?" I asked.

"Never mind," Melendez said. He tucked a large manila envelope under my arm. "Don't open this now. Give it to Mike. I'm going to hang around for a while. You need anything, whistle."

Melendez walked away into the shadows. I knew Mike had called him out to keep an eye on me. I didn't mind being watched over, and my brief conversation with him seemed to have been sufficient to establish my credentials with the detectives.

Various official types arrived in groups, most of them forensics lab people. They were all, like me, sleepy-eyed and casually dressed. I stayed out of their way.

Another black and white car pulled up. The driver officer was a big woman, looked like a power lifter. She and her partner could have passed for twins in the inadequate light. They were about the same height and weight, and the body armor under their shirts gave them nearly the same chest; flattened hers, padded his. The standard police equipment hanging from their Sam Browne belts made them walk with the same heavy, wide-armed gait every uniformed cop has. I found something very sexy about their androgyny and lifted my camera to capture them.

They had escorted to the scene a painfully thin, scantily attired young woman. She looked like a hooker, but she wasn't under arrest. At least, she wasn't handcuffed. Guido, with his videocamera taping, went straight to the newcomers, leading the detectives. I managed to maneuver myself in beside him.

"Get the officers with the girl," I said to Guido. "They look good, don't they? Mr. and Mrs. Cerberus guarding the gates to hell. Or, in this case, guarding one tiny flower of the night."

The woman detective conducted the field interview. "What is your name?" she asked the young woman.

"Gloria Griffin." Very straightforward. This flower had been through police questioning before.

"What can you tell us about what happened to Hanna Rhodes?"

Looking straight into Guido's lens, and without much prompting, this is the story Gloria Griffin told:

"Me and Hanna been partying at a rock house on Hickory Street. We were there, off and on, for three days. She said someone was looking for her and she was laying low, you know, staying off the streets a while."

"Did she say who was looking for her?"

Gloria shook her head. "I figure she owe some dealer. Around midnight, one o'clock, somewhere around there, she went out on the street to make some money, to buy her some more crystal. I went out with her. She walk up one side of Wilmington, I walk up the other, you know, going in opposite directions, but close enough so we could holler back and forth. I got me a date first and drove away with him.

"I was gone fifteen, twenty minutes when my date left me off again. I saw Hanna was talkin' to some dude in a blue car. Then she started to run away. She come down here by the school, lookin' for a way to get through the fence into the school yard. The blue car followed her. I see the dude get out of the car. I hear him lettin' two off, I see the flames shoot outta the end of his gun. Hanna don't say nothin', she just fall right down. This man, he revved up some and then he was gone. Then I see Hanna get up and start runnin' again. Come here across the street. That's all I saw."

I was close enough to Gloria Griffin to smell something like ether on her breath, the sharp doctor's-office smell of the cocaine freebaser. I asked, "Did you see the driver of the car?"

"Not close," she said, gazing across the street where the shooting had occurred before she turned her attention back to me. "When Hanna start runnin', I don't want to get too close. I'm thinkin' maybe this guy she owe money to has come collectin'. Somethin' like that."

The detective gave me the evil eye that meant she was in

charge. She resumed the interview. "What did you do when you realized Hanna Rhodes had been shot?"

"Girlfriend was scared. I run back to the house on Hickory Street. I had me some money then, so I got me some rock and smoked it."

"How do you feel right now?" I asked her.

"Mellow," she said, smiling. I hoped that it wasn't so dark that the tape wouldn't pick up the unfocused look she gave me. "I feel okay."

The detective asked, "Can you describe the car? Make? Model? Age?"

"That's the one." Gloria turned and pointed to Mike's blue Blazer.

I knew where Mike was at the time of the shooting, snoring beside my ear. Still, I felt very uneasy about Gloria pointing out his car. I felt very uneasy about anything that tended to tie Mike to this mess of a situation. Gloria was bombed, kept snapping her head up to hang in with us. The Blazer was the only civilian car within her range of vision: how easy to tag it when she didn't have another answer. I said, "Late model, American-made, four-wheel-drive car."

"Whatever you say," she said. "It was that one."

As Guido turned the camera toward Mike's car, I put up my hand and stopped him. He gave me a funny look, but he turned back around.

"Thank you, Miss Griffin," the detective said. "I know it's unpleasant, but we need you to identify the body."

The officers who had brought Gloria walked her up on the porch and had her look at Hanna's face. I stayed back because I didn't want to see it. Guido went right in with Gloria, his lens following her point of view, then pulling back to catch her reaction. I was still worried about the lighting. Guido and his techno friends at UCLA could do some computer enhancement, but low light punched up electronically always came out looking artificial. Flat.

Hanna must not have looked like a party under that sheet, because Gloria Griffin was nearly overcome when she took her look. With her hand over her mouth, she fled the porch. The roots of an old sycamore tree pushing up through the sidewalk tripped her, made her fall against the trunk of the tree. I heard her swear, and I saw her take something from the pocket of her shorts and put it into her mouth. Could have been anything, but it seemed to make her feel better.

Hector Melendez had seen her take it, too. When I sort of ambled in her direction, Hector Melendez sort of ambled along with me.

Gloria's hand shook too much for her to connect the match in her hand with the cigarette she put between her lips. I took the matchbook from her and lit the cigarette.

"Pretty bad?" I asked.

"Shit," she exhaled, leaning against the tree for support.

"How well did you know Hanna?"

"I know her my whole damn life. We grow up in the same neighborhood."

I caught Guido's eye and motioned for him to come over. When he was ready with his camera, I said, "You grew up with Hanna Rhodes?"

Gloria nodded. "Know her my whole life. She was my play sister. Our kids is friends, too."

"Tell me about her children."

"She have just one little girl. Yoandra. She's about ten now. Live with her grandmother."

"How old was Hanna?"

"Twenty-five, about. Same as me. We used to go to that school over across the street. But they never used to lock the gate all the way, you know. They let us go in and play. Guess Hanna didn't know they was locking things up these days so she couldn't get through."

"What a shame," I said. Hector's touch was warm through my sleeve. "I was wondering, Gloria," I said. "This date you had, he must have seen the shooting."

"He didn't see nothin'," she said, adamant. She lit a new cigarette from the glowing stub between her fingers.

"I'd still like to talk to him. Men notice cars better than we do."

She took a long drag. "I don't know nothin' about him. He just a date, you know?"

"A regular date?" Hector asked. "You're very pretty, Miss Griffin. You must have regulars."

She smiled in spite of herself, flipped her hair up off her neck, flirting with him. "Maybe I do."

"Was he a regular?" I asked. "Do you know where I might find him?"

"Maybe." She gave the three of us a keen appraisal. Then she looked down, dropped her cigarette, and stubbed it out with her toe. She took so long doing this, I thought she had forgotten about us. Finally, she said, "What I know will cost you two dead presidents."

The only dead presidents in my pocket were some George Washingtons. I looked up at Hector. "Two dead presidents, is that two hundred dollars?"

"That's what I say," she said. "Two of 'em."

Hector had glanced away, seemed to be smiling at something. Mike tells me a lot of war stories about things that go down on the job. I remembered one he had told me about Hector and dead presidents. I took hold of Hector's sleeve and said, "Hey, Gloria, you ever play Monopoly?"

"Maybe I did," she said, wary, as if she was afraid I was making fun of her.

"In Monopoly they have something called a get-out-of-jail-free card. In the game, the card's worth two hundred dollars," I said. Hector, on cue, took out one of his business cards with its big silver detective shield and his office phone number on it, and handed it to me. I passed it to Gloria. "Here's your get-out-of-jail-free card. Next time you get picked up on the street, you give this card to the officer, tell him to call Detective Melendez. It's a whole lot better than dead presidents."

She studied the card before she tucked it into the front of her halter top. Then she looked up and said, "His name's Tiny and he hangs up at the Bayou Barbeque. I see him there all the time."

"Thanks, Gloria," I said. The androgynous officers were walking toward us. "Thank you very much. If we want to talk to you again, where can we reach you?"

She smiled, coming on to Hector again. "You know where my office is. Up on that corner. You want to talk to me, just call my pager number."

She walked off to meet her escorts, swaying her narrow hips for Hector's benefit.

When Guido took the camera off his shoulder, he was laughing. "You two should go on the road with that card routine."

"It's already been on the road," I said. "Part of the Mike Flint repertoire, right Hector?"

"What other stories he tell you?" Hector asked. He was blushing furiously.

"Tons of them. When he told me about the get-out-of-jail-free card stunt, he said, 'Got us what we needed and no one laid a hand on the whore. That's called good police work, my friend. Good police work.' "

"That's called bullshit," Guido countered.

Hector laughed. "Same thing. With Flint, it's an art form."

Guido, who lives most of his professional life within the confines of university-directed tenets of political correctitude, visibly winced when I said "whore." He was suddenly not very amused.

"Can we go home now?" Guido asked me. "I've got the crime scene, the victim, the cops, the witness."

"Get the bystanders," I said. "And the cars on the street."

"Except the Blazer?" he said, sarcastic.

I reached into my pocket and switched off the tape recorder. "Everything except the Blazer. You have a problem with that?"

"No," he said, jutting out his chin like a defiant kid. "I don't have any problems. I'm having more fun than I've had since we camped out in the jungles of Salvador. At least here there aren't any biting bugs and at the moment no one's shooting at us. Just perfectly dandy. Doing this arty, interpretive shit is so much easier than working hard news; we don't even have to pretend we're looking for the facts as long as we get some hot footage. I always think patterns of light and shadow are more important than story content."

I ignored the insult, put it down to an unguarded flash of jealousy. Best friends often feel pushed out when a lover comes on the scene, comes between them. I had been noticing ever since I moved down that Guido seemed to bristle every time Mike's name came up. I walked away from him to give him space to cool off, but he followed.

"Hanna grew up in this general neighborhood," I said, moving past the tantrum. He had stung me deeply, and he knew it. Why belabor the issue? "She went to that elementary school across the street, little girl with pigtails, maybe. I like the way this is all coming together. With some luck and persistence, we may be able to hook up with Hanna's mother, or maybe the

school administration, and find some old pictures of her. Little
kid with gaps in her front teeth, cut to the body on the porch.
That would be beautiful, don't you think?"

"I don't know if beautiful is the right word, but it would be
powerful." Guido, chagrined suddenly, dropped his gaze, did an
unnecessary battery check. "Very powerful."

"I love you, Guido," I said.

"I know." He looked at me through his long lashes. "I'm
sorry."

"I know."

Gloria was driven away. She waved to us from the backseat
of the patrol car as she went past. I knew she faced an all-
nighter, what was left of the night, under questioning at Southeast Division. I hoped they would at least buy her breakfast
when it was over because she looked as if she hadn't eaten for
a long time.

The forensics people would probably be around the crime
scene most of the day with their tape measures, chalk, and little plastic bags. I overheard them discussing whether a gouge
on a metal fence post was a bullet impact or some other sort
of collision, maybe a hard encounter with a bicycle handlebar.
None of it seemed essential to our needs. Once Hanna had
been taken away in the coroner's van, there was no reason for
us to stay.

Guido, still chastened, walked me back to the Blazer, where
Hector was waiting. I had the envelope Hector had given me
tucked under my arm.

"Hector," I said, "did you know Wyatt Johnson?"

He shook his head. "I think he worked out of Hollywood or
maybe Hollenbeck. I don't know what he was doing down
here."

"Maybe there's something in his file."

"Could be," he said.

"What they're saying Mike did," I said, but Hector held up
his hands, stopped me from saying anything more.

"Mike Flint's the best," he said. "Don't believe anyone who
says otherwise."

"Thanks for coming out," I said. I offered him my hand, but
he gave me a long hug.

"Look after Mike," he said. "Because trouble is always looking out for him."

"I do my best. We'll have you and your wife to dinner as soon as we get settled in."

"Don't bother. I'll take you both out."

I kissed his cool cheek and pulled away. "Go home. Get some sleep."

It was a good idea. Guido talked all the way back to the Valley, on and on about a new video disk recorder he was trying to get a grant to buy for his department. He must have memorized all of the support literature, because I heard so much arcane technical detail that, had I tended at all toward the suicidal, I would have done myself in long before we reached the downtown interchange. I knew he was taking the responsibility for filling dead air space, atoning for his earlier outburst. It wasn't that he didn't like Mike, it was that he wouldn't have chosen Mike for me.

Guido declined my offer of breakfast when he dropped me off. It was still awfully early. I went into a quiet house, hoping for company. Someone was in the shower—I could hear the hot water pipes. There was fresh coffee in Mr. Espresso. But no one was walking around.

I put eggs on to boil, dropped a couple of slices of bread into the toaster, poured some coffee, and sat down at the table to look through the folder Hector had slipped to me.

Just as my toast popped, Mike came in the back door wearing running shorts and shoes and dripping with sweat.

He rubbed his salty, unshaven chin across the back of my neck as he looked over my shoulder. "What do you have?"

"Hanna Rhodes's rap sheet."

"Good." He pulled out the chair next to me. "I asked Hec to run it."

"And you asked Hec to come to the scene to watch over me."

"Didn't have to ask. He's my old partner. He takes care of me." He kissed my shoulder. "And mine."

If I hadn't been so tired, I would have challenged that "mine" remark. I wasn't in the mood for an argument, so I began reading to him from the rap sheet.

"Booked under five versions of her name: Rhodes, Hanna S.; Rhodes, Hanna Sue; Rhodes, Hannah; Rhodes, Sue; Farmer, Demetria. The charges begin with possession of a controlled substance, detained and released for lack of probable cause.

One year later, arrested for petty theft and trespass: occupying property without consent. Convicted, sentenced to jail, sentence suspended. Two months later, arrested for burglary. Convicted. With a prior, Hanna went to county jail for six months. Another theft charge, robbery this time. With priors, given a year in jail. Out on probation, arrested for disorderly conduct: prostitution, solicitation. Pled *nolo contendere*, convicted, sentence suspended. Again, picked up for prostitution, plea-bargained sentence to time served. Four more disorderly conduct/prostitution charges, all of them bumped or plea-bargained for a total of maybe six months time in the slam. Finally, felony theft with a prior, sent to state prison for eighteen months, got an early release and hit the streets again last Friday. End of record. What does it tell you?" I asked.

"She was a junkie. Hooking, stealing to buy shit. She has a juvenile record, too. But it's sealed. So, this paragon of veracity—if you believe the D.A.—has ten misdemeanor convictions and one felony over a six-year period. She's out of prison three days and she takes one through the chest. I'd say the miracle here is that she didn't take one a long time ago."

"How did you know she took one through the chest?"

"Talked to Hector." He pulled my by-now cold toast out of the toaster, buttered a piece, and began to eat it. "What bothers me is the timing of the shooting. I always have to look real hard at coincidence."

"If it wasn't a coincidence, who shot her?" I put in more toast.

"Hell if I know." Then, just when my coffee was finally cool enough to drink, he drank it.

I took the little revolver from my belt and laid it on the table between us. With my hand over the gun butt, I said, "Don't touch my eggs."

He put the revolver in his shorts waistband and poured more coffee. "But I like your eggs. I even like the dark circles under your baby blues. I'm really happy to see all of you safely back in this kitchen."

"Good," I said. I crossed my arms on the table, rested my head on them, and fell asleep.

CHAPTER
10

The director of dance at Casey's new school executed a magnificent leap, a gold-medal effort. But it was the prize-winning zucchini in the front of his flesh-colored tights that held the freshman dancers in thrall. Casey, sitting on the practice room floor with a dozen or so other new classmates, dropped her jaw and stared.

Because of Casey I have been around a lot of ballet, have seen a lot of stuffed tights. You get used to them, as you do tutus and other archaic accoutrements of dance. What gave me pause as the director went through his routine was Casey's reaction to his malehood: over the summer she had evolved from indifferent to awed. The change made me worry.

I looked around the practice studio at the other parents lined up against the mirrored walls. The attentive masks that had carried us through the boring academic portion of the school's orientation had dropped away as the demonstration by the director, his gifted young faculty, and the senior students began.

They performed for a tough, critical audience; every parent there had already invested a fortune in time, emotional support, and cash to prepare their young dancers for the privilege of attending this school. The sacrifices that had brought them this far had honed their expectations. I tried to pick out the mouthpieces, the vigilant parents who always kvetch when they are displeased. Every school, especially private schools, has nightmare parent police.

As the director *tour jeté*'d toward us, Mike leaned in and muttered into my ear, "Are we expected to tuck money in his jock when he dances over here?"

"Good idea." I passed him the first quarter's tuition check. "Any tips are up to you."

He glanced at the check and his eyes widened. As he re-folded it he said, "You're sure this is what you want for Casey?"

"Casey is sure. Look at her."

She had quickly gotten past the zucchini and was now fully concentrated on the dancers. I watched her hands subtly fol-low every movement because in her mind she was out there with the dancers.

The studio pianist ended with a showy arpeggio. The squeak and pat of ballet shoes on hardwood floors fell quiet. There was a moment of appreciative silence, and then equally appre-ciative applause. Before the applause had died, Casey had at-tached herself to one of the senior girls and persuaded her to demonstrate some movement from the dance she had just seen.

"We'll never get her away," I said.

Mike was watching Casey imitate the movements of the older girl. "She's really talented, isn't she?"

"Hard work and talent in about equal measure," I said, dis-tracted. I thought I had spotted a young man tall enough to partner her; a good sign. Casey's height would always be a hur-dle in ballet.

Casey pranced over, beaming. "Can I stay for a while? They're going to do a workshop for the seniors and Mischa said I could stay."

"Who's Mischa?" I asked.

"Mr. Karpov," she said, indicating the director.

Mike seemed dubious, but I asked, "For how long?"

"Until about five," she said.

I looked at my watch. Until five gave us three hours to kill. "We had planned to house hunt." I turned to Mike. "What do you think?"

"If it's okay with you, let her stay. We can look around this neighborhood for a couple of hours."

"We'll be back at five," I said to Casey. "Take care of yourself."

"Oh, Mom," she groaned, but she was too excited to get up a decent pout.

Mike grabbed her muscular arm before she danced away and pulled her against him. "Watch out for those guys. If I caught one of them out on the street in pantyhose like that, I'd have to arrest him for indecent exposure."

She laughed. "You're so weird, Mike." She left us then.

"You're so weird, Mike," I said, taking his arm.

"What? Did she think I was kidding?"

We went down to the school office to hand over the tuition and sign emergency medical treatment forms, give the nurse Casey's immunization records.

There was a form to list emergency contact numbers. After myself, I listed Mike's office, then Guido's pager. The fourth blank stumped me. Our former housemate, Lyle, was too far away to be of any immediate help, and he had no legal connection to help in the long run. I almost left the fourth spot blank, but after a pause, and as a matter of form, I wrote down Casey's father's number in Denver. Just writing the number made my palms sweat; Scotty was always a mess in an emergency. No matter what happened, I would not call him. I never, ever, wanted to go through a hassle involving him again. Ever.

When we left the school, we still had two and a half hours left. Pasadena was hot and smoggy. I was grateful that we were in Mike's Blazer and not my car, because he had air conditioning and I did not.

"Where should we start?" I asked.

"South Pasadena," he said, turning down Fair Oaks Avenue. "I think you'll like the area. The locals stopped the state from extending the freeway through town. Screwed up the whole county freeway system to save their old trees, but did they care?"

"My kind of people," I said.

"I thought so, too." He smiled as he reached for my hand.

"I'm glad the department put you in the cooler," I said. "It's nice to have some time with you."

"Just think, when I retire it'll always be like this."

"You wish."

He didn't argue.

I had no expectations about South Pasadena. In fact, I had never heard of the place until Mike mentioned it. As Mike drove south on Fair Oaks, I kept my eye on the odometer, measuring how far we were getting from Casey's school. When Mike turned down a side street, we were still within bicycle-riding range for a young athlete like Casey. And a city bus ran straight up Fair Oaks.

The neighborhood we drove through was dominated by large, well-kept old houses dating from the 1920s and 1930s. A typical upscale California architectural mix: graceful mission-style white-washed adobe and red tile cheek by jowl with trim Cape Cod cottages, stolid red-brick Georgians, the occasional French country farmhouse. There were real yards, neat green lawns and mature trees that filtered out the worst of the smog, made the air seem cooler. Very nice, I thought. Maybe too nice.

I tugged on Mike's hand. "Can we afford this?"

"We can probably find something in our range. Couple of guys at work live in the 'hood. Bud—you met Bud?—he thinks he has a lead on a place that isn't listed yet."

"The old cop fraternity," I said, squeezing his fingers. "Always takes care of their own."

"We have to watch out for each other," he said, "because no one else will."

"Oh, look," I said, pointing out the window. "Slow down a sec."

We were passing a beautiful old Iowa farmhouse-style woodframe on a sweeping corner lot. It had a "For Sale or Lease" sign pegged in the middle of the immaculate lawn. I knew it had to be beyond our budget, but just in case, and out of habit, I pulled a 35mm camera out of my bag and took some pictures out the car window.

I admit that I use the camera as an interpreter; I don't always know what I've seen until I have it on film. I wanted to pin the houses up on some wall for a while—pictures of them, anyway—get to know them.

Mike made frequent turns, apparently following no pattern, just cruising the neighborhood. He sped up or slowed down when he saw something—that's what I thought he was doing. I was seeing it all through the lens of the camera I held to my eye.

Even as I fell in love with the area, I was growing edgy, as

I do when there are big decisions to be made. Everything looked great, but were any of the neat-looking old men strolling on the sidewalks funny little old men who would bother my daughter? Were there sirens lying in wait for Michael behind the lace curtains? Were the sewers hooked up? Who would Bowser offend?

Mike seemed to be edgy, too, lost in thought, intent on the passing scene as he fiddled with the old handcuffs he kept dangling from his turn signal.

The cuffs were a standing joke between us. One night, just before we decided to cast our lots together, I cuffed him to the steering wheel and did him on the freeway while he drove. We both loved it, but it nearly got us killed. I had thought, now and then, when the magic grew cluttered with the daily chores, that I might try it again. Just for old time's sake.

I touched his arm. "Why don't you bring the cuffs in tonight? I'll lock you to the bed and make love to you until you scream for mercy."

"Uh huh." He smiled with his mouth, but his eyes were elsewhere.

I left him to his thoughts and raised the camera again. Mike's driving grew more erratic. I was about to say something when he sped into a turn and then, halfway through it, slammed on his brakes. The car behind us didn't make the stop in time and rammed us. I heard rubber bumpers connecting, but no grind of metal, no broken glass. The bump was sufficient to bang my camera into the side of my nose, though. I said, "Ouch," but there was no one there anymore to hear me.

Mike had bailed out his door, with the handcuffs, even before the bump came. When I turned around, I saw him at the driver's side of the red Toyota that hit us, roughly hauling out the driver. Mike twisted the man's arm behind his back, snapped a handcuff on one wrist, slammed him up against the side of the Toyota, kicked his legs apart, and then reached out and caught the free, flailing hand and cuffed it, too.

By the time I got out of the Blazer spewing coherent questions like, "Wha? Wha?", Mike was patting down this totally befuddled man whose questions more or less repeated mine, with some surprisingly clear obscenities thrown in.

Mike tossed the man's wallet, some loose change, and a

Swiss army knife onto the hood of his car. He flipped open the wallet, read the license, then threw it back down.

I still had my camera in my hand. I wiped away the blood running down from the side of my nose and I did what I do: I took pictures.

The prisoner was an overweight, middle-aged, ordinary looking fellow in shirt-sleeves. It was hot, but not hot enough to make him sweat that profusely. His glasses had been knocked askew and he tried to set them straight by using his shoulder. Mike fixed them for him.

"You have no right," the man seethed, straining against Mike's hold. "You can't do this to me."

"Sure I can. I just did." Mike's voice was controlled, but edged with something dangerous I had never heard before.

The man hissed, "Do you know who I *am*?"

"The license says George Schwartz, but suppose you tell me the rest of it. And while you're at it, maybe you could explain why you were tailing us."

"That's bullshit. I wasn't tailing you."

"Mike?" I said, wondering which one here was the lunatic. Mike only shook his head at me, as in, Go away. I was alarmed, but I still trusted that Mike knew what he was doing.

"Let me rephrase the question," Mike said to Schwartz. "Maybe you could explain why you were tailing us before I beat the dog shit out of you."

Schwartz wasn't taking in enough air to gasp properly. In his position, I would have passed out from either anoxia or impotent rage. He managed to speak: "I'm an investigator for the district attorney's office. Let go of me."

"Marovich?" Mike smiled evilly. "Now, why in hell would Mr. Baron Marovich want to tail me?"

"Ask him."

Mike yanked up the cuffs, making Schwartz wince. "I asked you three times now. Why don't you save us all some grief and just tell me what this is about."

"I don't know what it's about. Marovich told me to keep an eye on you."

"Since when?"

"Since you called Jerry Kelsey and tried to set up a meeting."

"I can't talk to my old partner without the D.A. putting the dogs on me?"

"I don't know."

I thought it was time for Mike to ease up. Poor Schwartz was hopelessly overmatched. He was about to lose the last of his dignity by crying or messing in his Dockers. I took a last shot of his face, then put down the camera.

"Mike?" I said again.

"Hold on," he answered gruffly, but he relaxed his grip on Schwartz.

"I can't decide what to do with you, Mr. Schwartz," Mike said. "I could charge you with harassment, threatening a police officer with a lethal weapon—if you can believe this piece-of-shit car could be lethal. There's a new stalking law we could try. Failure to signal before turning? How about plain old too-stupid-to-be-out-on-the-streets? Maybe I should just shoot you. What's your pleasure?"

Schwartz got himself together enough to answer. "This is bullshit, Flint. Total bullshit. Get these fucking cuffs off me right now or I'll have your ass."

Mike crossed his arms. "In a city as old as this one, there has to be a law still on the books against using obscenities in front of a lady. Now, if the lady declines to file charges, I'll have to let you go this time with a warning."

"Fuck you, Flint." Schwartz was building up some angry steam now.

Mike jerked the chain between the cuffs, not enough to hurt Schwartz, but enough to make him madder. "Here's the warning: You tell that asshole Marovich that if he wants to talk to me, all he has to do is pick up the phone. I'm a real cooperative guy. But if I ever see your ugly face, or any of his goons anywhere near my family again, tell him that hell will look like Club Med in comparison with what I put him through. If we're clear, Mr. Schwartz, you're free to go."

Mike gave Schwartz a shove as he let go of the chain. Off balance, Schwartz fell forward to his knees. Like a kneeling supplicant, he raised his face to Mike.

"Take these fucking things off me, Flint."

"You can keep them. A little souvenir." As Mike turned to walk away, Schwartz came up hurling his considerable bulk at Mike's back. My camera came up with him.

"Mike!" I yelled, snapping the entire sequence. I didn't need to warn Mike. He had set up Schwartz. He let Schwartz get almost within striking range, then he agilely slipped to the side at the last instant. Schwartz, in full flight and with nothing to stop him, crashed against the side of Mike's car. As he slid back down to the pavement, the cuffs etched a long gash in the blue paint.

Mike looked over at me. "Did you get it all?"

"Yes." I was so nonplussed I stood there frozen.

Mike pulled the slender key for the handcuffs out of his pocket and held it up to Schwartz. "Had enough, son? Come to papa."

Warily, Schwartz got up and backed toward Mike with his wrists extended as far as he could. Faster than Houdini, Mike unlocked the left cuff and snapped it over the spare tire rack on the back of his Blazer. While Schwartz swore—none of it very original—Mike went to his car phone, called the local police, and reported a collision. And an assault on a police officer.

A black and white cruiser came right over.

"He rear-ended me," Mike told the uniforms after showing them his badge. True, as far as it went. "I tried to talk to him, but he got froggy. So I had to cuff him. We have the whole thing on film. I'll send you copies."

By that point Schwartz had decided to get real quiet. Like a lamb, he climbed into the back seat of the police car. Maybe like a lamb saved from slaughter.

Mike waved to Schwartz as he was driven away. Then he turned to me.

"Okay," he said, "let's have it."

"Jesus Christ, Michael Flint." I opened up on him, standing right there in the middle of that peaceful street. "Of all the excessive uses of force I have ever seen, and I have covered my share, that was the single most reprehensible, unnecessary example of pure fascist-tactic police abuse I have ever encountered. What the hell were you trying to prove?"

Unremorseful, he put his hands in his pockets and shrugged. "He crossed the line."

"And what line was that?"

"My personal line. Think about it. Schwartz must have picked us up at the house this morning. Now he knows where your daughter goes to school. How does that make you feel?"

"I don't like being followed," I said. "But, my God, Mike, Schwartz isn't a criminal. He works for the D.A."

"So he says."

That gave me pause.

"And so what if he works for the D.A.?" Mike went on. "We're talking Baron Marovich, not Mother Teresa. I don't trust Marovich as far as I can throw him, and he outweighs me by thirty pounds. The point is, no one comes near my family. Even the Mafia has rules about that. *Capice?*"

"I *capice* okay," I said. "But I still say you went too far."

"Never laid a hand on him. Did what I needed to do to control the scene, nothing more. Everything strictly within department guidelines. You have it all on film. Besides, fuck him."

"Don't try to snow me," I said.

He smiled sheepishly. "You're mad, huh?"

"Yes I'm mad. You scared the shit out of me. See this?" I tapped the little cut on my nose. "I got hurt."

"Want me to kiss it?"

"Not yet. I'm still too upset. I've never seen this side of you. Is that the way you behave on duty?"

"When I need to. This time, I definitely needed to."

"I'm not sure how I feel about it."

"You'd better decide," he said. He was not in any way repentant. In fact, he was cocky. "I figure I've given Marovich fair warning. If I ever see him around you or Casey or Michael again, I'll shoot him."

"Bull," I said.

"No bull," he said. Then he held out his arms to me. "Come here."

I went over and put my arms around him because I needed to be reminded who he was, or who I thought he was. He still felt the same, had the same soft bristles at the back of his neck, the same little patch of missed whiskers on his chin. I had been feeling a little shaky ever since the cafeteria lunch at Casey's school. It was nice to lean against something warm and solid. To lean against Mike. My mind was in turmoil, but at least my body was comforted.

I looked over Mike's shoulder and saw the audience we had drawn, a group of five neighbors and one little dog that could be mistaken for a dust mop.

An elderly woman in bright walking togs, holding on to an

elderly man in similar bright attire, called out, "Are you all right, dear?"

"We're fine," I said.

"Are you lost?"

I looked up at Mike and started to laugh. "We're not lost," I said. "We're the new neighbors."

CHAPTER

11

All the rest of Tuesday I felt unsettled. My outrage over being followed had been chilled by the cool, cocky expression on Mike's face as he overpowered George Schwartz. It was some stranger who put the cuffs on Schwartz, not the Mike I knew.

Once we were home, I watched Mike's every move for clues, hoping, I think, that some gesture or turn of phrase would reveal to me something essential about him that I had missed, or reassure me that I had not been wrong. Expose him, redeem him, I didn't care which. I had to know.

My moodiness seemed to infect the household. Casey had come home hot, muscle-weary, suffering a rare crisis of faith in her own ability; the senior students had been magnificent, a tough standard to follow. Without saying much, and still in her dance clothes, hair hanging in damp strings, she had gone back out into the smoggiest part of the day to take Bowser for a walk.

Sitting close together in the cool gray living room, Mike and I went over the inventory of my stored furniture, discussing without much interest what we might want to ship down once we had decided on a house. Furniture was safe territory. I was afraid to bring up what was really on my mind, afraid of the outcome. Afraid that, if the answers weren't right, the furniture would never come out of storage. It was a relief when Michael came home and brought a bells-and-whistles distraction with him: Sly.

Sly belonged to all of us, a ten-year-old urchin Mike and I had gathered in off the street the previous spring. While Michael put away his school things, I followed Sly around as he followed Mike around. I eavesdropped on their conversation, dropped in my two cents now and then.

When we first met Sly he was a foul-mouthed, underfed little delinquent with more tricks in his repertoire than most career criminals acquire in a lifetime. After five months in a decent group home in Reseda, with Michael as his Big Brother and mentor, and with Mike running interference with the authorities now and then, Sly's sharp edges had noticeably softened. He was being transformed from a know-it-all old man into a vulnerable child. But he was still hungry all the time.

"This asswipe Fliegle's always on my case," Sly complained, slumped at the kitchen table while Mike made him a couple of predinner peanut butter sandwiches. "It's harassment, Mike. I'm gonna sue him."

"Fliegle's the math teacher?" Mike cut the sandwiches and set them in front of Sly. I poured him a glass of milk as an excuse to be there. "Are you turning in your homework every day?"

"I just don't get it. How'm I supposed to do those crapwad problems when I don't get it?" Dejected, Sly picked up his sandwich. "Anyway, don't matter what I do. Fliegle hates me." He took a bite.

"Fliegle wants you to learn something. If he didn't care about you, he wouldn't be on your case." Mike sat down beside Sly, listened to his grievances, acknowledged his frustration—school was a whole new world for the boy. Then he sold the teacher to the kid, pushed him even. When I left the room to answer the front door, they were laughing about Fliegle's weird mustache, agreeing that he was a good teacher.

Watching Mike with the child, I was moved. I was encouraged. Mike Flint would never coerce a kid to do something wrong; the charges were bullshit.

On my way out of the kitchen, I almost collided with Michael.

"I have tickets for the Dodger game," he said, following me to answer the door. "Can you and Casey come?"

It was Casey at the door, with Bowser. "Forgot my key," she

said. She unhooked Bowser's leash and followed him inside, both of them panting and hot.

"Michael has tickets for the Dodger game," I said.

"Can't," she said. "Homework."

I knew it was a lie, but I didn't make an issue. For nearly four years it had been just her and me. As much as we liked Mike and Michael, it takes a while to get accustomed to living with new people. Casey and I both needed a time-out.

"You men go ahead," I said to Michael. "Have fun."

I thought Michael looked as relieved that we weren't coming along as Casey did. I helped Mike find his binoculars and kissed everyone good-bye.

While Casey showered and dressed to go out to dinner with me, I took advantage of having a few minutes alone to make some calls.

I reached Baron Marovich's office and asked to speak with George Schwartz, just to see what I could learn. After a round of telephonic leapfrog, and under the guise of a loan rep trying to verify the employment of an applicant—that is, Schwartz—I was put in touch with Marovich's administrative assistant.

"Mr. Schwartz is on disability leave," she told me. "Has been for about two months."

"Paid leave?" I asked, absorbing the implications.

"Yes," she said. "You should call the county personnel office for verification, though."

I thanked her and went on to round two. If he was on leave from the D.A., then for whom was George Schwartz following us around?

I already knew from trying to track down LaShonda DeBevis that county personnel wasn't going to give me anything as useful as an address and a telephone number. Information was of no use: there were too many George Schwartzes in Los Angeles, doubtless many more in the commuter suburbs that fan out from the city for a hundred-mile radius.

Mike's badge number is 15991. I invoked it when I called the south Pasadena police and asked for booking information on Schwartz, George, white male, arrested for assault on a police officer that very day. Among the information I received, including Schwartz's booking number, was the address on his driver's license—he lived in Santa Monica—and a work telephone number. I dialed the number I was given. Intrigued, I dialed the

number a second time to make sure I had it right: the phone
was answered by campaign headquarters, Marovich for District
Attorney.

I didn't come up for air until about halfway through dinner
at a Chinese place in Sherman Oaks when Casey tapped her
chopsticks on the edge of my plate to get my attention.

"Earth to Mom," she said. "What's your estimated time of arrival?"

"Sorry," I said, taking her hand.

"What are thinking so hard about?"

"These accusations against Mike. There's something strange
going on."

"What are you going to do?"

I shrugged, tried to change the subject. "I saw a dance shop
on the way. You need some shoes."

Shaking her head, smiling at me to show she wasn't buying,
she said, "What are you going to do?"

I leaned toward her. "I'm going to visit the campaign headquarters of Baron Marovich. You game?"

"Hold on." She picked up one of the fortune cookies that
came with the check and cracked it open, read the fortune,
handed it to me. "Let's go."

The fortune said, "Make your own destiny."

Marovich campaign headquarters was on Victory Boulevard
out in Van Nuys. The campaign had taken over a vacant store-
front at the end of a block of vacant storefronts; quiet neighbors, but a busy intersection.

I could just make out "Valley Carpets and Floorcoverings,"
no more than a gold-leaf shadow on the big front windows to
tell who the last tenant had been. Campaign posters covered
some of the holes left by long-gone store fixtures. The huge
space was unevenly filled with rented desks and mismatched
chairs, tangles of telephone wires, a hodgepodge of computer
equipment and typewriters. The only luxury to be found was
the luscious seafoam-green carpet.

I scanned the dozen or so volunteers working the phones or
stuffing envelopes, picking my target. I passed on the retiree
with the bald head and bald-toed tennies, passed on the well-
coiffed matron and the earnest young pair I guessed were there
as part of a Poli-Sci 1A assignment.

I settled my attentions, finally, on a young man stationed off to the side, polished Gucci loafers on the desk next to half a take-out order of sushi. His clothes, which he wore easily, were subdued in color but extravagant in tailoring and, I was sure, in cost. Slacks, striped silk tie, custom-fitted white-on-white shirt rolled up to the elbows. In his manner I read good schools, good connections. Going places.

If money is the mother's milk of politics, then press coverage is surely the hand that rocks the cradle. I pulled out my press credentials as I led Casey over to my pigeon.

I think Casey liked his looks. She held herself tall, flipped her long hair over her shoulders.

"Maggie MacGowen," I said, holding out my press card to him. "My intern, Casey."

He brightened, took down his feet, swept the sushi into a desk drawer. Then he offered his hand to both of us in turn, giving Casey more turn than me. "Schuyler Smith. How can I help you?"

"I'm interested in your volunteers," I said.

"Media relations handles all interviews. If you'll leave your card . . ."

"Sure." I smiled, propped my hip against his desk. "All I'm doing at this point is deep background for a nonpartisan piece to run as filler on election night after all the rhetoric has been canned. 'Volunteers: Who Are They?'—something like that. Marovich is an old-time pol. I thought there might be some personalities to mine here."

Smith surveyed the mixed bag populating the room, smiling at some retort he was keeping private. What he said was, "The district attorney depends on citizens dedicated to his platform of a quality judicial system, of fairness . . ."

"Are you a volunteer?" I asked. "Or paid staff?"

"Full-time volunteer."

He must have read something into the glance I gave his Guccis, because he felt a need to explain further. "I feel so strongly about Mr. Marovich's candidacy that I took a six-month leave from my job."

"Paid or unpaid leave?" Already a familiar refrain.

He frowned. "You really should talk to media relations."

I made a little bow as an apology. "For background only. I'm curious, of course. A campaign on this scale takes a lot of bright-young-man hours." I glanced at Casey. "And bright-young-woman hours. The time represents quite a financial sacrifice. Your employer would risk violating election laws if he kept you on the payroll, risks his own productivity if he leaves your job open for you. I was merely wondering how you keep yourself in sushi and why you would put a career on hold and how you got your employer to go along."

He was eyeing my daughter, holding in his little gut for her benefit. "I'm fortunate to work for a firm with a social conscience. They feel that any sacrifice now is an investment in the future. Contacts made, friendships solidified."

"They pick your candidate?"

"Of course not." Still smiling.

"Who do you work for?" I asked. The law firm he mentioned was only too familiar. Jennifer Miller hung her credentials on the wall there. Baron Marovich was an alumnus.

Casey had wandered off to leaf through a stack of posters. Smith watched her. I was tempted to snatch him bald for his thoughts. Not so long ago, I . . . I believe the first sign of impending middle age is becoming invisible to men under thirty. I wasn't invisible yet, but I felt I was fading.

"George Schwartz," I said to get Smith's attention.

"Excuse me?"

"I understand George Schwartz has left his position with the district attorney's office to work for the campaign. Do you know him?"

"I know who he is. George works under the aegis of the executive staff. I don't see much of him."

"What does he do for the executive staff?"

"Leg work. I'm not sure."

"Know how I can reach him?"

"You might leave a message through Roddy O'Leary. Or call media relations."

"I'll do that," I said. "Mind if we speak with some of your volunteers?"

"Media relations will be in at nine tomorrow. You'll have to ask them." He was smooth, never let the friendly mien drop. I left him my card. Casey and I walked back out into the noise of city traffic, heads together, trying not to burst out laughing at the smooth of Mr. Schuyler Smith.

We had filled in some blanks, learned a few questions to ask. It was time well spent.

Casey was in no mood to waste the last night without homework at home. She came with me to my office in Burbank to help me get settled in. Sounds boring, but we were having fun, cataloguing video tapes before shelving them, taking turns with the TV, fifteen minutes of Satellite Network News, then fifteen minutes of MTV, with a few seconds of token groaning to serve as segue between sets.

We were five minutes into my turn when Ralph Faust came on with a breaking news report. I leaned forward from my seat on the office rug to hear every word. Casey was making labels and never looked up at the TV.

Demonstrators keeping candlelight vigil at Parker Center, police headquarters, have been for the most part orderly. Earlier some bottles were reportedly thrown at the front of the building after the Reverend Jimmy Lee Cook, in addressing the crowd—estimated to be between two and three hundred— suggested that if Charles Conklin were not freed immediately that it might be time to go back to the streets to give a message to the LAPD.

At a separate news conference in his office, District Attorney Marovich called for an investigation into the records of Detectives Mike Flint and Jerry Kelsey, identified as the chief investigating officers assigned to the Wyatt Johnson shooting. A recent survey by the police department identified the forty officers with the worst records of abuse and civilian complaints. Neither Flint nor Kelsey appears on the list.

Casey's head snapped up. "What did he say about Mike?"

"Junk," I said. I punched up MTV.

Casey gave me a quick, wise appraisal. "Why did you change the channel? They're talking about Mike."

"I don't want to hear it," I said.

"Oh, right," she said, reaching for the remote. "You mean, you don't want me to hear it."

SNN came back on the screen, running taped footage of the earlier interview Ralph had done with Marovich, Miller, and Burgess. Casey sat rapt this time, listening.

When the Reverend Burgess said, again, that Mike scared false testimony from two child witnesses, Casey threw down her pen in disgust. "The fat guy said Mike threatened someone."

"Casey, those people will say anything to get their names on the news. Look at them. You have a reporter desperate to keep his ratings, a politician running for office, an attorney looking for her thirty-percent cut of a potentially huge civil suit, and a pseudo-reverend sitting there with the address where you can send donations scrolling across his chest. Who do you trust, them, or Mike?"

"Don't get mad," she said. "It's like Mike always says, 'Who you gonna believe? Me, or your own lyin' eyes?' "

"You little wiseacre." I gave her a gentle shove and made a grab for the remote, but her arms are longer than mine. She held it beyond my grasp so I couldn't change from the news.

Burgess still dominated the spot. *Mr. Marovich listened to us, understood the implications of our findings right away. He has such confidence that the original investigation was tainted that he persuaded one of the city's big-dollar law firms to represent Charles Conklin on a* pro bono *basis. Without charging a retainer, Jennifer Miller will lead the defense.*

I crawled over and switched off the television. "Listen up," I said. "And be warned. If the D.A. succeeds in blowing this into a bigger issue, there will be press everywhere looking for juicy bits. If anyone comes near you, you keep your mouth shut and run."

I knew she had a sassy retort brewing, but the telephone rang and interrupted her.

"Another thing," I said, scrambling for the phone. "Don't give out anything on the phone."

I said, "Hello."

Bad news travels fast, especially when it travels by satellite. I had picked up the receiver with a sense of dread. I expected to hear on the other end an obscene caller, a local news person looking for fresh dirt, a concerned but nosy friend. What I got was my ex. And he was in high dudgeon.

"What the hell is going on out there?" Scotty ranted. "I saw the news. I want you to put Casey on a plane for Denver right now, Maggie, get her out of that overheated environment."

"Hello, Scotty," I said. "How are the wife and kids?"

"Merely contemplating the implications of what I just heard is like a knife through my heart."

"Through your what?" I didn't think he heard me.

"It's one thing if you want to destroy your reputation," he roared. "But to leave Casey vulnerable to the storm of criticism this mess will generate is absolutely unconscionable."

"How's the golf game?"

"The first time I hear my daughter's name linked in public in association with that reprobate Flint, I will haul you into court. With custody comes certain obligations, Maggie, that I seriously doubt you are fulfilling."

"Heard any good jokes?" I said calmly. Casey was watching me closely. "I heard one. What do you call a lawyer who can tie his own shoes?"

There was a pregnant silence.

"Gifted," I said. "I thought you might like to try that one at the office tomorrow. Let me know if anyone gets it."

"Are you insane?" He wasn't shouting any more so it was safe to pass him on to Casey.

"Yes, everything is fine." I smiled at Casey. "Casey had school orientation today. Here, I'll let her tell you all about it."

I handed the receiver to Casey. She covered the mouthpiece and said to me, "I could hear every word he said."

I whispered, "And he can tie his own shoes."

She took a breath. "Hi, Dad."

After that opening, Casey did a lot of listening, with a few "Uh huhs" and "uh uhs" wedged in, because she had no alternative other than hanging up. I could hear Scotty, but I didn't listen hard enough to discern what he was saying. I didn't need to. During our twelve years of marriage, I heard everything I ever wanted to hear from him. And more.

I went back to work cataloguing tapes, stowing them away. Now and then I glanced up at Casey to make sure she was all right. I watched her expression change from bored resignation to anger.

I said, "Remind him how much the call is costing."

She grimaced, took a breath, and said very loudly, "Dad! Will you listen to me?"

Apparently he wouldn't listen. She tried again.

"You don't know anything about it, Dad." Her assertiveness made me proud. "You don't know anything about Mike, either. Those people are just distorting everything for their own purposes."

She listened to some flak, then cut in again.

"You're wrong, Dad. Anyway, who are you gonna believe? Me, or your own lyin' eyes?" She slammed down the receiver.

I saw right away that the slam had been dramatics as much as frustration. She wasn't crying and that was a hopeful sign.

"You okay?" I asked.

"I'm okay." She stretched, reached up and touched the rim of the ceiling light fixture with her fingertips. "Dad's the one with the problem, Mom. I think he's jealous."

An odd idea. "Jealous of what?" I asked.

"Mike."

An odd idea that grew on me. Scott MacGowen had waited almost thirty minutes after our divorce was final before he married the lovely young Linda. Now she was pregnant with their second child. Pregnancy can be rough on men. Especially when they're over forty years old and facing a second go-round on the child-raising process that they hadn't much liked the first time. Too confining, according to old Scotty. Very messy.

I reached up and tickled the hard midsection of my one and only, nearly grown offspring, feeling a haughty smugness.

You make your bed, you lie in it. Four more years and Casey would be an adult, my daily mother work essentially finished. In four more years, in the matter of children, old Scotty would have barely climbed between the sheets.

"You ready to go home?" I asked. "Take a swim with me?"

She shrugged. "I'd rather go for pizza."

"Fine," I said. I didn't feel like eating, but I didn't feel like going straight home, either. While we straightened the room and turned out lights, I dialed Guido.

"Mpfh?" he said, picking up on the third ring.

"Sorry to wake you," I said. "You could have left the machine on. I just wanted to remind you we're going out to Central Juvenile Hall in the morning. I'll be by before nine."

"Nine's more civilized than three. Etta coming?"

"She didn't say one way or the other. If she wants a ride, she'll call."

He said something like mpfh again. I took it for good-bye and hung up.

The building was full of activity. Most of the tenants were free-lancers who rented offices downstairs and studio space upstairs by the hour. The studios were in use around the clock, usually bigger productions by day, small stuff at night whenever time became available.

Because the elections were only a month and a half away, the studios were solidly booked by political hack crews producing spots for the end-of-campaign TV blitz. All night long candidates walked the corridors in heavy makeup and perfect light-blue shirts. Working vampire hours.

I knew the people across the hall were doing spots for Marovich. I had seen them hard at it. After I locked my door, I stopped outside their office and listened. Someone was tuned to Satellite Network News, doubtless on the lookout for usable video bites to cannibalize from Ralph. Because Marovich would be footing the bills, I hoped Ralph gouged them more deeply for anything they used than the fifteen hundred I had cut for thirty seconds of Etta.

That was a cruel thought, I thought. I should give Mr. District Attorney Marovich a chance. Thinking, no time like the present, I knocked on the neighbors' door.

CHAPTER
12

I gained entry to my neighbors' office by pulling out a Pass Go card. That is, my business card. I knew my name would carry some cachet with another filmmaker, entrée at least, but the version I handed him read: Countryside Film Productions, Margot E. Duchamps—it's my legal name—and my San Francisco number. I also carry a version with my professional name—Maggie MacGowen—the one I acquired when a TV station genius at my first job decided that Margot Duchamps wasn't perky enough for western Kansas, and stamped me with my husband's name.

Circumstances define which card I pull out. Name recognition that might open certain doors, might get other doors slammed in my face. I play it by ear. My ear said Baron Marovich had acquired some idea who Maggie MacGowen was and would not be especially eager to speak with me, perky or not.

I learned from my across-the-hall colleagues that Marovich had a taping scheduled upstairs at ten-thirty. That gave me time to get pizza, take Casey home, and drive back again.

I needn't have hurried; it was nearly eleven before Marovich dragged into the studio for retooling—a fresh shirt and new makeup.

My card was on the makeup table among half-a-dozen messages when Marovich sat down on a high wooden stool and gave his face to the makeup woman.

Marovich was a surprise to me. I had expected the D.A. to be slicker than snot. Face to face, I found him to be very bright, very attractive, and thoroughly personable. We hit it off right away. I think that I represented to him the possibility of some free media exposure, which he cannily courted. He also seemed to like my legs, though he was having some trouble buying my reasons for wanting a word with him.

"I'm working on a documentary about a group of kids who grew up in the projects," I said. "Seems to me that every time I turn around I bump into Charles Conklin, or his tailings. If he's going to be a recurring presence, I need to have some blanks filled in. You probably know more about him right now than anyone. I'd like to use you as a source."

Marovich was getting the shine powdered off his face, so he couldn't frown properly when I said the C word: Conklin. But he got across his displeasure about the topic.

"Miss Duchamps," he said, hardly moving his lips, "I'd like to help you, but right now it's a question of time. I don't have any. My family thinks I'm a stranger, and the way things are going I won't see them again, awake, until after the first Tuesday in November. Obligations at the office, demands of a campaign—you understand, I'm sure, why I can't help you."

"Absolutely," I said. He couldn't turn his head and I didn't like talking to the side of his face. So I pulled up a second stool next to him, leaned my elbows on my knees and talked to his image in the mirror. "I understand how a campaign can put pressure on a family. Any time a parent is away from home for an extended period there can be disastrous ramifications. Take Conklin's son, Tyrone, as an example. Tyrone is in Central Juvenile waiting to be tried for murder."

He laughed. "Are you suggesting that if I don't go straight home my kids will end up in the slam?"

"Nope. I'm sure your wife is a paragon and has things well in hand. Tyrone Harkness's mother was a junkie."

"Might explain a lot," he said.

"It might. The two young witnesses against Conklin grew up on the same block as Tyrone. One of them was a hooker, the other one is a librarian. The question is, what made the difference?"

Mention of the witnesses made a shadow cross his face. But he still liked my legs well enough to hang in with me.

I leaned closer to him, aiming to project befuddled sincerity. "I find the 'what if's' to be absolutely compelling, don't you? What if Tyrone'd had a father who could provide him with a safety net, some guidance? Would the boy Tyrone is accused of killing be sitting down to dinner tonight with his family? Would his own two babies now have a role model and guide to see them safely through the perils of childhood?"

"Vicious cycle."

"Yes it is," I said. "Charles Conklin's conviction trails an endless wake of grief. If the man was innocent, if he was wrongfully deprived of all those years he should have been with his family, then it is truly a gross tragedy. But after 'oops,' what can be said?"

"Oops is a good start," he said, smiling, cracking the makeup that filled in his crow's feet. The makeup person was holding a white card behind his head so she could see in shadow, as the camera would, any stray wisps of hair. Marovich was being very patient with the fussing.

"Why do I feel I'm being interviewed?" he asked.

"Just conversation," I said. I picked up a comb, dampened it with hairspray, and smoothed some fluff that had breached the surface of his helmet of salt-and-pepper hair. "You do see the poignancy?"

"Uh huh," he said, dubious. "Let me first correct one misstatement. I have never suggested that Conklin was innocent. His guilt or innocence is irrelevant. What is relevant is this: Charles Conklin was convicted on tainted evidence. He has a right to a new trial. But after fourteen years, a trial would be an exercise in futility. Justice demands he be set free."

"Do you believe he's guilty?"

He shrugged. "Guilt is an altogether different issue."

I pressed, gesturing with the comb. "When you go on national television with that jackass evangelist and say nothing when he gets red in the face asserting Conklin's innocence, and you sit next to his defense attorney and nod when she lisps out her rage at the injustice of sending a poor lamb to prison, then it seems to me you express tacit agreement with them."

"I was merely one viewpoint on a panel," he said, defensive.

"An awfully quiet one. You looked like a fellow traveler. I heard no debate about fine points of the law, only protestations of the man's innocence."

He drew back to look at me directly. "Jesus," he said. "You're tough. In my defense I say again, guilt is not the issue."

"Maybe not in court, but in the real world guilt is absolutely the issue. The witnesses and the investigating cops, and I suppose the jail-house snitch, are taking a heavy beating. They stand accused of doing something corrupt and cannot defend themselves. They don't have your access to the media, and the media apparently is not interested in what they might have to say."

"You seem to know a lot about it." He eyed the comb in my hand, wary, maybe evaluating how much damage it was capable of inflicting.

I slipped the comb into his breast pocket. "You and I both know that Charles Conklin is a career criminal with a rap sheet about half as long as he is tall. Child molestation, pandering, dealing, theft, you name it. If he hadn't gone down for shooting Officer Wyatt Johnson, he would have tumbled on something else. Unless he got shot on the street first. Right?"

"If Conklin held to pattern."

"Tell me why, in all the fuss about this gross injustice, no one has mentioned Conklin's record."

"Because it isn't germane."

"What is germane, then?"

He picked up the stack of messages with my card on top, and started to rise. "The cops fucked up."

I rose with him. "Cops that fuck up attract a lot of press."

"Margot." The way he said it sounded like a challenge. "What is it, exactly, that you want?"

"I want to talk to the witnesses."

"Go ahead."

"I've tried. Hanna Rhodes was a body under a sheet before I connected with her. LaShonda DeBevis is doing a good impression of the invisible man. And I understand that when anyone tries to contact Detective Jerry Kelsey, your office puts out a tail. Exactly who does George Schwartz work for?"

"Margot," he said again, slowly, looking hard at my card. "I guess Maggie could be short for Margot."

"No. For maggot. My older brother and sister used to call me maggot."

"And MacGowen?"

"My husband's name."

.

I had not read him well. Once he made the connection, he was amused by me in the way a cat is amused when he has a rat squirming under his paw. I'd never been so sympathetic with rats before.

"Now I get it," he said. "I know what you want from me."

"What?" I asked.

"Absolution for Mike Flint."

"No." I matched his slow, considered tone. "I want the truth, the whole truth, and you know the rest of it. Don't feed me any more bullshit fine points of the law or fairy tales about dashed innocence. It is unconscionable the way you have exploited real people just to get your face on the tube as much as you possibly can before the election."

He flushed. "That's not what I've done."

"That's how I read it. That's how I will present it unless I am persuaded otherwise. I can have a red-hot package ready in time for the early news broadcasts tomorrow. Network news. With photos and footage. The lead will probably be some variation on 'Conklingate.' The theme will be boundless ambition. Where were you at two-thirty this morning, Mr. District Attorney, when Hanna Rhodes took a couple in the chest? Where was your investigator, George Schwartz? What the hell are you up to?"

He reacted the way a seasoned courtroom attorney should. He stonewalled all expression.

Roddy O'Leary, Marovich's campaign manager, came in just then, and I knew there would be no more discussion. Roddy was visibly unhappy to see me, but he came over and gave me a big smooch anyway.

"Working late?" he said, putting himself between me and the candidate.

"Normal hours for me," I said. "You know, no rest for the wicked."

He gave me a token chuckle. He said, "Studio time is expensive. You two want to debate, find a cheaper hall. Mr. D.A., they're waiting for you on the set. At their rates, every minute wasted is the equivalent of two-hundred direct-mail fliers. So, let's go do it."

Marovich fixed the knot in his tie as he studied me, memorized me. "Nice meeting you."

"LaShonda DeBevis," I said. "Get me access to LaShonda DeBevis."

"I don't have her," he said. He walked away shielded by the considerable mass of old Roddy.

"You'd have made a good she-wolf," I said to Roddy as I gathered my things, "the way you watch over your cubs."

"I do what it takes," he said. "Anything it takes."

"Anything?" I asked.

"What's on your mind?"

"George Schwartz. How far will you have him go?"

"Schwartz, you say?" Roddy turned his hands up. "Never heard of the guy. Nice talking to you, MacGee. I gotta go to work."

All the way home, I tried to sort what I knew from what I surmised. As always, the first column was tremendously shorter than the second.

Mike was in the kitchen with the telephone against his ear and a pencil poised above a notebook. The stills I had taken the night before were spread out on the table, along with stills made from Guido's videotape. I picked one up, a blow-up of the back end of a car. The quality was flat and fuzzy, but I could read the license plate. I could read license plates in eight or ten other shots as well.

"When did you see Guido?" I asked.

"Didn't. I talked to him this morning. He had this stuff sent over while we were at the game. For a commie, your Guido's damn smart. Hector says hi."

"Me, too," I said. "And Guido isn't a commie. He's a democrat."

"Same thing."

"I'm a democrat."

If he heard me, he didn't bother to retort. He was back on the phone with Hector. I got a soda from the refrigerator and drank it while I eavesdropped. Mike would read a license number to Hector on the phone. Hector was, I presumed, plugging the numbers into the Department of Motor Vehicles computer and sending back to Mike the names and addresses of the owners.

I rested my arm across Mike's shoulders and watched him write Ozzie Freemantle, 1931 112th Street. He thanked Hector and hung up.

I asked, "Can't Hector draw a suspension for unauthorized use of the files?"

"If he does, I'll make it up to him. Anyway, who's gonna beef him? Hec is a homicide dick working a case."

"But you're not."

Mike pulled me down to his lap. "But who's gonna tell?"

"Me," I said. "I just bawled out the district attorney for not playing by the rules. You think I'm going to live with cheating in my own home?"

"Damn right. If I'm a cheater, you'll live with it."

"You're pretty sure of yourself, Mike Flint." I nestled my face into the soft crook of his neck and closed my eyes while he rocked me. I felt sleep-deprived and would have been very happy to spend the next eight or so hours right there on his lap. "Pretty damn sure of yourself."

"Tell me about the D.A."

I yawned. "Later, okay? I have to be up early to get Casey to school. I'm going to bed now."

"I'm off, remember? I'll drive Casey."

"Okay, but one condition." I managed to stand up. "If anyone follows you, I don't want you to beat him up until after you have dropped off my baby. Got it?"

"Got it." He laughed.

I took him by the hand and gave him a pull. "Come on. Bedtime for cheaters."

CHAPTER

13

Etta didn't call Wednesday morning. I thought maybe she was still partying with Baby Boy. Or maybe he had worn her out so that she couldn't drag herself down the street to a pay phone. Whatever the reason Etta didn't call, I was relieved to be saved the long detour into Southeast L.A.

At eight-thirty, when I got on the freeway, the air was already hot and the sky was a ridiculously showy blue. The day's ration of smog still hovered in a low, dense brown layer along the ocean horizon, waiting for a change in the wind. At the tail end of morning rush hour, traffic down the Hollywood Freeway to Guido's house was heavy but moving steadily.

According to the news on the radio, the pro-Conklin demonstrators outside Parker Center had grown both in number and in volume. The police department had asked all of its workers to enter the building through the guarded, covered garage on San Pedro Street for their own safety. Two members of the police commission had nearly come to blows during last night's meeting called to discuss how the department would proceed. I turned the radio off.

Guido lives in a rugged canyon behind the Hollywood Bowl, his small gem of a house surrounded by groves of eucalyptus and dusty pine. Though he is only ten minutes from the festering armpit of the city—his description—once you turn off Highland Avenue and start up his winding road you are deep in wilderness. So, okay, maybe it's an illusion of wilderness and

locals dump their bodies off the side of his road with scary reg-
ularity. Still, at night coyotes howl at the moon from the rise
behind his house.

When I crested the top of his steep drive, I found Guido sitting on his front step in a patch of sunlight. Lazily, he got to his
feet.

"I was sitting here thinking," he said, sauntering over as I got
out of my car, "how nice it would be to drive up the coast today, maybe stop somewhere north of Malibu for a late breakfast. There's an antique camera store around Oxnard somewhere. Maybe it's in Ojai. I've been meaning to check it out. It's
gorgeous up there this time of year, orange trees in blossom everywhere."

"Nice try," I said. "It took me three days of fast talking to get
permission to bring the equipment into Juvenile Hall. I don't
want to go through that again, even for orange blossoms. Tell
you what, though. When we're finished with Tyrone, I'll take
you over to Lawry's California for huevos rancheros. I've always wanted to go there."

"Can't." He sighed dramatically. "They closed it down a couple of years ago. By the time I get to Ojai, the camera store will
probably be long gone, too. Listen to me, Maggie, *carpe diem.*"

"I like that." I clapped him on the shoulder. "How about,
Time and tide wait for no man, but Tyrone waits for us."

He bowed to me. "I'll put my shit in the car."

Central Juvenile Hall is on the Eastside, in Lincoln Heights.
The facility sits behind the massive County-USC Medical Center, sharing a dismal asphalt peninsula isolated by a freeway interchange on two sides and the Southern Pacific freight yards
on the third. Leftover land for human refuse: Central Juvenile
is the Big House for kids, where the hardest of the peachfuzz
hardcore being tried for murder as adults are kept. There are
some real mean little mothuhfuckuhs, to borrow from
Etta—or, as the county labels them, unfit minors—locked up
behind the block walls and barbed wire. The guards aren't
armed and kids break out all the time.

Guido and I, lugging about a hundred and fifty pounds of
equipment between us, were shown into Administration instead of the visitor center. We were escorted into a small conference room and searched until the deputy probation officers
were satisfied that we had nothing that looked like lethal

weapons and no keys to the front door hidden about our persons. We had already purged our gear. Over the years, and in various parts of the hemisphere, Guido and I had both been through some form of the search drill dozens of times. It can be the price you pay for access to the right subject.

Camera, lights, sound were in place half an hour before Tyrone was led in. When he came through the door we saw, to our dismay, that he had neither handcuffs nor shackles. I had expected the deputy probation officer to stay; they usually do. But for some reason, he went out and waited in the hall. Both Guido and I winced when we heard the conference room door close behind him, leaving us alone with six feet four inches of first-time killer.

I started with a little neutral icebreaker. "How are you, Tyrone?"

"Tee Bone," he contradicted, putting the emphasis on the second word so it rhymed with his name. "In here they call me Tee Bone."

His voice was deep, sullen. He was huge for fifteen, a muscular, sleek ebony man with a child's smooth cheeks and an old man's obsidian-hard eyes. I had seen his record, a steady escalation from curfew violation through joy riding, and on to crimes against people: assault, rape, car-jacking, then murder.

The county began offering Tyrone hospitality at age seven, when he spent four months at MacLaren Hall in El Monte, the facility for abused and abandoned children, because his mother forgot to come home for a while. After that it was easy time in Los Padrinos Juvenile Hall in Downey for petty crimes on a regular basis until Tyrone began using a gun.

At twelve the court sent him to Camp Miller in the scrub-covered hills above Malibu to serve eighteen months for aggravated assault. The ride north in the sheriff's black and white bus had been his first trip outside the central city. Apparently, the change of scene had not detoured him from his criminal path.

Tyrone got out of Miller two weeks before his fifteenth birthday, exactly three weeks before he pumped a load of double-aught buckshot into the chest of Kenny Jackson.

I clipped a small mike to the collar of Tyrone's coveralls. "What did you have for breakfast, Tee Bone?"

"Corn flakes and Tang," he said.

I looked over at Guido, who stood hunched beside a small video monitor with an earphone in one ear. I asked, "How's the sound?"

He nodded. "Little echo we can filter out. It's the cinder-block walls that do it. You look good. Tee Bone has a glow, but it's okay."

That probably meant that Tyrone looked as if he was sweating, even though he wasn't.

"So, Tee Bone," I said, "the questions we're going to ask pertain only to your family and your growing up. We will not discuss your pending case. We want to keep the tone like a conversation, very casual. Forget about Guido over there with the camera. Just relax, talk as you normally talk."

"Yeah?" he grinned broadly, checking Guido, a little male-bonding thing. "What I normally say?"

"Please," I said.

"What I normally say is this, take down my pants, bitch. Blow me."

I knew from experience that Guido is fast rather than strong. Under siege he can be counted on to get the camera and film out safely. Whenever possible, he keeps the camera rolling during his rapid retreat. It makes for very effective footage. Knowing this, however, gave me small comfort. If Tyrone attacked me, and that is what was on my mind as I sat there beside him, seeing the erection inside his county-issue overalls, the assault would be on the six o'clock news and Guido would be a contender for the Pulitzer. And I would be in intensive care watching it.

The glass panel in the door was partially blocked by the deputy probation officer standing outside. I knew he was unarmed, but he was big and he was only about fifteen seconds away if I screamed. I thought that for fifteen seconds I could take care of myself. I looked down at my notes, exhaled, started again.

"Tell me about your family, Tee Bone."

His answer was like a well-rehearsed recitation. "My mother? She a bitch. My grandmother? She a old bitch. My father? Well, he special. He a son of a bitch."

"Have you been watching the news? The district attorney is saying your father may get out of prison on a technicality."

"Oh yeah?" Finally I had hit on a topic that animated him. "He comin' out?"

"Are you close to your father?"

He shook his head. "I never remember him. He went up when I was little. All I know is this, he never sent Etta no money for me. Where is Etta? She say she comin' to see me."

"Have you communicated with your father? Maybe written to him?"

"I only get one phone call a day and I'm not much for writing. All I know, other people tell me. He went up for killing him a cop. In my set, that's cool, if you get what I mean."

"You received some extra status in your gang because your father killed a cop?"

"It's my inheritance," he said, emphasizing each syllable. I wondered who had said that to him.

"Your set is the Grape Street Watts?"

"Yeah." He flashed his gang's hand sign and I saw Guido move the focus in close on it.

To fill in information, I said, "Grape Street Watts is one of the most powerful gangs in the area that includes the Jordan Downs projects where Tee Bone lived with his grandmother."

"The *most* powerful. The *most* badass powerful." Tyrone used his fist on the table for punctuation, loud enough for the deputy to look in. "Grape Street rule the city. Anyone forget that, we show 'em."

"How do you show them?"

"Anyone dis me, I blow him away."

"Did Kenny Jackson dis you?" I asked.

"Yeah."

Switch the topic—I didn't want to be called in to testify against him. "The district attorney does not say your father didn't kill that cop, only that his trial wasn't fair. But if it turns out that he isn't a cop killer, will you lose status?"

"Don't matter if he done it. He done his time."

"Because of your record, you're being tried this time as an adult," I said. "It seems to me you've had a rather short childhood. Your mother died when you were ten. Do you remember living with her?"

"My mama?" Tyrone thought it over before he answered. "All I remember is this: she was stoned. You got to understand somethin'. When I stayed with her, I took care of her, not the other way around. Now and then, if she feelin' bad, she carry me over to James to stay for a while. It was real nice over at

James's. The house was real clean, he put the food on the table, real nice. Cook it on the stove, you know? Use dishes and forks and shit. He read to me, James did, put me into the bed every night. He walk me down to the school every morning, he pick me up by the door every day. He make me come inside the house when it get dark, make me take a bath. He don't let me take the Lord's name and shit. He real strict, but I kinda like being there."

"Who is James?"

"My granddaddy."

"James Harkness?" I asked.

"No. The other one. He my daddy's daddy. He have this market up on Central and Hunnerd-third."

"He still has a market?"

"Yeah. He make me turn myself in to the police this last time. Say the police shoot me dead if I don't turn myself in."

"How did you end up with Etta?" I asked, comparing Etta, who was anything but a model parent, to his description of James.

"It was the mothuhfuckin' police kep' carryin' me to Etta," he said, showing a flash of his grandmother's influence. "They keep takin' me over to her. They say to her, your girl stoned, your girl in jail. Here, take the kid. Mos' the time, she keep me a while, buy me a new shirt or something, then she let me go over to James."

"Why didn't the police take you straight to James if he was so good to you?"

"You ax me that, shows you don't know nothin'. If one of my set kill one of your set, you gonna turn some kid over to me? Fuck no. You gonna keep him away. Well, my daddy kill one of the police's set. They kep' the county from lettin' James have me."

"That's how you see it?" I said. "The police are just another gang?"

"Ain't they?"

I couldn't look over at Guido because the tape was rolling. Instead, I took a breath. "You were very young to have a relationship with the police. How did the police treat you? Did they dis you?"

"Now they do. Back then, they was okay. This officer come by all the time, see I'm okay or not. He carry me around in the car, buy me stuff to eat and shit. You know, like ice cream, shit to wear. But this officer, when I say take me to my granddaddy, he say, no, he make you into a cop killer, too, like he done your daddy."

The question had to be asked, "Do you remember the officer's name?"

"Yeah. Officer Flint."

I looked down at my notes again for help. I found the track I wanted, but no salve for what I was feeling.

"According to the probation department," I said, "you joined the Grape Street Watts before you were ten years old."

He shook his head at my ignorance. "No kid that little can get in, man. You gotta prove yourself, you know. Gotta be strong enough to take care of things."

"But you were hanging with the gang."

"Yeah, they let me hang with them. Like a little brother, you know? I do shit for them, they do shit for me, like if anyone try to get in my face. It ain't safe to be out there all alone."

Because it was such a good line, I said nothing for a long moment while Guido came in tight on Tyrone. It is far easier to edit out silence than to edit in a reflective pause.

"Tell me about the future, Tee Bone," I said when Guido signaled me. "Where do you want to be when you're eighteen?"

Tyrone's eyes filled suddenly and he looked away, out through the window that had no view except asphalt and a few rows of barbed wire. It took effort, but I could see the fifteen-year-old child in there beyond the hard eyes, vulnerable under the massive muscle structure. Finally he gave his full face to Guido's lens.

"When I get outta here," he said, "James gonna take me away. We gonna live up in the mountains or some place. Not like Camp Miller, but far away. Get away from my set. Go fishin' and shit. Get clean again."

"Your probation report says that you have two children, Tee Bone. By two different teenage mothers."

He nodded.

"Do you see them?"

"When I can. Can't see them when I'm locked up."

"For a moment, I want you to picture yourself in that clean place in the mountains with James. Can you do that?"

"Yeah."

"Look closely at that picture," I said. "Are your children there with you?"

The question startled him like a physical nudge.

"Are they there?" I repeated.

"No, man. They can't come where I'm going."

CHAPTER

14

"Spill it," I said to Guido when he slammed shut an aluminum case. "Tell me what's on your mind. Don't take it out on the equipment."

"I hate to bring it up," he said, and tossed me the Tyrone videotape to stash in the insulated bag. A deputy probation officer was holding the door, impatient for us to gather our things and leave. "I'm sure there's nothing to it."

"To what?"

"Mike Flint," he said. "It seems, I don't know, sleazy somehow that his name keeps coming up in connection with this project. If you can still call it a project. I've always loved working with you because you imbue your subjects with a certain nobility; the way you handle everything. But this time it's different. Jesus, Maggie, what are we doing? Finishing a commissioned film or trying to save Mike's ass?"

"It's a great ass," I said, holding back. "Well worth saving."

"That's your answer?"

"Part of it. But only part. If there is a nobility about my work—thank you—I believe it is because we work from a loose outline and let the story evolve organically, depend on the interviews to give it shape and focus instead of holding ourselves confined to some prefab script. That's what we're doing here, letting a story evolve."

"Which story, Maggie? The kids, or Mike?"

I picked up a roll of masking tape and fumbled around look-

ing for the cut end. "The complication with Mike arises because I asked him to give me some contacts. That could be in-
terpreted as a conflict, I suppose. It's also called networking.
Mike is a great resource. He worked in the ghetto for a lot of
years and he knows people. I mean, really knows people. You
have to admit that what we have now goes far beyond the
standard sop about ghetto youth. Charles Conklin is an evil,
but magnificent catalyst. I don't apologize for anything."

He wanted to scrap. "Yesterday, I felt like scum, Maggie,
when I made those blow-ups for Mike. Like one of J. Edgar
Hoover's red-hunting goons. I snitched off every car on 112th
Street. I gave Mike crowd pictures, too. Little old ladies in their
jammies. Shit. What's he going to do with them? Draw circles
around their faces and put them in the subversives file?"

"Why don't you ask him what he plans to do?"

"I don't think Mike likes me."

The best I could do was to say, "Mike thinks you're a genius."

Guido started humming "That's What Friends Are For."

"The problem here is one of bias," I said, taping up a coil of
extension cords. "When Mike gave me Etta, he should have
given me James, too."

"No, please, Maggie," Guido sighed. "I'm hungry."

"I bet we can find some really terrific barbecue in Southeast.
Somewhere around Central and 103rd."

"No," he said, adamant.

"You brought up the issue, Guido. To be fair, we have to talk
to James."

"That's not what I meant," he said, hefting the recorder. "I
don't want to eat down there. Feed me now and I'll be your
slave all day."

"I'm ashamed of you," I said. "Slavery is not politically correct."

I took him out Sunset to Barragan's in Echo Park for heuvos
rancheros. As I dug into the trencher-size platter the waitress
set in front of me, I realized it was the first time in a long time
that I'd had any interest in food at all. I more than made up for
the lapse, with Guido keeping up bite for bite. As skinny as he
is, he has always been a big eater. We worked through our
massive entrees, the beans and rice, two sides of chips and
fresh salsa, and finished off with cold flan. When there was

nothing left, I let out my belt a notch, leaned back in the uphol-
stered booth, and sighed. Guido was pouring out the last of his
Corona beer.

"Ready now?" I asked.

"When you are," he said, and finished his beer in a long
swallow. "Fueled and happy, I am yours."

We drove straight down the Harbor Freeway to Century
Boulevard. The morning scene was very different from the
night. The streets teemed with people going about their business, oblivious to the squalorous backdrop. Women in bright
dresses or skimpy halter tops and stretch pants led flower-like
little girls by the hand. Little boys, in baggy shorts and high-top
basketball sneakers that were surely too heavy for their skinny
legs, jived and hustled irreverently among them, laughing and
teasing all the time. It was a parade. Knots of men hung out on
the sidewalk to watch it pass by.

Two churches had "Free Charles Conklin" banners tacked
up over their front doors. Identical banners.

We passed the corner on Century where Wyatt Johnson had
been shot fifteen years earlier, and continued on two more
blocks to Central. Three short blocks down Central we found
103rd Street, and Unity Market on the corner. I hadn't noticed
it on any of my trips to Etta's.

Since leaving the freeway, we had passed gutters dirty with
litter, not a small quantity of human litter, too, sleeping it off in
doorways, loitering anywhere there was something to lean
against. In stark contrast, the immediate area around Unity
Market was spotless. There were no weeds growing through
the cracks in the freshly swept sidewalk, no trash at the curb
or blown up against the side of the building.

Most of the neighborhood market and liquor store owners in
Southeast had plastered over their display windows and strung
razor wire around any openings or vents. The Unity, however,
had an open front to show off bins of fresh fruits and vegeta-
bles, cut flowers in big cans. There was a smell of fresh coffee.
It all seemed to belong to a different, a gentler place.

When Guido and I walked up from the car a man I guessed
to be in his sixties was helping an elderly woman select or-
anges. They had a little discussion about each orange before
putting it into a paper bag. The man was very patient, courteous to the point of courtliness. He was a big man, a command-

ing presence. He wore blue jeans and sandals, a short, colorful batik tunic, and an embroidered Muslim cap on his short, nappy gray hair.

"Good morning," he greeted us. "How may I help you?"

"We would like to speak with James Conklin," I said.

"There is no James Conklin here," he said. He looked me over with uncomfortable yet not hostile, intensity. "But if James Shabazz will do . . ."

"I am Maggie MacGowen, Mr. Shabazz. This is my colleague Guido Patrini."

"I know who you are, Miss MacGowen. I am an admirer of your work. On several occasions I have shown your films at F.O.I. evenings at the temple."

"What is F.O.I.?" I asked.

"Fruits of Islam. Lessons on family living. I have shown *Latchkey* several times. *Aged and Alone* as well. We who are in the middle must take the responsibility of caring for the little brothers and sisters as well as our elders."

The old lady shopper said, "Amen, brother James," and moved on to the fresh broccoli.

"You have rare insight, Miss MacGowen," he said. His stare made me uncomfortable. "And compassion as well."

"Thank you," I said. I knew I was blushing and would not look at Guido, but I gave his arm a pinch.

"What brings you here?" Shabazz asked. "Are you working on a film?"

"Yes, I am," I said. "We want to talk to you about your grandson, Tyrone Harkness."

"My grandson?" He was taken aback.

"Tyrone told me you are his 'daddy's daddy.' That's why I assumed your name was Conklin. Is Charles Conklin your son?"

"I suppose in the sense that all of Allah's children are the sons and daughters of all mankind, then the young brother is my son. But I have no children of my own. Would you like to come inside and have a cup of coffee?"

I looked at Guido.

"Maybe something cold," Guido said, meaning another beer.

We followed James Shabazz inside. The market was immaculate and attractive, a cross between a health food store and a 7-Eleven. There was no alcohol of any kind, nor anything like a hot dog in the deli case. Three teenage boys in big white aprons were attentively helping customers, keeping things in order, and working the register. A sign over the check-out counter said, "Allah provides."

Shabazz filled three paper cups with unfiltered apple juice. As he handed one to me, he said, "How is Tyrone?"

"Considering where he is, I suppose he's all right," I said. "He spoke of you with real affection. He told me you're going to take him away from the city when he gets out."

He smiled. "I was talking about helping him enter the Kingdom of Allah, but Tyrone seemed to think I meant summer camp."

"What is your relationship to Tyrone and his father?"

"Let me show you," he said, and led us out through the back of the store to a patch of asphalt off an alley. Bright, crude murals covered all of the facing walls. Paint-spattered tables and easels were folded up against a small shed at the side.

"I have this little parking lot here," Shabazz said. "After school there isn't much for the youngsters to do. Idle hands and minds go looking for trouble. Every child needs structure to his life, something productive to do with his time. Years ago, we started offering afternoon programs to any young ones who wanted to drop in. Crafts, music, dance. Educate them to their heritage, give them structure.

"Growing children are always hungry," he said, smiling like the fond uncle. "To keep their strength up, we serve them snacks, too. Feed the body along with the spirit.

"We saw that some kids only came for the food. Charles Conklin was one of those—could not entice him away from the table. He got breakfast and lunch at school—and that's all that kept him in school. What he ate here was all he would have for supper. When I learned that sometimes he did not have a safe place to sleep at night, I offered him sanctuary, as I later offered sanctuary to his son."

"You saw something redeemable in Charles?" I asked.

"Charles?" Shabazz considered the question for a moment before he answered. "The little brother never had a chance, Miss MacGowen. The streets reached up and sucked him in, consumed him whole when he was still a baby because there was no one to hold him away. No one. Your question, did I see something worth redeeming in him? All of Allah's children can find redemption. But a boy who would put a bullet in the back of a man's head to steal his car for an hour's ride, who would take his own girl child into his carnal bed, a boy like that was beyond my power to help."

Guido looked nauseous.

"Mr. Shabazz, did Charles Conklin ever talk to you about the shooting of Officer Wyatt Johnson?" I asked.

"No. The others did. But never Charles."

"What others?" I asked.

"The little girl who found the body came to me. She told me Charles shot a man. I was the first to call the police."

"She told you?" I leaned closer, needing to pull something more from him. "And you believed her?"

"Ten-year-old children lie about stealing candy, or did they brush their teeth. They don't lie about murder, Miss MacGowen. I walked her back to the place where it happened and she showed me."

Guido chimed in, "What was a ten-year-old kid doing out alone after midnight in the first place?"

"I told you." Shabazz pointed an accusing finger at Guido. "No structure. The child's mother worked in the café across the street from the filling station where the shooting occurred. Couldn't afford a sitter and she didn't want the girl to stay home alone, so the child would walk over after school and sort of hang until quitting time—midnight, one o'clock. The mother did her best to keep an eye on her. She was a good child. Went to church, got through school. Works for the county libraries now."

"LaShonda DeBevis?"

His face lit into a broad smile. "Do you know LaShonda?"

"I want to talk to her, but I can't find her. Can you help me?"

"I will ask around."

"Do you know Hanna Rhodes?"

His smile was suddenly a deep frown. "I never knew much about Hanna. She was a street child, like Charles. Had no safe place to go home to. Have you talked to her? What's become of her?"

"I'm sorry to be the one to tell you, but Hanna is dead."

"Dead, you say?" Asked the way a man visiting home after years away inquires about the old neighbors. Reverent pause in recognition of the fact, not necessarily grief or sadness. "How did it happen? Drugs or a man?"

"Maybe a combination of the two. She was shot night before last."

"Night before last?" Shabazz looked around the spattered lot as if there were some answers inscribed in that chaotic mix of colors and shapes. "So recently? I haven't seen her around, walking on the streets, for a long time. I assumed she had passed a long time ago."

"I'm sorry," I said again, because there was nothing else to say.

He shook himself. "It was inevitable. She was walking the streets selling herself for drugs when she was twelve, thirteen years old. Dead depends on your definition."

"Were the two girls friends?"

"No. LaShonda's mother wouldn't have allowed that. What brought the girls together that night was the weather. It was cold. They had a little fire going out behind the filling station. That's where they were when the officer was shot."

"Why didn't La Shonda go across the street to her mother instead of running five whole blocks to get you?" I asked.

"She was afraid of Charles. All the children were. She knew Charles wouldn't hurt me."

I took Guido's arm. "Do we have batteries?"

"What if I say yes?" Guido asked.

"I want to shoot some background footage at the murder scene." I turned to Mr. Shabazz, smiled at him. "Want to be in pictures, Mr. Shabazz?"

He smiled his assent. It was his turn to blush—I saw red rise up in his oak-colored face. "What do you propose?"

"Walk us through the scene as you remember it."

He laughed a nervous laugh. "Do you pay scale?"

"I'll give you a copy of the finished tape for F.O.I.," I said. "Fair enough."

I turned to Guido. "How much time do we have on the batteries?"

"Easily an hour. If I'd had some warning . . ."

"Then let's do it," I said.

"My pleasure," Shabazz said. He charged one of his teenagers to watch over the store and, after checking his reflection in the glass door of a soft drink cooler and adjusting his cap, he came out into the glare of midday with us.

Guido had sweated off his breakfast beer by then, so he

drove, with Mr. Shabazz in front with him. I sat in back with a camera out the window, taping the route Shabazz had taken that night with LaShonda.

With the viewfinder in front of my eye, I asked, "Did you grow up in the area, Mr. Shabazz?"

"This is Watts," he said, again as if I should have known better. "There were no Africans in Watts when I was a child. Things changed after the world war. I came here after Korea— the navy discharged me in Long Beach."

When we got back up to Century, Shabazz pointed to an abandoned lot on the corner of Clovis Avenue.

"That's the place. The filling station went out about the time Mr. Reagan came into office. There was a body shop in here for a while, but it didn't last more than a year or two. The corner is notorious."

Nothing was left of the old station except a few thousand square yards of cracked asphalt and the gutted stucco shell of the office and service bay. A chain-link fence that had been erected around the property had been pushed into rusted, pleated heaps. Campaign posters plastered to anything upright, competing for attention with the ever-present graffiti.

There was enough of the old station building left to offer some shelter. It had obviously seen regular use: the dim interior was cluttered with liquor and beer empties, discarded mattresses, little piles of toilet paper and dried feces. Every surface, even the broken asphalt, was covered with elaborate, overlapping gang tags that defined overlapping gang territories: Eight-Tray Gangster Crips, Rollin' 90s, Grape Street, Kitchen Crips, Black Bishops, Be-Bop Bloods, Black P Stone.

I had the newspaper account of the shooting of Wyatt Johnson in my mind as I looked around. On the corner of the lot there were two concrete pads, the remains of the public telephones where Johnson would have placed his last call. The distance from the telephones to the restroom where he died was maybe thirty feet. A short last mile.

I knew the scene would look good on tape. Heat reflected off the faded pavement in shimmering waves that, with the heavy smog that was now in place overhead, would give everything a silvered, chiaroscuro effect. Colors would have a thin, hard quality. Very urban.

Guido had been casing the scene, too.

"What do you think?" I asked.

"Depends on the tone you're aiming for," Guido said. "This background is fine if what you want is war zone. But I think it's distracting. Too ominous, you know? The night of the murder there was a functioning business here. This is something else. I say walk it through to get perspective, but keep the background in soft focus."

"Let's try it," I said.

We stood a few yards from where the office had been. I positioned Shabazz so his side was to the building, his back to traffic moving down Century Boulevard. Guido checked it through his lens, repositioned us both a few degrees. Then he hefted the camera to his shoulder and said, "Century and Clovis, Shabazz and MacGowen. Go ahead, Maggie."

"Mr. Shabazz," I said, "the shooting death of Officer Wyatt Johnson fifteen years ago went largely unnoticed by the press and by the public. Yet the ramifications of that shooting have been large, affecting lives for several generations. What can you tell us about the events of that November night?"

"It was after midnight," Shabazz said, seeming very comfortable with the camera aimed at his face. He had a natural sense for drama. His cultured speech took on more ghetto flavor as he got into his narrative. "A little sister came to my house and woke me up out of bed—I have an apartment over my store. She said some brother was shot up at the filling station. She said Pinkie did it. I knew Pinkie to be Charles Pinkerton Conklin, a boy who sometimes stayed at my house before he was sent to prison. She said, 'Don't let Pinkie get me.'"

"She was afraid of him?"

He nodded. "She had reason to be. I suppose on the streets now he would be labeled scandalous. Fifteen years ago we called him a delinquent. Always in trouble."

"What did you do?" I asked.

"I told the child to show me."

"Will you show us?"

"Around here," he said. He narrated as we walked. "It's trashy here now, and it was trashy then, too. Henry Woodson— he owned the station—kept some old wrecks in back he cannibalized for spare parts. A couple of Cadillacs, I recall, and a Bonneville." He pointed out where these had been, dark oily patches on the ground. "Drunks used to climb into the cars to sleep. The girls should have known better than to be messing around out there, but they got a little fire going in an empty oil barrel and they were trying to keep warm."

Shabazz stopped and looked around for bearings. Then he held out his hands in front of him, defining a big circle, maybe the oil barrel. "The girls were just about here when they heard the shots. Even fifteen years ago shots weren't unusual. But the children were scared, so they started to run toward the café across the street where LaShonda's mother worked. They ran smack into Charles as he backed out of the men's facilities. They saw a gun in his hand. And they saw Officer Johnson lying on the floor inside."

By then we had walked all the way around to the Clovis Avenue side where the restrooms had been. The doors and plumbing were long gone, most of the interior walls were gone, too. Standing opposite the restroom door, I could see daylight through the far wall of the old service bay.

Shabazz pointed toward the floor. "This is where the officer was lying when I saw him, face down with his head between the bowl and the sink. There were six bullets in his back and his head, I hear, but all I could see was blood."

We had to step aside so that Guido could play around with what I was sure was an arty interior pan. He didn't need us for that, so I moved away where the human smell was not so intense. Mr. Shabazz came with me.

I asked him, "Mr. Shabazz, even if he was an armed, streetwise cop, would a nice boy like Wyatt Johnson use a public restroom in a neighborhood like this after midnight?"

He blushed a little again. "Maybe not for the purpose it was intended. No one has ever answered why he was here. He was not robbed, you know."

"Maybe the girls interrupted Conklin before he could finish some kind of business with Johnson," I said.

He shook his head. "They met him on his way out."

Guido joined us. "I don't know how much time we have left, Maggie. Better give me your parting shot now."

I looked around, chose open space for a backdrop. With James Shabazz next to me and Guido's lens two yards in front of me, I said, "Mr. Shabazz, when Tyrone Harkness was still in diapers, his father was sent to prison for the rest of his life. If he had not been convicted of that crime, how do you think young Tyrone's life might have been different?"

Shabazz shook his head. "No different. If Charles had not been sent up for that murder, he would have served time for something else. The most positive influence he could have on his son's life was his absence from it."

I paused for fade-out. Then I said, "Miss anything?"

"Let me think," Guido said, flexing his arm, stiff from supporting the shoulder-held camera. "We have Mr. Shabazz I.D.'ing Conklin as the shooter. No, I guess that's everything."

"Real funny, Guido," I said. His words gave me a hot spot in the pit of my stomach that had nothing to do with Barragan's salsa.

Shabazz said, "A private joke?"

"He's needling me," I said.

"Go ahead, Maggie. Ask him if he knows Mike Flint."

"Officer Flint?" Shabazz said. "Of course I know him."

Guido raised his camera again. "Tell us about him."

"I have been watching the news," Shabazz said, hesitant, as if feeling his way through a mine field. "I heard the names of Charles Conklin and Officer Flint linked."

"I don't have much juice left, Mr. Shabazz," Guido said. "So, cut to the chase. Did Officer Flint coerce, threaten, bribe, intimidate LaShonda DeBevis and Hanna Rhodes to make them identify Charles Conklin as the man who shot Officer Johnson?"

Shabazz stroked his chin and posed for Guido, giving him a three-quarter profile. "I can't answer that. Even if he did nothing overt, certainly Officer Flint's size, his color, the authority of his position intimidated the children. I was not present during the questioning, I do not know whether he told the girls what to say. This I know, the truth they told was dangerous to them, and they would not have told it unless they were equally afraid to hold back. Does that answer your question?"

"No," Guido said. "She wants to know if you like Officer Flint. Do you think he is redeemable?"

Shabazz smiled. "Do you like him, Miss MacGowen?"

"Yes I do. Very much."

"Then, let me say this. Officer Flint operates under his own code. Now and then his code is in direct opposition to the laws he and his fellow officers have sworn to uphold. From my experience, Officer Flint did not always bother with the niceties and delays of due process."

"You're begging the question," Guido said. "Yes or no. Do you like the guy?"

"Put that way," Shabazz said, "the answer is no. I detest him."

CHAPTER
15

" 'A truth that's told with bad intent, Beats all the lies you can invent,' " I said.

"Deep." Guido yawned. "Very deep. Where'd you get it?"

"William Blake."

"Deep and mystical. The question is, who's telling the truth?"

"All of them. None of them," I said. "The big question is, what is the intent?"

"Heavy." Guido was hot, so I had bought him a couple of beers for the road. He finished one and opened the other, but he was already too sleepy to hold it upright. Wasn't necessarily the beer. Guido sleeps like a cat, short naps whenever he can get them. The last thing he said to me was, "Fix the air conditioner, will ya?"

I put Eric Clapton in the tape deck and headed west on Century. Guido paid no attention to where I was going. He dozed, now and then rousing himself enough to sing toneless harmony to the choruses. He didn't notice when I bypassed the Harbor Freeway and continued west when I would have turned north to take him straight home.

I found the Lennox branch of the county library in a small county administration compound on Lennox Boulevard, next to a sheriff substation.

It wasn't until I pulled into the parking lot behind the library that Guido sat up and looked around. "You lost?"

"No," I said. "I thought we might drop in on someone."

He was fully alert as soon as he opened his eyes. "Like who?"

"LaShonda DeBevis's former co-workers. Won't take long." I opened my door.

"I'll wait," he said. He got out of the car and found a tree to sit under.

Inside the library a couple of classes of what looked like first- or second-graders were getting their first library cards, handing in signed permission slips, printing their own names in the space the librarian showed them. The big rug in the children's section was covered with little ones who had finished the process. They seemed more intent on the stiff new cards they clutched than on the story being read to them. Happy, proud faces.

I went to the information desk and handed the librarian there my business card, the Maggie MacGowen one. She was a tall, slender black woman, with lace on her collar and flecks of silver coiling out of the bun at the back of her neck.

"I'm researching a film," I told her. "I want very much to speak with LaShonda DeBevis. I know she isn't here anymore, but I hoped someone would be able to put me in touch with her."

"I can't give you an employee's home number." The librarian frowned over my card, apparently trying to make some connection in her mind, or reach some difficult decision. "I believe LaShonda is out of town for a few days, but I will call her for you and leave your message."

"Thank you," I said. "I can't ask for anything more."

She was still holding my card up as I turned to leave. "Maggie MacGowen," she said, and glanced at the kids on the rug. "You said you're making a film?"

"Yes."

"*Latchkey*," she said. "Are you that Maggie MacGowen?"

"I made *Latchkey* three years ago." I moved closer to her, because she seemed very troubled. Close the physical space sometimes, you close off certain doubts.

"It's so strange, you asking about LaShonda just now," she said. "Is she in some sort of trouble?"

"LaShonda is a witness to trouble. In the beginning I only wanted to talk with her about the neighborhood she grew up in, but so much has happened that I'm concerned about her. I want to find out whether she's all right."

The librarian gave me a second visual interview, made her decision about me. "I suppose I'm being overly dramatic." She tucked my card under the edge of a stack of books. "I've worked with the library system for many years. Sudden transfers just don't happen. Odd. Very odd."

"How does LaShonda explain it?" I asked.

"I haven't spoken to her, and that's odd, too. One of the other librarians said she heard from someone in personnel that the move was for LaShonda's protection. Protection from what, I don't know. If she was in trouble, she would talk it over with us; we're very close here. I know that transfer instructions came down from someone in the county with more authority than a head librarian."

Story time was over and two-dozen little kids in the six- to seven-year range surged up to the check-out counter with their arms full of precious books, clutching the bright covers against their damp tee shirts. They tried to use library voices, but their excitement bubbled through, charged the atmosphere. Truly, the library trip was a grand new adventure. As a group, they were clean, but just adequately dressed, thrift-shop patina on the sneakers. I wondered how many of them had books of their own at home.

The librarian had been watching the kids with the same sort of awe that must have been on my face. "Excuse me," she said, rising from her desk. "More hands are needed."

"Thanks for your time," I said, and followed her as far as the counter.

As she opened book covers and fed them into the laser scanner, she said, "I'll deliver your message."

"That's all I can ask," I said.

"Miss MacGowen," she called as I walked away. "If you hear from LaShonda first, ask her to call me."

I left her surrounded. Librarians have a reputation for being meticulous with details. And with people. She was worried about LaShonda, and not because the transfer had not been according to standard procedure.

"Have a nice visit?" Guido asked, wiping sweat from his face as we got back into the car.

"A good visit. But damn, I'm still in a going-calling mood, little buddy. Guess we'll have to drop in on someone else."

"Like who? Like maybe a bar I know in Santa Monica Canyon? Watch the end of the ball game?"

"Better than that," I said. "Old Jerry Kelsey's retired. Bet he has the game on the tube."

" 'Splain this to me, Lucy."

"Don't you want another version of the girls' story?"

"Absolutely not."

"When Mike tried to call Jerry Kelsey, the D.A. or his campaign put a tail on him. I want to see what happens if we actually show up *chez* Jerry."

"How well do you know this Kelsey guy?"

"I met him once," I said. "Mike had to deliver some papers to him and I rode along. You'll like him a lot—a real space cadet. He pensioned out on a psycho disability four or five years ago."

"Psycho?"

"Stress-related."

"Boy, am I relieved," Guido groused as a matter of form. "Most mass murderers have stress-related problems."

"Mike said he was a boozer."

"Uh huh." Guido slouched down in his seat and watched out his window, trying to seem annoyed, but I knew he was faking it. Guido is the nosiest person I have ever known. That's part of what makes him so much fun to work with.

Jerry Kelsey lived in Palms, on the Westside, almost under the San Diego freeway. He had an arrangement with a construction company that gave him space to park his trailer in their equipment yard rent-free in exchange for keeping an eye on things. I'm sure it was a good arrangement all around. Rents on the Westside are high and ex-L.A. cops don't come cheap as security guards.

I saw the construction lot below us, got off at the next off-ramp, and circled back down Sepulveda.

After he rear-ended us, George Schwartz had said that he followed Mike because he tried to get in touch with Jerry Kelsey. I drove past the trailer slowly, stopped briefly beside the gate, showing myself. When I didn't attract any apparent notice, I pulled away from the drive, circled around the block through a neighborhood of small postwar apartment buildings.

During work hours, the neighborhood was very quiet, a few cars parked along the street, now and then someone walking along the sidewalk. Smog dulled the sky to a yellowed silver, made the air heavy, like a bowling alley after a tournament, curled the big leaves of the desiccated sycamore trees. Guido wasn't complaining, but I knew he was as hot and uncomfortable as I was.

We didn't pick up our tail until we made a second pass in front of Kelsey's trailer.

I wondered when George Schwartz had made bail. And who had paid it.

I pulled into the equipment yard through the open gates. Schwartz, still driving the Toyota, front left fender still showing traces of Mike's blue paint, drove past the gate, U-turned, and parked at the curb across the street. He made a point of being seen. He scared me, and I knew that was the point. I half-expected him to get out of his car, wouldn't have been surprised by a confrontation. But he stayed put while Guido and I made our way across the hot gravel toward Kelsey's double-wide.

"Look dangerous," I said to Guido. "At least stand up straight."

"We should have a camera."

"That would put Kelsey off." I patted my bag. "I have a recorder running."

Jerry Kelsey opened the door before I could knock. He was tall, a thin-shouldered man with a paunch like a basketball under his polo shirt—a heavy drinker's belly. He also had a serious case of what Casey called hair denial: a long swath of hair combed up from one side and plastered over his shiny bald pate. The thick lenses in his wire-rim bifocals gave him a vacant, owlish stare. My impression was, he wasn't happy to have company.

"Jerry," I said, offering my hand. "Maggie MacGowen. Remember me? Mike Flint's friend. Nice to see you again. This is my associate, Guido Patrini."

He said, "Mike?"

"Mike Flint?"

"Come in," he said. When he turned around, I could see the lump made by the handgun tucked into his belt at the back. Guido saw it, too.

I turned just as I stepped into the cool gloom of the trailer, saw Schwartz drive away.

Kelsey was leaning out to hold the door open for me.

"George Schwartz a friend of yours?" I asked.

"Who'd you say?"

"George Schwartz."

"I thought you said Mike Flint."

"I did. I just wondered whether you knew old George Schwartz. Works for the D.A.?"

Kelsey combed his skinny fingers through that long hank of stiffened hair, tugged on the far end of it, but apparently didn't achieve enlightenment from the effort. He seemed merely impatient for me to get inside, out of the glare and reflected heat coming off the gravel. He touched the back of my shoulder to hurry me.

The trailer was bigger inside than it appeared from outside. A lot of room and very little furniture. Besides a big-screen television and a recliner chair, there were a card table, a few folding chairs, and an old upright piano. On the floor beside the chair was an untidy stack of dog-eared masturbation lit.

"I was in the neighborhood," I said. "Thought I would drop by and see how you are. All this fuss about Charles Conklin has a lot of people upset."

"You want a drink?" he asked.

"Okay," I said. I didn't want a drink, but it seemed to me that if I accepted I was entitled to a reasonable amount of time to down it, time to talk. When Jerry was out of sight in his small kitchen, Guido made a show of dusting one of the folding chairs before he would sit on it.

Jerry came back with three nearly full tumblers of what I found to be straight scotch, a single ice cube clanking in each glass.

"Cheers," Jerry said, tipping his glass to us. "Have a seat. I won't say make yourself comfortable, 'cause these chairs aren't much to sit on. Never bought any real furniture. I don't get much company unless it's poker night. Besides, I don't plan to be here long."

"Where are you going?" I asked.

"Oregon. Bought a lot up there. Soon as I get things squared away, get my financing together, I'm going up to build. Won't be long now. L.A. used to be one hell of a city, but it's a cesspool now. And getting worse." He raised his glass. "Getting worse."

Guido sipped his scotch. After the first taste, I only held mine. Jerry drank heavily from his, but seemed to pace himself, put himself on a timer. He was mentally spacy, but steady-handed. A lot of long-time drunks keep themselves just on the edge all the time without slipping over into sloppy inebriation. I thought that was what I was seeing.

"So," I said, "how do you feel about Charles Conklin getting out?"

"Who did you say you are?"

"Mike Flint introduced us, remember? I'm a friend of Mike's."

"Oh, yeah. The new squeeze." He took another long drink. "Mike and I go way back."

"Mike talks about you all the time," I lied. Mike had had a lot of partners over the years. When he referred to his partner he usually meant the person he was currently working with or someone close from the old days, like Hector or Manny Tenwolde, a partner who was shot by a suicidal neighbor a dozen or so years ago. To Mike, Jerry was nothing more than a man he had worked an early case with. There was no bond there.

I milked that tenuous tie. "Mike tells me stories about the old days in Southeast, about moving from patrol to detectives."

"Yeah?" He smiled into his glass. "We were a good team. Solved all of our cases, mostly. I mean, some you never get. Transient comes in, commits a crime, moves on. Or the mob. Can't get a handle on those guys. Some people you just never get."

"If I remember," I said, "Wyatt Johnson was the first murder assigned to Mike after he made detective. Nice to begin with a collar."

"Uh huh. Not much of a case. Matter of knowing which heads to thump, but we brought it in. Mike ever tell you about the time we found a mummy in the trunk of some old guy's car? We worked on him for a good week before we got him to tell us it was his wife. Been dead six or seven years, just riding around town in the trunk all that time."

"What do you mean, you worked on him?" I asked.

"Persistence, that's all." Jerry grinned. "Shit, he was older than dirt. I was afraid if we touched him or moved too fast the old guy'd croak on us." He'd raced his ice to the bottom of his glass, and won. He reached for Guido's half-full glass. "Can't wait for her to catch up. Let me freshen that for you."

On his way to the kitchen, he winked at Guido. "She as slow on the uptake as she is with that drink?"

Guido gave me a sidelong, horrified glance. When Jerry had trotted out of sight and was rattling ice cubes in the next room, Guido leaned into me, reeking of booze. "This is a bundle of laughs. You're not going to get anything out of him. Let's go."

"Don't be in a hurry," Jerry said, coming back into the room. The scotch had put a funny bounce in his step, but obviously hadn't impaired his hearing. I couldn't figure him out. I decided he was lonely and needed some company. Any company.

Jerry and Guido talked about the ball game without much energy. I excused myself to use the bathroom, took a quick look at the untidy single bedroom while I was gone. Overall, it was a sad place for a man to end up, barren of evidence of attachments or accomplishments. Transient.

When I got back to the living room, I was ready to leave. Guido was intent on a double-play in progress on the big-screen, so I sat down again to wait it out.

A knock on the fakey-wood front door was a welcome interruption. Jerry got up from his recliner and went to answer, but he left his eyes on me, as if I might evaporate or something if I got out of his sight. Even when he opened the door, he kept watching me. He pushed open the door and came back to his chair without so much as greeting the person standing on the stoop.

I stood up when I saw who it was. Jennifer Miller, Conklin's *pro bono* attorney, looking cool and professional in a navy-blue suit. On television she had looked taller. I pegged her live as five-two in heels, max.

"This is cozy," I said.

She gave me a stern appraisal. "Who are you?"

"An old pal," I said. "The real question is, what the hell are you doing here?"

"She screens my company," Jerry said. "She's my adviser."

"She can't be. She's Charles Conklin's lawyer." I set my glass on the floor and stood up to tower over her. "When the Bar Association hears about this, Miss Miller, you'll be disbarred for egregious breech of ethics."

Miller seemed struck dumb.

Jerry Kelsey chuckled as he reached for my drink. "You sound like a lawyer your own damn self. I thought you was some kind of decorator or something."

"Close enough," I said. "I suggest, Jerry, that if you're expecting some sort of gratuity from Miss Miller so you can move out of town, you should take your payment up front, before she's indicted. I have to leave now. I have a complaint to file."

Guido thought this was pretty funny and giggled inanely, but I felt heartsick. When we walked out, the lovely Jennifer Miller was right behind us. I hung back, waiting for Miller to catch up while Guido, his step none too steady, went straight to the car.

As she picked her way across the gravel, Miller tottered on her heels like a kid playing dress-up. She did seem young. Certainly undercooked to have been handed such a high-profile, media-rich case by a major law firm. Someone had to be keeping close tabs on her. Real close, like a puppet with a fist up its bottom.

"I am not his legal adviser," she called out to me.

I wheeled on her, startled her. "You should have said that in front of Jerry. He thinks you're his adviser."

She tried to take the offensive. "What are you doing here, anyway?"

"None of your business. How did you know we were here? Did George Schwartz call you?"

She leveled a poker player's stare at me, an I'm-holding-at-least-a-full-house-but-I-won't-let-on-to-you blank gaze. "George Schwartz?"

"Right." I folded my hand because I was fed up with her bluff. I turned and started to walk away again. "Whatever you're up to, kiddo, it looks bad."

"Let me explain." Miller started after me, but had to stop to dump a pebble from her shoe. I liked the visual when I glanced back to check on her, took a camera out of my bag, and got a quick shot of Miller with Jerry Kelsey's trailer in the background, and Jerry Kelsey's face in the window watching her.

I went on to my car. She limped after me, calling, "Miss MacGowen, just a moment, please."

I gave her time, leaning against my open car door. Guido

was trying to get his seatbelt buckled, but he couldn't seem to get tab to meet slot.

Miller pleaded. "I'm afraid that you have the wrong impression."

"Do I?" I made sure Jerry was still watching from his window.

"Detective Kelsey is . . ." She paused to think. "Emotionally challenged."

"Does that mean he's a lunatic?"

"No." She had to think again, and whatever was going on in her thoughts made her seem angry, exasperated. "He isn't a lunatic. He just needs to be protected. Jerry is an essential witness and I need to keep an eye on him. He doesn't always know what he's saying."

"He seems lucid enough."

"He thought you were a decorator, Miss MacGowen. Yesterday he got lost coming home from the store."

"Yesterday, who did he think you were?"

"He didn't recognize me at all." Tears welled in her eyes. An odd reaction, I thought. And then I began to feel bad for picking on her. Not real bad, just sort of bad.

"I'm offering you some advice," I said, "because I think someone is using you badly. That raggedy old cop isn't your responsibility. If you think he can't take care of himself, then find his family or call the social services people at the police department. But stay away from him until this case is resolved."

She sniffled a little. If I could make her cry, then any vulture in court, a witness like Mike for instance, would shred her. I hoped she had a second career in mind when this one collapsed.

I got into the car and, after I had buckled in Guido to keep him from falling out, I gave Miller a parting word. "I fully intend to file on you. There is too much at stake for me to be nice about it. I hope you do spring Conklin. And I hope you win a big-time wrongful imprisonment case against the police in civil court. And I hope you get the usual thirty percent cut out of it, because Mike Flint could use the money."

"I don't understand," she said.

"Mike is going to sue you for defamation, libel, slander, and just for being too naive to be out on the streets alone. Don't bother to put your fee check in the bank. Endorse it straight over to Mike." I started the car and drove off, leaving her to fend off a flurry of loose gravel.

I said to Guido, "Jennifer Miller seems bright enough. So why is she behaving so stupidly?"

His only response was a snore. I've never known Guido to snore. Over a period of some hours he had consumed most of three beers and a quantity of scotch. Usually, he can hold his drink. Then I began to feel a little guilty. I had kept him out all night a couple of nights ago and worked him hard all day, in the heat. He was in good shape, but maybe I had worn him out.

The news station on the radio was taking call-ins commenting about the continuing demonstration in front of Parker Center. The easy rock station was full of commercials, the classical station was interviewing an aged diva. I played with the tuner until I found classic oldies, turned the volume low, opened all the windows, and avoided fast stops so I wouldn't awaken Guido.

Guido didn't stir all the way out Santa Monica Boulevard and up Highland. I missed his company, maybe, but I wasn't concerned about him until I stopped in front of his house and tried to shake him awake. I couldn't rouse him.

"Guido," I said. "You're home. Quit fooling around." I lifted his eyelid. His pupils were fully dilated. It was too bright a day for fully dilated pupils even if he had his eyes closed. His breathing was shallow but regular, his pulse all right. He had a flush. Who didn't? It was a hundred degrees out.

I fished his keys out of his pocket, went into his house for some cold water and a wet towel. When I came back he hadn't moved, but his breathing sounded funny to me. I wiped his face with the towel and drank the water. The car was an oven. I had to get him inside where it was cooler.

Guido is about my size, but he's all muscle. I managed to hoist him out of his seat and get him over my shoulders fire-rescue style. He was so heavy—dead weight—that I nearly fell three or four times before I got him into the house and laid him on the cool Mexican tile floor. My fingers had made deep red marks on his arms where I held him, but he never complained or groaned or even sighed in my ear. I was scared to the edge of stupid panic.

My strained back muscles hurt too much to straighten, so I crawled to the telephone, dialed 911, and asked for paramedics. While I waited for them, I sat on the floor beside Guido, talking to him, holding him, listening to his chest, waiting until I had to help him breathe, going over in my mind the routine for CPR. I kept trying to get him to wake up.

The paramedics arrived within five minutes, first an ambulance with a two-man crew, backed up by a fire truck. I ran out to meet them, to urge them to hurry. The first paramedic was out of the ambulance before it came to a full stop. He was a big man, about my age, in midnight-blue uniform and yellow rubber gloves.

"What happened?" he asked as we ran back inside.

"I don't know," I said. "He fell asleep in the car. I can't wake him."

The paramedic knelt beside Guido and began taking vital signs. He sniffed Guido's breath.

"How much did he have to drink?"

"Not enough to pass out," I said, feeling defensive. "Some scotch and a couple of beers."

"Drugs?"

"No."

By then the second paramedic had come in. "O.D.?" he asked before he had even looked at Guido.

"She says not."

"Guido doesn't do drugs," I said, not adding any more or asking whether they considered marijuana consumed with banana nut ice cream now and then to be drugs. "He rarely even takes aspirin."

A couple of the firemen, massive men, sauntered in out of the heat to look on with vague curiosity. I overheard "O.D." in their quiet conversation.

"Look," I said, rising to my knees, "he didn't take any drugs. He had a couple of beers—two and a half beers stretched over several hours. Then he had a scotch, a tall one, and part of a second. He was fine when we got in the car. A little wobbly on his feet, but he was lucid."

Sometimes a single word hits you like a dictionary. Jerry Kelsey seemed lucid. I remembered holding a glass of scotch like a prop while I tried to get something useful out of him. Guido drank his scotch. One tall one and part of a second.

CHAPTER
16

"Huevos rancheros everywhere," I said. Guido was nearly the same color as the hospital sheets. Maybe paler. "Lab analysis of your stomach contents may take a week."

"S'okay. I'm not going anywhere." The plastic drainage tube down his throat made him difficult to understand. "I'm going to sleep for a week."

"Not in the hospital you're not," I said. "At these rates, my credit card will only keep you here through tomorrow. If you still want to sleep after that, I'll get you a suite at the Four Seasons. Be cheaper, and they have cable."

He managed to smile. "I woke up, saw where I was, thought you'd driven us through a brick wall. Thought I was dying."

"Not yet, my friend. We still have things to do." I had an obstruction in my own throat, a logjam of emotions. I felt relief that he was all right and guilt that I may have put him in harm's way. And I felt bereft. Whenever any thought of losing Guido managed to rise through all the fuss involved in getting him to the hospital, signed in, pumped out, I felt nearly overwhelmed with sadness. I gripped his icy fingers.

"I called your mom," I said. "She's on her way."

"I want to sleep some more." He yawned. "My throat hurts. Let me sleep."

"Go ahead." I smoothed his blanket up under his chin and stayed beside him until he was softly snoring again. The doctor's best guess was that he had taken a heavy barbiturate. Not good in combination with alcohol. The police were pursuing the source. I was clear what had happened, the question was, why?

I waited until Guido's mother arrived, explained the situation to her as well as I could, and then I left her in charge of further fussing and pillow fluffing.

My benefactor network had left a message that the Reverend Burgess was scheduled for an interview taping. I intended to crash the session in hopes I would find something useful. And if I did, I had no fear about embarrassing the hand behind the signature on my checks. As long as I could use the information to bring the network viewers, I could flog them raw.

Burgess drove up just as I was getting out of my car. I didn't want to scare him away from his interview by confronting him in the parking lot, so I went on up, stationed myself near the elevator to watch for him.

Burgess showed up right behind me, a demanding, balding little rooster from the instant he stepped into the studio. He came carrying a garment bag and a Styrofoam head with a toupee pinned to it. He wanted the staff to provide him with, in this order, a cold Dr. Pepper, a dressing room with a shower, a consultation with the sound and lights technicians, hypoallergenic makeup. Everyone began to scurry—not to accommodate him, but to get out of his way.

I sidled up to him and said, "Gloria Swanson don't live here no mo'."

"Who are you?" he said, checking me over for labels.

"I don't know what you've been watching or who you've been listening to, but the post-Reagan, tight-budget reality around here is the same as it was over at SNN: You get your own drink out of the cooler in the corner, you change in the men's dressing room down the hall. Anything you don't want to lose, keep an eye on." Then I pointed to the stiff little hairpiece he held out in front like a trophy. "And all pets must be on a leash."

"You've got a smart mouth on you." He was smiling when he said it. I decided maybe he had untapped potential.

"If you're carrying a clean shirt," I said, "don't put it on until your face has been painted. And don't try to tell the technical staff their business or you're likely to go out on the airwaves looking and sounding like Frankenstein's spare parts. I'm giving you the best, and probably the only, advice you're going to get around here. By the way, nice car."

I turned my back and left him standing alone with only his extra hair for company. I knew he would be ignored until the staff had decided he had been sufficiently punished for his pushiness.

I asked the assistant director to call me when everything was ready to roll, and went downstairs to waste some time with Lana Howard, my independent-projects producer. We talked about Guido and what had happened, about the background music I wanted to use in my project, about graphics and promotion, and planting spring bulbs as soon as the weather cooled. A very productive forty minutes.

When I arrived back upstairs, Leroy Burgess was seated on the news set with the generic male city-affairs reporter on the staff. Burgess wore a pale blue suit and a clerical collar. His hairpiece was glued in place a precise three inches above his combed eyebrows.

The director, Jack Riley, was an old friend from my Latin American correspondent days. He had been a field cameraman then. A big guy; in the days before little hand-held video-cameras, the shooter was always the tallest and strongest man on the crew. I went into the director's booth and sat down next to him in front of his massive instrument console.

I planted a friendly pat on Jack's back. He responded with more inviting body language than I wanted to deal with, so I backed up a bit.

He said, "Like old times, Maggie."

"Yes," I said, "back in the jungle together."

"You have some interest in this character Burgess?"

"Indeed, I do. Pretend I'm not here. I only want to listen."

A red light began flashing on the console and Jack turned to attend to it. Jack communicated with his cameramen and his on-camera "talent" via tiny ear sets connected to a microphone that extended up out of his board. When the microphone was turned off, conversations in the booth could not be heard on the set. Almost as good as being a speck on the wall for eaves-dropping purposes. I was behind the lights that shone in Burgess's eyes.

When the interview began, most of what Burgess had to say was a rehash of the stuff he had given to Ralph Faust. In his defense, most of the questions asked were the same, too. The tone was sympathy for poor Conklin, outrage at police abuse, and the failures of our justice system.

I was worried about Guido in the hospital—the doctor had assured me he would be fine once he had slept off the drugs—and I was feeling frankly bored by the proceedings on the set. I rested my chin on my hand and listened to the reporter go through his schtick.

Jack nudged me. "Whuzzamattah?"

"Same old same old," I shrugged. "He's given the same interview to every station in town."

"Have anything to offer?"

I suggested a question that was immediately, electronically transplanted into the reporter's shell-like ear. Like magic, it came out of the reporter's mouth.

"Mr. Burgess," the reporter intoned, "your investigation has taken many months, involved a good deal of travel and other expenses. How is your program financed?"

Burgess sat up straighter, beamed brighter than he had while discussing the legal details. I knew we had hit the A topic. "We are privately funded, mostly by donations from good citizens interested in seeing an injustice exposed to the bright, purifying light of day. 'The truth will set you free,' sayeth the Lord."

Jack directed his on-camera mouthpiece, "Rephrase it. Push him."

I was proud of him. I gave his arm an approving nudge.

The talent asked, "How much funding would an investigation of this nature require?"

Burgess blustered over a few syllables before he composed himself again. "It's too early to say. We still have a long way to go. A long way. Anyone who wants to help can call . . ."

I took the microphone and planted a new query that interrupted the pitch for money. The reporter was startled by the new voice, but recovered in a hurry.

The question: "Mr. Burgess, if the court decides that Charles Conklin's conviction was flawed, and he is released from prison, will he file a civil suit against the city and the police?"

Burgess frowned. "Charles lost fourteen years of freedom and earnings. His children grew up without him. No dollar amount can repay him. He should be compensated, but what price tag can you put on fourteen years?"

"I imagine that price tag will be substantial. Well into the millions. The attorney will take, one expects, the standard thirty to fifty percent. What will be your interest in the award?"

Burgess grew hot under the lights. He equivocated. "The people who put Charles Conklin behind bars must be served notice that this community will not tolerate misuse of power. I would like to see the punishment come out of the pockets of the men responsible and not from public funds."

"Will you have a share in the award?"

Burgess was trying to peer beyond the lights, looking for us. "Only what is appropriate."

I turned to Jack and said, "The truth will set you free."

Jack put his finger against his microphone switch and asked me, "Anything else?"

"Ask about Conklin's plans should he get sprung."

The question was, "Charles Conklin has been in prison for fourteen years. In the event he is released, has he spoken of his plans for the future? Will he return to his former profession? What of his family?"

Burgess's eyes grew misty on cue. "As I said, more than anything else, Charles has missed watching his children grow up. They are all adults now, or nearly so. To capture some of what he lost, Charles has told me how very much he wants to work with children when he gets out. Do something in the arts. Teach peace."

The reporter furrowed his brow. "What line of work was he in?"

Burgess was quick. "For Charles, the answers all lie in the future."

Jack said, "Maggie?"

I grinned at him. "It's your show. Ask your own damn questions."

Into the mike he said, "Close him."

I stood up. "One thing you can do for me, though. Get a shooter to follow Burgess out of the studio, get a shot of him with his car."

"Why?"

"Background. Some variety to talking heads."

"Don't lie to me."

"I saw him drive in. His conveyance surprised me."

"Yeah?"

"Besides, I want that celestial blue suit recorded for posterity. I'll be beholden to you if you get me a copy of this interview and the grand exit. Like, today sometime."

"How beholden?" he asked, gripping my thigh through my jeans.

"Be careful, Jack," I said. "Anita Hill is a personal friend of mine."

"Damn," he said.

CHAPTER
17

My family, plus one, Sly again, were just finishing dinner when I walked in. Sly had his hair combed back in imitation of Michael, his idol.

"How were things in math today?" I asked Sly.

As always, he turned his foxy face to Michael before he said anything. "Hangin' in."

"How are things at home?"

"Food's shit, but okay."

"He's eating regular." Michael tweaked the boy's flat midsection. "Look at this belly bag."

Sly, delighted by the attention, slapped Michael's hand away. "Faggot."

Mike reached up for my hand. "Hungry?"

"No." In the back of my throat I still had the smell of the huevos rancheros Guido had deposited on his floor. I got a diet soda from the refrigerator and sat down at the table between Mike and Casey. "Casey, how was the first day?"

"Good." She wore sweatpants over her leotard, her hair was still trapped in a tight ballerina bun. Bowser lay on the floor under the table, resting his head on her foot. "My geometry teacher is a major jerk, but the rest of them are okay. Dance is going be really, really hard. But good."

"I hope so," I said.

"The L.A. Ballet Company is coming next week for *Nutcracker* tryouts," she said, enthusiasm gaining momentum. "I don't know if I'm going to try out. Mischa says I'm too tall for the Clara part. Everything else is *so* boring. The snowflakes and sugarplums are really lame. Think I'll wait until the Joffrey comes in January."

"Auditions for an L.A. show, I hope? I don't want you on a tour for another year or two. Or three. Or ten."

"We'll see," she said, picking up her dinner plate. "They probably won't want me anyway." Her tone said this was only token self-deprecation. Lack of confidence is not one of Casey's problems. With Bowser following her every movement, she pirouetted to the sink and rinsed her dishes.

"Wish they'd let me have a dog." Reverently, Sly stroked the dog's back. "Hey, Michael, how come you don't have a cool dog like this?"

"Why do I need a dog, squirt, when I have you?"

"Faggot," Sly giggled.

"So, Michael," I said, "were you able to petition the class you needed?"

"No. I ended up with Asian lit just to fill my schedule." He glanced at Casey, gave me a sardonic smile. "Teacher's a major jerk. But the rest of them are okay."

I laughed. "Glad to hear it."

Casey rolled her eyes. "You are so funny, Michael. Not!"

"Can you play volleyball on your toes?" he asked her.

She sneered. "Of course not."

"Can you play at all?"

"I'm okay. Good enough to beat you."

"Prove it." He gathered his dinner things and stacked them in the sink. "There's a game out back tonight. Show me your stuff."

Sly, not to be neglected, chirped up, "I can beat you both."

"Oh yeah?" Michael wadded the foil from his baked potato into a ball and flicked it to Casey. "See if you can get it from her, squirt."

In the small kitchen they played keep-away. Casey and Michael, who towered over poor little Sly, teased, feigned, mercilessly held the foil ball out of his reach.

Michael passed high to Casey. She reached for it. Sly hit the back of her knees, pinched her butt, and, when she fumbled the ball to swat him, intercepted the ball and was out the back door with it.

"You little creep." Casey flew out in pursuit, with Bowser, barking, close on her heels.

Mike reached back from his chair and snagged Michael's arm before he could get away. "We're going to go look at a house in South Pasadena before it gets dark. You interested?"

"Can't. Sly's still flunking math, needs a tutorial." He jogged out to catch up with the others.

Mike watched him with a misty-eyed wistfulness saved for transitory pleasures, moments that will too soon pass. He sighed and turned in his seat, smiled at me.

"Quite a kid," he said.

"The best." I started picking at his dinner salad. "What's this about a house?"

"Old place in South Pasadena, belonged to Harriman's grandmother. Remember Harriman? Works Hollywood vice. So, the house has been vacant for a while. Some snag in probate. He's offering us a break on the rent if I help him do some work on it, get it ready to sell eventually."

I tried to hold back mental pictures of some grandma's dark old house with cabbage-rose wallpaper and antique plumbing. You can live with almost any inconvenience for a short time, but a short time didn't interest me. I asked, "How long can we have it?"

"Long as we want."

"Until you retire?"

"Long as we want."

"Cozy arrangement," I said.

He leaned back. "I told you, we look after each other."

I decided to reserve judgment as to how well they looked after each other until I had seen the house.

Mike hadn't finished his pork chop. I set aside his empty salad bowl and picked up the chop. He watched me with a dreamy sort of look on his Bogart face.

I said, "How was your day, cupcake?"

"Stimulating. I did the laundry and caught up on my soaps. Drove the carpool, did the marketing, fixed dinner. Usual routine. How was your day?"

"Routine," I said, moving on to the ends of his baked potato. "I interviewed a murderer in Juvenile Hall, a Black Muslim in the ghetto, and an old psycho cop. Watched a TV taping. Guido you know about."

"Guido I know about." Mike picked up the empty serving dishes and turned away from me toward the sink, but not before I saw something dark cross his face: fear, despair, frustration, they all seem to come out of the same emotional pocket. For the last few days, ever since Conklin's name came up on the news, Mike had become moody, unusually changeable. And quiet.

Mike was scraping dinner scraps into the garbage disposal when I came up behind him and put my arms around him, pressed my hands against his flat middle and my cheek against his hard back.

"Guido's okay," I said.

"I know."

"And I'm okay."

"I know."

"It's you I'm worried about. What makes your face so sad?"

He turned off the water and the disposal and stayed with his back to me, his damp hands covering mine. He said, "I can't stand being locked out. I want to go back to work. If I had a day—just one single day—I'd get this pile of manure case bagged and delivered and out of our lives."

"I'm sure you would. But you just told me your people look after each other. Trust them to bag your manure this time. Trust me."

"There are a lot of things I like you to do for me," he said in his tough-guy mode. "Working my case just doesn't happen to be one of them."

"I'm not working your case," I said.

"Could have fooled me." From the mail pile in the corner, next to the basket of market coupons and take-out menus, he pulled a manila envelope like the one Hector had given me a couple of nights earlier. This one was thicker. A yellow sticky note on the front of it said, "Mike, give this to Maggie. Let's get together soon. Hec."

"Mash notes?" I said.

"Take a look."

The envelope had copies of Wyatt Johnson's personnel file and the police report of his murder, about fifty pages stapled together. The cover sheet on the report warned, "Confidential. Operations-Headquarters Bureau. The Chief of Police considers this report to be highly confidential. Administrative use is limited to concerned staff and command personnel of the Los Angeles Police Department. Any other use is forbidden by the District Attorney. This report is not to be reproduced or copied. This report has a registered distribution."

"Sounds intimidating," I said. "Is it routine warning?"

He shook his head. "Only on officer-involved shootings and internal affairs cases. This is strictly in-house info."

"How much trouble can Hector get into for bringing it out?" I asked.

"Lose his job. His pension. Wife'll probably walk. That's why this report doesn't leave your hands. It doesn't show up in a movie."

"I didn't ask Hector for anything," I said. "What does he expect me to do with this?"

"I wouldn't know. He left the envelope on the doorstep and took off. Now you have the files, suppose you read them."

Wyatt Johnson's personnel folder was interesting only because I had never seen a police employment file before. Johnson had graduated near the top of his police academy class in physical tests and on the firing range. Academically, he was in the lower third. After his rookie period on patrol, he transferred to traffic out of Central Bureau.

"Not a go-getter," Mike said. "Traffic is easy duty."

"He had good evaluations," I said, reading through them. "Courteous, prompt, and clean. A note here from an accident victim praising his helpfulness and professionalism. A genuine paragon of police virtue."

"Not quite," Mike said. "I see he got beefed. He drew five days for hitting the hole."

"Excuse me?" I said.

"He was caught sleeping on the job and got suspended for five days without pay. It's no wonder. See these?" He pulled out half-a-dozen work permits. "He was king of the part-time job. Until he got caught sleeping and had all his permits revoked, he had the okay to moonlight at, count 'em, six security jobs."

"Not all at the same time," I said.

"No. Probably worked more than one at a time, though. Look at his personal data. He's a kid, twenty-four years old. He's buying a house, buying a car, has a wife and baby. Keeping up with that takes a helluva lot more income than a rookie cop salary. If he's like the rest of them, he works his eight-hour shift in uniform, then he goes straight to his next job and works eight more. On his days off, he works a third job. Doesn't leave much time for sleeping."

"Or for wife and baby. Did you have part-time jobs?"

"Shit, yes. Used to work morning watch, get off around seven in the morning. If I had court I'd find a place to grab a nap until I was called—sleep in my car, any empty office. One time a bailiff let me into a courtroom during lunch break and I slept on the judge's bench. I'd collect overtime days doing court, take the days off and work security for the movie studios on location shoots.

"Most of the time, I'd go from my patrol shift straight to my next job, work five or six hours, then I'd go pick up Michael and coach his baseball team—I coached him until he was in high school. Eat dinner, take a nap, then go back to work and start all over again. I'd never get more than three, four hours of sleep in a stretch."

"Hard on a marriage."

"Too hard." Dewy eyes again. "I wanted my family to have everything I never had. Nice house in a good neighborhood, new cars, the best schools. I wanted my son's mother to be home for him. My problem was, I didn't really know how to make that happen. Had no model to work from."

"Maybe not," I said. "But you did a great job. Michael is a wonderful man. You're a wonderful father."

He had a crooked, almost shy smile. "You should hear my ex's version before you say that."

"No thanks." I turned back to the files.

"I worked nearly every waking hour, but I never made her happy."

"Maybe if you'd been home more."

"Once I had a mortgage, I couldn't get off that treadmill."

"I know how that is. Sometimes you have to make a leap, even if you can't see where you'll land. I did it once." I was picking at the remains in the salad bowl. "During the last few seasons that I worked network news, I pulled down six figures a year for reading copy off a Teleprompter. I persuaded myself I was no better than a whore—tease up my hair, paint my face, and try to give the viewing audience a hard-on so they wouldn't turn the channel before the commercials came on. Sounds ridiculous when I say it now, but that's how I felt. So, I did the noble thing, and I quit.

"The first year I was an independent, I earned minus forty-thousand dollars and loved every minute of it. We nearly lost our house. My husband didn't make the leap with me, though. He was so worried about impending fiscal disaster that he started losing his hair. He couldn't get it up for a while, either. And you know what?"

"I'm afraid of what you'll tell me," he said. "But what?"

"That year I quit, Scotty made nearly two hundred thousand dollars all by himself. You'd think it would be enough to buy groceries, wouldn't you?"

"You'd think."

"Which brings us back to the point here. It doesn't matter what you earn, it's what you're used to spending. Now, look at this nice young cop, Wyatt. Surely he and his family had become accustomed to a certain standard. How did he cover his obligations when he couldn't work overtime?"

"Probably did what everyone else does. Cut back, put the wife to work, lie about the number of extra hours you work. Why? What are you suggesting?"

"Nothing. But it bears looking into. It still bothers me that that boy scout was in a public bathroom in a crummy neighborhood, in the middle of the night."

"Maybe he was so worried about fiscal disaster that his hair started falling out and he couldn't get it up." Mike started to tickle me, holding me with one strong hand so I couldn't get away. It had more to do with control than with fun. "Maybe he was looking for a hit man because his wife kept bringing up shit that bore looking into. Maybe he had to pee."

I wasn't laughing when I got away from him. My sides hurt from his tickling. "Mike, did you ever get beefed?"

"Not for sleeping on the job." His voice sounded tight. I knew I was treading the line. I didn't know how to phrase the next part of the question on my mind because I was afraid of the answer. Mike answered before I had to figure out an angle.

"I was a street cop for a lot of years, baby. Things go down that you can't always handle according to the book. I did what I had to do to control the situation, keep innocent people from taking too many lumps, weed out some of the creeps. So, yeah, I got beefed."

"For excessive force?" I was pushing it.

"That's what the sheet says." He gave it to me in slow, white-hot speech. "I gave my baton to a rape victim once and let her beat the crap out of her attacker. I took two weeks on that one. I broke my flashlight over a guy's head when he drew a gun on me. Judge said I should have shot him and threw the case out. I got into my share of fights. A blow by blow make you happy? Is that what you want?"

I had backed up against the sink, as far away as I could get without leaving the room. He was big, he was fierce. Any kid in the room would be reduced to blubbering and tears—I understood that right away. Grown men and women would think twice about taking him on. He could scare me if I let him. But I faced him down, moved into him because it was all wind and fire. Mike would never touch me, that I knew that for an absolute certainty.

I said, "There's only one thing I want, Mike."

"Let's have it."

"I want you."

CHAPTER

18

I was right about the cabbage roses, great big pink ones with dark green leaves. Lying under the ugly wallpaper and the many layers of paint slathered on the original woodwork, under the army-blanket-gray carpet, I saw a beautiful turn-of-the-century California craftsman-style house ready to be rescued.

When Mike pulled back the heavy damask drapes in the living room, I was sold. One entire wall was floor-to-ceiling glass doors that opened onto a brick patio shaded by an enormous avocado tree.

The house had been built around three sides of the patio and every first floor room had similar tall glass doors. The wing to the right was a single empty room large enough for a pool table or a grand piano. The left wing held the kitchen and dining room. Beyond the patio a lush, sloping lawn and a formal rose garden separated the house from a free-standing cottage and the garage.

"Bowser would be happy," Mike said.

"We'll take down the drapes," I said. "They spoil the windows."

"If we decide to take the house," he said.

I said, "Uh huh," and walked out across the patio to explore the kitchen.

I was already in love, so maybe I didn't see things with an appropriately critical eye. The kitchen looked as though it hadn't been touched for probably twenty-five years, and then touched lightly. I thought that all it needed to be functional were a microwave, some fresh tile grout, and Windex to clean the patio doors. Mike had some questions about the old copper plumbing. I left him with his head under the sink and wandered upstairs by myself.

What attracted me to the old house was clean design, the feeling of openness created by tall ceilings and windows everywhere. All of the rooms were large spaces that seemed to flow around the open center. Even the upstairs bedrooms.

There were two bedroom suites, both with decadent green and mauve art-deco tile bathrooms complete with claw-footed tubs. Both suites also had adjoining sitting rooms with balconies that overlooked the yard. I thought we could easily convert one of the sitting rooms into a third bedroom so that Michael and Casey would share a bathroom. Though maybe sharing a bathroom with Casey was asking too much of anyone.

The master suite was a few square feet larger and just a little more opulent than the other rooms. The big discovery there was the small granite fireplace opposite the huge bathtub. Right off, I thought of a few possibilities.

I went out to the landing that overlooked the entry, watched the gathering dusk wash the house in soft, blue evening light. When I couldn't see the cabbage roses any more, it was easier to visualize the house as it would be when the walls and the floors had been stripped, when our furniture was in place, our pictures and treasures installed. It seemed a natural merger.

Mike came out of the small powder room tucked under the stairs and looked up at me, his hair bright silver in the last glow of daylight.

"Plumbing is old," he said, drawing together his brows. "I'm not sure about the wiring, either. Power has been off for over a year."

"Come up," I said.

"It's dark."

"See what I found."

"The electrical service isn't our problem," he said as he climbed the stairs toward me, grousing all the way. "Unless it screws up. All your video stuff, the kids' computers and stereos, a microwave—the wiring was never meant to handle that kind of a load."

When he got to the top step, I grabbed a handful of his shirt-front and, walking backward, pulled him along the hall. "None of that matters, baby."

"You don't care if the whole place leaks and shorts out?"

"No. We'll fix it." I led him into what would be our bedroom. A warm, fragrant breeze blew in through the open windows and swept the upper branches of the avocado tree against the side of the house, a brisk sound like an old lady with a new broom.

We went over to the window and looked out across the lawn. When I took a deep breath and sighed, Mike looked down at me and smiled. "You like it?"

"The bathtub is big enough for two."

"But if the pipes leak . . ."

"We'll heat water in the fireplace."

He turned again to the windows. "I took a look at the little house in back. It's just a single room with a bath. No kitchen. If we update the wiring, you could use it for an office."

"There's a good room downstairs for an office. If the little house is nice, maybe Michael would like to make bachelor quarters out of it. Give him more privacy."

"Hmmm," Mike said. "Hmmm."

"You could put up Casey's barre in the extra room up here. Then everyone would have plenty of space."

This time when he said, "Hmmm," he was nodding.

I leaned against him and he felt so solid. Solid like the house.

I've never been able to keep my hands off Mike, not from the first day I met him. I cannot rationalize the chemistry thing between us. From the beginning, it was, frankly, something new and damned surprising for me.

At some point in history, I must have felt passion for my ex-husband. Otherwise, how would we have gotten together? But by the time we reached the point of splitting up, I could not remember ever feeling anything for him stronger than vague and constant annoyance.

Time does play tricks on the memory. Just the same, I knew for an absolute certainty that the raw, hungry lust I had for Mike Flint was, for me, an unprecedented affliction.

I reached up under his shirt to find bare skin. "Don't you think we should baptize our room?"

He laughed softly. "What did you have in mind?"

"Make love to me."

"Should I go down and get the handcuffs out of the car?"

I pulled his shirt off over his head. "Sure. I'll cuff you to the balcony railing and have my way with you."

"You got it backwards." Mike was a wrestler in high school. I reached for his belt buckle, but before I saw his move coming, somehow I landed on the floor pinned beneath him, nose to nose. "I don't need cuffs to hold you down."

"Right," I said, breathless. "But I hoped you had more in mind that holding me down."

He did, and we well and fully initiated the room, blessed the house. Anointed ourselves in accumulated rug dust. When we got back to the condo in the Valley, we looked as if we had dug right into the grime of restoration. Made a commitment to it.

Michael and Casey were in the dining room doing homework when we passed through. They exchanged scandalized glances when they saw us.

"Where's Sly?" I asked.

"We drove him home," Casey said. "How's the house?"

"Beautiful," I said. "You can ride your bike to school. Mike thinks he can have it ready to move into in about a week. Michael, do you think you can tolerate sleeping on the couch that much longer?"

"I think so." He seemed tremendously relieved by the announcement. I wondered, if we hadn't found a place so quickly, how long would his charity and good humor have lasted?

Bowser crawled out from under the table, from his usual perch next to Casey, and began sniffing Mike and me. His tail wagged delighted approval with the variety of smells we had brought him to sample.

"Can we go rent a video?" Casey asked.

"Not on a school night," I said.

"I'm bored."

"Read a book. Take a walk. Come for a swim with me."

She looked up at me with utter disdain. And so did the dog. "I finished my homework."

"Congratulations," I said, kissing the top of her freshly washed head. "I have some work to do in my office. If you don't want to swim, maybe you'd like to come with me and be useful."

I had not tempted her.

Mike said, "Casey, after I get cleaned up, I need to go to the mall, pick up some things. You haven't seen the mall yet. Would you like to come along?"

Casey looked from him to me, her face happy again. "Mom?"

"If you want to go, go."

Ten minutes later, Mike's hair still wet from his shower, they went. It took me a few minutes longer to get washed and changed. The house was quiet when I was ready, some unedited tapes tucked into my bag. I found Michael stretched out on the couch with headphones on.

I shouted his name.

He took off his headphones. "What?"

"I'm going to spend a couple of hours editing an interview. Would you like to come?"

He nestled down among the cushions. "Another time."

I understood. He was enjoying some blessed aloneness while he could.

All the way down Ventura Boulevard, I was enjoying the prospect of having my work space at home again. No more commuting, no more rent. I would be more accessible for Casey, especially with her school only a couple of miles from the house. Best of all, I was thinking as I pulled into the nearly deserted parking lot, I wouldn't be working alone at night.

I went upstairs first to check my studio slot for the following night. A special-education expert named Linda Westman was coming in to discuss the relationship between learning disabilities and growing up in a war zone. I picked up my mail—most of it junk—stopped at the ice cream machine before I went down the hall to my office.

The hall walls needed paint. The carpet needed cleaning. The whole building was an unloved, transient haven. I had never bothered to notice before. Now that I was a short-timer, I saw it all with a more objective eye. With pleasure, as soon as arrangements were made for the house, I would call the rental agency and tell them they could start looking for a new tenant.

When I put my key in the door, my first thought was that

even the locks were cheap; sloppy works. But I had installed new locks of my own. Good ones.

Sometimes we have to listen to that little inner voice that may have picked up on some tiny nuance; something about the easy way the new locks turned set off the alarms. I pushed the door open and hit the lights without stepping inside.

My office, at first, seemed exactly as I had left it the day before. But things had been touched: The middle drawer of the old wooden desk had to be lifted just so to make it close all the way. Someone who didn't know that had last closed my drawer. The shelved tapes were meticulously aligned, the shooting notes on the blotter were stacked with the corners nice and even. The usual dust was there, the trash had not been emptied. I am not meticulous about straight corners and aligned edges, the night cleaning crew had not been in to straighten anything.

The real clincher that set off the adrenaline rush was, the message light on my answering machine was not flashing. I took a pencil out of my bag and used the eraser end to punch the replay button. The day's usual collection of messages began spieling out.

Right away, and using the pencil to dial, I called Michael.

"Check the doors," I told him. "Make sure everything is locked. Until your dad gets back, don't let anyone, *any*one in."

Then I paged Mike. While I stood by the telephone waiting for him to call me back, I saw that the power light on one of the tape players was glowing. I pushed play and watched Etta on the courthouse steps during the three minutes, twelve seconds—according to the VCR timer—that it took Mike to get to a telephone.

"What?" he said when I answered his call.

"Someone was in my office."

"Is it tossed?"

"No," I said. "Barely touched. Whoever it was put a tape in the VCR, listened to my phone messages, went through my desk and the tape files. I don't know whether anything is missing. Or added. It's damn spooky."

"You're there now?"

"Yes. What should I do?"

"Bolt the door and wait for me."

I used the time to make another call. Lana Howard was at home.

"What's the progress?" she asked me.

"Everything's great," I said, hauling up enthusiasm for her benefit. "A film always needs time to find its stride. At this point, we are in full striding glory. A few in-studio interviews and a follow-up or two, and then we're ready to give it form. It will, I say with all modesty, knock your socks off."

I was watching Etta on the screen again as I talked. "The reason I called, though, is, something interesting has come up in the process and I want to run it by you."

"Sure." She sounded eager.

"This Charles Conklin business?"

"Yes. Great story." Sounded like real enthusiasm. "Really great. So many human interest elements there."

"You don't know the half of it," I said. Her enthusiasm seemed to be that of a convert, and my job would be the difficult one of re-education. Lana first, the entire viewing public next. "And the half you don't know involves Baron Marovich, the murder of a prostitute, the shooting of a cop, media manipulation—stop me when I've peaked your interest—high-level perjury, breaking and entering and, if we stretch it, child abuse."

"I don't know, Maggie. How long is this piece?"

"I can do it in sixty seconds, I can do it in sixty minutes. Depends on what you want. Before you make a decision, though, you need to know that someone is after my data. My office was broken into this evening. I have a feeling that the sooner I get something on the air, the safer I'm going to be."

"Really?" Dramatic expression. "Are you in danger?"

I fudged here. "I have been followed. Guido was doped. He's in the hospital right now. My gut feeling is, someone is desperate to stop certain information from being made public. Now, you've been in this business almost as long as I have. You know that the more someone doesn't want you to give some piece of information, the more that information needs to be broadcast. We're not talking personal dirt here. We're talking misuse of the public trust. And the election is six weeks away."

"How soon can you have something for me?"

"If I can use the network facilities and borrow an editor, I can have something that will singe the paint off your nose by noon tomorrow."

She didn't need to think it over. "Just tell me what you need. If you can have something for me by noon tomorrow, I'll schedule a lunch meeting and screen it for the editorial board."

After good-bye, I turned off Etta, ejected her tape, and slipped it into my bag.

I heard Mike and Casey coming down the hall. When I opened the door, they looked as if they had been in a foot race. They surveyed the office, both of them disappointed that there was nothing to see. Mike was carrying a large fishing tackle box.

"They were here after seven o'clock," I said. "The last message on my machine was from Guido's mother giving me an update on his condition."

"How's Guido?"

"Asleep, but okay."

Mike had opened his tackle box. He took out a large soft-bristle brush, a plastic bottle filled with dark graphite powder, and a roll of wide clear tape. With these tools, he lifted prints from the buttons on the answering machine and the VCR, from the light switch and the door knob. Then he took out an ink pad and made a set of prints from me and a set from Casey.

"If you find a stranger's prints," I said, "what will you do with them?"

"Run them through AFIS."

Sounded like a garden pest, but it was the state's computerized fingerprint identification system. Anyone with prints on file with the state, from school teachers to convicted ax murderers, was in the computer.

Mike lifted more than a dozen clear prints. Most of them were mine or Casey's. The four or five that did not compare, he put into a small brown envelope and tucked into his tackle box.

"I'll follow you home," he said.

"Okay," I said. "But, if you'll be okay watching over Casey and Michael tonight, I have some work to do at the network production facility. I need to pick up some material from home, then I'm gone."

"How long do you think?"

"My deadline is noon tomorrow."

He was upset, maybe angry. "All night? What are you doing?"

"I'm putting together a teaser for the evening news broadcast. The D.A. says he has new affidavits from the Conklin witnesses. But no one has seen them. I have affidavits of another sort, and I want to get them on the air as soon as I can, before this business gets any uglier. Breaking into my office was going too far. I have a bad feeling that whoever was in here tonight knew I was occupied at seven o'clock. I don't keep regular office hours. No one knows when I'll drop in." I glanced at Casey and felt hot all over. If someone knew where I was, they probably knew where Casey was, too. And Michael.

Mike said, "What are you going to do?"

"I'm not sure until I get into it, but I'll put together a sixty-second package for broadcast. Maybe it will flush out something useful."

Mike reached over to take my arm, bring me in closer. "You shouldn't go out alone. I'll call someone."

At ten, I had Casey tucked in and my materials gathered into a big box. Mike waited outside with me until my escort arrived, a black and white unit with two uniformed officers, then he went inside and I heard the deadbolt shoot home behind him.

My escort followed me back through Burbank to the network studios. Their spotlight saw me all the way into the building.

Lana Howard was waiting for me at the security desk. She made a crack about the lengths I would go to one-up the usual limos the talent used, but I saw that any doubts she had about the gravity of my new project evaporate when she saw my police tag. I wasn't about to tell her that if Mike wanted me to have an escort, I would have an escort, whether I was coming in to draw mustaches on the portraits of the studio execs in the foyer or to save the universe from certain destruction. She was impressed, and that was enough.

CHAPTER
19

Usually, it's far easier to make an hour-long or two-hour-long film than it is to make one that lasts only a minute. It is not especially difficult to condense the facts. I had put together enough evidence—including the shot of attorney Jennifer Miller at Jerry Kelsey's place, with Kelsey's face perfectly framed in the window behind her—to show the broad audience gross manipulation of the facts relating to Charles Conklin. The real difficulty lay in eliciting an emotional reaction in such a short time without resorting to the usual knee-jerk images: a waving flag, bodies on the street, starving orphans. I could explain, I could make people believe. But, in a sixty-second package, could I make anyone care?

By ten-thirty Thursday morning I was mentally numb and half-blind. With the help of a very patient and capable editor, I had what I thought was a good piece. I borrowed a portable tape player from him and drove over the pass to the hospital to show Guido.

"You look like hell," Guido greeted me.

"You look like you've had a holiday," I said. "Get the nurses off your bed and let me climb in. I'm exhausted."

The two perky nurses who were ministering to him—one feeding him broth, one adjusting an IV—scowled at me as if I had invaded their zone. I further upset order by pushing things aside on his bedside table to make room for the video player. I plugged it into the same socket as the heart monitor, put in the tape, walked around to the side of the bed without all the IV apparatus, climbed up next to Guido, and stretched out.

"Excuse me," the little brunette nurse whispered, scandalized. "Patient beds are sterile."

"I'm sorry, Guido," I said, sliding one of his pillows under my head and crossing my legs atop his white blanket. "You would have made a wonderful father."

Guido told his nurses, "It's useless to argue with her. Come over and see what she brought to entertain us."

I started the tape. I watched them watch. And was gratified by their reactions. When it was over, I rewound it and played it again. The nurses stayed through the second run.

"That is so scummy, what they did," the brunette spat. "Really, really scummy. How did they think they could get away with it?"

"Exactly the point I hoped to make," I said.

Guido wrapped his arm around me, pulled me close to him, and kissed my forehead.

"I'm proud of you," he said. "Hard facts, vivid images, steady build to the tagline. You did it without being self-indulgent or melodramatic. I think you're getting dangerous, but it's damn good. What are you going to do with it?"

"Lana Howard is taking it to her editorial board at noon. If she talks it into the rundown, look for it on the news at four, five, and six. Anything you would change?"

"Not a nanosecond."

The brunette nurse's face lit up. "You'll be on the news?"

"Probably," I said.

"If you'll excuse us," Guido said to her, "Miss TV Star and I have some things to discuss."

The nurses left us alone but left the door open.

I asked him, "When are they going to spring you?"

"Now. Soon as the doc signs me out."

"Want me to wait and drive you home?"

"Yes. If I call my mom, she'll stay at my house for days shoveling pasta down me and cleaning cupboards. I don't have the energy for her ministrations."

"I think I owe you at least some taxi service," I said.

He waved off the suggestion of debt. "What's new?"

"Plenty." I opened my bag and took out the police file on

Wyatt Johnson's shooting and turned to the follow-up report that Mike had written a year after the shooting.

"This is so interesting," I said. "Reads like an old *Dragnet* script. Wish I could figure a way to use it."

I took a sip of Guido's water and started reading aloud to him the straight, flat, prose description of the scene in the service station men's room that November night in 1979.

" 'On 11-6-79, at 0045 hours, the victim, Los Angeles Police Department Officer Wyatt Johnson, a male black, twenty-four years of age, was found mortally wounded in the men's restroom of a service station on the corner of Century Boulevard and Clovis Avenue, in the City of Los Angeles. The victim had been shot six times through the chest and abdominal area. Four bullets exited the victim's back and two deflected off his fourth and sixth thoracic vertebrae and exited through his right side. The motive for the shooting is unknown. The weapon was not recovered. No slugs were located at the scene or recovered from the corpse during autopsy.

" 'At 0120 hours, detectives responded to the crime scene. The crime scene was being protected by the first officers on the scene.' " Their names and serial numbers were listed. I didn't recognize any of them, and I didn't read the names to Guido. " 'The weather was dry and clear, with the temperature in the low forty-degree range. The crime scene was illuminated by three single globe mercury vapor lights at the intersection and a double-tube fluorescent light attached to the eaves on the east side of the building. The area is commercial with multiple-family residences to the south.

" 'Detectives observed the victim, supine, face downward, on the floor of the men's restroom with his head wedged between the toilet bowl and the wash basin and his feet extending out the open doorway.' "

I held up the hand-drawn diagram of the scene showing the orientation of the body, and then several black and white photographs of the blood-spattered room and the dark river that poured out from under the victim. According to the diagram, the room was three feet by four feet, barely wide enough to open the door without banging into the wash basin. To myself, I read through the description again before I turned to Guido. " ' He was shot from the front and he fell forward.' "

"There wasn't room to fall any way but forward."

"Right," I said. "The shooter had to be straddling the toilet or else he was wedged into the corner between the toilet and the wash basin."

"Your point?"

"Wyatt Johnson would have literally fallen into the shooter's arms. Look at all the blood in these pictures. In the interviews with the girls, they never said anything about seeing blood on Charles Conklin."

Guido gave the pictures a closer look. "It was dark. The lights were sodium vapor and fluorescent. Both of them distort color, make red look black or brown. If the shooter wore something dark or some kind of print, I can see blood getting past notice. Unless it was shiny."

"There are bloody footprints and handprints everywhere," I said, pointing them out in the pictures. "A lot of people passed through that small space—James Shabazz, police, paramedics, the same assortment we saw dancing in attendance on Hanna the other night."

"Dancing's a good description. Looks like Arthur Murray charts on the floor."

"I wonder what they did with the prints," I said.

"That is not allowed!" The rebuke came from a tall, dark imperious man wearing a starched white lab coat. The pocket badge labeled him as Dr. V. K. Sadgopal and he stood at the end of the bed glaring at me and Guido snuggled together over the report.

Guido tightened his hold on me. "If you don't like it, then expel me from this place."

Dr. Sadgopal slapped his clipboard down on the end of the bed and reached for the privacy curtain. "If your vital signs are normal, Mr. Patrini, you may leave." To me he said, "Excuse us."

I got off the bed and went over to a chair in the corner. Very pointedly, the doctor pulled the curtain around Guido's bed, excluding me, but also giving me a private corner of my own.

I slouched down into the plastic-upholstered chair, crossed my legs, and searched through the report until I found the original witness statements. The interviews were handwritten by the detectives on a printed form: name, residence, phone, business, physical description, where, when, and by whom interviewed, and signed at the end of the account by the witnesses.

I started with Hanna Rhodes. She had told the first detectives who questioned her, "I was at the filling station with my friend, LaShonda. I heard someone let off five or six. I saw the man run out of the toilet. I don't know who he was. Tell him I said I never saw him before."

LaShonda said more or less the same. When she was asked why she ran all the way to James Shabazz's house instead of calling the police, she said, "I don't know. I was scared."

Tucked among the interviews I found the chronological record, the log of every action taken during the investigation. There were fifteen or so handwritten pages of telephone calls, follow-up interviews, leads, trips to canvass and recanvass the crime-scene neighborhood, autopsy findings, the booking of physical evidence. The record was meticulous, showed consistent effort, but for an entire year there was no result, no suspect identified.

The first entry for November 1980, 0830 hours, was, "Case assigned to Dets. Flint and Kelsey," written in Mike's neat, all-caps hand.

From the log, I knew everything Mike and Jerry did on that first day. Fifteen minutes after they were assigned to the case, they were at the crime scene, canvassing. The rest of the day they re-interviewed all of the witnesses on record they could find, and listed new contacts derived from those conversations. Every day for a week, they talked to the same people.

I went back to the stack of interviews, leafed through them until I found what the witnesses had told Mike. Every day for a week, everyone involved said just about the same thing: everyone heard the shots, no one recognized the gunman.

Mike was persistent with LaShonda DeBevis and Hanna Rhodes. Every day he contacted them, visited them at school, saw them at home. By the end of that week, I thought, to those kids Mike would either be like a member of the family or a nightmare that wouldn't go away. Whichever way it fell, there was no change in their story.

There was progress, though. By the second day, Mike and Jerry were responding to telephone tips that came into the station. Someone remembered seeing a green Bonneville with gray primer paint on the right front door in the area on the night of the murder. Mike requested that patrol officers stop any cars of that description and identify the driver.

On Monday of the second week, Mike returned a call placed from the jail ward at County-USC Medical Center. I recognized the caller's name—the jail-house snitch in the case. The next entry was the first appearance of Charles Conklin's name. Mike ordered a computer run on Conklin's records with the city, the county sheriff, and with Compton police. He also ordered booking photographs from the sheriff and from Compton. That afternoon, Mike and Jerry visited Conklin at his parents' home.

All that week, twice a day, and sometimes three times, Mike interviewed Conklin or went by his house looking for him. He interviewed Conklin's family, his employer and former employer, his neighbors, girlfriends and home boys, his parole officer, the clerk at his corner liquor store, and the snitch. Every day, the very last thing Mike did was make contact with Conklin.

I had no idea what Jerry was doing during all of this. There was a blank on the interview form to list all persons present. Mike's name was on every interview sheet after he was assigned the case, Jerry's on very few. So, I thought, maybe Jerry's skill was in an area outside the interview room. Or, maybe he was out serving subpoenas—cop-speak for hitting the bars during the day.

On Friday morning of the second week, Mike picked up the booking photographs of Conklin he had ordered. He made a "photo display card" with six different men's faces, and recorded that Conklin's face was in position number five on the card. The rest of the day, Mike and Jerry made the rounds of their witnesses, showing every one of them the display card. Several recognized Charles "Pinkie" Conklin as a man who lived in the neighborhood and was "one badass dude," by consensus. But no one, not LaShonda DeBevis nor Hanna Rhodes, connected him to the murder scene.

Mike went to Conklin's house first thing Monday morning. The house was vacant and the landlord, who lived next door, had no idea where the Conklin family had gone. No phone, no forwarding, with two weeks paid-up rent. Just gone.

At 0830 hours, eleven-year-old LaShonda DeBevis told Mike that picture number five was "Pinkie," the man she saw running from the restroom immediately after she heard shots fired. She gave a new interview: "I was afraid he would kill me or do me like I hear he did some girls I know. He is nasty. I saw that man lying in the toilet and I saw all his blood just pouring out and I saw Pinkie run by me with a real mean look on his face. I didn't want to make Pinkie mad at me so he'd do me like that with his gun. That's why I didn't tell the police nothing. If he ever comes back, I hope he don't kill me."

Hanna Rhodes spilled it at noon: "Me and LaShonda was back there and we heard the gun, like I say before. We go start to run over where her mama work because we was scared. But we run smack into Pinkie. He was running out of that toilet where he shot the man. Me and LaShonda look at that dead man and we start screaming and then she run right off. I didn't know what to do next. I think Pinkie has another gun and he shoot me, too. But he go get in that old green car of his and he drive off. I go jump into this old Cadillac is parked there and I climb down in the back and cover up in some old rags and things and I stay there until LaShonda and James call my name and say, 'Get over here.' "

Mike and Jerry had a meeting with the district attorney late that afternoon. The district attorney issued a 187 warrant for Conklin's arrest. At that point Conklin was officially a wanted suspect, and all shift rotations at the Southeast Division were looking for him. Three days later, around dinnertime, he was pulled over on a routine traffic stop—driving erratically in a green Bonneville with gray primer paint on the right front door. He was arrested by the patrol officers when they ran his name through the computer.

After the arrest, the log continues for several pages as Mike and Jerry helped the district attorney put together an evidence package for Conklin's arraignment. They ordered Wyatt's autopsy photos and reports, asked for an aerial photo of the crime scene to be made, searched through DMV files for any records on the green Bonneville. They stayed in contact with their witnesses and tried to milk more from them, tried to find others who might suddenly remember something that happened that night.

Mike logged in receipt of a lie detector test administered to the snitch in an unrelated case. I found the photocopy of the test report. The results were inconclusive. In the opinion of the examiner, the snitch did not register appropriate physiological responses, suggesting he was an accomplished liar.

One year and two months after the murder, Charles Conklin

was held to answer the charges at a preliminary hearing. A trial date was set. During the three-week interim, Mike and Jerry served subpoenas and held their evidence and witness package together. During the trial, they chauffeured witnesses, ran errands for the D.A., and testified.

The trial lasted five days. The jury convicted Charles Pinkerton Conklin to life in prison for the murder of Officer Wyatt Johnson. End of file.

As I read the detective reports and the witness interviews, my mind's eye saw it all as if it were on a big, color screen. While I was trying to figure an angle that would let me use the file without getting Hector into trouble, I was vaguely aware of a lot of movement on the other side of the curtain. I never heard Dr. Sadgopal leave.

When the curtain was drawn open again, Guido was alone, dressed in the same soiled shirt and jeans he had been wearing when I brought him in the day before. He bowed to me and said, "Ta da."

"You're a mess," I said. "Stay put for twenty minutes. I'll go find you a clean shirt. Maybe the gift shop has something."

"Don't bother. Get me out of here."

The heat, the bright noon sun, drug residue all conspired against Guido. He had been enervated when I told him about the office break-in. He smelled quick money from tabloid TV and talked about expanding my tape to fit their format. The money interested me, but not as much as reaching a big audience did. We were going to spend the afternoon working on something. But by the time I turned up his street, he was worn out, ready for a nap.

I went inside with Guido on the pretext of needing to use the bathroom. I wanted to make sure that no one had been there tampering with his tapes or equipment.

My techno friend, Guido, living alone in the woods without close neighbors, had installed a very sophisticated video-based security system. None of the cameras had been tripped or tampered with. I know, because I checked every one of them. Feeling something of an alarmist, a relieved alarmist, I double-checked that everything was reset before I left him.

I was at the studio during the editorial meeting, but I was upstairs, holed up again with a couple of production staffers, making some changes in the tape.

CHAPTER
20

Network facilities are notorious for leaks, so I prefer working either on the street, or in private. But without Guido, and without time, I had to accept the network's largesse.

On that day, the big studio name worked for me. Beth Johnson, Wyatt's widow, overcame her reluctance to talk to me when I threw in an offer of coffee in the network commissary. She left work and came right over.

Beth rode up to the sound stage in an elevator with her favorite talk-show host. I'm not sure whether he was her favorite when he stepped into the elevator or acquired the status during the ride. He certainly had her all atwitter by the time she stepped out on the fifth floor.

Beth's robust happiness surprised me. I don't know what I had been expecting, a grieving young widow I suppose, because all that I knew of her came from a single newspaper story about her husband's funeral. An old newspaper story, I had to remind myself. To me, the shooting of Wyatt Johnson was new information, part of a situation that was still developing.

Beth Johnson was no longer the sylphlike woman in black in the news photo. She was now plump, still very pretty, a feminine woman dressed in a flattering bright pink and turquoise silk suit. Her hair and makeup were perfect. I was flattered she had taken some extra effort on my behalf. From what I knew of her, I calculated her age to be around thirty-seven, though she looked much younger. Her skin was beautiful and unlined.

"My name isn't Johnson anymore," she said when I introduced myself. She tried to seem blasé, but she glowed with excitement. She spoke with a pleasant southern drawl. "I got married again a couple years after Wyatt died. I'd just as soon you don't use my husband's name. You can still call me Johnson."

"Johnson would be less confusing for the viewers," I said.

The set we were given to use belonged to a morning talk show, looked like a big farmhouse living room. The space was too big, so I had asked the crew to move a couple of high-back chairs, a lamp, some silk plants over in front of a fake window that looked out into a tempera-paint garden; an illusion a million light years away from the cement and asphalt real world outside.

Beth seemed to enjoy the fuss with microphones and lights, held up her face for the woman who came to powder some shine off her chin. I gave myself over to the same makeup woman, let her paint over the circles under my eyes, add a little sunshine to my cheeks, mousse up my flat hair.

When everything was set, I put my hand over Beth's, felt the nervous tremor. I said, "Just relax and talk to me. In a few minutes you'll forget all these people are here eavesdropping."

"I'm used to it," she smiled. "I have the nosiest neighbors in the world."

I laughed to be polite, thought I sounded artificial. "Tell me about your life now, Mrs. Johnson. What sort of work do you do?"

"Same as always. I work in a bank, in the loan department. I've been there since I married Wyatt and moved to California."

"You have one child from your marriage to Wyatt Johnson. Tell me about him."

"Wyatt Junior, he's in college now. A good boy. We had our rough times, like everyone does bringing up kids, especially a widow woman. But he's a good boy. A serious boy, like his daddy. A good, Christian boy."

"How old was he when his father died?"

"He was a baby. Not even four years old. He never remembered his daddy at all. Sometimes when I think of all Wyatt missed out on, watching his boy come up, well, it breaks my heart all over again."

"Tell me about Wyatt Senior. What sort of man was he?"

"Like I said, he was serious. He was real smart, too. Wanted to be somebody. His folks couldn't afford to send him to college, so he went into the army for a couple of years to get his GI Bill. That's when I married him—when he was stationed at Fort Polk in Louisiana. Soon as he got his discharge, Wyatt came home and joined the police. For a boy without an education, it was the best job he could get. Better than the post office."

"Did he enjoy police work?"

She frowned. "Not very much. They were hard on black officers back then. Said a lot of racial things to him. But with what they paid, and all the benefits, he couldn't hardly quit."

"He worked part-time jobs to supplement his income," I said.

"Yes he did. Wyatt grew up in Willowbrook. He wanted something better for his family. So we bought a new house outside the city, out in Cerritos. Then we had the baby and I could only work part time—with the cost of baby-sitters, clothes, transportation and all, I saved money every day I stayed home when the baby was little. It was nice being at home—we had a real nice house. But that house payment . . ." She waved her hand as if something smelly had passed by. "It nearly killed us. Wyatt wanted to go to college, maybe go to law school at night later on. But he spent all his time working extra security jobs just to keep our heads above water."

I said, "At one point, the police department asked him to quit his part-time jobs. How did you manage financially?"

"I went back to work full-time and Wyatt started working morning watch so he could be home with the baby when I was gone. I sold Avon Products on the side—you know, to the ladies at work and in my church. Still, it wasn't enough.

"Then Wyatt got into some business deal with some other officers—selling vitamins or something he told me. Just like me selling cosmetics from a catalog. I didn't like his hours, but pretty soon, one way and another, money started coming in. At the time he got himself shot, we were doing okay."

The memory of the burden, her loss, maybe all of it together, pulled down her initial buoyance. I leaned forward to bring her eyes up again for the camera. In a soft voice, I said, "Mrs. Johnson, let's talk about the shooting. I have seen where it occurred—one of the roughest neighborhoods in the city. Do you have any idea why your husband was there?"

Slowly, sadly, she shook her head. "He was working morning watch, like I said, so he was used to being out all night. A lot of police are like that, out real late. Besides, it was difficult for him to go out during the day, because of the baby and all.

"It was his day off," she said. "I thought maybe he was selling his vitamins to other officers, you know, at midwatch or after their shifts. That's all I could think. He didn't go out to bars or anything like that." She grew defensive. "Wyatt was a family man."

"Did he know Charles Conklin?"

"My husband was a Christian. The only way he would know a gentleman like that man was in his official capacity as an officer with the Los Angeles Police Department."

"Did you speak with the investigating officers?"

"Oh, yes. All of them. They all asked the same question you did, what was Wyatt doing down there. I told them the same as I told you."

"Has the district attorney spoken to you about the shooting recently?"

"No. The only one has called me is the detective."

"Mike Flint?"

"No, the other one. Detective Kelsey. He asked that same question. Did Wyatt ever say where he was going that night, who was he going to see? What did I know about it? I told him no, don't know, and nothing. And that is the truth."

"A few minutes ago, you said this vitamin business was profitable. Do you remember the name of the company or the other officers who were involved?"

Long, thoughtful pause. "No, I don't. After Wyatt had passed, it took me some time before I could go through his things. He used to carry his samples in an old gun case, 'cause he could lock it up. I was looking for the samples and thinking there should be order forms and records—like I had to keep when I sold products—but there was nothing. I was expecting a representative from the company to come asking for an accounting. I called his partner about it, but he didn't know what I was talking about. In those days, I wasn't thinking real clearly. The only reason I looked into it was because I was hoping there was maybe some money owing Wyatt. We sure could have used it."

"You never heard from the vitamin company?" I asked.

"I had other things to worry about."

I said, "Times were difficult for you and your son after the shooting?"

She nodded. "The police were real good to us. The Police Memorial Fund helped out with the burial expenses, helped me pay my bills until I could sell the house. They set up a scholarship so little Wyatt could go to college like his daddy wanted for him. Every now and then, one or the other of them would come by, make sure we was okay.

"When my boy was around fifteen or sixteen and I was having some trouble with him—didn't get along with his stepfather—I could not have gotten through but 'cept they take him under their wing, so to say. Talk sense to him, man to man. I have to say, the police take care of their own."

"So I understand," I said. The cant had a familiar ring. "Did your husband spend his off hours with other police?"

"Had to."

"Why? Was there some pressure to socialize only with police?"

"Nothing like that. It was because of the hours he worked. That's all."

I made a note to get the names of his old pals. They might shed some illumination on dark corners here, talk about vitamin consumption if I was lucky.

Watching me askance, Beth said, "My mama would say a well-brought-up young lady should know better than to mention a certain subject, but I hope these microphones aren't so touchy they pick up the sound of my stomach grumbling."

I got the message and unclipped her microphone. "Thank you for your time. The producer wants the privilege of your company in the commissary."

Beth went downstairs with an assistant producer, who promised me he would give her an insider's tour. I went home.

The condo was deserted when I walked in around one o'clock that afternoon. Mike had left a message on the machine telling me that he was at the house in South Pasadena, with Bowser, and planned to pick up Casey from school at four. According to the clock on the bedroom wall, that gave me three hours of quiet to sleep. I thought about taking a bath first, but didn't want to waste the time.

I traded my grungy clothes for one of Mike's oversize tee shirts and folded down the bed. Before I climbed in, I dialed Mike's pager and punched in 96, our code that everything was fine—on a push-button phone, *yo* is spelled 96. Unless he had something important to tell me, he wouldn't call back.

I slept like a rock and woke up about halfway through *Oprah*, L.A. time. The first thing that occurred to me once I had figured out where I was, was that I had forgotten to eat all day. Half-awake, I shuffled out to the kitchen in Mike's shirt. My hair felt stiff and gummy from the studio's moussing. It stuck out in strange ways. There was night-gravel in the corners of my eyes.

I was marginally coherent enough to assemble a peanut butter and banana sandwich, pour a glass of milk, and find an unbruised apple in the crisper. I gathered this feast together, with the apple balanced on top of the glass, and headed back toward the bedroom with the intention of watching the rest of *Oprah* while I ate. But the doorbell detoured me.

The apple rolled off the top of the glass, making me stumble a step or two trying to retrieve it. I kicked it out from under an end table and picked it up. Between the glass, the sandwich, the apple, I didn't have a hand for the door, so I clamped the sandwich between my teeth and turned the knob.

The woman on the doorstep was too beautiful to be an ordinary walking-around-in-public mortal. As tiny as she was, she still filled her exquisite linen suit with voluptuous curves. Everything about her bespoke a natural perfection, the lovely posture, her short, dark sculpted hair, the subtle use of makeup and jewelry, her expensive little pumps. When she said hello, her gaze was fixed on the sandwich hanging from my lips.

Beyond basic maintenance and good haircuts, I never really give much thought to my appearance. When I was a news anchor my face, figure, and hair were network property. I was regularly painted, back-combed, sprayed, tinted, recreated—I even let them talk me into having the hump on the bridge of my nose surgically edited so that I fit better within an industry standard for color, size, sex, voice, bones. When I went independent, I gave up as much artifice as I could. For most of my own projects, I wear a blue oxford cloth shirt and a nearly naked face. I prefer it.

A disdainful expression marred the perfection of the creature on my doorstep. Just once, I wished I had opted for the hair wash instead of the nap.

"Is Mike here?" Her voice was honey.

With a mouthful of peanut butter and banana, the best I could do was shake my head.

"When do you expect him?"

I set all of the food on the closest end table and tried to work the bite of sandwich off the roof of my mouth so I could swallow. I washed the biggest mass down with milk. Sounding like a boxer who forgot to take out his mouth guard, I said, "Want to leave him a message?"

She smiled the way clean people smile at panhandlers when she asked, "Who are you?"

"The maid. Who are you?"

"Mrs. Flint."

I thought she was too young to be Mike's mother. And far too good-looking; his mother had been dead for three years. That left two possibilities. I said, "Mrs. Flint number one, or Mrs. Flint number two?"

She said, "I'm number two," and laughed when she heard the way that sounded.

"You're Charlene," I said. Here was the source of all the gray carpeting. "I don't expect Mike for another hour. Would you like to come in and wait?"

"If you don't mind. I should have called, but I found myself on a job not far from here and thought, hell, no time like the present. If it weren't so damn hot, I would go sit by the pool and wait."

I stepped back to let her in. "No time like the present for what?"

"I heard Mike is planning to move. I thought I should make arrangements about picking up my things." She seemed a bit wistful as she looked around the living room, and not very happy as she watched the wet ring grow around the milk glass on the table. "Do you know where he's moving?"

"He'll tell you about it." I closed the door behind her. "Look, I have some serious housekeeping to do before Mike gets home. Why don't you make yourself comfortable. I'm sure you know where the kitchen is. Help yourself to a drink or something. I'll be a few minutes."

"Fine." She ran her hand slowly, possessively, over the back of the gray-tweed sofa. "Needs recovering."

I said, "Excuse me," picked up my sandwich, and left her. If she absconded with the furniture, I wouldn't mind.

A shower, hair wash, quick blow-dry, some blush and mascara, fresh white denim shorts from The Gap, and a sleeveless shirt knotted at my waist, the black leather thongs I bought in Italy several years ago, and I was ready for a second face-off with Charlene.

She was sitting straight-backed on an ottoman in the middle of the room, holding a glass of white wine. Her slim ankles were crossed, her toes pointed. I am not jealous by nature, and I have no interest in cat fights. But, as I said, she was small. All it would have taken was one good shove.

As I walked into the room, she gave me a wide-eyed appraisal. "I knew you weren't the maid, but . . . ?"

I offered my freshly lotioned hand. "I'm Maggie Mac-Gowen."

"I should have called," she said again. She was embarrassed. Or maybe she wasn't so cocky once our hairdos reached parity; I will match haircuts with the best of them.

I heard the back door. Bowser bounded into the living room first, panting, his heavy fur littered with leaves, his nose brown from digging in fresh earth. He gave me a token hello nudge on his way past and headed straight for Charlene, she of the pastel linen suit. She did her best to get out of his way, but Bowser is good at his work. He sampled her crotch and lapped his tongue across her mouth in one fluid sweep.

I said, "Sit, young man." Instantly, as always, he obeyed and dropped back onto his broad haunches. He stayed, but he kept his eyes on Charlene.

Casey, Michael, and Mike had all stopped for cold drinks on their way through the kitchen. They came into the living room like an electric surge, the three of them laughing and talking at once. Casey still wore dance clothes. The men were in filthy work garb, covered with dust and paint chips that left a trail on the gray carpet.

Mike saw Charlene first. He registered only mild surprise. Exactly the right reaction, from my point of view.

"Char," he said, acknowledging her with a lift of his chin. I got his sweaty arm draped around my shoulders. "So, you two have met?"

"Yes." Her smooth exterior couldn't cover the apparent rush of strong emotion that passed through her when Mike walked in. It wasn't peanut butter that caught in her throat.

Michael, uncharacteristically awkward, pointedly stayed back, beside me. He said only, "Hello."

"You've grown so tall, Michael," Charlene said, smiling at him in the formal way adults smile at very young children. "You're as tall as Daddy now. Maybe taller."

Michael's only response was to turn a furious red. I reached through that uncomfortable silence for Casey's hand. "Charlene, this is my daughter, Casey."

The exchanged hellos and a handshake as light as the collision of two falling leaves.

Casey backed up toward Michael. She gave his shoulder a thump to get his attention. "You want the first shower?"

"Go ahead," Michael said, watching Charlene. "I'll use Maggie and Dad's bathroom."

On their way out, I overheard a whispered, "stepmother." Casey turned her head to make an amended appraisal of Charlene before she went through the hall door with Michael.

"What an attractive pair," Charlene said. "Casey is lovely."

Mike said, "What brings you out to the Valley?"

"A decorating job. I heard your name on the news. Are you all right?"

"Sure. It's nothing."

"Same old departmental bull, right?" Her laugh was unconvincing. "Mike knows so many ways to find trouble."

"I like trouble about as much as the next guy," he said. There was nothing friendly in his tone. "But even trouble has some rules. How's what's-his-name?"

"I wouldn't know," she said, dropping her eyes.

I chimed in, "Charlene wants to pick up her things before we move."

"Like what things?" he said, cold steel.

"I'm sorry." She set her glass down. "I'm really sorry, Mike.

I should have called." She looked around with sad longing in her gaze. "This is such a lovely room."

"A real showplace," Mike said. "Talk to Maggie if you want any of this custom-made junk. It doesn't fit the new house very well. We'll probably dump it at a garage sale."

He kissed my cheek. "I need to get in line for a shower. Nice to see you, Char." He left the room.

CHAPTER
21

"What rule did Charlene break?" I stretched a Band-Aid around a cut on Mike's thumb.

"You don't fuck your husband's partner."

"That's a good rule," I said. "How'd you cut your thumb?"

"Drapery hook. We got rid of all the drapes and pulled out the old carpet. House looks better already. Tomorrow, a couple of the guys are taking a few days off to help me strip the walls. We'll start painting Saturday. What color?"

"Guess we should have asked Charlene's expert advice while she was here."

He curled his lip. "I want a home this time, not some fucking model house. I want furniture I can sit on, put my feet on, get potato chip crumbs all over without someone getting all pissed. And I want some color. I learned how to spell monochromatic, but I never learned how to like it."

"In that case, I see very soft, neutral peach for the walls and off-white for all the moldings and wood we decide not to strip down to its natural color."

He smiled. "You decided that in a hurry."

"That's how I see it," I said.

"Come to the paint store with me and show me what you have in mind."

"I don't have to go with you." I put the Band-Aid box back in the medicine chest. "Just drop your pants and show the paint man your naked behind. Most beautiful color in the world."

"The things that come out of your mouth," he said with a laugh. I caught him stealing a peek at his rear in the mirror.

"Nice to hear you laugh again," I said.

Then from the nether regions of the house, I heard, "Mo-om."

I went to the door and called back, "I'm in the bathroom, Casey."

"Telephone."

I had turned off the ringer on the bedroom phone when I took my nap. I picked up the receiver.

"Maggie? It's Lana. Just want to keep you on top of things. To give you time for your new edits, we're running your package tomorrow beginning at four. We'll run trailers on the story during daytime programming, so it should get a lot of attention. I screened the first version for the producers of *L.A. Hot*, our midnight issues show. They're really interested in an expanded format. Will you talk to them?"

"For tomorrow night?" I asked.

"Could be," Lana said. "I think the topic says 'late night.' These guys also produce a Sunday morning interview show. They're thinking about bringing you on because of the political campaign angle. Talk to them."

"I'll talk to them." I wrote down the number she gave me, but I wasn't ready to have my face attached to the story. Because of my connection to Mike, I was vulnerable. My research was good, the issues raised were legitimate ones. Still, I had to be careful.

While Mike dressed, I went to the kitchen to start dinner, stir-fried leftover pork and steamed rice. I was slicing zucchini when Michael came in, dressed in shorts and a polo shirt.

"Need some help?" he asked, picking up a peeled carrot on his way past me.

"I need some company. Sit down and talk to me."

He pulled out a chair and straddled it backwards.

"So?" I said. "Tell me about school. Have you met anyone?"

He flushed slightly. "I have a date tomorrow night with someone I met in Asian Lit."

"Ah, fate plays a hand. She's nice?"

"She's . . ." He paused. "She's interesting."

"And beautiful?"

He put his hands up on the back of the chair and rested his chin on them while he thought that over. Finally, he turned to me. "I prefer interesting. What did you think of Charlene?"

"She's beautiful," I said. "I think she has strong feelings for your father. And, I think Bowser was a lot happier to see her than you were."

"I was that obvious?" He turned away to cover his chagrin. "She was actually sort of nice to me today."

I peeled another carrot and began chopping it.

He said, "Char was always jealous of me and Dad, because we were so close. She made him choose between us."

I said, "Exit Char."

He raised his big gray eyes to me—Mike's eyes. "You'll like my mom, though."

My face must have given me away.

"Trust me." Michael laughed knowingly. "You'll like her."

"Uh huh," I said, and segued to celery. "Meeting one ex-wife filled my quota."

"You don't have anything to be afraid of. For my dad, three times is the charm. No one has ever made him as happy as you do."

I set my knife aside, feeling touched by the tenderness in his tone as much as by his words. "Thank you, Michael. I love you, too."

He laughed. "Is that what I said?"

"Close enough."

I kept my appointment with Linda Westman, the learning specialist, because it was easier to keep than to cancel on short notice. I had booked independent studio time and studio technicians, and would have to pay union scale whether we showed up or not.

My project had evolved a long way from its original focus, but what Linda had to say could still be useful. If not on this film, then maybe on something else.

Linda Westman was an easy interview. Whatever she might have been feeling, she looked calm and professional on camera. Dark brown hair with a comfortable amount of gray, expressive brown eyes, a well-tailored, teal blue suit made her photogenic.

"I have worked with kids like Tyrone Harkness for almost twenty years," she said, chin up, shoulders straight with a slenderizing half-turn to the camera. "It doesn't matter how bright they are, kids from disorganized families are destined from the first day of school to drop out, to lose job after job, because no one teaches them the organizational skills necessary to get to school or to work on time. You must learn how to get up at a certain hour, budget the time it takes to wash, dress, eat, gather school materials, and proceed directly to school."

Her intensity edged her forward in her seat. " 'On-time-ness' is not a goal that can be reached with a good lecture on promptness and a reliable alarm clock. It must be taught consistently at an early age. Parents who go to work every day, who serve meals on schedule, and enforce bedtime, these parents teach time-management skills by example.

"Until he was sent to Juvenile Hall, no one ever told Tyrone when to eat or sleep or what time to get up so he could get to school on time. He ate when he was hungry, slept when he dropped. And school? He got there when he got there. Listen to his language. When he speaks, he uses only the present tense, as if he is without past and without future."

I said, "Tyrone told me how he plans to go away to a better place. That doesn't sound like present-mindedness."

"You're right, it doesn't," Westman said. "But I'll lay odds that he was repeating a story someone else told him. 'Someday, son . . .' But Tyrone doesn't have any idea where someday is. Was he getting organized for his move? Did he have a plan of action worked out?"

"He was in Juvenile Hall on a murder charge."

She raised her hands as if to say, I told you so. "Tyrone kept getting caught by the police because he never planned his crimes. He might know that the best time to rob is bank is when it opens at ten, but he would have no idea how to get there at ten. Arriving sometime between eight and noon for a ten o'clock appointment is not precise enough for success, even for a bank robber. His crimes tended to be crimes of opportunity, because he didn't know how to carry off a timely plan."

Linda Westman gave me good background to use. I was glad I hadn't rescheduled. We talked for a good hour, and could have taped a second, if I'd had the time. When the lights were turned off, she stood up and stretched.

"That was fun," she said.

"You're a natural. You should be in sales."

She laughed. "All teachers are salesmen."

On our way out, I offered her a soda from the machine instead of taking her out for coffee somewhere. I needed to be home. She invited me to drop by her classes at Juvenile Hall some morning, and dictated her schedule to me. Without setting a date, we said good-bye.

As soon as I walked into the house, Mike and Michael went out to buy paint. Casey was in the hall, working out on her barre. I sat down on the floor out of her kicking range to watch.

"So?" I asked her. "What do you think?"

"About?"

"School, the house, Los Angeles, Monsieurs Flint, life?"

"I like the house," she said. "It's pretty old, but Mike showed me how he's going to make a studio for me. That's cool, but why does Michael get a whole house of his own?"

"You're too young to fly so far from the nest."

"Oh, right. His house is only in the backyard."

"Michael is an adult, Casey. If his school tuition wasn't so expensive he would be living away from home. Don't you think he needs his own place?"

"That's one of those trick questions. Yeah, I think he needs his own place. But so do I."

"You'll have two big rooms to yourself. Much more space than the cottage."

"And it's right next to you."

"Yep." I leaned back against the wall. "Show me some of your stuff."

"Watch this." She unfurled one of her amazing legs up from the side until it was straight up, nearly touching the ceiling. "I can finally do it. Mischa showed me how to lengthen the hamstring."

"Looks like it hurts," I said. "The ceilings in the new house are taller."

She snapped her leg down. "Do I have to go to Dad's this weekend?"

"That's the agreement. You haven't been to Denver for over a month."

"One more week?"

I held my hands up to her. "That's between you and your dad. But isn't it easier to go now than later in the semester? When do you start weekend workshops?"

She crumpled to the floor beside me. "I hate going to Dad's. Linda hates me. The kid's a brat."

"I thought you liked being a big sister."

She gave me a withering glare.

I leaned my head against the wall. "All weekend we're going to be house painting. Is Denver worse than house painting?"

"You know what I really want to do? I want to spend the weekend with Lyle in our *own* house." From out of nowhere, she started to cry. "I want to see my friends."

I put my arm around her and pulled her head down to my shoulder. "You've had a lot of changes to get used to all at once."

"I hate this crappy condo," she sniffed.

"Me, too," I said.

She looked up at me, surprised. "You do?"

"Sure. What's to love about it except the people in it?"

Casey wiped her face with the tail of her tee shirt. "Michael told me what a bitch his stepmother is."

"Is she worse than Linda?" I asked, using her shirt to get a wet spot she missed.

"Actually." A pause to think it over. "Linda's okay. Ever since she had the baby, she hasn't been as jealous of me and Dad. Sometimes she's almost nice to me."

"So, what about Denver this weekend?"

She took in a deep breath and exhaled it. "I guess."

"Pack tonight. I'll have your bag in the car when I pick you up at school tomorrow. We'll go straight to the Burbank Airport. Plane leaves at four-thirty."

She said she was hungry, so we got into the car and drove down to Ventura Boulevard for ice cream cones at Ben and Jerry's. We window-shopped while we ate them. The Santa Ana winds had calmed down, letting in a little ocean breeze to take the edge off the heat wave. The sidewalk still radiated some warmth a couple of hours after sunset, but we didn't have to hurry through our chocolate-cookie-crunch cones before they melted.

Linking my arm through hers, I said, "I miss our ocean view."

"I miss walking down to the marina to hear the steel bands," she countered.

"I hate the smog."

"I won't miss San Francisco fog, though," she offered.

"I like Mike."

"Me, too." She smiled into my face, a smudge of ice cream at the corner of her mouth. "We're going to be okay, Mom."

Out of the mouths of babes.

CHAPTER

22

All day Friday, I drove around with Casey's suitcase in the back of my car. I found myself looking at it as if it were some kind of time bomb, set to go off at four-thirty.

Casey had been flying alone to Denver for regular, court-ordered visits for almost three years. I dreaded every trip. One time, the plane had had engine trouble and had to turn back after take-off. Twice, Scottie had misplaced her and she hadn't arrived home on schedule. At that point I had quit worrying about not having a pension; I knew I wasn't going to last long enough to collect one.

According to the custody agreement, Casey had to spend sixty days a year with her father until she reached her sixteenth year. At the end of October, Casey would be fifteen.

First thing in the morning, I had a long talk with the producers of *L.A. Hot.* They gave me a lot to think about, but I wasn't ready to commit to them.

Around noon, when I got to my office, I found a series of messages on my machine from Ralph Faust at Satellite Network News. The tone increased in urgency as the morning progressed.

I called Guido first, found him at work in his trailer at UCLA. He said was feeling a hundred percent again, but would fake something if I needed him. I told him about the *L.A. Hot* conversation.

"Don't give away the store," he said. "Run your minute on the news, then let's see what surfaces."

I put his advice away with a lot of other unsolicited information I had been offered.

I called Ralph.

"Jungle drums are beating," he said in his smarmy tone. "Word is, you have some dynamite shit relating to Conklin."

"Says who?" I asked him.

"What do you have?"

"The thing is, Ralph, you gave me a pretty good lesson on media ethics the other night." I was speaking slowly, intentional counterpoint to his hyper state. "I may be, as you said, a baby in this industry, but I'm a quick learner. Besides, I may already have a buyer."

"Be careful, Maggie. Conklin is a buzzer today, but by Monday he could be a dead story. I'm ready to talk time and money right now. Big time, big money."

"I'll put you in the line-up, Ralph. I have your number. We'll talk later." I hung up.

The phone began to ring immediately. Thinking it was probably Ralph, I let it go onto the machine, heard the hang-up.

I slipped the tape of James Shabazz into the player, then I dialed Guido.

"Sorry to hear about your relapse," I said when he picked up. "Guess you went back to work too soon."

"Oh yeah? How serious is it?"

"I need you," I said. "Will you collect all the project tapes and stills you have at your house and bring everything to my office? We have a lot to do and no time to do it."

"You must be right. I came back to work much too soon. There are a few things I really need to deal with, though, so give me a couple of hours. I'll be there as soon as. Keep the faith."

I paged Mike. While I waited for his return call, I listened to Shabazz and paced.

"What's up?" Mike asked when I picked up. The connection, from his car phone, was fuzzy.

"This thing I've been working on?" I said. "Well, a piece of it's going to be on the news today. Starting at four."

"Congratulations. What is it, some kind of promotion for the documentary?"

"Don't congratulate me. I should have told you right away, but I want to be able to say that you had no input and no prior knowledge."

"What the hell?" He was worried then.

"I've made a short rebuttal to the assertions of the district attorney and the reverend private eye. I hope it offers enough to keep Conklin from becoming a media heart throb."

Mike's voice sounded overly controlled. "Am I mentioned?"

"Mentioned? No. But Jerry Kelsey is."

"How'd he get so lucky?"

"I had a serious lapse in my professional detachment."

"Oh?"

"It has to do with a serious personal attachment."

"I love you, Maggie," he said. "Have you gone and gotten me fired?"

"I hope not. There is a shot of your back for maybe two seconds. Half the women in the city will probably recognize it, even with clothes on it, but not to worry. I need you to warn Hector. And don't forget to watch at four. I'll be at the airport seeing Casey off, then I'll be in my office maybe by five—depends on traffic."

"Wouldn't miss this one," he said. "Hector's here, working on the house with everybody. We'll go find a TV at four. Be all of us together when we get our pensions yanked."

I laughed. "You're so dramatic." One thing I have learned, though, is that short-timer policemen don't joke about losing their pensions.

When he said good-bye, Mike sounded weary.

For maybe fifteen minutes, while I waited for Guido, I lay on the floor with my eyes closed and thought about how we were going to proceed. The general framework was clear to me. In my mind, I began fleshing out the framework, recreating a night fifteen years ago, putting meat on the major players. I had nearly everything that I needed on tape or in a still photograph. Everything except LaShonda DeBevis and a few background details.

I followed LaShonda's telephone number trail again, starting at the Lennox Library, then Hacienda Heights, finally Valencia. No one had seen or heard from LaShonda, but all of them took a message to have her call me if they did hear anything. I didn't know what else I could do.

My back-up shooter, Thieu, called and reminded me that we had scheduled a shoot in Reseda—Charles Conklin's younger brother, Bartholomew. I lied and said I hadn't forgotten, that I was on my way. I left a note for Guido and headed out the freeway to meet Bartholomew Conklin.

"Pinkie? Pinkie was always scammin'." Bartholomew was on his lunch break from his mail delivery route in Reseda. He was a long, thin, athletically built man. He had shaved his whole head, but I could see from the relative smoothness of the dome that he was nearly bald, anyway.

Visually, it was a good scene: against a backdrop of gray smog, the many-colored streaks of passing traffic, the stationary red, white, and blue postal service Jeep parked at the curb, Bartholomew's summer uniform of post-office-blue shorts and short-sleeved shirt, white knee socks and black sneakers. He leaned against the Jeep, long legs extended, crossed at the ankle. Casual, good-humored.

I was worried about the traffic noise, so I attached a body mike to him. The battery pack and cord were concealed inside his shirt, the mike itself was a tiny black clip on his collar. Thieu filmed him from over my shoulder so that Bartholomew would have the entire screen.

"What do you mean by scamming?" I asked.

"You know, always trying to get something for nothing," Bartholomew said, squinting into the sun. "Pinkie is the laziest sombitch on earth. If he spent half as much time working as he spent figuring out how to make other people work for him, he could be a rich man instead of a con."

"He had young women working the streets for him," I said. "Is that what you mean?"

"Could be." He studied his feet for a moment. Even when he started to talk again, his focus was off to the side, an oblique response. He said, "One time I remember, Pinkie was short on cash, didn't have a job, wasn't about to go out and look for one, either. Took to hangin' up by the 7-Eleven. Just stand there all night, panhandling some so he could buy a beer now and then. But watching—that's all, just watching and waiting. Like a fox waits.

"Then one night he's standing there, sees what he's been waiting for all that time. He sees two dudes go in, hold up the place. He watches it go down, slides himself over to the dudes' car, and waits for them to come out. They come out in a hurry with a grocery bag full of money. He pulls his gun, high-jacks them, takes the money they stole, drives away in their car. They were still standing there like fools, trying to figure what the hell happened, when the police drove up and arrested them."

"What happened to your brother?" I asked.

"Nothing. Not one thing. Who's going to take the word of two thieves that they were held up?" An embarrassed laugh. "Pinkie is bad, but he's good at it. If you get my meaning."

"Are you close to your brother?" I asked.

Bartholomew shook his head. "Nowadays, you would say we were a dysfunctional family. Back then, well, no one ever said anything. Anyway, I never spent much time with Pinkie. I was enough younger I couldn't hang with him.

"Most of the time, Pinkie was in jail for one thing and another. And when he wasn't in jail, he was out on the streets looking for trouble. No, we're not close."

"Do you talk to him?"

He shrugged. "Nothing to talk about."

He was reflective, a nice transition to the next question. I said to him, "By all measure, you're a successful man. You finished high school, you've worked at the same job for over ten years. You have a home, wife, children."

"Pension, health plan, two-car garage." He said this with an attractive, humorous lilt. "You make it sound boring."

"Not as boring as prison. You have the same background as your brother. What made things so different for you?"

Again, he was thoughtful. When he had an answer, he looked straight at me. "My father was the meanest bastard on this earth. A bodacious drunk. Beat us, hurt us, called us every name in the book, and then some. Beat all us kids, beat our mother, too. Why she stayed with him, I don't know, but she did. The thing is, Pinkie, being older, well he took the worst of it. By the time I came along, the old man was plain old worn-out. Running on empty. I had a couple of older sisters to protect me some, too. Being the baby, I guess, saved me.

"When I was about five or six, my mother died and, if it was possible for things to get worse, it got worse. Sometimes, you know, good things come out of bad, because it got so bad that people had to take some notice. The school called the police about the condition we were in when we showed up. The County came and told my father he had to give us up. Pinkie was already living on his own. My sisters went to live with my aunt in Oakland. And I was taken in by a saint, older man who lived in the neighborhood; fed my puny body, fed my undernourished soul."

There were tears in his eyes and Thieu came in close to get them. "You said I'm a success. Well, if that is true, then all the credit belongs to Brother James Shabazz."

I repeated the name, "James Shabazz," because I knew it was coming.

In these stories I had collected, Charles Conklin and James Shabazz were point-counterpoint. William Blake came to mind again, speaking of the tiger: "Did he who made the lamb make thee?" Bartholomew gave me a lot to think about.

Bartholomew had only a forty-minute break, so the entire meeting was short. I was back at my office within two hours of the time I left.

When Guido finally arrived, he had his arms full of materials and his own ideas. During the course of the afternoon, we had some noisy clashes, but productive ones. My strength is the message, his the craft. Together we make one hell of a filmmaker. And, together, that afternoon, we did what we do best.

When I left to pick up Casey, the vision was clear. I left Guido hard at the mechanics of execution.

I had Casey excused early from her last class—dance studio—so that I could take her by the house to say good-bye to Mike and still be on the freeway by three-fifteen. In the car, she pulled on Levis over her leotard, shook out her ballet bun, and brushed her hair into a long, smooth fall. With fresh makeup and a light sweater draped over her shoulders, she was ready to travel. One-inch shy of being six feet tall, she looked much older than her fourteen years.

My first thought when we saw the South Pasadena house was, I hoped the neighbors were of a forgiving nature. There was a massive dumpster parked at the curb. All the old carpets and drapes lay in dirty heaps on the driveway. Everywhere, there were tools and building litter. And beer cans.

The work crew was a noisy, happy collection of off-duty police friends of Mike, and his dad, Oscar. Oscar was knee-deep in a ditch in the front yard with two other men, working on water pipes and a six-pack. He stopped swearing long enough for Casey and me to get out of earshot.

I hadn't met most of Mike's friends, though they all seemed to know who I was when I walked into the house. They were friendly toward me, and curious. But it was my daughter who caught their collective eye. I restrained myself from throwing her sweater over her head and rushing her back out to the car.

Through the chaos, the beauty of the house was beginning to emerge. The hardwood floors were being sanded down to a natural honey color, and the cabbage roses were on their way out. The smell of paint-stripper was overpowering, the scum it created was a mess. But the result was going to be exceptional.

Bowser saw us and wandered in from the backyard to say hello. He took his place beside Casey and followed us through the house.

"What do you think, Casey?" I asked.

"No ocean view," she said, measuring the height of the ten-foot ceilings with her eye. "But it's okay." High praise from a fourteen-year-old.

We found Mike on a scaffolding set up in the living room, wrestling with a rented wallpaper steamer. Sweat poured down his face, plastered his shirt to his chest. There was a liter bottle of Evian at his feet, but the dropcloth on the floor under him was littered with empty beer cans. When he saw us, he turned off the steamer and climbed down.

To Casey he said, "All set?"

"I guess," she said, dusting off her hands. "What a mess."

"By the time you get back Sunday, it'll be a showplace." He grabbed a length of paper towels and wiped his face and arms. "Hot work."

I said, "We just came to say good-bye."

"Bye," Mike said. Without touching her, he leaned forward to give her a chaste kiss. "Take care of yourself. You have my pager number. Need any heads ripped off, you call me."

"So weird," she tsk'ed. "You two finally get a weekend alone, and this is how you spend it. Very romantic."

He laughed. "Ms. Wiseass, Junior. Don't miss your plane."

"Is Hector still here?" I asked as Mike walked us outside. "Couple of things I want to clear with him."

"He's on a beer run. What's the problem?"

"No problem. I used some of the photos, and this and that,

from the reports he gave me. Nothing from the reports themselves shows up. On camera."

"If he has some objection, it's too late to do anything about it. Right?"

"Yes."

"So we'll just wait until four before we panic."

"Good idea," I said. I kicked through a stack of cans. "Do me a favor and give a Breathalyzer to anyone who picks up a power tool."

The tough guy said, "We know what we're doing."

"Bye," I said. I kissed his damp, whiskered chin.

Casey had been smiling at us the way fond parents regard slow-learning children. "You two are so cute."

Mike sneered, but he was flattered, I could tell. We left him standing on the curb waving to us.

On our way to the freeway, we drove through the first burger place we came to so Casey could refuel the carb levels and get a cold drink. All of her anxiety from the night before about going to Denver seemed to have vanished. I thought she seemed almost eager to get on the plane.

"Have fun," I said when I kissed her at the boarding gate. "I'll be waiting right here Sunday night."

"Bye, Ma. It'll be nice to get out of the heat for a couple of days. I'll miss you."

I said, "You better."

She turned away and walked her ballerina walk down the ramp, with every male eye fixed on the rock-hard curves in her jeans. I felt like slapping every one of them.

When I got back to my office, Guido had tapes running on four screens at once with the sound off. I saw Hanna Rhodes under the flowered sheet, Tyrone Harkness in Juvenile Hall, James Shabazz walking around the war zone that had been a service station, Linda Westman in the studio upstairs. Occupied with the images on-screen, Guido handed me a slip of paper.

He said only, "She called."

When I read what he handed me, I do believe I felt the skies open up and the sun shine through. *She* was LaShonda DeBevis and she had left a phone number.

I went to the phone and dialed. "When did she call?"

"Right after you left." He was grinning evilly. "I told her you'd be back by five."

I got no answer, and no machine. I said, "Damn."

Guido began to chuckle.

"What is it?" I demanded.

"She just went into the can. I had her come straight over."

LaShonda DeBevis, in the flesh, walked in from the bathroom.

"Miss MacGowen?" she said. "I understand you want to speak with me."

The LaShonda in my mind was a scared little ten-year-old girl. Before me I saw a very grown-up, sophisticated-looking young woman. She was about my height, very slender, with café-au-lait skin and lightened, straightened hair.

"You were difficult to track down," I said, offering my hand, holding on to hers when I caught it. "You seemed to have disappeared into the library system."

"I guess maybe I did." She had a slight southern accent, but had lost the ghetto-speak that appeared in her police interviews. "From out of nowhere, I got a transfer Friday. Before I went to my new assignment, I was notified I had been transferred again. With all the budget cuts going on, I didn't question this circumstance very closely because I was just happy that I still had a job. But when the third transfer came, I knew something was wrong. No one had any answers for me. It just seemed that some computer wanted me moved around. The area supervisor gave up trying to figure it all out and sent me to work at the county media center in Downey until he could get to the source of the confusion. So, that's where I've been, staying with an aunt in Downey, going to work every day."

I led her over to the sofa. "I'm glad we finally connected. We have a lot to talk about."

The subject matter was painful for LaShonda. I could see remembered grief and terror in her expressions as she told me what she saw the night Wyatt Johnson was murdered. She seemed eager to help us, as if, I thought, watching that nightmare night played out to its end might make it all finally go away.

Her memory of the night of the shooting was clear. Of course, she had been over those events many times. She gave us not only her perspective on the shooting, but also had a few things to say about other people we had interviewed, Etta and Shabazz among them.

LaShonda was very bright, and eager to be useful any way she could. We were short on time, and here was another set of hands and eyes. Guido put her to work.

At six, it occurred to me that I hadn't heard from Mike. There were several possibilities: he hadn't found a television, the film had been dumped from the rundown again, he saw it but it was no big deal, or, he saw it and he was so angry he wouldn't speak to me.

As a check, I turned on the news. The lead story was about the restive crowd of demonstrators outside City Hall demanding the immediate release of Charles Conklin. A smaller, angrier group had gathered at the corner of Normandie and Florence where the riots had begun a couple of years ago. There had been some bottle-throwing, someone had set a fire in the intersection before a phalanx of police in riot gear swept everyone away.

We were the follow-up story. The anchor was a handsome, well-known local. He gave the camera Look Number Four from the anchorman's handbook, Serious Concern, as he introduced my film.

He read from the teleprompter, "At a press conference Monday, District Attorney Baron Marovich leveled charges against the police, alleging that undue pressure had been placed upon witnesses to a cold-blooded shooting of a police officer fifteen years ago, coercing those witnesses to wrongfully identify Charles Pinkerton Conklin as the killer.

"According to the district attorney, Charles Conklin should not have been sent to prison fourteen years ago. The case of Charles Conklin came to symbolize for our city, and for all of America, flaws in a justice system's guarantee of equal protection to all. Again, in the spotlight, came disturbing evidence of police excess.

"While the community expressed its outrage over this matter, a second side of the case has come to light.

"Renowned filmmaker Maggie MacGowen, while working on a documentary for this station, came across information that not only casts doubt upon the district attorney's version of the case, but also raises questions as to his motives in supporting Conklin's claims.

"Here, in a network exclusive, we offer Miss MacGowen's findings. We will let you, our viewing audience, decide."

"Fuck," I said. "I didn't want to hear my name."

Guido shushed me as my film faded in.

Ralph Faust owed me for his overuse of the Etta Harkness tape. I had taken repayment by lifting a healthy chunk from the SNN show he did with Baron Marovich, Jennifer Miller, and Leroy Burgess. I let Ralph Faust introduce the major players. On the screen, the four of them are sitting in a tight half-circle. Once their names and credentials had been established, I froze the frame, reduced it, and moved it up to the top right quadrant of the screen, a miniature like a postage stamp in the corner. Marovich alone, just his face, stayed behind to fill the remaining three-quarters of the screen.

Marovich is seen talking, but the voice heard is mine: "The District Attorney is in the middle of perhaps the strongest political challenge he has faced since his first, and unsuccessful, run for public office in 1979." Marovich is replaced by a full-face shot of George Schwartz.

I continue: "George Schwartz has been an investigator with the district attorney's office for twelve years. According to Schwartz, he was asked by the district attorney to tail one of the original detectives assigned to the Conklin case. Again, according to Schwartz, the surveillance was ordered after the detective attempted to make telephone contact with his former partner on the case. Mr. Schwartz rear-ended the detective's private automobile, and angrily confronted him."

The still shots I had taken of George Schwartz in South Pasadena begin to move through their sequence: Schwartz turning, his face ugly and contorted as he runs at Mike, assaults Mike from the rear. I stopped before Mike stepped aside and let Schwartz fall. I had also cropped the handcuffs until the last frame, when Schwartz was being put into a South Pasadena police car. His Toyota's dented front bumper is clear in the foreground. In sum, it is a wonderfully damning three seconds.

Fade to Jennifer Miller taking her turn in center screen, my voice: "The defense attorney for Charles Conklin works for a major Los Angeles law firm, the same law firm that employed Baron Marovich before his election to public office."

The foursome in the top corner begins to move, Leroy Burgess begins to speak, but the larger part of the screen is still Jennifer Miller. Burgess says, in his resonant baritone: "Mr. Marovich listened to us, understood the implications of our findings right away. He has such confidence that the original investigation was tainted that he persuaded one of the city's big-dollar law firms to represent Charles Conklin on a *pro bono* basis. Without charging a fee, Jennifer Miller will lead the defense."

The foursome freezes. Split the screen again, Jennifer moves left, my voiceover as Jerry Kelsey fills screen right. "Retired Detective Jerry Kelsey has been accused by the district attorney of coercing the young witnesses to lie in order to gain a conviction of Conklin." Pull back, spread the screen so that the original full photograph is seen. Clearly Jerry Kelsey, framed in his trailer window, is looking at Jennifer Miller standing in his front yard.

"When this reporter tried to speak with Detective Kelsey at his home, attorney for the defense Miller arrived. She was identified as the 'advisor' for Detective Kelsey. Charges of gross ethics violation have been filed against Miller. To this date, no one outside the district attorney's circle has successfully questioned Detective Kelsey.

"There were two witnesses to the killing," I say. Wyatt Johnson's bloody body in black and white replaces Kelsey and Miller. "In 1979 LaShonda DeBevis was ten years old when she came upon this scene. Hanna Rhodes was eleven. According to the district attorney, both witnesses have recently recanted their original testimony and signed new affidavits, denying that they identified Charles Conklin as the man they saw at the crime scene. The affidavits are unavailable. And so are the witnesses.

"Since Friday, no one, neither co-workers nor close friends, has heard from LaShonda DeBevis.

"Hanna Rhodes, the second witness." Juxtaposed next to Johnson's corpse, Hanna's shrouded body, her own stream of blood blending with his in the middle of the screen. "Monday night, Hanna Rhodes was gunned down just blocks from the service station where this case began fifteen years ago. Since her release from prison Friday, where she was alleged to have retracted her identification of Conklin, Rhodes had been hiding out in a Hickory Street rock house in Southeast Los Angeles. She told friends someone was after her.

"Charles Conklin, the center of this controversy, has remained silent to this point. Who is he?" Bring up Charles

Conklin's booking photographs, three of them, each clearly labeled, from three different police departments: Los Angeles, Compton, the county sheriff. His rap sheet fades through the photographs. Slow scan down the rap sheet, slow enough to read rape, crime against child, burglary, pandering, murder.

After the gray and white of the computer printout, a flash of color that is James Shabazz. I am only visible as a blue sleeve beside him. My voiceover: "James Shabazz was a sometime foster father to Charles Conklin."

On the tape, I asked him, "You saw something redeemable in Charles?"

"Charles?" Shabazz was thoughtful here, appearing careful before he spoke. For reasons of time, I edited out a few seconds of his answer. "Your question, did I see something worth redeeming in him? All of Allah's children can find redemption. But a boy who would put a bullet in the back of a man's head to steal his car for an hour's ride, who would take his own girl child into his carnal bed, a boy like that was beyond my power to help."

Fade James. The foursome in the top corner again comes to life. Leroy Burgess takes his turn center screen. He is leaving the network studio with a garment bag over his shoulder and his empty toupee head held in front of him like a torch. He's smiling self-consciously for the camera, hurrying, head down as if he's been caught doing something naughty. I ask in voiceover, "Why has Charles Conklin's case suddenly appeared in the media?"

As Burgess in the center of the screen begins to jog, wearing his clerical collar, Burgess up in the corner speaks. "Let me clear up one misconception here. I'm not a priest or an ordained minister of any kind. I never said I was. Sure, I wear a clerical collar. That collar opens a lot of doors to me that wouldn't normally open for a private eye."

He opens the door of his rental Cadillac and gets in. His voice says, "I'm not a flim-flam man. Leroy Burgess is not getting rich off the misfortune of others. My organization, Pastoral Crusade, is completely nonprofit."

As Burgess drives away, sunlight glints off the shiny Cadillac. Fade to black.

It takes a while to describe action that in fact occupied exactly, and only, sixty seconds.

LaShonda applauded.

I stood up and bowed. "Okay, LaShonda, it's your turn. You ready to do an interview for me?"

"All right." She ducked her head shyly. "What are you going to ask?"

"First, did you recant your identification of Charles Conklin?"

She shook her head. "All I did was, I said I never actually saw him pull the trigger. But that's what I said in court all those years ago. I heard the shots. I saw Pinkie run out of the restroom. I saw the dead man's feet sticking out of the restroom and his blood running into the driveway. After that, all I saw was nothing until I got to James's house."

I said, "You didn't see anyone else?"

"Only Hanna."

"Were you bribed by the police?"

"I was very young," she said. "As I remember, the officer told my mother there was a reward for catching the man who killed the other officer. He said if my testimony helped convict Pinkie, I might get enough from the reward to buy a new bike. I don't know if that's offering a bribe or not."

"Who made the offer?" I asked.

"The tall one."

I looked at Guido. "Mike?"

Guido stood up and stretched. "Better record her. Want me to see if there's studio time available?"

I said, "No. Let's keep this just us."

While Guido fussed with lights and LaShonda checked her makeup, I paged Mike.

I went over to a locked cupboard, took out a handycam, put in a fresh tape. Then, with the camera running, I asked, "What did you see on the night of November 6, 1979?"

CHAPTER
23

At seven, I still hadn't heard from Mike. I reached Michael just as he was leaving the house to pick up his date.

"I saw your story on the news," he said. "Pretty spooky."

"Very spooky. Stay watchful. If you get home before your dad or me, call me here at the office. The way things are, I don't want you to be home alone at night."

"Don't worry. I'm spending the weekend at my mom's. Didn't Casey tell you?"

"Not in so many words." Vaguely, I remembered her saying something about me and Mike being alone for the weekend. "Be careful anyway. Any ideas where I might find Mike?"

"No. Sorry. Probably just has his pager turned off."

"Probably," I said, followed by good-bye.

LaShonda and Guido announced that they were hungry. I was hungry, too, but I didn't want to leave in case Mike called. The two of them went to dinner without me, promising to bring me back something.

When the door was locked behind them, I took out a large schedule book and began plotting out our post-production requirements, making a work schedule, what Linda Westman would call a time budget.

Almost immediately, the phone began to ring. Lana Howard called to say the response to the broadcast amounted to a groundswell. Jack Riley said he was impressed anew by my wickedness. Baron Marovich's campaign chair, Roddy O'Leary, announced that he planned to sue me. An anonymous caller promised to blow my fucking head off. Ralph Faust invited me to dinner with his people to talk about a job.

I used the phone myself twice, to page Mike again and to make sure Casey had arrived at her father's house in Denver. After that, I left it on the machine and monitored calls, paying only enough attention to listen for Mike.

Around nine, about the time I was thinking Guido and LaShonda were taking a lot of time to eat, I got up. Feeling restless, I turned on a tape player, scanned through LaShonda's interview until I got to the part that kept jabbing me.

"He scared me," she said, referring to Mike. "I was just a little kid. My mother always told me to watch out for strangers, and he was a stranger to me. I had never spoken to a white man before he came by. He was big, he talked different from the people I knew, sounded just like my teacher, and she scared the you-know-what out of me every day. I can't say whether the officer did anything, or said anything that I would see as a threat if I heard it now, but back then, everything he said seemed like a threat. But I was still more scared of Pinkie.

"I remember talk about a bicycle." She dropped her head so her voice faded. "My mother got mad whenever I asked her about it. All I know is, I've never had a bike in my whole life. Never learned to ride one.

"And I remember the day I finally told the officer what he wanted to hear. He came by school and told me Pinkie was gone, and if I wanted to keep him away forever I had to talk."

I asked: "Did you tell him what he wanted to hear, or did you tell him the truth?"

"A little of both."

I was concentrating so hard that I startled when I heard a knock on the door.

"Who is it?" I shouted.

"Jennifer Miller," came the answer, but quiet, pressed close to the doorjamb.

I thought it was a prank, but I turned off the tape and went to the door. "Are you alone?"

"Please. I don't want to be seen here."

I opened the door enough to make sure she was indeed Ms. Miller and that she was alone, then I opened it enough to let her slip in.

Jennifer had been crying. Her face was all ugly blotches, her hair was a mess, and her perky blouse slopped out over her waistband. I led her over to the sofa. When she set her purse on the floor at her feet, I hefted it to make sure she wasn't packing something lethal.

I asked, "Can I get you something?"

"Yes. Cyanide."

"Ice or straight up? Maybe mixed with scotch?"

She almost smiled. She raised her swollen eyes to meet mine. "My career is finished. Thanks to you."

"Thank yourself. What brings you here?"

"Stupidity. When I saw your hatchet job on me, I was so furious I wanted to confront you, make you retract everything you said about me."

"Something changed your mind?"

She began to laugh. "Traffic was bad. I took out my angst on the other drivers. Now I can't think of anywhere else to go but here."

"Home?" I offered. I went to the rented refrigerator and found her a root beer. "What about your own office?"

"Can't." She took the can from me. "Everyone is gunning for me. This is the last place anyone would look for me. I need some time to think."

I was standing in the middle of the room. "Do you want to talk about it?"

When she shook her head, I went back to my calendar and tried to pick up the thread. The telephone rang, the machine clicked on. As soon as I knew it wasn't Mike, I turned down the volume a few notches, and went back to my work. I had no more than found where I left off when Jennifer said, "I knew better."

I didn't look up. "Did you?"

"This case was supposed to be a major step up for me. Major. I knew from the beginning Conklin was assigned to me only because none of the partners or senior staff in the firm wanted to touch it. But I took it. I thought—it sounds so naive—I thought I could make my chops on it."

"The gangbangers call that getting jumped in," I said. "They beat the crap out of you and if you survive, they let you join their set."

She laughed softly, bitterly. "I didn't survive."

"That's the point," I said. "If everyone survived, what kind of initiation would it be?"

"I'll be disbarred."

I didn't say anything to that, but what went through my mind again was my father's favorite old saw, "You make your bed, you lie in it." What I said was, "If it's such a big case, why wouldn't anyone else touch it?"

"Because of Baron. He had too much involvement, too much interference."

"Too much ego," I said.

"Definitely," she said. "I saw the pitfalls, but there was merit."

"And there was media."

"Yes, there was media." She had the grace to blush. To busy her hands she picked up a bag of Doritos Guido had left on the sofa, took out a few chips, fiddled with them.

Eyes fixed in space, she said, "We didn't expect a vigorous challenge. We weren't ready for it. We weren't ready for you."

"You didn't do your homework, Jennifer," I said. "Or you would have been smarter about the target you picked. You can take cheap shots at the police department all day and the public will roll for you. Bad cops make good press because everyone likes to hate the police right now. I would have stayed out of it and clucked my tongue like every other politically correct asshole in town. But you made your big mistake when you named the cops, and got it wrong."

"We didn't get it wrong."

I said, "Oh?"

"I may have fucked up trying to hold it all together, but I stand by the allegations against Flint and Kelsey. They coerced their witnesses to lie."

I stayed calm. It took effort, but I stayed mellow. I knew she was a lawyer and had a lawyer's skew on facts and implications. Then I took some of my own old advice and did some silent counting. When I passed ten the second time, I got up and stretched. The telephone had rung twice more. No Mike.

"So, Jennifer," I said, "can I get you something else to drink? Something a little stronger than root beer? Guido already has a stash around somewhere."

"If you are."

There was half a bottle of chardonnay in the refrigerator. I found two more-or-less clean glasses and poured. I let her get some of it down before I said, "Charles Conklin is quite a guy."

She responded with a shudder.

"Spent much time with him?"

"He's a client," she said. "I can't discuss him."

"I understand," I said. I sipped my drink, walked around the room a little. "I don't know anything about you. Are you married? Do you have children?"

"Divorced. One child. He's three. How about you? You work so late. Do you have children at home?"

"Two teenagers. One's mine, one's my lover's. Great kids. I love them to death." I smiled, a phony-feeling smile. "Kids are hard work, so difficult to do the right things. You want to protect them. You want them to be independent. They should know about the real world, but you don't want to scare them about people."

"It is hard."

"I know one thing. I wouldn't want a man with Charles Conklin's record moving in next door." I tipped my glass to her stony face, gave her a phony, us-pals laugh. "Did you hear about his career plans when he gets out? Burgess says he wants to work with children. Like a coyote works in the hen house. If I were you, I wouldn't take your baby to the victory party, Jennifer."

She followed with a non sequitur. "I didn't suborn Jerry Kelsey."

"What did you do?"

"Whatever was necessary to keep him in town—he's a material witness. I delivered some groceries, ran some errands on his behalf, made sure no one harassed him. Especially the police."

"Who dopes his scotch?"

She drew back. Either she was a better actress than I had thought, or she was a better lawyer; same thing. From her reaction, she didn't know what I was talking about.

"Jerry's scotch is laced with barbiturates," I said. "He must have been taking downers for a long time because he has built up a powerful tolerance to them. That day Guido and I went to his house? Guido drank two scotches and slept for two days. My question is, does Jerry dope his own, or is it delivered to him that way? I know he wasn't in the kitchen long enough to dissolve a big dose into our drinks. He was serving premix."

She deflated. "I can't talk to you."

"Yes you can." I sat down close beside her. "That's why you came here, Jennifer, to talk to me. You looked up out of your gloom and you saw me hanging on the cross over your head and you knew I could save you. As Jesus told his transgressors, the first one among you who confesses her sins gets the big lollipop, the rest of you get the stick."

"You're mixing metaphors," she groaned. "And you can't make me say, 'Let's stick it to them.' "

"But that's the idea, isn't it? You want to defect. You want to snitch off the others and come out a hero."

"I want to salvage my career."

"I'll do what I can, but I have a price."

"Why am I not surprised?"

"I want copies of the witness affidavits. I want you to be straight with me."

Every time the telephone rang, it made me jumpier. I listened through the beep, impatient for the caller to begin speaking. I could only half concentrate on anything else until I knew who was on the other end. The call was another hang-up.

Jennifer said, "It would be unethical for me to release confidential documents."

The phone rang again. The machine clicked and beeped, and then I heard singing, a familiar slightly off-key baritone. "Maggie, M-M-M-Maggie, you're the only g-g-g-girl that I adore."

I picked it up, pathetically relieved. "Hi, big guy. What's happening?"

"Nothin'." Mike drew out the word. "Wanted you to know you're the most wonderful woman in the world. I miss you. I really, really miss you."

"Sounds like you've been partying. Where are you?"

"We all came up to the Shortstop to watch the news. Had a coupla beers. Did I tell you you're the most wonderful woman I ever knew?"

"Close enough." It was like talking to a dopey child. He was bombed. He had been drinking beer at the new house, so he had probably been relaxed when he got to the bar around four. It was now almost ten and he was relaxed to the point of sloppiness. I asked, "Are you still at the Shortstop?"

"Oh, sure. Bunch of the old guys came by, so we watched you again. Not you, but you know what I mean. Maggie, you're . . ." Words seemed to fail him so he started humming.

"Is anyone there sober?" I asked.

"I'm sober," he said, a small attempt to be huffy about the insinuation.

"More sober than you?"

"No. I'm the designated driver."

"Great. Stay put. I'll be there to get you as soon as I can."

"I'll be waiting," he sang. "I'll wait for you until the sun comes up if I have to. I'll wait until hell freezes over. Maggie?"

"Yes, baby."

"I love you, Maggie." He seemed a little weepy.

"I love you too, baby. Just don't go near anything with fast moving parts until I get there."

"I would never look at another woman."

It took a few attempts to make him say good-bye. When I hung up, I was in a hurry.

"Jennifer," I said, "this has been fun. But I gotta go."

"May I wait here?" she asked. "It's so peaceful."

"Sorry," I said. "I wouldn't feel comfortable."

"I understand. I shouldn't have asked."

She gathered her things and waited while I wrote a note for Guido and turned out lights. As I locked the door, as a precaution in case she had ideas about spontaneous re-entry, I said, "My associate will be back in a few minutes."

"Was that him on the phone?"

"No. That was my lover. You know my lover, don't you?"

She seemed to search through her memory banks before committing herself. She said, "Do I?"

"Maybe not. When can I see the affidavits?"

"I'll slip into my office now and run you copies."

"You know the only way to save yourself is to join the winning camp."

"I know," she sighed.

"Have a messenger deliver the papers here, tonight. The guard up front will take care of them until I get back. Right now, I need to fetch Mike home."

"Mike?" she said.

"My lover," I said, and shot the bolt. I didn't give her the rest. She should have known.

CHAPTER
24

The Shortstop is a bar out on Sunset Boulevard in Echo Park, just below Dodger Stadium. The owners aimed for a baseball motif, but because the police academy sits at the edge of the stadium parking lot, it is the off-duty cop crowd that has given the place its character and rowdy reputation.

There was a big crowd spilling out onto Sunset, about half of them women in short Spandex or tight jeans. Wherever there are police, there are women looking for them. Mike says the uniform is the turn-on. I say it's availability.

The closest parking place was two blocks away. It was a crappy neighborhood by day, scary as hell by night, with or without police nearby. I locked my bag in the trunk and slipped my keys into my jeans pocket. I wished, just fleetingly, for the little automatic Mike had forced on me a few nights before. I had to settle for walking with a purpose.

I was propositioned, as a matter of form, by a young hunk who was sitting on the curb heaving into the storm drain. I thanked him for the offer and walked on.

A couple of parked cars rocked to the rhythm of backseat love, and one pair of outdoorsy lovers were going at it in the recessed doorway of a closed dry-cleaning shop. They were doing a lot of heavy-duty verbalizing that bespoke the man's failure to give the situation a firm approach. I thought he was compensating with some creative alternatives to the old in and out, but she did not seem impressed.

The bar was smoky and dark and vibrated with a country plaint from the jukebox. I couldn't find Mike at first. A few bobbers and weavers standing at the bar inside the door made perfunctory come-ons. I wondered if they were the appointed greeters or just the outgoing type. When I asked for Mike, I got nowhere with them.

The bartender was a big man who kept a sharp eye on things, a retired cop. I had heard that police brass and city fathers had come down hard on him a few times after noisy brawls made the Metro page in the *Times*. He worked hard to overcome the bar's bad reputation. All over the paneled walls he had hung signed, framed glossies of substantial types from Tommy LaSorda to former police chief Daryl Gates.

The bartender asked if I wanted a drink and when I told him I only wanted to find Mike Flint, he made himself scarce.

I went through to the first room, small tables and a few chairs, a lot of standing room and all of it filled—men and women in about equal numbers. The smell of liquor, perfume, people in close quarters on a hot night, could have been bottled and sold under the label "Lookin' for Love."

I was looking for Mike. And I hadn't found him.

There was a second room in the back, on the far side of the bank of lockers the management gave to women customers for their purses. I had to wedge my way through the passageway, dodging hands that grabbed my rear, smiling off lines that represented damn good effort and years of practice. I appreciated the effort. I appreciated the attention. But all I wanted to do was find Mike and get the hell out.

The back room was as full as the first, noisier and smokier because it was smaller. There was a pool table in the middle of the room, but there wasn't enough available space for anyone to play. I recognized Mike's group off in the far corner by their grubby work clothes, and began making my way back toward them.

Finally, I saw Mike. He was sitting on the banquette at the far side, talking with a cluster of maybe half a dozen of the guys. I knew that he had been drinking, knew that drink explained why he found all the jokes so funny. Drink probably also explained the sweet young thing sitting on his lap.

Mike has a soft spot for chicanas, especially chicanas in short, flippy skirts. He says they have an assertive way about them that he likes. The one on his lap was being assertive about nuzzling my favorite soft spot on his neck. His focus, blurred as it was, seemed to be the guy gang and he was holding her as a matter of form, to keep her from falling onto the floor. Holding her like a habit.

Once again, I wished for the automatic he had locked away in the closet.

I heard my name pass through the crowd, and then I lost sight of Mike because everyone stood up and faced me. I was grabbed from behind and boosted up onto the pool table. I was confused at first, thinking these were ridiculous lengths to go to protect a brother officer from being caught dirty. When I had regained my balance and was standing on the table, I saw Mike's face beaming up at me as he joined the others in applause. The little dear was still clinging to him, more like a fungus than a friend.

Someone yelled, "Speech," and I finally realized that this was an accolade because of the news broadcast. As the vanquisher of a common enemy, I made a deep bow. Then I climbed down and went over to Mike.

Through the din, I yelled, "Who's your friend?"

"Olga," he beamed, and patted the arm wrapped around his middle. "Olga, meet the love of my life."

Olga hissed.

Hector was at my elbow. I smelled beer on him and his eyes had the same dreamy glaze that Mike's had.

"It was great what you did, Maggie." Hector pulled me into an embrace and planted a sloppy kiss on me. He was weaving. I knew that if I let go of him he would fall on his face.

I caught a glimpse of Mike watching us. His eyes had cleared. Actually, they flashed. Elaborately, I paid no attention to him, or to the female attached to him. He reached through the mob to put a hand on Hector's shoulder.

Gazing up into Hector's face, I said, "What's with Mike? He looks cranky."

"I don't know what it is. Ever since I fucked Charlene we haven't been really close."

That was the first time in my life I wished I was as drunk as everyone else.

"He doesn't blame me," Hector was saying. "Not like it's my

fault. She came on to me. She's so-o beautiful, what's a poor sucker to do?"

I disentangled myself and propped Hector on the broad shoulders next to us. Mike was weaving some himself. Olga seemed to be getting mad that she had lost his attention. When I smiled at her she mouthed, "Bitch." To Mike she snapped, "You said you wasn't married," and flounced off to try her luck elsewhere.

When Mike listed precariously to the left, I righted him. I said, "Ready to go home?"

"That was one hell of a piece of work you did." His words slurred. "We watched it three times. Three times all the way through."

"Good thing it only lasted a minute," I said, taking his arm. "You smell like *una noche de amor*, amigo. Let's go get you cleaned up."

He draped an arm around my shoulders and let me forge the path of least resistance through the standing crowd. Besides beer and cigarette smoke and sweet young thing, he smelled like a hard day's work. I liked it.

The fresh air outside made him reel. I hadn't a clue where his car might be, so we headed toward mine. I said, "If you're going to throw up, I'd rather you do it here than in my car."

"Me?" Shocked offense. "You think I'm drunk?"

"I hope you are," I said.

"You're pissed about Olga."

"No."

"Damn." He seemed dejected. "It would be easier if you were pissed. Go ahead and yell at me. I'll feel better."

"What's the point? You're so drunk, in the morning you won't remember anything I said. Like yelling at an amnesiac. Why waste the effort?"

We passed a new set of lovers in the dry cleaner's doorway. He said, "How can I make it up to you?"

"Make love to me right here, right now."

His step faltered as he thought over the proposition. Then he stopped, appealed to me with tears in his eyes. "Sorry, baby. I don't think I can."

"Exactly," I said.

I woke up early Saturday morning, sorted my arms and legs from Mike's, and took the cotton out of my ears—he's a fero-

cious snorer when he drinks. The air conditioner had been set
too low and I felt a little chilled. The chill disinclined me from
swimming laps, so I slipped into running things and headed
down the hill toward Ventura Boulevard.

Some fog had drifted into the Valley, a cool, moist, gray in-
fusion into the rising heat. For the first mile, I ran stiff and
heavy-footed. But I found my stride at about mile two and ran
easily among the residential streets north of the boulevard, falling into place among the mass of weekend runners.

Because I didn't know the area, hadn't clocked the streets, I
couldn't set a distance goal. Instead, I timed myself. If I didn't
get lost, I figured to arrive home at just about the same time
the coffee was set to be ready.

I didn't push myself, so I beat both the paper boy and Mr.
Espresso by about two minutes. I was listening to telephone
messages from the day before when I heard the paper thunk
against the garage door.

I paused the answering machine, bored with it. In one way
or another, every caller had offered me something: a job, an interview, sudden painful death. I had been through it all before
and wanted none of it.

It was nice to have the house to myself for a while. Even
Bowser was gone—Mike left him locked happily into the yard
at the South Pasadena house, with food and water, he promised. I traded my hot running shoes for the ratty moccasins
Mike keeps by the back door and slogged out for the paper.

Maggie MacGowen had made page one, part one, column
right. I spread the paper open on the kitchen table and glanced
at the lead paragraph while I heated some milk with the little
steam chingow on the espresso maker, made myself a big cup
of café au lait. When I sat down, I was ready to concentrate.

The "dark and stormy night" school of journalism is very
tiresome. I wanted straight news. What I got was a clumsy met-
aphor using the heated-up weather to define the heated up
D.A.'s race, and then Maggie MacGowen came and threw a cold
bucket on the leader, Baron Marovich. I managed to sort out
the essentials.

Reached in his downtown office late last night, according to
the reporter, Marovich denied every allegation of creating a reverse Willie Horton in order to get attention for his campaign.

He labeled me an example of media gone amok, a dangerous propagandist and dirty-trickster, tried to tuck me into his opponent's camp. I had to read ahead to get his opponent's name, because it had slipped my memory.

The story continued on page twenty-three, half a column giving a synopsis of Marovich's campaign history and some of the unfair-campaign-practices charges filed against him over the years.

Overall, the coverage was okay—I knew it would send Marovich into the stratosphere—but the best part was a little sidebar, a short, related bit of information set off within an attractive gray border. The headline was: "When Career Criminals Go Free." The story gave details of a few of the more horrific crimes committed by convicts after they were released from prison on legal technicalities. Charles Conklin was not mentioned anywhere in the sidebar.

I called Guido, woke him up, gloated with him about the story. He was happy, though I thought he wasn't as chatty as usual. He didn't prolong the conversation beyond the essentials. I also thought I heard someone else in his bedroom.

There were some muffins in the freezer. I put one in the microwave, made a second cup of coffee with milk, and was halfway through it when Mike made his stumbling entrance.

By the time we got home the night before, Mike had been at the point of crashing. It had been difficult enough to get him from the car and into the bed. Beyond taking off his belt and shoes, I hadn't bothered wrestling off his clothes. Still wearing his dirty work clothes, unshaven for the second day, face puffy, eyes red-rimmed, he was a charming sight.

He shuffled the last few steps to the kitchen table, aimed a shaky hand, and grasped my coffee cup. After he finished it in one long swallow, he shuddered. Then he looked at me.

"Wha' happen?" he said.

"Olga," I said.

"Oh, yeah." He sat down and raised the empty cup to me for a refill. "Have mercy. I haven't had that much to drink in years. Never again," he moaned. "I'm too old."

"It happens to us all, big guy."

"How come you're not mad?" He frowned at me. "Don't you love me?"

"It's not your fault women keep falling into your lap. I understand the attraction."

"Uh huh." He looked at me askance, suspicious.

"Hector explained all that to me last night. A woman offers herself, what's a poor sucker to do?"

"Oh my God." He had color in his grizzled cheeks again. "He told you about Charlene?"

"Not in detail. She threw herself at him. He's a gentleman, he had to catch her. Is that how it went?"

"More or less. She was pissed at me for taking Michael's scout troop camping when she had some kind of gallery opening. Old Hector didn't know what hit him."

"You didn't hit him?"

"Nah." The tough guy was making a comeback. "Like you said, it wasn't his fault."

I slid the paper in front of him. "Our story made the front page."

He looked at it dumbly, eyes not working in concert. "I need my glasses. Read it to me."

"It'll keep," I said. "Are you hungry?"

"I'm getting there."

I poured him about half a quart of juice and started frying eggs. Normally, Mike takes great care of himself, runs, watches what he eats. But that morning he was completely out of the loop. He ate four eggs, hashbrowns, a stack of toast, and a whole grapefruit. I don't know where he put it, but it seemed to start the juices flowing again. When he finally crossed his fork and his knife on the edge of his plate, he looked like a potential survivor.

"So," he said, leaning back in his chair, rubbing his chest, smiling up at me. "What's the plan today?"

"The plan is no plan. I've hardly seen you all week. Can we just hang together for a while? You know, like a date?"

"Sounds good."

"I'm going to take a shower." I dumped my coffee dregs into the sink. "Would you do one favor for me? Would you listen to the phone messages and see what you think about them?"

"What I *think* about them?"

"Couple of them sound like serious death threats."

CHAPTER
25

"It was after the Watts Festival one year, maybe the first year they held it, I don't remember. Twenty years ago I guess." Mike picked up a big plumber's wrench from the shelf and set it in our shopping cart. We were cruising a hardware warehouse for a few essentials, some elbow joints, socket plates, a lot of spackle; our date. "Anyway, all of us who worked the festival—police and sheriffs—we went down to this vacant lot afterward, street dead-ended at the Artesia Freeway. They were still building the freeway so there was no one around, just a lot of dirt. Used to be a nice neighborhood, till the freeway took it out.

"So, we got some cases of beer and went down there, built a fire, starting unwinding. Pretty soon the girls started coming. I don't know who put the word out, but you never saw so many girls."

"Women," I said.

"Girls," he said, sorting through a bin of spackle blades. "It's my story, so they're girls."

"Pig," I said.

"Exactly. Back then, we were pigs, they were girls. You gotta know the language of the times or you're not going to get this story at all."

"I'll try to keep up." I was pushing the cart. The story was hard to listen to, more truth about Mike than I really needed at the moment. That's exactly why he was telling it, a sort of test to see where I drew my line, how much truth I would take in before I stopped loving him. I had tried to change the subject a couple of times, but he always came back to the ugly day in the cul-de-sac.

"People were doing the dirty deed all over the place. Everywhere you looked, naked bodies."

"What were you doing?" I asked.

"Just hanging. My partner got lucky on the hood of our car. I was sitting inside watching his little white ass pumping against the windshield in front of my face. Just pump, pump, pump. Funniest thing you ever saw."

"And you just sat there?"

"Yeah." He handed me a brown paper drop cloth. "So, I'm sitting there and this girl comes up to me and she says, 'I'll do you right here. Anything you want, but I won't take it in the ass.' "

"And did she?" I felt squeamish hearing all this, squeamish the way I felt when batons and fists entered his stories. We had moved a long way from the Olgas always trying to sit on his lap to where this conversation began.

"No," Mike said, looking at the shelves. "She told me she'd already done ten guys by mouth. That really did it for me. I didn't want her breathing the same air as me."

"She did this for pay?"

"Nope. Just for the fun of it."

"Was she pretty?"

"Not bad."

While Mike was busy with wood putty, I walked away from him, pushed the cart over a few aisles to the cupboard knobs display because I didn't want to get into something with him. All day there had been an edge.

Mike and I argue back and forth all the time—cop, Berkeley liberal; natural foes. It's usually a lot of fun. We both posture and exaggerate our opinions just to jerk the other's chain. This story disturbed me. Especially the just-for-fun part.

Mike came up behind me. "Find something?"

"No." I bent down to look at the knobs in the bottom row because I didn't want to look at Mike. I heard him take a big breath.

"It was a long time ago, Maggie. Things were different then."

"Did I say anything?"

"You didn't have to."

I straightened up and turned to face him. "I love your stories. You know I do. This one's hard to take."

"I'll watch what I say."

"Don't do that. I would be bereft if you thought you had to censor yourself for me. It's just, that girl gives me chills. I need to think about it a minute."

"Bereft, huh? If that story bothers you, you'd never make it on the streets."

"Sure I would. It's not the story—I went to college, I saw my share of naked people doing *it*—it's your perspective. She wasn't a *girl*, for chrissake Mike, she was a human with a big problem."

"Is this a male-female thing?"

"Not really. It's more a cop-civilian thing. I think this one belongs in the excessive-shit pile with the fat hooker, Queen Esther, you wrestled to the ground and sat on, and that guy Philip you gave a head full of dummy bumps for resisting arrest. Good stories, but I have trouble putting you in the picture with them."

He closed up on me the way he does when he feels defensive, shut me right out. I hated it. He bent down and looked at the knobs in the bottom row because he couldn't look at me.

I said, "Find something?"

"No."

I sat down on the floor cross-legged beside him and looked at the ranks of cupboard knobs, from Shaker-plain to rococo. "I like the white china ones. Very simple."

He said, "Too simple."

"We don't need any knobs," I said. "You know what we need?"

"Pulls?"

"Lunch."

He gave me a sidelong, narrow-eyed glance, still defensive.

"We need lunch," I repeated. "And then we need a nap. What do you think?"

"We should go by the house and see how the guys are doing with the painting."

"Lunch first," I said, and stroked the underside of his chin, where the muscles were set and hard. "Then a nap."

"Where do you want to eat?"

"At home. I want to eat at home. You and me, like a date, re-member?"

First thing I did when we got home was take the telephone off the hook. I didn't listen to any messages, and I didn't pick up the mail. We made sandwiches and carried them into the bedroom to watch the first game of the Dodger double-header while we ate. He was very sweet, very attentive. Very polite, like with someone he didn't know very well.

Propped up on pillows, we had a little party, got potato chip crumbs everywhere, argued about was the runner out on sec-ond or not, should LaSorda retire, and who was going to win the division. He began to relax with me again. And I relaxed. I was out before the seventh inning stretch, sleeping with my face against Mike's tummy, his arm draped across me.

I woke up once, came to enough to notice that the television was off and Mike was asleep beside me. The second time I awoke, the sun was low in the sky and I was alone. I got up, groggy, and went out looking for Mike.

Mike wasn't in the house, nor had he left a note. The tele-phone ringer was off, the message tape had been erased, the mail had been sorted. In my pile there were only a picture postcard from my parents—they were on vacation in the East—a reminder from Casey's orthodontist, and a check from the tenants in my San Francisco house. I stuck the card on the refrigerator with a magnet.

I called security at my office building and asked whether an envelope had been left for me. The man who answered said there were several envelopes in my mailbox. He was holding a telegram and a big bouquet of flowers—he'd tried to call but couldn't get through. I had him read me the card on the flow-ers.

"Congratulations, Ralph and the staff at SNN."

"Keep the flowers," I told the guard. "Give them to your wife if you have one."

I thanked him. Then I went in and took a shower to wake up.

Just for a change, because I probably had not worn a dress for at least a month, I slipped into a flowery sundress I had bought for a friend's outdoor wedding in June. Feeling vamp-ish, I also put on some mascara and blush, went into Casey's bathroom and borrowed some eye shadow. When I had finished, I was a vision. Home alone, but a vision.

I missed Mike.

I waited around for about half an hour, puttering. I felt so restless, though, that I traded my three-inch pumps for sandals and went out for a walk through the condo grounds. Waiting around is hard for me.

I was sitting by the pool in the long, deep shade of early evening, chatting with a neighbor couple, when I saw Mike's Blazer come up the drive. I excused myself and ran down the sloping lawn to catch him, my skirt billowing around my legs, light and cool. When Mike saw me, he stopped in the middle of the street to wait.

"Why, Miss Scarlett," he said, leaning out his window for kissing, "aren't you pretty?"

"Yes, I am," I said. He wore slacks, a sportshirt, and a secretive grin. I touched his arm. "You're mighty pretty your own damn self."

"Climb in," he said. "We have reservations at the most exclusive eatery in town."

"Do you need a tie? Do I need heels?"

"No, and no. Just climb in."

I had to brush dog hair off my seat. "We should go check on Bowser."

"We'll do that right now; it's on the way. Don't worry about Bowser, though. He's fine. So fine, he doesn't want to leave his new yard for anything."

Mike drove us east to the Pasadena Freeway, then dropped down into South Pasadena.

"Is this restaurant a new discovery?" I asked.

"Old place, new discovery."

He pulled up in front of the house and parked beside the dumpster. The yard was still cluttered with building materials, but the trash—the old carpets and drapes, mostly—had been cleared away. No beer cans, no men.

Looking up at the front I had a sudden sort of electric jolt as I realized, truly realized for the first time, that this was *our* house. Me, Mike, Casey, and Michael. And Bowser. Not playing house, not shuffling back and forth between my house and his house, but living together in this place for two and a half years. Mingled furniture. Mingled destinies. Suddenly it scared me. Suddenly it looked like commitment. Might as well have been a ring on my finger.

I hung back while Mike unlocked the door, then I followed him inside, staying a few steps behind, making a little space between us.

The only light came from the tall back windows. Twilight, filtered through the leaves of the old avocado tree by the patio, painted the walls and the floor with delicate blue lace that moved with the breeze. I stepped into the shadow pattern, like wearing a veil as I crossed the room.

Bowser pressed his nose to the glass, tongue hanging out, tail wagging, happy to see us. I opened the door for him.

"What time is our reservation?" I asked.

"About now," Mike said. I couldn't see his face in the failing light.

"Let me say hi to Bowse," I said, "then we can go. How far is it?"

"Not far."

Someone had given Bowser a new tennis ball. He dropped it on my foot. Mike went back inside as I stepped out onto the patio to throw the ball for the dog to fetch a couple of times while I checked his new water dish, poured some fresh kibble into his new bowl. He was more interested in having his head scratched and his stomach rubbed than in eating. He kept looking into the house behind me, and I knew he was searching for Casey.

"Casey'll be home tomorrow, old man," I said. He sighed and lay down and looked up at me with pathetic big eyes.

Mike came out through the dining room doors. I saw the flicker of candlelight behind him, heard Wynton Marsalis's trumpet, "Taking a Chance on Love," with his father Ellis accompanying him on piano, as soft and lacy as the shadows. Mike held his hand out to me. "Time to eat."

Out of nowhere, I started crying.

"Don't worry," he said, coming to me, gathering me against his crisp shirtfront. "I didn't cook the dinner. You'll be okay."

"It's not the food that worries me." I wiped my eyes and walked in with him.

Mike had made a small table out of two sawhorses and a couple of planks, and covered them with a starched white cloth, filled an empty juice jar with roses from the backyard and set it in the middle. There were two places set, and two folding chairs. The only light came from the candelabra on a ladder beside the table. The music came from a CD player on the bare floor.

Mike pulled out my chair with an elaborate flourish. "Madame," he said, and kissed the back of my neck when I sat down.

Before he could go away, I pulled him down to me by the hand, brought his face to mine. "Everything is beautiful," I said. I still had a lump in my throat and a vague sense of foreboding.

"You only think so because it's dark in here. Couple more days, though, and it will be beautiful."

"I wasn't referring to the house." I raised his hand to kiss the backs of his fingers.

"If you don't stop now, the food will get cold."

"Better call the waiter, then." I let him go, but he lingered long enough to curl my toes before he went to fetch the caterer-wrapped meal from the kitchen.

Salad, pasta something, chocolate mousse, and fresh raspberries. It looked nice, but I could hardly swallow anything except the dry champagne. I couldn't take my eyes off Mike across the table from me. The thing is, I was trying to imagine growing old with that face beside me, across from me, all around me all the time. It is a world-class face, so I must be a hard sell. I was very unsettled

Mike's plate had hardly been touched, either. Marsalis, *père et fils*, were playing "The Very Thought of You."

Mike watched me, without saying anything, as I picked up my glass of champagne and walked with it over to his side of the table. He leaned back in his chair and looked up at me, questions in his expression. When he held out his arms to me, inviting me onto his lap, I shook my head.

"Dance with me," I said. As he led me around the freshly sanded floor, I kissed him, beginning at the point of his chin and working along his wonderful, craggy face all the way to his ear. When I got there, I whispered, "I love you, Mike."

He responded by nuzzling my neck. I had chills that had nothing to do with the breeze coming through the open windows. From somewhere, while we danced, he pulled out a small gold box and offered it to me on his upturned palm. My stomach did a roller-coaster fall; I was grateful I had foregone the pasta. I lost the music and stepped on his foot.

"What is that?" I asked. I didn't really want to know, and I did not touch the box on his hand.

"Open it," he said, smiling like a kid at a birthday party, embarrassed when the birthday girl got to his gift, but excited, too.

"I don't know," I said. "I don't trust small boxes."

"Open it. Trust me."

Well, I trust Mike, so I did it, I opened the box. Inside, under the cotton, I saw a flash of gold in the candlelight and nearly chickened out. When I finally pulled away the cotton, I found a shiny new key attached to a gold heart by a heavy chain. The heart was engraved with an M and had a clear stone set on either side of it. It was pretty. I think I was relieved it wasn't a ring, but I can't be sure.

"Whose M is it?" I asked, holding it up, spinning the heart in the flickering light. "My initial, or yours?"

"It's ours. This is the key to the front door of our house."

"Thank you."

"What did you think was in the box?"

"I hadn't a clue."

"You were nervous about it." He said this with tooth-sucking, teasing sureness.

I said, "Are you going to dance with me or are you going to try to pick a fight?"

"Of course, there are a lot of M words. I guess it could stand for a lot of things. Want me to list a few?"

"No."

"I want to talk about M words." He took me in his arms again and danced me across the room and out onto the brick patio. His voice was next to my ear. "There's, mar . . ." He drew it out sadistically. ". . . igolds. And, marbles. Don't forget Margot—a funny name to give a little baby."

"The only thing funny here is you, big guy."

"Ready to dip?" He dropped me backward, pulled me up again, finished with a spin that brought us face to face. With our noses almost touching, he said, "Margot Eugenie Duchamps MacGowen?"

"What?"

"Marry me."

CHAPTER

26

Fire lit the sky for miles. Like a giant pointer, a fat white plume reached up out of its center and disappeared into the cloud cover. Six helicopters circled the area, shining their big spots down into the middle of the red glow, saying, "Here it is." We could see exactly where the fire was. The problem was getting to it.

The freeways for miles on all sides were nearly impassable, the surface streets were at gridlock. We were near Overland Avenue, somewhere on the Westside, trying to find a way through. Mike blasted his horn in frustration before he gave up and veered off to drive the shoulder. He bounced us through potholes, over road debris and various car parts. It was uncomfortable, scary as hell, but we did progress past the solid, unmoving mass of cars.

"You weren't friends?" I asked, holding on to the dash.

Mike frowned as if he'd swallowed something distasteful. "No. He's a one-way kind of guy. I don't think he has any friends. Something about him, the things he talks about, I guess—I don't know. I worked a tough case with him, but I kept my distance."

"What kind of things?"

"Schemes." He nearly sideswiped a station wagon to avoid a crater. When the Blazer stopped bouncing, he took a breath. "Always involved in some sort of deal, gonna get rich, gonna blow town. Nothing ever seemed to pan out, though. And he was a lush."

I was trying to relax; the worst thing you can do in a collision is brace yourself—snaps your bones. I asked, "Was he competent on the job?"

"Maybe he was once, or he wouldn't have been promoted. He knew what to do, but he'd get drunk, lose track of things. I was new to the division and he sort of attached himself to me. Probably because no one else would work with him."

"I read the Conklin investigation files. I didn't see his name on much of it."

"Totally H.U.A. all the time."

I said, "I forgot my glossary."

He risked taking his eyes off the road long enough to give me his tough-guy smirk. "Head Up Ass."

I said, "Oh."

"It was a piece-of-shit case to begin with. The trail was a year old. Jerry asks to be assigned to do the year review, the lieutenant doesn't trust him, but he has to give him something to keep him busy. So the lieutenant says, sure, take it on, and here's the new kid on the block—me—to be your bun boy. I knew Jerry didn't expect a damn thing from me. For damn sure he never thought I would pull it together."

There was open space in the middle of the next intersection. Mike, holding down the horn, blasted through it to effect a left turn. We took a lot of the evil eye and not a few middle-finger salutes, but we made it.

When we were back on the shoulder, I said, "There is a body?"

"Yes."

I picked up the telephone. "What's Michael's number?"

"Why?"

"I have to talk to him."

"He's okay, Maggie. Calm down. Michael and his mom went up to her folks' place in Arrowhead."

"How do you know?" I asked.

"I already called."

Mike rode the center line down Rose Avenue, crossed Sepulveda in the no-man's land between the end of a red light and the flashing on of a green. Fire trucks, police cars, paramedics vehicles, and news vans blocked the street, and we were still two blocks from the equipment storage yard where Jerry Kelsey kept his trailer. Where flames still shot ten feet into the air.

By a combination of skill and dumb luck, Mike got in among the official vehicles without major damage and found a place to stop.

I was out of the Blazer and running toward the storage lot, ankle-deep in dirty run-off water, a fine spray falling from overhead, when Ralph Faust grabbed me, spun me around.

"Hold on, Maggie," he said. His grip hurt my wrist.

I said, "Let go."

Through the fence I could see flaming oil barrels and construction equipment, the hole in the ground where the gasoline storage tank had been. Jerry Kelsey's trailer was nothing more than a molten mass, a black smear on the gravel.

I smelled booze on Ralph's breath. He might have smelled wine on mine. Mike had been beeped at the beginning of our second bottle of champagne. In the middle of the argument.

"We did this, you know," Ralph said. "We started it."

"What do I hear?" I asked, cruel sarcasm in there. "Sudden compunction? You never turned around before, saw the human wreckage in your wake?"

"Don't be mad at me."

"Have to be mad at somebody." I was looking around for Mike. Finally, I spotted him talking to the coroner's people. I pulled against Ralph's grip, but he held firm, drew me against him. I heard heavy sighing in his chest.

I looked up into his face. I whispered, "It's only a fire. You'll be all right. Let me go."

But he seemed unable to comprehend.

"Was Kelsey in there?" I asked.

From his pocket he took a shoe, a little navy pump, about a size five or six. The toe was blackened, the leather was wet. I took the shoe from him. Casey hadn't worn anything that small since she was in about the fourth grade; the thought a reflex. My daughter is always my first thought when something scary happens.

"Where did you get this?" I asked him.

"I was standing over there by the gate with a film crew, and it just floated by." He pointed with his free hand. "Just floated by."

I broke then and ran to Mike. He caught me, too, but more to hold me away than to keep me. I offered the little shoe to him. I said, "Where is Jennifer Miller?"

Mike looked over at the technician leaning against the coroner's empty van. "One body?"

"So far," was her response.

"Male or female?"

"Don't know," the woman said. "Firemen saw it inside the trailer, but it's still too hot to get a better look. No hurry. Victim isn't going anywhere—charred beyond, from the description. Just hope there's enough left to x-ray. Have to wait."

Mike took me aside, walked me back toward his car. "Did you hear her? You have to wait. I need to talk to some people. Can I trust you to stay put for a while?"

I dropped back. "Did you say stay put?"

He sighed. "Just don't get hurt, okay?"

"I'll try."

"Jeez," he muttered, and jogged off toward the police command post.

Staying on the perimeter, away from the firehoses, I walked back to the news vans, found the one sent out by the network I had been working with. Jack Riley was inside the cab, talking on the phone, watching the fire in air-conditioned comfort. He climbed out when he saw me.

"When did you get here?" I asked.

He shrugged, "Five, ten minutes ago. Lot of fuss isn't it? I just don't get the big deal about a fire. I mean, it's nice and bright—good color—but they're doing prime-time interrupts for some bulldozers and a watchman? Probably started it himself smoking in bed, or tossed a butt in the wrong place. The petro people are going to dump their load on the oil barrels in a minute, then it will be all over."

"Jack, don't you know who the watchman is?"

He toned right down, opened up, ready to rethink things. "Should I know?"

"Jerry Kelsey. One of the detectives in the Conklin case."

"Oh." With some enthusiasm. "He's the corpse?"

"Don't know. Adds a little fuel to the story, though, doesn't it?"

"I'll forgive the ghoulish attempt at humor." Jack was thinking fast, as usual, putting something together. "You've got a handle on the deep background, don't you? I mean, you knew this guy."

"I met him. I used a picture that I took right there in front of his trailer in the piece that ran last night."

"Now we have a story I like. I want you on camera, Maggie." His new enthusiasm moved us toward the film crew across the street. They were just standing around, gossiping with the weekend news talent.

"What do you want me to do?" I asked him.

"Give me a break." He gave me a shoulder nudge. "You know what to do. Let's just do it before we lose the fire."

Jack had a short verbal scuffle with the talent, who was getting one of his first shots at a prime-time story out of the fire. He was young and smooth-looking, and eager. He suggested that instead of turning everything over to me, he interview me, though he hadn't a clue what questions to ask. It was his turn, dammit, and he wasn't going to give it up.

"He's right, Jack," I said. "You're screwing with his résumé. This is his fire to report, and I'm an interloper. What if he introduces me, nods his head here and there, and closes? We'd all be happy, right?"

That's the way we did it. The two of us stood in tight, with the camera three yards in front of us, the fire about sixty yards behind us. Even at that distance, I could feel some of its heat. The entire scene was lit red.

After the intro—he did a good job, said everything I told him to—I gave a brief rundown on Jerry Kelsey, retired cop, and why he lived in the trailer, how I met him in relation to the Conklin case. I was careful to mention Marovich, twice, getting in a dig about his tight race for reelection.

Then I laid what I hoped was the bombshell, peppering it shamelessly with attention-getting buzzwords: "Twice this week, fatal tragedy has struck among those originally involved in the Conklin murder conviction.

"During the early hours of Tuesday morning, young Hanna Rhodes, a witness to the slaying, was cold-bloodedly gunned down in the Southeast Los Angeles neighborhood where she grew up. Locked out of the school yard where she had once played, Hanna Rhodes was felled by two blasts to the chest." Melodramatic, sure. But the entire scene seemed to call for Grand Guignol.

"Fourteen years ago," I continued, "it was Hanna Rhodes's eyewitness testimony that sent Charles Conklin to prison for life. The senior detective assigned to the case, the detective who first heard her account, was Jerry Kelsey.

"Behind us, you see the inferno that has consumed the modest trailer home of Detective Jerry Kelsey. The coroner informs us that firefighters have found an as-yet unidentified corpse among the ashes of Detective Kelsey's trailer. It is still too hot for them to go in for a closer look, to attempt to identify the deceased.

"On Monday afternoon, a court hearing is scheduled on behalf of Charles Conklin to evaluate the testimony of Hanna Rhodes, to scrutinize the procedures used by Jerry Kelsey to elicit that testimony nearly a decade and a half ago. In light of the double tragedies, how much crucial testimony has been quieted? Quieted forever."

I backed from the microphone that was being held in front of my face as a signal for the talent do his thing. He was good, stayed with the dramatic tone. As the camera pulled in close to him, I slipped away.

Mike was standing near Jack Riley watching me, grinning sardonically as I walked up to him.

"So?" I said to Jack.

He seemed pleased. "The station is already re-running your special report."

"When did I get upgraded from sixty-second bit to special report? Does the pay go up, too?"

Mike said, "I thought I told you to stay out of trouble."

"I thought I told you not to tell me what to do." I leaned against him. "Did I leave out anything?"

"My name," Mike said.

"Must have slipped my mind," I said.

Mike was called away by the coroner. I stayed and had a long talk with Jack before I walked back to the car to make some calls. I wanted to find Jennifer.

I had no home number for Jennifer. No one answered at her office. Not knowing anywhere else to try, I called Baron Marovich's office and left a message, and then called his campaign headquarters out in the Valley and left another message for Roddy O'Leary. I gave them both Mike's mobile number. Then I called James Shabazz, to fill him in.

Jack had been right. As soon as the petroleum-fire crew appeared, the party was just about over. Street traffic had caused some delay for the foam tankers, but when they came, they moved right in with their big hoses. At the same time, an aerial tanker dove in overhead and dropped its red slime on the flaming oil barrels. The blaze disappeared, but the stench of burning petroleum and rubber lingered.

The helicopters, one by one, turned off their spots and swooped away, leaving us in an eerie darkness. The flashing lights of the official vehicles, the floods set up by the news people, the streetlights, could not penetrate the dense black smoke beyond a few yards. Nonessential personnel began to go, each one leaving the scene darker, quieter. I watched them all, waiting for Mike to come back.

We were among the last to leave. The coroner wouldn't be able to get to the corpse until daylight. Official identification and cause of death could take weeks. There was nothing left for us to do.

I felt a tremendous adrenaline letdown, exhausted and excited all at once. We stopped by my office to pick up the mail on the way home. Back on the freeway, Mike was quiet, lost in thought or reluctant to restart the argument. The ringing of the car telephone startled us both.

Roddy O'Leary was angry. "What do you have against Baron? He's a decent guy, he's done a good job for the county. Why are you crucifying him?"

"We both know the answer to that, Roddy."

"What's it going to take to make you stop?"

I said, "The truth."

"Whose truth? Dang, Maggie, you know as well as anyone does that truth is a slimy bastard—keeps changing its shape. You have a version, Baron has a version, that fucking con has a version. You've taken some pretty dirty shots at Baron. You're killing him in the polls."

And killing you, I thought. A campaign director's price is set by his last campaign. Lose one, move back two spaces. For Roddy, a loss in the D.A.'s race would probably eliminate any chance of getting a governor-race gig, even state assembly would be reaching.

"I want a debate," he said. "I want you on TV, give Baron a chance to answer."

"Sorry," I said, "debate isn't my format."

"You owe him."

"I don't owe him a goddamn thing. And I'm not going to debate him."

Roddy was persistent. "Ralph Faust says he'll give us air time. Thirty minutes tomorrow afternoon, replayed at eleven."

"If I do it," I said, "the format is discussion, not a debate. And I bring a friend or two with me."

"Who?"

"I'll let you know, if I decide to go ahead."

Mike thought it was a bad idea to have a face-off. After he let me know that, he had nothing more to say. All the rest of the way home, and while we got ready for bed, he was like a mute. Very unusual for Mike.

I didn't get to the office mail until I sat down on the bed. In the middle of the stack, there was a plain envelope with my name hand-printed on the front. There was no note inside. Nothing except copies of the affidavits dated the week before and signed by Hanna Rhodes and LaShonda DeBevis. I passed them to Mike.

All he said when he read them was, "Hmm." Then he rolled over and went to sleep. Or pretended to.

CHAPTER
27

Sometime in the middle of the night, Mike turned on the light beside the bed and sat up.

"Why not?" he asked.

I hadn't been sleeping, but the light still hurt my eyes. I rolled over against him, buried my face in the pillow behind his shoulder. When the fire interrupted our first go-round on the topic of marriage, I had hoped against logic that it wouldn't come up again. I said the only thing I could think of, "I love you too much."

He gave this some consideration before rejecting it. His tone was sharp. "Try again."

"I don't ever want to go through a divorce again."

"I didn't ask you for a divorce."

"Aren't we happy, Mike?"

"I know I am."

"Why mess things up?"

"How is getting married going to mess up our happiness?"

I sat up then, pulled the sheet up under my chin, wrapped my arms around my raised knees. I said, "How did you feel about getting called to the fire?"

He looked at me askance. "After twenty-two years on the job, I have seen my fill. The only thing that gets me through it anymore is knowing that in two more years, five months, there won't be any more roll-outs. No more nothing but peace."

"The problem is," I said, "I haven't seen my fill. I love the roll-outs." I put my arm through his. "We're great together now, baby, because we are still in the thick of things. But what will happen in two years? You'll be off walking on your deserted beach, and I'll be in the trenches in Mogadishu or somewhere. I've been in a sort of holding pattern as long as Casey is still at home. My plan has always been that as soon as she's on her own, I'm out of here. I won't have to accept pissy domestic-themed projects anymore to pay the bills. I can do, I can go anywhere."

All he said was, "But . . ."

When there was no follow-up, I asked, "Will you come with me?"

"To Mogadishu?"

"To anywhere."

"If I came with you, what would I be doing?"

"Guess you have to figure that out. Then, you have to decide whether that's anything you want to do for the next God knows how many years."

He put an arm around me and pulled me close. "What's wrong with walking on the beach?"

"Nothing. There are beaches all over the world. I hear Mogadishu has a great one."

He said, "Hmm."

"We're in different places in our lives right now, Mike. In two years, five months, who knows? Can't we just be happy being happy?"

"I don't know." He reached over and turned off the light, turned his back to me. "I don't know."

In the morning, early, Mike took me up to the hills above the Griffith Park zoo for a run. Mike has both greater speed and better endurance than I have. I run to keep everything from falling apart, he runs as a challenge, always pushing his limits. I should have known better than to stand my five miles three times a week up against his eleven miles a day, even for an easy Sunday morning outing.

For my benefit, Mike set us on a nice, slow pace. At first, it was fun. There was a dense, gray marine layer overhead that kept us cool. We ran through a rugged canyon filled with dusty scrub, withered sycamore trees, and poison oak flaming red and orange to mark the coming of fall. Now and then, little brown squirrels or packs of stray cats would dart across the pavement in front of us.

For such an out-of-the-way spot, there was unusually heavy vehicle traffic—the canyon is a major pick-up spot for gay men—so we had to hug the roadside. All the way up, the sides of the narrow, two-lane road were lined with parked cars, young men hoping to make a connection. Some got out to pose on the hoods of their cars, others sunbathed in bikinis in the pull-outs—like statues in a wooded garden.

Most stayed inside their cars and made eye contact with the men slowly cruising by. No one gave Mike or me more than a nod. Not that Mike would have seen a nod; his eyes never left the center line.

I enjoyed the run for a while, but the operative word for the course he set was *up*. The slope was steep, and it was all up-hill. After the first few miles, I was straining to keep up, he was straining to hold back. As long as I could, I tried to cover the effort it took to hang in. But by the time we came out on top, I was breathing hard and the long muscles in my thighs were beginning to cramp.

Mike slowed, ostensibly to admire the magnificent view of the city laid out below us. "Beautiful, huh?"

I managed to nod; my chest burned.

Mike was breathing easily, running like a machine. He said, laughing, "There are three million stories in the big city. Rape, murder, mayhem. But I'm off, so let them go to it."

When we hit the down slope, another set of muscles took over so I wasn't in as much pain. After a while, I began to get my wind back. Just when I thought I would be able to make it back to the lot where we had left the car, he said, "Want to do some sprints?"

I knew he knew how tired I was. I managed to say, "Go ahead."

Grinning, teasing, he said, "You can do it."

"Beast," I gasped, and dropped back to a walk. He ran in big circles around me until I thought I would have to shoot him. Finally, wounded ego overcame pain, and I began to run again.

As soon as we left the path along the hill crest, we dropped down into heavy shade, and the air felt sweeter, moister. It was blessedly peaceful. There were small animals and birds. I saw occasional lover-pairs walking off together deeper into the undergrowth, for privacy. Now and then a mountain cyclist came by.

Mike said, "Ever see a better place to run?"

I said, "No ocean view." And that ended the conversation. All in all, it had been a punishing run.

Mike needed to put in a painting shift at the house, and I thought maybe we both needed some time off from each other. I made other plans.

Ralph Faust wanted my answer, now, about whether or not I would appear with Baron Marovich that afternoon. For a number of good reasons, I didn't want to do it. Certainly, I wanted to talk with the D.A., but I preferred a little private one-on-one with him, hash things out with no audience to pander to. With the fire at Kelsey's and being tailed by George Schwartz as recent history, I had to think carefully about where that private meeting would take place.

I made one call, to Hector, before I called Marovich and told him where I would be if he wanted to talk.

I folded a load of clothes, put a new load in the washer, did a few other chores to give Hector some time. When I pulled into the lot at the LAPD Hollywood Division an hour later, he was waiting for me on the covered ramp that leads into the back of the old brick station house. He walked down to meet me.

"Thanks for coming," I said.

He chuckled. "It was either meet you or work on the sprinkler system with Mike's dad. Believe me, you're a whole lot better company than Oscar."

"I won't tell Oscar you said that," I said. "The message you left yesterday, you said you had some reports for me?"

He opened the back door. "I'm not sure what you're looking for. Be a whole lot easier for me if I did."

"Be easier if I knew, too."

We walked down a long, narrow hallway lined with framed, autographed movie posters—this was Hollywood Division.

Generally, the detective room looked like every other detective room I had seen: overcrowded with mismatched, scarred desks and chairs, ranks of no-color file cabinets, boxes and stacks of papers on every available surface.

Two things gave the big, open room some character. The first was the movie/TV presence in the form of signed cheesecake black and white glossies taped on nearly every desk and cabinet. The second was the big wooden, hand-carved, somebody's-father-in-law-got-a-router-for-Christmas signs suspended by chains over each section. Very rustic. I wondered what old Dad must have thought as he carved "Rape," "Robbery," "Homicide" for the boys and girls down at the office.

Hector's desk was in a back corner under the homicide sign. He pulled up a chair for me, cleared a space on his blotter, and opened a thin file. He handed me five computer print-out sheets, each with a line or two of type.

He said, "AFIS reports from the prints Mike lifted in your office. Tell you anything?"

"Plenty." The computer had identified Ralph Faust, Jennifer Miller, Eusebio Kino, who was the building's night janitor, Guido Patrini, and an unknown as sometime visitors of mine. I pulled out Jennifer's print-out. "Mike lifted the prints Wednesday. As far as I know, the only time Jennifer Miller was in my office was Friday night."

"Interesting." Hector set her print-out aside. "I can't do anything about it. I can't bring Miller in if this is all I have. I can't even show for a certainty there was a break in."

"I wish you could bring her in," I said. "But not for jimmying my lock. Has anyone spoken to Jennifer since last night?"

"No. Friday morning, she asked her ex to take their little boy for the weekend—said she had to work through. Security at her office building signed her in at eleven Friday night, signed her out twenty minutes later. The guard at your building ID'ed her as the woman who dropped off an envelope for you at midnight. From there, cold trail. She's scheduled to pick up the kid around six tonight. If she doesn't show . . . Well, I guess that will tell us something. Kelsey hasn't been located, either."

"Any word on the corpse in the fire?"

He shook his head. "Nada. It takes time."

I caught myself before I let loose with something sarcastic. What I really wanted was a TV detective with sixty minutes, minus commercials, to bring everything together. The real-world delays were aggravating in the extreme. I said, "Show me what else you found."

"Property dispo card," he said, pulling out a photocopied evidence log. "You wanted me to dig out the prints from the John-son murder scene and run them through the system."

"Right." I pulled my chair closer.

"There are no prints anymore. All of the hard evidence was tossed out years ago."

"Say it ain't so," I said.

He smiled. "Think about it. We don't have room to store all the crap from every case forever. Every six months to a year, the property room does a routine audit and asks the detective in charge of a case what he wants to do with his evidence. Look at the card: Fingerprints, shoe prints, some clothes—all consigned to the incinerator." He ran his finger down a column. "See, property disposed per whoever's signature that is, that badge number, that date."

I said, "Jerry Kelsey's badge number, the date is the same as Conklin's sentencing date. Jerry sure was in a hurry to clean house, wasn't he? Could he do that?"

"Absolutely. The assigned detective is the one responsible for the evidence. It was stupid to act so fast, though. Kelsey's lucky there was no appeal on the conviction."

I looked up at Hector. "I believe people make their own luck."

"Yeah?" He laughed softly. "Guess I do, too."

"There are no spent shells listed in the log."

"Don't see any."

"Inside a tiny room, Johnson took six slugs at point-blank range. No slugs recovered from the body. No shells found. Where are they?"

"Who knows?" He said this with a worldly sort of disdain. "Souvenir hunters, maybe. Maybe the killer picked them up, or whoever cleaned up after swept them out. Bigger things than shells get overlooked all the time."

"Oh," I said. "Have anything else for me?"

"Not really. Mike had questions about a couple of the vehi-cles at the Hanna Rhodes scene. But I think I've cleared them all. I talked to Mike yesterday. Want to go over them?"

As I leaned over the list, Hector suddenly slid it back into the file and quickly slid the file into his top desk drawer, locked the drawer. Eyes down, he muttered, "Your man's here."

Baron Marovich was wending his way toward us through the

ranks of desks. Wearing soiled tennis garb, and looking wary, he said, "Good morning."

"Thanks for coming," I said. "You know Detective Melendez, I'm sure."

Hector offered his hand, "Mr. District Attorney."

Marovich was only marginally courteous in this exchange. He said, "I should have recognized the address you gave me, Mac-Gowen. What are you doing in a police station?"

"It seemed like neutral territory," I said.

"Hardly neutral," he said. "Can we go somewhere else?"

I said, "No. I feel safe here. If you would be more comfortable in an interrogation room with a tape running, maybe Detective Melendez can set it up."

Marovich seemed stretched, pushed near the point of ignition. "Give me a break. Let you have a tape? Use it for fucking voice-over material. Just tell me, what's the score here? Are you coming with me to SNN? You going to play fair for once?"

I left some space for the air to settle. He had been noisy enough to attract the attention of a couple of plainclothes officers who were walking through. In a low voice, I said, "I think it's time for the two of us to talk, alone. Plain talk, no campaign manager, no video camera."

"That's unresponsive."

"Off the record talk," I said.

Marovich turned to Hector. "Can we get some coffee?"

Hector looked at me, I shrugged. He walked over about three desks, crossed his arms, watched us from that remove.

Marovich turned his simmering wrath on me. "So, talk."

"Just tell me," I said, "how someone as smart as you got into such a stupid mess."

That got his back up. "I wasn't aware that I was in a mess."

"Have you seen the polls? Have you seen your opponent's new commercials? 'Why does D.A. Marovich want to put a convicted killer back in your neighborhood?' "

He sighed and sort of caved in on himself. He dropped into Hector's chair.

"I need to know how Charles Conklin came to your attention," I said.

"You know the answer to that. I had a meeting with Leroy Burgess."

"You wouldn't give a con man like Leroy Burgess the time of day."

"He was channeled by my staff."

"Office staff? Or campaign staff?"

He scowled. "Does it matter?"

"It matters very much," I said. "Of course, sometimes it's hard to tell one from the other. Couple of days ago, Mike Flint filed a claim against George Schwartz's insurance. Know what he found out? The car belongs to George's current employer, the Committee to Reelect Baron Marovich. Isn't it fraud to accept employment when you're out on disability? Knowing Schwartz's status, doesn't that make you party to fraud?"

"Fuck," was the answer.

"Let me tell you how I think this scenario unfolded. If I'm wrong, you correct me." I sat on the edge of Hector's desk. "You hired an old pro to run your campaign. Roddy O'Leary did his usual precampaign study: Who are the voters and what gets their attention? Sixty percent minority population, eighty percent minority anger with the police. Roddy went out looking for an attention-getter and he found Conklin for you. White cops, black suspect—it looked like a natural way to plug into the voter's *angst*, get a load of votes on the cheap. Then Roddy went out and did his worst—on your behalf—stirred up the community."

"Bull," he snapped. He swiveled his chair away from me, but he stayed in the chair when I half-expected him to walk out.

I said, "All you had to do was get a judge to agree that there had been improprieties in the original case. Procedural policies change—what case doesn't have improprieties when you look at it years later? Get a wrongfully convicted man released, you become a hero to eighty percent of the sixty-percent community. Another advantage to using an old case was, the judge probably wouldn't be too picky. Conklin had already served a longer term than most murderers get anymore."

I was talking to the side of his head again. "For insurance, you found a case involving the murder of a cop, because cops usually go after cop killers like bull dogs after red meat, and to hell with the niceties of due process, to quote a friend. Because of that, you assumed police excess. Or Roddy did."

He turned his chair back around. "You can't deny there was excessive use of authority."

"You can't prove it," I said. "Not with the affidavits I read."

"I have the departmental files on Kelsey and Flint. They both have excessive force complaints on their records."

"So what? You told me that Conklin's previous record was not germane to the issue of a fair trial. The same principle holds for Kelsey and Flint, does it not?"

"Police are held to a different standard."

"As they should be. But saying that doesn't change the facts: Your research was lazy. This was not a typical cop killing, and you should have known it. There was a good investigation, but no dogs-and-posse manhunt for the killer of Wyatt Johnson. No revenge slugfest. And no traditional twenty-one-gun police send-off. You know why?"

He cocked his head to one side, narrowed his eyes at me.

"Because the department and the family didn't want the attention," I said. "According to his wife, he was out selling vitamins. You're a man of the world. Tell me about the kind of vitamins sold in ghetto men's rooms after midnight. Then again, maybe he lied to his wife about why he had to be out at night—wouldn't be a first."

Marovich seemed to pale. "You miss the issue."

"You want me to go on TV with you? You want to match files? You bring Kelsey and Flint and I'll bring Conklin." I looked at Hector, who was listening, trying to keep a poker face through all of this. "I have a nice montage made from the Monday news broadcasts. I'll bring that, too. Front shot of Parker Center, angry mob, D.A. nodding while some lunatic says it's time to go back to the streets to give the police a message."

Marovich said, "That's not the way it was."

"That's the way it looks. There was a second demonstration down on Florence and Normandie—the old riot flash point. You're the legal expert, but what you've done, using Conklin to stir up the public, looks to me a whole lot like conspiracy, inciting to riot."

"I'm not clear," Marovich said. "What is it you want?"

"Not much," I said. "I'm offering you a shot at redemption. And I want an hour with Charles Conklin."

That bomb cleared the air: both Hector and Marovich laughed.

When he got his breath back, Marovich said, "Go right

ahead. But first, you have to find his attorney, then you have to
get her approval. I can't help you."

"I thought you had some influence with your old law partners. Guess I was wrong."

"Guess so." He rose as if to leave. "We'll discuss it this afternoon." He glared at Hector. "In public."

I stopped him by saying, "I've already called Ralph. I won't
do a taping with you."

"I don't get it."

"We both have too much to lose. I've been watching your
wheels turn. I know that by air time you'd have a point-by-
point rebuttal ready to demolish me. Then I would have to take
you down with me, so what would be the point?"

He gave me an evil leer. "The exercise might be fun."

Hector threw back his head and laughed again.

I turned to Hector. "Weren't you looking for some coffee?"

"There's a pot right over there," Hector said. "Help yourself."

Marovich said, "You offered me a shot at redemption. What
did you mean?"

"If Jennifer doesn't show up by tomorrow, Conklin's hearing
will be postponed until he finds new counsel. Could take—
when's the election?—six weeks to bring new counsel up to
speed. By then, to borrow from Ralph, Conklin will be a cold
story. Six weeks gives you some breathing room."

He was shaking his head as I spoke.

"One question," I said. "Is your old law firm giving you a flat
campaign contribution or are they tying the amount to their
take in Conklin's civil suit?"

"That's slander."

"So, sue me. Roddy has already threatened to. It's only slander if what I said was false. I don't have to remind you that
campaign contributions are a matter of public record."

"Do you remember the question?"

"Yes. Save yourself. Go on the air and confess, shed some
Jimmy Swaggart tears. Apologize to the people you hurt, show
the voters how your innate compassion made you want to believe a man's sad tale, left you vulnerable. Do that, and I'll help
you out."

"Help me?"

"I've made a little film, *Anatomy of a Lie*. And you're not the
star."

CHAPTER

28

"I only stopped by for some tapes Jack Riley left for me," I said. My arms were full. I was trying to effect an escape from Lana Howard's office without either a major spill or a commitment to a long-term employment contract. I didn't have a hand for the door, and she wasn't about to open it.

"Think about it, Maggie," she said, whispered tones—a churchlike hush. "Office space, the best facilities, regular paycheck. Use of the letterhead."

"I like what I'm doing, Lana. I have to admit that the money is a temptation, but a regular paycheck can be tighter than a noose."

"I understand that. I understand how important it is for you to maintain control over your projects. But we both know that big world out there can get pretty cold. A regular paycheck can make a damn fine blanket." She sauntered over to the burlwood cabinet that held her wet bar; the office was opulent. She took out a pitcher of fresh-squeezed orange juice and poured two glasses—two sparkly clean glasses—offered one to me. "What would it take to bring you in from the cold?"

I set down the tapes on a corner of her leather sofa to accept the juice. She was watching me, slow smile growing. I respected Lana, respected her judgment. All through this brouhaha I was involved in, she had shown me the best qualities I would want in a boss: flexibility and daring. It wouldn't be hard to work with her on a regular basis.

A network job? I ran through the lists of pros and cons, but the heading over both sides ran something like, "You've already spent your advance check twice over, Casey's tuition is due the fifteenth of every month and the money you're being offered is obscene."

Lana reached for my empty glass. "Maggie?"

"This is what it would take: I sign with you for two years, five months. Two two-hour projects a year on assignment, six short-subjects on topics of my choosing. I have full editorial control. If the network chooses, for whatever reason, not to air any of my projects as-is, the project reverts to me so I can sell it elsewhere. Beyond that, I want the network to rent and furnish my home office space for my use, and I want Guido Patrini hired as a consultant."

Lana wrapped me in a big, blanket-like hug. "You're going to like it here, Maggie."

"That's it?"

"I have to run it by the board, but I think we'll come to terms. Welcome aboard."

All I could think to say, was, "Damn."

I gathered the tapes again and went upstairs where Guido was working with a staff editor.

"You're not going to believe what I just did," I said.

"That's highly likely." He was watching the time on a piece of LaShonda's interview. "What now?"

"I got myself hired as a network slave."

He jumped as if startled. "Say it ain't so."

"Got you a slot as a consultant."

"I have a job," he said, pausing the tape, turning to face me. "It seems to me it wasn't so long ago we both burned out in a place that looks and smells a whole lot like this one."

"Independent projects only," I said. "And they'll let you use the letterhead. That should help your love life."

When he glanced at LaShonda's face on the screen, his features went all mushy. "My love life's just fine, thank you."

I said, "You slut."

"Mike called," he said. "Thanks for reminding me."

Guido didn't know where Mike was, so I dialed his pager and left the number of the phone on the console beside me. Mike took almost a minute to call back.

"Etta's been trying to reach you," Mike said. "Said she'll be home all afternoon."

"I'll go by and see her," I said.

"Want company?"

"Always."

"Thought maybe it was time to take a closer look at what it is you do."

I felt suddenly all mushy inside, myself. "I'll meet you at the new house in fifteen, twenty minutes."

I gave Guido a lot of instructions and a big kiss, and ran out to the parking lot.

The South Pasadena house was getting new trim paint, including the front door. I walked through a maze of scaffolding and ladders to get inside where the dog, lying on his belly in the foyer, watched the ceiling painters. Old Bowse's big brush of a tail was tipped in a combination of Desert Sunset, the color of the door, and Peaches and Cream, the color of the walls.

I grabbed Bowser by the collar and asked the painters above me, "Anyone seen Mike?"

In unison, "Backyard."

I led the dog out and closed the doors behind me.

Mike and Michael were carrying an unfamiliar oak dresser along the walkway between the drive and the cottage. There was a U-Haul truck parked in the drive. With Bowser at my side, I walked across the lawn toward them.

"What's this?" I asked, pushing in a dresser drawer that had fallen out.

"I'm moving in," Michael said. "Go inside, take a look."

"Yeah." Mike was grinning like he was up to something. "Go take a look."

Too nosy to listen to warning voices, I went inside. I don't know exactly what I expected, hard rock posters maybe, or nudes on the walls. The cottage looked great, rug on the polished wood floor, desk and bookcases to match the dresser, a couple of chairs. And a very attractive woman around my age smoothing a new-looking spread on the bed.

"Hello," I said, grabbing Bowser's collar before he could give her his customary muzzle-in-the-crotch greeting.

She stood up, smiled while she gave me close inspection. "Maggie?"

I had to move further into the room so that Mike and Michael could wrestle the dresser through the door. They set it against a side wall and Mike, wiping his face, came up beside me.

"Maggie," he said. "Meet Leslie. Michael's mom."

She offered her hand, smiling broadly. "I've heard a lot about you. And about Casey."

Michael laughed. "Don't worry. I only tell Mom the good stuff."

"That's a relief," I said. It was so strange to look into this woman's face; echoes of Michael's face. I felt neither awkward nor competitive, as I had when Charlene showed up on my doorstep. Only curious. Leslie was, in several ways—in height and build, and in general manner—a darker version of me.

I said, "The cottage looks wonderful, Michael. After spending a week on the couch, the privacy should be a relief."

He looked around at his new quarters. "I don't know. I got used to the company."

"Couches," Mike said, as if some switch had been hit. "The dealer Charlene works for has made an offer on all the condo furniture. Anybody want any of it?"

Michael said, "I don't have room for anything else."

I said, "No," trying to make it sound like a casual no and not a thank God, get that gray shit out of my life no. I had already spoken to my old tenant, Lyle, about taking my furniture out of storage and sending it down.

"Les?" Mike said. "You have an empty room now. Want anything?"

She snickered. "Think about it, Mike." Then she turned to Michael and draped an arm over his shoulders. "What's left in the truck?"

"The dresser was the last of it."

"Then, let's go get your car, turn in the truck."

"Where are you sleeping tonight?" Mike asked Michael.

"Thought I'd have a farewell run on the couch." Michael gave his dad a hug, then, to my delight and surprise, came over and hugged me, too. "I'll be home after dinner."

Arm in arm, Mike and I walked out to see off Michael and his mother. As the truck backed into the alley, I said, "I like her."

"So do I." The way Mike said it didn't bother me at all.

On the way down to Southeast, we stopped at a mall and bought Etta some gift certificates at a department store she had mentioned fancying. Welfare recipients are supposed to report any windfall they receive. I wanted to give her some share in my own windfall, but in a way that wouldn't get her into a hassle with the county. Gift certificates was the best I could come up with.

"You mean they're going to pay our rent?" Mike asked, scowling his disbelief as I explained Lana's offer.

"A big part of it. You can start socking away more of your salary for retirement."

His sly glance was a tip-off. "So, you do plan to stay put for a while. Every time I go home, I check the closet to make sure your stuff's still there."

"You do not."

He didn't seem very happy, so I didn't press him.

It was about one when we got to Etta's. There didn't seem to be anyone home. I wrote a note telling her where she could reach me at four, and was tucking it into her screen door when I heard her call out.

"Look at who's here." Etta, dressed as for church in a flowered sheath dress, tottered toward us on her high heels. She had a beer can in one manicured hand. "Girl, I been tryin' to get ahold of you for two days."

"What's up?" I asked. But she turned her attention to Mike.

"Won't you give this lady some sugar, Sugar?" She pressed her impressive bosom against Mike. "Been such a long, long time."

"You look nice, Etta," I said, asserting my presence. "Where's the party?"

She preened. "Party's at Miz Rhodes' house. Had the memorial for Hanna this morning after church, asked some of her closest friends to come by for a little lunch. That's where I was when I saw you knockin' at my door."

"Is that what you called about?" I asked.

"No. I wanted to tell you I don't care no more if that motherfuckin' Pinkie gets out the jail or not. Tyrone copped him a plea. He's goin' to jail his own damn self so I don't have to worry after him no more. He don't need no father where he's goin'. And he damn sure don't need no Pinkie, neither."

"What did he draw?" Mike asked.

"Much as he could. He's goin' to the Youth Authority till he's twenty-five." Etta finished her beer. "Hope he uses that time to turn himself around, finish school maybe."

"I hope so," I said, though I couldn't imagine how growing to manhood in that hole could change the course he had set for his life.

Etta crumpled the empty can. "Don't stand out here. Come on in and pay your respects to Miz Rhodes, get yourself a little refreshment."

"I've been trying to reach Mrs. Rhodes. I want to talk to her about Hanna," I said. "But maybe this isn't the time."

"No time better. I told her all about you."

I took a camera from the back of the car, loaded it with a new tape and a battery fresh from the recharger, and passed it to Mike. "Best way to get a closer look at what I do is to look through the lens. Just remember that the camera has a slower eye than you do. If you make abrupt movements, you get blur."

"That's it?" he said, fiddling with the buttons.

"We'll work on the fine points later." I caught up with Etta.

Outside the Rhodes apartment there were a few guests sitting on folding chairs, holding paper plates heaped with food. They nodded to us, made low remarks to Etta that I didn't catch and she ignored.

The living room held maybe fifteen more people, about half that number again in the kitchen and dining alcove. Etta parted the crowd and led us through.

"Miz Rhodes," she said in mournful tones. "Look who's come to pay respects."

Mrs. Rhodes was a small, attractive woman wearing a simple black dress. She looked young to be mourning a granddaughter.

I started to say something like how sorry I was for her loss when she set upon Mike.

"Why, officer," she said, her voice rising in pitch at the end. "You was such a nice lookin' young man. How'd you get so old?"

"Hello, Mrs. Rhodes." Mike combed his fingers through his white hair. "It's been a while, hasn't it?"

"Not that long. What happened to you?"

He blushed. "Guess it's my line of work."

There was general polite laughter. Mike shook a few hands

that were offered, exchanged greetings with old acquaintances, let himself be led to the buffet table.

Mrs. Rhodes took me aside. "Etta says you were asking about my Hanna. What was it you wanted to know?"

"About what she saw the night Officer Wyatt was shot."

"Lot of people been asking me about that. Hanna was living with her mama back then, so I don't know anything about it except what people talked about later. I don't think you can trust in the truth of a story once it gets told over and over so many times. Do you?"

"Not usually," I said. "Who has been asking you about Hanna?"

"Well, the police, of course. Someone came, said she was with the district attorney. Little tiny girl. I couldn't figure her as a district attorney."

"Was it Jennifer Miller?" I asked.

"Something like that. There was someone else from the district attorney, wanted to look through Hanna's room, but Hanna didn't have a room here. Then the other officer—not Officer Flint—he came by, too. What's his name? I'm not thinking very clearly today."

"Officer Kelsey?"

"Could be." She nodded. "And some people came, said they were from the newspapers or the TV. Etta says you're from the TV."

"In a way. I know it's a bad time to ask you for anything. But Hanna is one of the subjects in the film I'm working on. If you have any pictures of her, I'd like very much to see them. Maybe old school pictures, something more recent."

"Mm hmm." She puffed out her bottom lip, furrowed her brow and studied me. "Why?"

"I want Hanna to be more than a corpse on someone's front steps. She was someone's little girl once. I want people to know that."

Mrs. Rhodes nodded while I spoke. "I lost all I had in a fire some years ago; that's when I moved out to California to be near my daughter. But maybe there is something. Hanna left a little box of things with me when she went to prison. I don't know what's in it; private things, you know. I was going to look at it later, but you might as well see, too. It's in the closet in the other room."

I walked with her down a short inner hallway to her immaculate bedroom. The double-size bed was covered with handbags and hats, a few wraps—just like parties at my parents' house.

Mrs. Rhodes reached up to the shelf of her small wardrobe and took down a carton that was about a foot square. She cleared a space on the bed so we could sit with the carton between us.

"When Hanna's mama died, Hanna started using my address, but she never really lived here except for a day or two off and on." She pulled off the brittle old masking tape that sealed the carton and pried up the flaps. "I had rules, you see, about the way a young lady should behave in my home. Hanna preferred the streets to my rules."

Mrs. Rhodes lifted out a folded Girl Scout scarf and a few faded construction paper folders that looked like school projects. There was a blonde Barbie doll with matted hair and a few of her outfits, all of them frayed with use. And mementos: a pencil from Disneyland, some seashells, several movie ticket stubs, a candy cane reindeer with pipe-cleaner antlers, a matchbook from a Sizzler, a ceramic box with "Be My Valentine" painted on the chipped lid.

Mrs. Rhodes said, "When something special happens to a young girl, she likes to keep a souvenir of it."

I found the small store of treasures to be very sad. Was this as special as it ever got for Hanna?

Cheap costume jewelry filled a coffee can. While Mrs. Rhodes sorted through what looked like report cards, I went through the coffee can. Plastic baubles, adjustable rings with colored glass jewels, dangly earrings all tangled together. I pulled them out in a mass, dragging out with them a long bead-chain, and started to separate them to keep my hands busy.

"Here are some school pictures." Mrs. Rhodes laid out a handful of wallet-size portraits. "Hanna must have traded with her friends; I don't know who most of these children are. This one's Hanna. I would say maybe third or fourth grade."

Hanna had a long, heart-shaped face, still a few front teeth missing in her cocky smile. Her hair was done in an asymmetrical Afro. I said, "Very cute."

"Yes, she was." Mrs. Rhodes had no tears. "She was a pretty

little child. Not an exceptional child in any way, except to her mother and me. But she was pretty. Wild and pretty."

"May I borrow the picture?"

"If you like."

"And this?" I held up the disentangled bead-chain. There were five spent .38 shells, pierced and hanging on the chain like charms. The shells were stained with brown, as if rolled or dropped in a pan of paint. I could see fragments of fingerprints.

Mrs. Rhodes fingered the shells. "What is that?"

"A little souvenir, I think. Something special did happen to Hanna."

CHAPTER

29

"I had it all wrong," I said. While Mike put away the camera in the back of the car, I held the brownie he had carried away from Mrs. Rhodes's buffet table. "I listen to your rowdy stories and I have to remind myself they're ninety-two percent pure bull. Now and then I forget to do the math, so I get suckered right into believing them as told."

"What are you talking about?" He took back his brownie. "You saying I'm a liar?"

"Yes. And I'm saying I'm deeply chagrined for entertaining for even a moment any notion that you might have abused LaShonda and Hanna. I walked you into that house wishing we had stopped to get your body armor, because the way you talk about what you used to do in the good old days—kicking butt and taking names later—I'm thinking it might get real ugly when these people set eyes upon you. But it was like a neighborhood reunion in there, Sugar."

"You should have been chagrined, Miss Berkeley-has-a-big-dictionary. Hell, I know all their kids. Arrested most of them. We're family."

"Exactly my point." I jabbed him with a finger. "Maybe you arrested eight percent of their kids. For jaywalking or something. The rest? Ninety-two percent pure bull. Some tough guy you are, Flint. You swagger in and swap brownie recipes."

He laughed and I got a chocolatey peck on the lips before he unlocked my car door for me and opened it. As I climbed in, the string of bullet shells dangling from my neck tinkled like a wind chime. I pulled up the chain and looked at the shells again, being careful not to touch any of the brown stain I was certain would prove to be the blood of Wyatt Johnson.

"You know you can't keep those," Mike said, closing his door behind him.

"I know." I let the chain fall back against my chest. LaShonda had run right away in a panic, but Hanna had stayed behind, and not hidden in some old car, either. Not until later. It took a fairly cool head to scramble over and around the bleeding, dying body of Wyatt Johnson to collect her souvenirs—like collecting seashells.

The coroner thought it had taken Wyatt Johnson a minute or two to expire; long enough to pump out a lot of blood. Had Wyatt spoken to Hanna? Had he explained how powerful those spent shells could be—a ticket to the gas chamber if they could be tied to the shooter's firearm? She was street-wise. Had she figured the angle all by herself? The big question on my mind was, who had she told? Who had known she had to be silenced?

"You're quiet," Mike said.

"I was wrong about something else."

"Two admissions in one day? Unbelievable. Did you and Mrs. Rhodes smoke something funny in that back bedroom?"

"I had persuaded myself that there had to be a second person in the restroom with Wyatt Johnson."

"There was." He chewed the last of his brownie. "You've got the proof of that hanging around your neck. Hanna went in there."

"Before that. Bart Conklin told me how his brother used to hang around waiting for someone to commit a robbery, then he'd go in and rob the robber. Because of the missing shells and the way the body was lying, I thought someone must have been in the restroom with Wyatt. I thought maybe Conklin had interrupted Wyatt making a deal with someone, and ripped them off. Or tried to. And that the girls didn't see the third man because they ran off. But Hanna would have seen him. Nosy little thing, she hung around."

"I keep telling you, Wyatt was just taking a leak. It's that simple." Crumbs in his mustache eroded his air of authority. "Trust me, this is how it went down: Conklin sees Wyatt drive up in a nice car, and because he's an asshole, he wants it. He follows Wyatt into the can, tries to hold him up. It goes wrong, Wyatt gets shot, Conklin runs the hell away. Period. He didn't even know he'd killed a cop until he heard it on the street later."

I must not have looked like a buyer. Mike sighed heavily as he turned from me to start the car. "I know you want something bigger, Maggie. But that's all it was. Just a crappy heist that went wrong."

I said, "But," before I accepted the futility of arguing a point I was not clear on.

Mike turned onto Ninety-second Street. "Now that you've seen the new color on the walls, how do you like it?"

I said, "I wanted Kelsey to be there somehow."

"That night? No way. You want a big drug deal, or some undercover scam, or at the very least a loose woman. But you can't make it, baby. Not with Wyatt. Not with Kelsey, either."

"Kelsey looks guilty. There's more to his involvement."

He laughed. "If looks could convict us, we'd all be in the slam. The only thing Kelsey was guilty of back then was drinking on the job. And another thing: You're never going to know any more about what happened that night than you do right now. So, I want you to think about Wyatt's family for a minute. Is it nice to go around suggesting things you can't substantiate? It makes them feel bad, and what does it do for you?"

I slouched down in the seat and watched the scenery for a while. Maybe I would have to accept what he said about Wyatt, but Jerry Kelsey was guilty of a whole lot more than drinking on the job. I just didn't know what. And for sure I was not ready to argue that one with Mike.

It was Sunday afternoon. Every church we passed leaked music. Family groups in their Sunday finest strolled along the streets. Very festive. But all I could see was LaShonda running off in a panic, and Hanna, braver, more street-wise, going in for a better look. Gathered up the bullet shells as her prize, blackmail currency if she got wise enough. Was she hiding herself in that derelict car, secreting her new treasures, or just taking a nap when James Shabazz called her name?

I said, "Mike?"

"Thought you went to sleep."

"Hanna's new affidavit is a fraud."

"I know."

"Someone didn't want her to say so."

"I know."

"That's why she died."

"Uh huh."

"What else do you know?" I asked. But he just smiled, all the way to South Pasadena.

We rejoined the painters at the South Pasadena house. A brother-in-law cum electrician had installed an upgraded electrical service. I spent the better part of an hour with him in my new work space, showing him where I needed outlet strips along the baseboards. I talked him into removing a piece of the hardwood floor so that I could have some recessed outlets in the middle of the big room. Before he got away from me, I also talked him into some strip lighting.

When I had pushed him as far as I dared, I joined the cadre of painters upstairs and worked on windowframes for a few hours.

There were people all around me, but I was left to my own thoughts for the most part. These men had been working together for three solid days. They seemed to have run out of chitchat and had moved on to topics that were more quiet, more serious, more personal. I was something of an outsider. I didn't mind and I didn't want to intrude.

At around five, Mike made a sandwich run. When he came back, everyone gathered under the avocado tree to eat and rest. When I heard Mike's summons, I put the lid on my paint can. But I stayed upstairs after the others had gone down.

Voices from the yard drifted up through the open balcony doors. With their baritone laughter for background music, I pulled out my big bag and sat down with it in the middle of the floor. It took some searching until I found the two documents that had been at the center of my thoughts. I put them side by side on the drop cloth beside me and studied them.

Both statements were short. Hanna's first statement had been dictated to Mike, who handwrote it on a printed interview form. I read it through again.

"Me and LaShonda was back there and we heard the gun, like I say before. We go start to run over where her mama work because we was scared. But we run smack into Pinkie. He was running out of that toilet where he shot the man. Me and LaShonda look at that dead man and we start screaming and then she run right off. I didn't know what to do next. I think Pinkie has another gun and he shoot me, too. But he go jump in that old green car of his and he drive off. I go jump into this old Cadillac is parked there and I climb down in the back and cover up in some old rags and things and I stay there until LaShonda and James call my name and say, 'Get over here.' "

I was having a lot of trouble putting aside my partiality for Mike. I had admitted favoritism from the beginning. Even after factoring that in, for me the handwritten, ungrammatical, uncorrected document had far more credibility than the slick, typed, centered, spell-checked page that Jennifer Miller had sent me. If it was legit, then saying that Hanna had changed her mind surely must be taken literally: The language did not come from Rhodes, Hanna, five-time loser, sixth-grade dropout.

The affidavit began, "I was eleven years of age on November 6, 1979. I have forgotten some of the smaller details of the events which occurred that evening. In sum, however, my memory is very clear.

"I was at the above-named service station with my friend, LaShonda DeBevis. At approximately twelve-fifteen a.m. we heard shots fired. I estimate that five or six shots were fired. We were very frightened so we began to run, seeking safety. As we came from the rear parking area, we encountered a man in dark clothing leaving the service station restroom where the shooting occurred. I saw his face clearly, but I did not recognize him. I knew I had not seen him before, nor have I seen him since. Charles Conklin was known to me at the time. The man who ran from the men's room was not Charles Conklin.

"I identified Charles Conklin only after relentless pressure and threats to do so from Detectives M. Flint and J. Kelsey. They frightened me. When they offered to buy me a new bicycle, I signed their prepared statement."

Dated and signed in the Frontera State Prison for Women. The witnesses were Leroy Burgess and George Schwartz.

I put the papers away and began cleaning my paintbrushes.

"Maggie?" Mike came in with a wrapped sandwich in his hand. "Jennifer Miller just picked up her son."

I exhaled a breath I think I had been holding on to for a couple of days. I didn't know Jennifer Miller very well, and what I knew of her I didn't respect very much. The magnitude of relief

I felt upon hearing this piece of news caught me off guard. I asked, "Can we talk to her?"

"Not yet. They took her in for questioning."

"Where's LaShonda?"

"With Guido," he said. "She's okay."

He furrowed his brow, made the deep crease that reminded me of his dad. "We miss you downstairs."

"I'm sorry," I said, hearing reproach. "I didn't mean to be antisocial."

I took him by the hand and walked down with him. We joined the circle on the lawn, finding a place next to Hector. Mike sat down with his back against the big tree, and I sat with my back against him. The conversation moved from the Dodgers to the department's teams for the Baker-to-Vegas run, always with references to old stories that formed a sort of code for their jokes and their affection for one another. My only contribution was to laugh now and then. I wasn't aware how often I was checking my watch until Mike caught my arm.

"Going somewhere?" he asked.

"Casey's plane comes in at nine," I said.

He turned my arm to look at the watch face. "It isn't even seven. Relax. After the sun sets, then you can start worrying."

Hector said, "The place is shaping up. When you moving in?"

"Tuesday, Wednesday." Mike smiled contentedly as he looked up at the house, the fresh trim paint shining in the sun.

"We'll have you all over for a house-warming next weekend," I said. "Bring your significant others."

With a wicked gleam in his eye, Hector said, "I'm bringing my new girl. Her name's Olga."

"By all means bring her," I said. "I'd like to show her around the kitchen. Show her my new knife sharpener."

Mike put his arms around me and knuckled my shoulder. "What should we put back here? One big table or a couple of smaller ones?"

"How about a pool while we're at it?" I said.

Hector was staring at me, so I turned to him. "Don't you like to swim?"

He seemed to shake himself. "You brought up something this morning with Mr. D.A. Marovich. I was thinking maybe this wasn't the best time to talk about it."

"We're all family," I said.

"I made a few calls." Hector shrugged, as if to say he hadn't made much effort. "Found a guy—you know Phillips, works out of Newton?"

It took a few minutes for everyone to remember Phillips and tell some sort of story about him before Hector could go on.

"So, Phillips says he knows this George Schwartz pretty well. Says he's been a tweeny for Marovich for years, never does shit for the D.A.'s office, only works for the boss himself. Does the dirty work, handles damage control. Phillips hates the guy. He says whenever Schwartz shows up, the case will get nasty, because that's the way Schwartz likes it. Phillips also had a few things to say about Schwartz working for the Marovich campaign and some of the stuff he's been up to for the boss."

I got up and stretched. "Doesn't matter. I don't frankly give a damn about Mr. Baron Marovich and his campaign now that Conklin isn't a usable issue."

"Say what?" Mike frowned at me.

"The judge has to throw out his case."

The moans and guffaws were like a Greek chorus—the one just before the hero leaps off the precipice or cuts his heart out. I appealed to the assembled. "What did I say?"

"Sometimes you democrats don't get the big picture." Mike knuckled my shoulder again, harder this time, and without a smile. "Do you know the judge?"

I felt a clutch inside; I had never thought to look into the judge who had agreed to hear the petition, and that was a big lapse.

"Find out what law firm he came out of," Mike said.

I said, "Oh," because that seemed to cover the territory. I mentioned Jennifer's firm and got a new round of the chorus.

"Judge throws this out now, he'll look like a fool." Mike was the tough guy again. "You need a little refresher course in big city politics? Section One, Subsection A of the city charter says, 'The facts, although interesting, are irrelevant.' Remember that and you'll do okay."

I said, "I thought Subsection A was, 'Anything worth fighting for is worth fighting dirty for.'"

"No." He laughed. "That's Sub B."

"Now that you've explained things to me, I have something to concede," I said. "You ready for it?"

Mike looked up at me, skeptical. "Three in one day is over quota."

"Yeah? Well, I think you were right. From the beginning, it was a simple heist. And I don't mean the shooting of Wyatt Johnson."

CHAPTER
30

Casey's plane was early. I had only been waiting for half an hour when she came down the ramp. I took her carry-on bag from her and put my arm around her narrow waist.

"How was your weekend?" I asked.

"Boring," she said. "What happened here?"

"Not much." Give her time to decompress. "Your new room is ready. Lyle is bringing down your furniture."

"Bringing?" She lit up like Vegas. "He's coming?"

"And . . ." I drew it out, corrupted by Mike. "Stacy and Lisa are riding down with him. They're setting out right after school Thursday and spending the entire weekend."

Casey was happy beyond words. I was delighted to have brought her such good news about her best friends, but I was also thinking that three fourteen-year-old ballerinas would be a houseful, even for a weekend.

Just as I stepped onto the escalator, Casey gripped my arm. "Can they come to school with me Friday?"

"If it's okay with Mischa."

"Wouldn't it be fantastic if they applied? They could live with us all the time."

Fantastic just would not come out of my mouth.

"Except," she said, struggling to pull something out of her backpack, a new sort of light in her eyes, "Dad got me this."

She handed me a slick brochure from a very fine professional ballet company. There was an application attached. Young Dancers Program. In residence. In Houston.

I wanted another shot at enthusiasm for running a dancer's dorm in my home. In South Pasadena.

All I could think to say was, "It's expensive, Casey."

"Dad wants to pay. He says he's been doing a lot of business in Houston. He could see me more often."

Fighting back tears, I put the brochure into my bag. "We'll look into it."

The condo was quiet. Mike and Michael had gone to the movies. Casey took her shower and went straight to bed. I dumped the contents of Casey's suitcase into the washer before I turned on the kitchen television to watch the replay of Ralph's Sunday afternoon interview. It was a rerun; Baron Marovich had stood up Ralph, too. I was deciding between opening a bottle of wine and going to bed when the call came.

"Maggie?" Jennifer Miller sounding fragile. "I'm at Parker Center. Will you come and get me?"

The request hit a wrong chord. Usually people call on friends or family after a police experience. I was neither. "Surely someone in your firm would come if you called."

"Please. I don't trust anyone else. And I really need to talk to you. I'll meet you in the lobby."

I didn't trust her, didn't fall for the tremor in her voice. I simply wanted to know what the next act would be.

Right after I told her I would come, I paged Mike. I didn't know where he was, but his pager went off in the bedroom. I followed the sound, found the pager still attached to the jeans in the pile of dirty clothes he had left next to the hamper. At that moment I decided to buy him a pocket telephone and an answering machine for his car phone.

I needed to go, but I wasn't about to leave Casey in the house alone; I've seen too many movies to fall for that one. I called Guido.

"Do you still have company?" I asked.

"Who wants to know?" He was oddly suspicious.

"I need a babysitter. Do you know a nice couple I might engage?"

"No. I'm a singleton. Will that do?"

I said, "Admirably. It won't be for long—Mike should be home soon."

When he came, Guido gave me only token argument about going out alone. I was headed for police headquarters, I reminded him, what could be safer? He did try to stall me, though. I knew he was hoping Mike would come home so he could tag along with me. Guido needs regular adventure.

Company would have been nice, but I was afraid that Jennifer would skitter away if I didn't come alone. I prepared myself for several contingencies. The belt of my pants didn't fit right when I was ready to go, but I felt up to the challenge.

Downtown Los Angeles becomes a ghost town at night, especially on weekends. Still, there was a sparse crowd on the tight-budget lawn in front of Parker Center. The demonstrators were long gone, their turf taken over by families waiting for their loved ones to make bail after weekend peccadillos.

I parked in a well-lighted passenger-loading zone right on Los Angeles Street, tempting fate and the traffic officers by opting for security over legal details. Jennifer had been watching for me. I had no more than locked the car when she burst out the front doors of the station and came down the wide walkway at a run.

I was back in the car with the motor running when she slipped into the passenger seat. As she reached for her seat belt, I watched a shudder pass over her.

"I hate that place," she said. "Thanks for coming."

"Did they book you?"

Taken aback, she asked, "For what?"

"Arson comes to mind."

"They only asked questions. Can we go?"

"Sure," I said. "Tell me where."

"Hancock Park. Las Palmas and Third." She directed me to head out Wilshire.

"Glad to see you intact," I said. "And with both shoes."

She glanced at her hiking boots and seemed puzzled. The boots fit with her jeans and plaid flannel shirt, the cap pulled low over her short hair. The night was warm for hats and flannel, the day certainly had been.

"Where have you been?" I asked, weaving through light traffic. I saw no one behind me.

"I needed time to think." She sat up and looked around, got her bearings before she slouched back down and closed her eyes. "My parents have a place at the beach. I took a lot of long walks, did a lot of thinking."

"And?"

"I came to some conclusions about what's essential. The bottom line—every line—is this: I have a son to raise. I'll do whatever is best for him in the long haul."

"Which is?"

"You're a mother. What would you do?"

"In your place? Leave town, start over." I thought of Tyrone's words. "Get clean again."

"That sounds easier than it is." She pulled her purse up onto her lap. It was big and soft-sided, full. When she opened it, I put my left hand on my belt, watched her root out a pack of gum, put a stick into her mouth. She wadded the wrapper and dropped it into the open purse. "I have worked so hard to get where I am. Think of yourself, Maggie. Can you imagine abandoning everything you've accomplished and starting over?"

"I've done it before," I said. "I could do it again if I had to. The world is full of possibility. You might surprise yourself, Jennifer."

She took a deep breath, tested a small laugh. "I've had all the surprises I need for a while."

"Am I taking you home?" I asked.

She said, "Yes," while looking out the window and not at me.

I knew her address, on Avenida Mariposa in San Pedro. San Pedro is a long way from Hancock Park, where she was directing me. She told me when to turn off Wilshire. I put on my turn signal, but before I left the lights of Wilshire for some dark side street, I reached over and lifted her purse off her lap, weighed it. It was light, but I threw it into the backseat anyway.

"Why'd you do that?" She seemed nonplussed.

"Too crowded up here. Need a little room to move around." I slowed, watched the street.

"When you came to my office Friday," I said, "I wondered how you managed to find me. I've only been in town a few days. I'm not in the directory. Hell, I'm not even on the building directory yet. So, I went through the short list of people who might have told you: Baron Marovich and Roddy O'Leary knew. So did Ralph Faust.

"When you came in, you mentioned traffic slowing you down. But you didn't say anything about calling around for my address." I smiled at her. "But then, you'd already been to my office. The police lifted your prints on Wednesday."

"Oh damn." She buried her face in her hands.

"You're not very good at skullduggery, counselor. What were you looking for, anyway?"

"Whatever I could find. I had to know what you had and try to figure out why you got so involved."

I was incredulous. "No one told you?"

When she said, "No," she sounded betrayed and angry.

"Someone used you, big time." I was still watching the street, slowing to let cars pass me. "Who?"

"Tell me first. Why do you care if this degenerate gets out of prison or not?"

"I don't care, as long as he stays away from me and mine."

"Then what is it with you?" Finally, some heat from her. "It was all going really well. You fucked it up."

"I could say I'm a newsman. It's my job to expose idiots who will foment a riot to get a few more votes or a big money judgment. But that would be a lie." I slowed when she pointed to the Third Street sign, signaled my turn. "The truth is this: Every morning when I wake up, the face I see on the other side of my pillow belongs to Mike Flint."

She spat, "Shit," as she hunkered down in her seat, turning away from me.

"I gave you all the clues, counselor. You should have figured it out. Someone should have told you; Marovich knows."

I turned right on Third. The open, dark expanse of the Wilshire Country Club golf course was ahead on the left. "Is anyone home at your house?"

"No. My son is with his dad. Turn there, on Hudson."

As I made the left onto Hudson, I leaned forward enough to slide Mike's little .38 with the filed-off hammer all the way out of my waistband without her seeing it. I held it down in the space between the seat and the door, with the hammer cocked. Jennifer I could deal with—a good elbow shot would take out a creampuff like her. I was more concerned about outsiders.

"There," she said, pointing to a gated estate that backed on the fairway. The houses around it were enormous; not the sort of neighborhood where people walked around or hung out behind screen doors. Mature trees interfered with the streetlights. Overall, dark and deserted.

I pulled to the curb but crept along ten or so yards beyond the gate she had pointed out, moving so slowly my speedometer didn't register.

"Back there," she said. "You went too far."

I was watching both the windshield and the rearview mirror, checking out the sides. "You can walk from here."

You know about curiosity and the fate of the cat? When I told my mother, years ago, that I was abandoning my degree in philosophy to go into the news, she thought it was a natural move.

"Go poke around someone else's closets," she had said. "Get paid for it."

That's why I didn't push open Jennifer's door on the move, roll her out onto the pavement, and drive on. I had to know who was there waiting for us, whose patsy Jennifer was.

He came from behind, out of the landscaping like a dark current in the shadows, stayed low as he moved around to my side of the barely rolling car. I heard the snick of the latch on my car door, felt the first sliver of night air as he opened the door.

My right foot hit the brake as my left hit the door, ripping it from his grip. I saw the shiny muzzle of the gun he held in firing position, used the instant of his confusion to bring up my .38 and aim it, using that shine as my target. My aim was low—the bullet ripped through his Adam's apple and threw him backward. Made him bounce on the black asphalt.

All around, porch lights snapped on. With my little gun held ready for a back-up shot, I screamed, "Call the police."

Jennifer was fast. She was out her door and running before the man stopped twitching and gurgling.

"Freeze, Jennifer," I said, but not too loud. Just in case she wanted to do the rabbit-in-the-rifle-sights routine, I was ready to oblige. She stopped, collapsed into a heap, and began to weep. That's when I really wanted to take her out.

It was a *good* neighborhood. I heard sirens within twenty seconds. When the first black and white rumbled up the street, Mike's little revolver was on the car seat and I was six feet away from it, standing over Jennifer.

Roddy O'Leary still held his Luger in a death grip.

CHAPTER
31

"I picked the lock." The only good part about what had happened was where it happened: within the jurisdiction of Hollywood Division. When the police took me in for questioning, I told them I needed Detective Hector Melendez, now. He sat on the near end of the table in the interrogation room during my grilling.

"The .38 was in a locked case in the closet," I said. "Because there had already been two deaths related to this mess, I was afraid to go out, alone, unarmed. I picked the lock on Mike's gun case and took his gun. He wasn't home and he knew nothing about it."

The hardnose, Detective Valenti, had one leg up on a chair, rested his arm across his knee showing a lot of starched shirt cuff. I thought he was posturing for my benefit. So did Hector. When no one could see him, Hec would roll his eyes or wink at me, as if we were co-conspirators. I could have kissed him.

"Do you realize," Valenti said, "that the weapon was not to code?"

I had answered the same question three times. I looked Valenti in the eye and said, "All I know is, it fit in my belt and it kept me from getting my face blown off."

Hector stood up then, took a step to put himself between me and Valenti. "It's a straight case of self-defense. Let the lady go home, get some rest. If you think of any more stupid questions, you can call her tomorrow."

Valenti started to get his back up, but when Hector faced him down, he shrugged it off. "Go on home," he said. "We'll be in touch."

Mike was waiting for us in the detective room. He had his feet on Hector's desk, snoring into his chest. I knocked his leg, caught it in mid-air as he startled awake.

"Take me home, sailor," I said, letting his leg drop.

"Why didn't you wait for me?" was all he said.

"And get you into more trouble? Put your pension at risk? No, big guy. I thought it better to sacrifice myself."

He got rid of a lot of saved-up air.

"Take me home," I said, feeling so weary I was weepy.

I walked down the hall of movie posters between Mike and Hector, fighting the urge to give in to the shakes that had threatened to seize me ever since the shooting. Maybe I would have let go if Baron Marovich hadn't come in the back door just then, walking between his own pair of police escorts. He blanched when he saw me and his reaction brought me up straight, made me angry.

"Look, Baron," I said, doing one of Casey's pirouettes for his benefit. "Two arms, two legs, all her faculties intact—you big dumb fuck."

The D.A.'s escorts both took an arm, held him back when he seemed ready to charge at me. He said, "Never know when to stop, do you, MacGowen?"

"It's all over now." I gripped Mike's arm. Holding him was the only way I felt strong enough to face Marovich. Later, I knew there would have to be tears, when realization replaced adrenaline. When it happened, I didn't want Marovich to see it. I made myself smile at him. "Be interesting to see your polls after this news gets out."

The district attorney's handlers began moving him forward again. I didn't want to get within striking range—either his or mine—so I broke from my handlers and ducked out of the hallway, headed up a flight of stairs that opened on the left. At the top of the stairs I saw the door to the female officers' locker room. I went in.

The floor of the locker room was cluttered with big, blue equipment duffels overflowing with body armor, batons, helmets, riot-size sacks of plastic wrist restraints marked with the owner's badge number; ready for the riot that wasn't going to come, this time. I grabbed a handful of rough paper towels, went over to the rank of sinks, pushed aside the baskets of hair dryers, curling irons, gels, mousses, sprays, and wet the towels.

My only plan had been to spend some time alone while I calmed down. I scraped off the remains of the paraffin that had been used to lift gunshot residue from my left hand for evidence. Then I pressed the damp towels to my face.

Something happened to me after I saw what I had washed from my face, saw the front of my blue shirt in the stark fluorescent light; pale pink stain, spots of dark brown.

The detectives kept asking about peripheral details, who, where, how. No one had given me time to think about the actual shooting, to talk about what I *saw*. It was all over so fast. From memory, I played it back more slowly.

The bullet exploded Roddy's throat, destroyed it, shot flesh and blood and bits of bone spraying into the night like many-colored confetti. I had felt his debris, cold, sharp needles on my face, and the sting of gunpowder tattooing my hand, was deafened by the sound, dazzled by the streak of blue-green light.

I was on the wooden bench between the lockers, sobbing into the crook of my elbow, when I felt arms around me. My head was gently pressed against a firm, uniformed bosom that smelled of perfume.

"You want to talk about it?" she asked, patting my back.

"No," I gasped.

"First kill?"

I nodded, snagging my hair in her badge.

"It's rough. I shot a man during my rookie year, left him a paraplegic. It was his fault—brandishing a loaded firearm—I had to stop him. Still . . ." She kept patting. "Heard you took him clean. Left-handed."

I snuffled, used my arm in lieu of handkerchief.

"You a lefty?"

I said, "No." I admit a tinge of something verging on pride had crept in.

"I brought in your woman passenger," she said. I straightened up so I could read her badge, D. Rukowski. "Know what we found in her bag?"

I said, "Besides chewing gum?"

"Chloroform. She had a Baggie with a saturated wad of cotton. Best guess is, she was supposed to sing you a lullaby so there wouldn't be a struggle when O'Leary took you out. Wouldn't work, though, if the bag was in the backseat."

"I threw it in back." I managed to get to my feet, got some new towels to wipe my face. "The way she was fussing with her purse, I thought she had a tape recorder in there. Or a hypodermic. They used drugs once before."

Officer Rukowski squared my shoulders, brushed my damp hair from my forehead. "You played it smart, honey. Old Flint's out there wearing a groove in the floor, pissing and moaning, saying how lucky you were. You tell him luck had nothing to do with it."

Mike was going to say a lot more than how lucky I was. A lot more. Just thinking about the barrage to come wore me out. I sagged back down. "I can't face him."

"Sure you can." She stood and reached for my arm. "Go fix your face."

I pulled myself together the best I could, borrowing a comb and some blush from the collection on the counter. Then I unbuttoned a couple of buttons to show a little cleavage—emergency ammo—and walked out.

"All set?" Mike took my hand, the one that had killed Roddy O'Leary, and folded it in his. He didn't say another word about it all the way home.

It was after three when we got home. Michael and Guido were playing chess at the dining room table.

Guido said, "Maggie?" in a tentative way, rising from his chair.

"Everything's under control," I said, leaning against Mike. Michael came over and kissed my cheek, squeezed my free hand, and made the tears start all over again.

"I know you feel awful," Mike said. "You're going to feel awful for a while. Go ahead and cry."

"I never imagined it would feel so bad."

Mike took over where Officer Rukowski left off, patted my back. "If it makes you feel any better, you probably saved Jennifer's life. O'Leary wasn't about to leave a witness, even if she was in on it."

"I know. He was aiming at her when I shot him."

Mike said, "Oh?"

"If I hadn't been armed, he would have hit us both, her first, then me." That's just about the point where anger began to dispel shock. "For what? To protect the election scenario? To add a plum to Roddy's résumé?"

"To save his butt," Mike said. "He'd already killed two people and you were closing in on him. Hector ran his DMV and his credit cards."

"So?"

"Last Tuesday he rented a dark-blue four-wheel drive that looked a whole lot like mine. Turned it in early Wednesday."

"Ah," Guido chirped, connection made. "Tuesday night, that flower of the evening said the guy who shot Hanna was driving a car like Mike's."

I looked up at Mike, started to laugh. "Roddy blew it on deep background all over the map. But, damn, the idiot should have known who he was messing with, when he tried to set you up, cupcake."

"Yeah." Mike winked at me. "Don't mess with the big boys."

"I wasn't talking about you."

He nudged me, started to laugh, too.

Michael had the family furrow between his brows. "Dad, you know, this is the first time I ever heard you talk about what you do at work."

Mike flushed a furious red. "I'm sorry, son."

"Sorry for what? It's more interesting than I thought. I sort of imagined you drove around giving people tickets. You're a strange guy. I like it."

"Oh, Jeez."

"I was thinking of going into teaching, but . . ."

"I don't want to hear it," Mike said.

"Teaching, police work," I said, "they're pretty much the same thing. People shooting at you all the time."

Michael asked, "How do you get into the academy?"

CHAPTER
32

My mother called at nine o'clock on Monday morning—nine o'clock Boston time. She and my father were there on vacation and had seen my name in a wire service item that ran in the local papers, "Filmmaker Slays Attacker."

"Should we be hysterical?" she asked.

"No," I said. "Whatever you read, it's a lie."

She chuckled. "I read that you were a renowned and gifted filmmaker who shot a carjacker."

"Thirty-three and one-third percent a lie, anyway. You can decide for yourself which third of that you want to throw out."

She grew serious. "Are you all right, Margot?"

"Shaken, but untouched."

"Your father, feeling nostalgic, wonders, do you need bail money?"

"Not this time, Mom," I said. "Just bring me home some lobsters."

After speaking with my dad and repeating virtually everything I had said to Mom, I went outside to fetch our morning *Times* to see whether they had something to say.

I had made the first page of the Metro section, just a short piece with very few details, not even the names of the victim and my passenger. The paper had gone to bed before there were many details to learn. It would be different later. I would see to it.

Before word got out, before all her friends heard about it, I had to talk to Casey and explain what had happened the night before.

There was a period after her father and I separated when Casey was morbidly afraid for me all the time, worried that something would happen that would take me away from her. For two weeks, I had hardly been able to leave the house. After a reasonable time she overcame her fear, but with reservations I had to be careful to respect.

It was nearly time for her to get up, anyway. I went in and sat on the end of her bed with Bowser and talked it out with her. She was at once dubious, and frightened, and sympathetic. When we had gotten to the end, she made a half-hearted attempt to feign illness and stay home—the old pattern—but gave it up when she remembered she wanted to ask Mischa whether her friends could come to classes with her on Friday. When she left with Michael, she seemed fine.

Detective Valenti picked me up at eight and took me in for more questioning. I would have preferred to drive myself, but my car had been impounded as evidence. Valenti's attitude toward me had softened considerably overnight. I thought someone must have gotten to him, filled him in. And I thought that someone was Hector.

Mike had been told by his lieutenant to stay away, so *in loco amantis*, Hector was there. During all of the questioning he worked at his desk no more than six feet away from us.

Valenti and I made sketches, went over the crime scene photographs, talked about the minutiae. He asked a lot of questions about my "relationship" with Roddy O'Leary that I found irksome. Overall, it wasn't bad.

We had our heads together over a city map while I retraced the route I had taken from Parker Center, when I heard a door open and then a familiar voice. I got up and went across the big bullpen, following the voice. Hector followed close behind me.

A detective in shirt-sleeves was carrying two cups of coffee into a small interrogation room that was tucked into a dogleg in a back corner. He handed one of the cups to Jennifer Miller.

"Good morning, counselor," I said, leaning against the doorframe.

Jennifer wasn't particularly happy to see me, but she didn't duck, either. She was wearing one of her perky suits and her hair and makeup were freshly done. That is, she hadn't spent the night in jail.

"How are you this morning?" she asked.

"I haven't decided."

Hector put a gentle hand on my arm and drew me back. "Valenti needs you," he said, making a lot of eye contact. Trusting Hector, I acceded. On my way out, I said to Jennifer, "Let's do lunch."

"Not today," she said, sitting with the posture of the victor waiting for his laurel wreath. "Remember? I have a *habeas* hearing scheduled at two."

Before the door closed again, Hector was inside with Jennifer.

I went back to Valenti with a white rage rising. "What is she doing here?"

"Same as you," Valenti said. "She's your witness."

"Only by miscalculation. She tried to get me killed. Why wasn't she held?"

He was shaking his head while I ranted, waiting for me to wind down. "I'll tell it to you as she told it to us. She asked you to pick her up at Parker Center, take her to an address on Hudson Street in the city. When you stopped at the address to let her out, a man approached the car and opened the driver's side door. You raised a weapon and shot him. Mrs. Miller did not know you were armed, she did not see his weapon. The name of the victim was familiar to her only because she has followed election coverage. Mrs. Miller says she has no memory of ever meeting Roddy O'Leary."

He crossed his arms over his chest and leaned back in his chair, as in, end of story.

I cleared my throat and leaned nearer to him. "A couple of things. Why did she want to go to Hudson Street if she lives in San Pedro? And, what was she going to do with the chloroform in her purse?"

"What do you think?"

"I think she lured me to a dark area, planned to gas me so I wouldn't make a fuss when her colleague blew me away."

He was shaking his head again. "She didn't want to go home to an empty house, so she directed you to her parents' place. And, there's nothing illegal about carrying chloroform in that quantity—bug collectors do it all the time. She says her son has a sick hamster. She was going to euthanase it."

"You checked this out?"

"Mom and Dad have her graduation picture on the piano. The kid has a hamster, but whether it's sick or not . . ." He shrugged. "And another thing. She says you had previously mentioned to her that an employee of the victim, election staffer named George Schwartz, had been stalking you. She said you had taken pictures of him on several occasions to document the fact. She said you even had him arrested once."

Jennifer was good. Her vulnerability crap just kept sucking me right in.

Valenti was studying me with a devilish light in his eyes, a crooked smile growing from the tough-cop sneer. "How long you known Flint?"

"A while."

"I worked a couple cases with him here and there. He's a good guy. Great sense of humor."

I didn't say anything. Everyone has a Mike story, it was Valenti's turn to tell one. They're funny stories, but I wasn't in the mood to be jollied.

Valenti was grinning wide now. "Outside of me, he's probably the best detective in the city. You know why? Because he can read a person like the label on a pack of weenies. You can't hide any of your shit from Flint, 'cause you've got everything he needs to know right there on your wrapper. It's a gift. Sometimes it takes the rest of us a little while to catch up to him. You know what he always says? 'Who you gonna believe?' "

"I know, 'Me, or your own lying eyes?' So, who are you going to believe?"

Still studying me carefully, he said, "It's a gift, the way Mike can read a person."

I reminded him I needed my car, so he made some calls and got it released. He drove me over to the crime lab garage just east of the civic center and waited to make sure there were no glitches.

Because I was in the building, I paid a visit to my old friend Sharon Yamasaki, a senior investigator with the coroner's office. I wanted to know what progress had been made identifying the body found in the remains of Kelsey's trailer, anything that had been discovered about the fire itself.

Sharon seemed genuinely happy to see me. Most of her work involves moving official documents from one side of her desk to the other, so I offered her a potentially interesting diversion. She put aside her heavy case load to go hunting for me. I was in her office, halfway through a cup of coffee, when she came in with a couple of files.

"Everything is preliminary," she said. "There's no positive I.D. yet, but there is a profile. The deceased was male, early to late fifties, probably Caucasian, five feet nine to six feet tall, slender build. So far, there are no inconsistencies with the dental records of Detective Jerry Kelsey. Considering the condition of the remains, we may get no closer than that."

It wasn't really news, but I felt a jolt of something akin to pain. What made me sad was the notion that there probably was no one close enough to Kelsey to arrange a proper funeral.

Sharon sorted through a stack of forms. "The medical examiner was looking for some indication of state of mind, weighing the possibility of suicide over murder. The arson people put that notion aside.

"The prelim arson report indicates the fire's point of origin was directly under the living room portion of Kelsey's trailer. One end of an ordinary garden hose was placed into the gasoline storage tank situated in the yard, the other end of the hose was placed under the trailer, a distance of fifty-three feet. A lit votive candle was placed under the trailer a few feet from the end of the hose. Once the arsonist had begun the siphon effect of the gasoline at the tank end, he had the time it took for the gas to run through the hose and reach the candle at the other end to get the hell away. Then, to use the technical language, kaboom."

Elegant, yet simple. Anyone who had seen the layout of that equipment yard could have planned it.

I rose. "Thank you."

Sharon got up with me, walked with me toward the elevators. "I understand we have another acquaintance of yours in residence at the morgue."

"Word gets around," I said.

"It does when the brass takes special interest." She held the elevator door open. "The D.A. was on the horn first thing this morning. Wants a twenty-four hour lid put on public statements coming from the crime lab. Idiot forgets we're civil service. I personally know three people who called the *Times* to make sure they knew exactly what he wanted a lid put on."

I invited Sharon and her husband to the housewarming on Saturday and went back down to the garage. Just in case anyone changed his mind about releasing my car, I took it out of the lab garage and reparked it in the lot under the civic center mall.

The Conklin hearing was scheduled for two, giving me maybe an hour and a half to kill. I took the stairs up to the street level and caught a Dash bus to Chinatown, walked around the neighborhood.

I first met Mike Flint in Chinatown.

Ever since the night before, when I watched Roddy O'Leary make his explosive bounce across the pavement, it worried me that thoughts of death had taken up very assertive residence at the front of my mind. I couldn't shake an unfamiliar sense of melancholy, a distressing preoccupation.

I'm sure that feeling of doom was why I ended up where my story with Mike had begun, because of all that I hold precious, Mike is in the top two. I stood for a while next to a six-foot plaster Buddha on Hill Street, watched the tourists and the locals go about their shopping, moving at two speeds: tourist stroll versus Chinese housewife sprint. I just stood still like the plaster Buddha, thinking things over. When I decided it was time to walk on, I felt much better.

The Dash dropped me right in front of the courthouse twenty minutes before the scheduled two o'clock hearing.

The hall outside the appointed courtroom was dotted by clusters of media teams and their captives; it was like homecoming. Mrs. Rhodes and Etta had their heads together with Ralph Faust. LaShonda and James Shabazz huddled with Jack Riley's news team. Beth Johnson and a tall young man I guessed was Wyatt, Jr. stood with a third video crew. Leroy Burgess had two cameramen all to himself.

I ducked at least a dozen microphones that were thrust into my face, and made it, frazzled but intact, into the courtroom.

Mike was there, in suit and tie, sitting in the back row with Hector. When they saw me, they did some negotiating with their neighbors to clear a seat for me between them.

I slid my hand under Mike's elbow. "Are you allowed to be here?"

"I don't give a fuck."

"Boy, and I thought I was having a bad day."

He squeezed my hand. "Are you?"

"Yes."

"That's two of us."

The defense entered the court, Jennifer Miller in the same suit she had been wearing earlier that morning, a bit wrinkled in the lap, makeup faded, hair in need of a comb. I glanced up at Hector. "Did you at least give her enough time to go to the bathroom before she had to be here?"

All innocence, he said, "Guess I forgot."

The district attorney came in and took a seat behind the defense table. After him came the media crowd from the hall, stumbling around the news pool's camera emplacement in the middle of the aisle to get to the last available seats. I did not see Leroy Burgess come into the room.

Finally, Charles Conklin was led in by the bailiff.

Though I had seen his old booking pictures many times, I would never have recognized him on the street. Conklin was prison-yard buff, huge arms and shoulders, and tiny, undeveloped legs. He seemed uncomfortable in his new clothes. The sport coat fit tight, his slacks were too big in the waist and too long. His dress shirt was buttoned up to the neck, but someone had forgotten to get him a tie.

I thought that Conklin had a very strong sense of his star status. He waved to the crowd, preened for Jennifer, gave Marovich a complicated two-handed handshake.

The judge, a distinguished-looking senior, came in from chambers carrying a thick notebook identical to the one in front of Jennifer. After the bailiff announced the opening of the session, the judge asked Jennifer to state her case.

"From the beginning," she said in a sweet, cultured voice, reading from notes placed on a lectern, "the police investigators grossly manipulated the case against Charles Pinkerton Conklin. They threatened the children who witnessed the killing of Officer Johnson, forced them to identify my client. They withheld evidence from the defense. They made a mockery of the system of justice they swore to uphold."

She went over the case witness by witness, reading into the record the new affidavit signed by Hanna, but saying only,

"Your Honor, the second child witness also signed a revision of her original testimony."

I looked around for LaShonda, saw her shake her head and whisper to her neighbor, James Shabazz. What Jennifer had said was true in its words, but not in its intent. And so she went, point by point through the case, skating the edge of truth.

With every point, Mike grew angrier. When his name was brought into the proceedings, Hector reached behind me to grip Mike's shoulder. Mike set his jaw, gripped my hand so hard it throbbed.

The district attorney was called to give his expert analysis. I swear he was staring at me during his testimony describing a flawed investigation and a flawed prosecution. He laid the heaviest blame on the police, neglecting to mention that he had been part of the original prosecution team. *Mea culpa* for believing the police, was how I read him.

There was no opportunity for rebuttal. The police were not called. Mike was not asked to explain his procedures, or to answer the charges placed against him.

LaShonda, the surviving witness, wasn't even mentioned by name.

No one said anything about the man who had been killed. I imagined Marovich explaining that *lacuna*, "The loss of a man's life was not germane to the issues here."

The testimony lasted barely an hour before Jennifer, in tones that were almost weepy, closed. "Your Honor, Charles Conklin is an innocent man. He was an innocent man fourteen years ago when he was sentenced to life in prison because of a deeply flawed trial. We ask the court at this time to grant our writ of *habeas corpus* and release this man from custody."

Jennifer sat down and the judge took out his own set of notes. The entire hearing had been only a formality, because he obviously had his decision prepared in advance.

After scolding the police for their misbehavior, the judge faced Conklin.

Conklin was scared. He had sweated through his new coat. He shook, he dabbed at his eyes with a large handkerchief. He did not face the judge, did not look over at Jennifer.

"Mr. Conklin," the judge said, "on behalf of the state of California, I apologize to you for the gross injustice that has been done. No legal cause exists for your continued imprisonment. Your writ of *habeas corpus* is granted. The defendant is ordered released directly from this courtroom. You are a free man."

I got up with Mike and slipped out the back door. Jack Riley ran out after us, dragging a cameraman with him.

"Detective Flint, will you give us a statement?"

"Damn right," Mike said. I was afraid he was winding up to deliver a scorcher that might embarrass him later, but his statement was both brief and controlled.

"I stand by my original investigation. I absolutely believe that he's guilty. All this hearing did was throw out the first verdict on a technicality, it didn't declare Conklin to be innocent. Far from it. There is no statute of limitations on murder. The man should be retried. That is the proper procedure in a case of procedural error."

Mike walked away toward the elevator as the courtroom began to spill into the hall, every significant player trailing a camera crew. As the din rose, Jack pulled me closer.

"Listen, Annie Oakley," he said, "Lana wants to do a special about last night's shooting. But not here. Meet me at the studio before five."

"I'll try."

The D.A. walked by, distracted Jack. "Gotta go," he said.

This time, I grabbed him. "Innocent man freed is a tempting story, but don't get suckered into it. Go over and talk to LaShonda about the contents of her affidavit. She'll help you see what's screwy."

From Jack's reaction, I must have been babbling. "Maggie, you had your say last Friday. This is Monday. Conklin is Monday's story."

"Whore," I said.

"Ratings," he said.

He trotted off to join the mob swarming around Jennifer and Conklin. As I walked away, I heard Jack's distinctive voice, "Congratulations, Mr. Conklin. How does it feel to be a free man?"

CHAPTER
33

Los Angeles (WP).

Police investigating the shocking, violent death of Roderick J. O'Leary, director of the re-election campaign for District Attorney Baron Marovich, late Sunday night in the exclusive Hancock Park section of the city, have uncovered evidence that suggests the shooting may have been a tragic accident.

Documentary filmmaker Maggie MacGowen, who fired the fatal shot, may have been startled by O'Leary, who was known to her, and mistaken him for a stalker. Police records show that during the past week MacGowen had complained that a man identified as George Schwartz had been stalking and harassing her. On several occasions she photographed Schwartz in her proximity, hoping to discourage him. After a minor collision, when Schwartz rear-ended her vehicle, MacGowen had him arrested by South Pasadena police.

Police arrest records identify Schwartz as a county worker currently on personal-necessity leave for undisclosed reasons. He was described by co-workers as a quiet man who lives alone. Schwartz was not available for comment.

According to sources, MacGowen was driving a friend to her home on Hudson Street near the Wilshire Country Club late Sunday night. A witness reported that O'Leary, who was armed, opened the door of MacGowen's parked car, perhaps frightening her. MacGowen drew her own weapon and shot

O'Leary, fatally wounding him. O'Leary died at the scene be-
fore paramedics arrived. No charges have been filed.

In recent years, there has been an increase in the number
of violent attacks on celebrities by obsessed fans. It is not
known when Schwartz first became interested in MacGowen,
or whether they were acquainted. Through a spokesman,
MacGowen said only, "It would not be appropriate at this
time for me to comment."

There was more, most of it looked to be a recap of Roddy's
career in politics, but I didn't bother to read it. I threw the paper into the nearest trashcan. Then I went right back and retrieved it. The outline of the article had a familiar ring. For
damn sure, no one from any news medium had contacted me
about the shooting. And Marovich got scant mention.

A black stretch limo swept away from the curb in front of
the courthouse, carrying Conklin and his defense team to a victory party at the Biltmore Hotel. It was half-past four, coming
up on happy hour, I thought. I also thought I wanted to see just
how happy people were going to be at the Biltmore party.

The hotel was only five blocks from the courts, straight
down Grand Avenue. I walked it. It was rush hour. Traffic was
so heavy I had to do a little window shopping now and then to
keep from beating the limo to the hotel.

Inside the hotel, I followed a train of news people up the
massive central stairs to the ballroom. My party invitation was
the camera I took from my bag and an extension cord I had
picked up off the floor.

In the ballroom, there were more news people than civilian
guests. But then, I wondered—and not without some
bitterness—how many friends would a man have when he'd
been in jail as long as Conklin? And when his offspring were
themselves in jail, well, who was left to help you celebrate except his Dr. Frankenstein and the news whores? Me among
them.

There was a sumptuous buffet set up along one side. My always ravenous colleagues had queued up for mini soft tacos
and sizzling fajitas. Thirsty after my walk, I bypassed the food
and headed for the bar.

James Shabazz and Etta were there. James, carrying a fruit
kabob in one hand and a soda water in the other, kept me com-

pany while I waited in line. "I'm surprised to see you here, Miss MacGowen."

"I hate to miss a party. This looks like a good one."

"The man has something to celebrate."

"Indeed." I ordered a scotch on the rocks, changed my mind and had a glass of wine. "You know Pinkie better probably than anyone here. How long do you think he can stay out of the slam this time?"

"How long?" James gazed across the room to where Conklin was holding forth in front of a rank of cameras. The innocent man had an arm around Jennifer's slim waist. She was smiling, making a show of listening to him, but her body language betrayed her revulsion. "How long depends on how closely they watch over him. My estimate is, they'll keep him clean long enough to get through his suit against the police department. After that? He'll stay clean until his money is gone."

"He's friendly with you?"

"Seems to be."

"How would you feel about setting up an interview for me?"

"For what purpose?"

"The film. I've taped his son and mother-in-law, about half his neighborhood, it seems. I think he deserves equal time."

James studied me for an uncomfortable moment before he decided. He raised his soda water to me. "I'll see what I can do."

Baron Marovich came in without entourage. Almost by stealth, he walked up to Conklin, shook his hand, mugged with him for the cameras for less than a minute. I watched him bow his head to whisper something to Jennifer, I saw her blanch. She recovered her poise quickly when someone called her name, turned her attention again to the barrage of questions.

"Will Mr. Conklin file suit against the city? Where does he plan to live? What is the first thing he plans to do as a free man?"

The way Conklin kept eyeing Jennifer, I thought the answer to that last question was damned obvious.

With no more fuss than the waiters who moved through the crowd clearing away dirty dishes, Marovich cleared himself away through the service doors.

I gulped my drink, gave James's arm a squeeze, and slipped out the same way.

I caught up with Marovich waiting for the freight elevator in a back hallway. When he saw me, he laughed in a sad, resigned sort of way. The hair was still perfect, but he looked exhausted, pale eyes nearly transparent, deep dark circles below them.

"You," he said. "Everywhere I look—you."

"I hoped we could talk."

"I need a drink," he sighed. "What do you say?"

"Fine, as long as it's in a public place and we drink out of the same bottle."

Like Jennifer, he blanched. "I had nothing to do with doping Guido Patrini. I know you'll have some difficulty believing me at this point, but I had nothing to do with the Kelsey situation."

"Situation?" I asked.

"Drinks first," he said.

We went down to the elegant lobby bar.

While the waiter waited, Marovich asked me, "Do you like champagne?"

"For celebrations."

"Then, it's champagne."

I said, "You can't expect me to celebrate what just happened in court."

"No," he said. "This is my very own party."

We had icy Dom Perignon in crystal flutes, and tiny canapes. The background music was vintage Ray Charles. The setting was perfect for an auspicious occasion. And clearly, this was an occasion. I just didn't know what it was about. Marovich watched the bubbles rise in his glass and then he tipped its rim to mine.

"What are we celebrating?" I asked.

"The end."

"But it isn't over. Lawsuit, book deal, movie rights—it's just beginning."

"Not for me." He pulled a folded sheet from his inside pocket and handed it to me. "My office issued this statement at five o'clock this afternoon."

My watch said ten after.

The single sheet was heavy bond, the district attorney's letterhead. Over Marovich's signature, I read, "I have worked for the city and county of Los Angeles for the last eighteen years, fortunate all that time to be able to perform work that I love.

So it is with some sadness, but no regret, that I announce my decision to withdraw from the race for district attorney.

"I do not have the heart to wage the brutal, personal, negative campaign that it would be necessary to wage to prevail over my opponent. I have closed my campaign offices and ordered my staff to immediately cease all campaign activities.

"At this time, it is my intention to retire from public office to spend more time with my family. I wish Godspeed to my opponent."

No mention of the untimely demise of Roddy O'Leary in the announcement. I asked, "Why?"

"You just read why."

I handed back his bombshell. "I also read today that I've been pursued by a deranged stalker, so don't push any more fiction on me. What happened? You have a talk with Jesus?"

"I had a meeting all right. But it wasn't with Jesus." He flicked the caviar garnish off a canape before he ate it. "Campaign staff pow-wow. I can't win. It's as simple as that."

"You still have five weeks to pull off a miracle."

"I'm out of the miracle business." Marovich finished off his glass in a long swallow, moved forward in a chummy posture. "I had nothing to do with what happened last night, Maggie. I fired Roddy yesterday."

I said, "Uh huh," as in, liar.

"I did. Hardest scene I ever went through. 'Everything I've done for you,' he says. 'Conklin will pull up the polls,' he says, 'get the momentum going again.' Couldn't take it anymore. I fired his ass."

"About time," I said, and refilled Marovich's glass for him.

"Had to do it." A black, sardonic laugh. "He was going to be indicted, anyway. I knew you wouldn't leave him alone until you had him up for murder. I cut my losses."

"Better hope you did it in time. Why are you talking to me, anyway? Aren't you afraid how I might use what you say?"

Suddenly he looked old rather than exhausted, his star luster fading. When he spoke, there was sad resignation in his voice.

"No one's listening, Miss MacGowen," he said. "I'm history as of five o'clock. I'll get a few gasps over the news, but by tomorrow, after the follow-up, in-depth a.m. edition bullshit, I'll become invisible. No one will care about anything I did. By day after tomorrow, ninety percent of the people who wept for Conklin on the news tonight won't even recognize his name. You know how it works."

"Three people are dead."

Eyes evasive, he said, "Roddy ran amok."

"He's dead, so he's taking the whole rap?" I felt sick.

"Police have found evidence linking him to two killings, Hanna Rhodes and Jerry Kelsey."

"We all know about the immutability of evidence, though, don't we?" I meant to be sarcastic, but there was a catch in my throat that made it sound bitter, injured. "For a long time, I tried to figure out why, in the middle of the political fight of your life, you would resurrect an old case that was such a potential bomb. Finally, it came to me."

"Drink up," he said.

"Remember the story about the peasant's daughter who had to spin straw into gold or the king would kill her, kill her father, too?"

"What?" Off guard and wary.

"That's what happened to you, isn't it? You had to turn a disaster into political gold, or die."

"You're telling me a fairy story?"

"There are great moral lessons in those stories. That's why we read them to our kids, you know." I filled his glass again. "So, this peasant girl lies and cheats, trades her firstborn to get some elf to do the actual work for her and save her neck. Then, as her reward, the king marries her. The reward for the elf? She gets him killed."

"What's the moral? Cheaters prosper?"

"Hell no. She made her bed, she had to lie in it ever after—I'm not sure about the happily part. Every night, she had to fuck this greedy king who had held a death sentence over her." I smiled up at Marovich then. "I think she got her punishment, don't you? She couldn't divorce the king. You can't divorce this mess by resigning from the race or putting everything on Roddy's ticket."

Reaching for his wallet, Marovich motioned the waiter for the check. "I need to get home. My wife will be worried."

There was a light drizzle falling on the street outside. The air had turned suddenly chilly. Marovich pulled his coat collar higher, rubbed his hands together. "The heat's gone. We always get a little rain after the Santa Anas."

We were walking back up Grand toward the courthouse parking garage. The sidewalk was still crowded. People caught by the sudden change in the weather covered their heads with whatever was available: briefcases, newspapers, jackets. I thought the rain felt wonderful; I was light-headed from the wine.

While we waited at a corner for the walk light, I asked Marovich, "What are your plans?"

"I don't have any."

The light changed and he took my arm as we started across the street, a genteel habit I thought.

"Miss MacGowen," he said, then he started over. "Maggie, I know where your loyalties lie. I know you don't care much for me. But you have to believe me when I say this one more time: My motives were sincere. The conviction of Charles Conklin was flawed. All I ever wanted to do in a quiet, legal way, was to get the conviction set aside, to have a rehearing. To salve my conscience."

"Quiet for you is calling a press conference?"

"I didn't call the press. Burgess did. Then Roddy tried to run herd over anything that came out. Like you say, spinning shit into gold."

"I have never seen your name in any of the Conklin case files. Why was Conklin's conviction on your conscience?"

"The snitch." He still had his hand through my elbow. "Flint and Kelsey's case hinged on the word of a snitch. Flint got good information from him, solid stuff he needed to put together a case."

"So?"

"So, the snitch was a plant. Kelsey knew how the shooting went down, but he couldn't get anyone to talk to him. He gave the snitch a few of the essential details, paid him off with a little help during his sentencing. It happened all the time in the old days."

"Where did you come in?"

"Kelsey helped me out with the same snitch on two other cases. One of them turned out to be a bad conviction. The guy died in prison before I could fix things."

"When?"

He shrugged. "Couple of years ago."

"I thought we agreed, no more fiction."

"Am I lying?" Offended.

"You're fudging. When I used to go to confession, the priest never let me blame my friends for my sins. You've laid blame on everyone but yourself. Isn't it time for you to take your own rap?"

"I quit. Isn't that enough?"

"Not for Hanna Rhodes, or Jerry Kelsey, or Roddy O'Leary. Not for Mike, either. Save yourself, come clean."

His sigh was not a denial. The drizzle turned into showers, eroding the perfect contours of his hair, wilting his shirt. I was thinking about the load he had been carrying, thinking what a pathetic pud he was to believe he could have pulled it off, when he gripped my arm more firmly.

"You're tough. But I feel better talking to you. If you don't have plans, you want to get a bite somewhere?"

"Won't your wife be worried?"

"Yes, she's worried." He wiped rain from his eyes. "I called her, told her my decision to resign. She's worried I'm going to be underfoot for a while."

"I have to go home," I said, shivering now, soaked through. "My family is expecting me."

The garage ramp was slick, oil mixed with rain. I was concentrating on keeping my footing, but he was intent on me, studying me with such intensity that I grew uncomfortable. He seemed to be looking for some answer that maybe I was withholding from him.

I saw my car down an aisle to the left, almost by itself now that most workers had left for the day. Standing next to the attendant's booth, I pulled my arm from Marovich's grasp and, stepping away a few feet, offered him my hand.

"It's been interesting," I said. "Be careful on the road. No one down here remembers how to drive in the rain."

He smiled, took my hand, held it in a warm grip, reluctant to let go. "Don't think too badly of me. I only wanted the same thing your Mike wanted, just to get the bad guys off the street."

"I'll tell him," I said. "But don't expect a Christmas card."

CHAPTER
34

Jennifer's San Pedro house was a small restored bungalow, about halfway up a steep hill lined with similar restored bungalows. There was good art on the walls, expensive, deep rugs on the hardwood floors. The view of the Los Angeles harbor from her living room windows reminded me of the view from my San Francisco house, minus a couple of bridges.

I walked quickly through the front of the house, using only the light from the large bay windows to find my way around, and staying in the shadows.

I knew Jennifer hadn't been home for a few days, but the house had the sharp pine scent of recent cleaning—hired help. There were only two bedroom doors, ergo, no live-in, so I moved without worrying about the noise made when I stepped across the bare wood spaces between rugs.

Jennifer's son's room was orderly, smelled slightly of rodent piss. I could see the place on his desk, next to a bag of feed, where he kept his hamster when he was at home.

When I looked into the child's room, I felt for the first time like the thief in the night I was. While I would almost relish being caught and forced to explain why I had jimmied Jennifer's dining room window and climbed through, I had very different feelings about the boy learning that his space had been invaded by a stranger. Without going in further than the doorframe, I shut his door and crossed to the second bedroom.

Jennifer's room was larger than her son's and had a better

view of the harbor below. Everything was tidy, feminine in a business-like way.

Old houses never have enough closets. Jennifer had broken through a bathroom wall into some sort of back passageway, and converted that space into a walk-in closet. I went into the closet, shut the door, and turned on the light.

All of her clothes were arranged by function, length, and color, with work suits filling an entire side rack. She preferred two suit labels—both expensive—and wore a size four. Her shoes also were sorted by color and function: sports shoes, boots, flats, neat little pumps that coordinated with her neat little suits—all of the pumps from the same shoemaker.

I photographed the shoe rack, made a close-up of the color gap between black and gray, then took a shot of the rank of jacket sleeves. When I put my camera away in my bag, I tucked a pair of her pumps in beside it.

Jennifer had a desk in a corner of the dining room. There was no Rolodex, so I turned on her computer, found the tools file, and loaded her address book from the disk. She had none of the key players listed by name, which I found strange: Why wouldn't an attorney have the district attorney's office number in her files? I typed in the number for Marovich campaign headquarters and asked for a search. The tag came back: she had listed the number under pizza. I printed the file, made a back-up disk, and got the hell out.

A smooth caper; I was back in my car within five minutes from the time I had climbed through her window. As I turned off her street, a private patrol car turned in. The driver looked at me, but probably dismissed any thought of someone who did not fit the burglar profile in his training manual.

Down on Gaffey Street, outside a club, I stopped at a pay phone and called home again.

"I need to go by my office," I told Casey. "Tell Mike."

Up the Harbor Freeway hitting eighty, slowed on the Hollywood to seventy, over the Cahuenga Pass and into the Valley in thirty minutes, easy.

I dropped my film at an all-night, one-hour developer a block from my office, and tipped the clerk twenty bucks to deliver the prints to me on her break.

There were a lot of cars in the office lot and people walking around outside my building. Lighting was good. But I parked in

the fire zone next to the front door and asked the security
guard to escort me down the long hall to my office, to come inside with me and look around. When I was satisfied that everything was as it should be, I thanked him, bolted the door
behind him, and set to work.

Guido gave me some advice by phone before he hung up in
frustration and drove over. Mike arrived at about the same
time, with both of the kids. I put them all to work and re-
warded their diligence with not-very-burned microwave pop-
corn and canned soda.

It was fun. Everyone had a task. Michael and Casey began
repacking the tapes Casey had just finished filing, getting ready
for the movers again. Mike and Guido bent together over a
computer image manipulator. The only difficulty we encountered was agreeing on the music to play on the radio: Michael
wanted headbanger, Casey preferred the Russian classics that
sent Mischa into raptures, Mike held out for country, and
Guido wanted, as always, jazz. We compromised on reggae.

My assigned area was Jennifer. Guido had brought along a
fun new piece of equipment that made prints from videotape.
I ran through miles of fire videos that Jack had given me, isolated a shot of Ralph Faust: Ralph looking like Prince Charming weeping over Cinderella's tiny slipper—a size six, navy blue
pump on his palm.

I made a series, zooming in closer with each print, Ralph
holding the shoe with the fire as background, his hand with the
shoe, the shoe alone, the scuffed heel only.

I was still playing with variations when the pictures I had
taken in San Pedro were delivered. I sorted through them,
picked four, put them on the stack accumulating on the table
beside me. Onto the stack I added the pictures I had taken outside Kelsey's trailer, Jennifer stopping to dump gravel out of
her shoe. I played with the sequence, then I laid them all in a
line on the floor. At the end of the line, I arranged the stolen
shoes to match the angle of the first shot.

"Mike?" I said. "Where is that shoe I gave you at the fire?"

"Evidence locker somewhere. Why?"

"Can I have it?"

"Not a chance." He came to peer over my shoulder. "Jesus.
Good match. Where'd you go shopping?"

"Jennifer's closet."

Mike's face turned a dangerous red. "Just don't tell me about it."

"Not much to tell."

I asked Guido to make a tape of the prints. When he finished, I changed the angle of the shoes a few times, having him tape each alteration.

You walk a mile in your shoes and they begin molding to your feet, show where the toes and bunions are, bend over your instep in a particular way. The shoe on Ralph's hand, the shoe on Jennifer's foot, the shoes on my crappy office carpet all had the same characteristic big toe bump. Like a fingerprint.

I was editing the tape, fiddling with the sequence and form, when Mike summoned me. He had commandeered a tape player.

"See this?" Like a proud new father, he started the tape. He had taken the shot of Jennifer's coat sleeves hanging in her closet, superimposed it over her shoe rack, manipulated the scale using the computer, so that the black sleeves lined up with the black shoes, the gray sleeves with the gray shoes, the navy blue sleeves with empty space. Over the space, he had laid the image of the battered navy blue pump in Ralph's hand.

"I'm impressed," I said.

He shrugged. "I do this shit all the time. It's the way you put together any case. Except, I hang tight until I get a warrant so I can actually use what I find. Question is, what are you going to do with this foot thing when you're finished?"

"I'm going to blackmail Jennifer."

"Yeah, sure," he said. But from his tone I knew he wasn't at all sure I was kidding.

"I didn't have a warrant for this, either." I tossed him the tape I had made of my Biltmore conversation with Marovich. "Marovich spilling his guts. Can't use it in court, but it's interesting. He mentions you, big guy."

"Jeez," Mike muttered, but he slipped the little tape into his shirt pocket.

"I have a legal question for you," I said.

"A little late for that, isn't it?"

"Say you're a lawyer, defending a client."

"Never happen," he said, a reflex.

I punched his arm, almost gently. "Say you're a lawyer defending a client for crimes in which you participated."

The know-it-all sneered. "Jennifer was in grade school when Wyatt Johnson got shot."

"Wrong crime. Baron Marovich has retained Jennifer to defend him. He's facing a campaign fraud charge, according to the docs on Jennifer's desk. He has an appointment tomorrow with the U.S. attorney to discuss Roddy's crimes, and Jennifer is going with him."

"No shit?" Taken by surprise. I love it when I can drop one on him. "Really?"

"Really."

"Well, Baron will get one tight defense," Mike said. "If he goes down, he'll sure as hell take her with him."

"Poor Jennifer," I said. I handed him the print-out I had made at her house. "But we can bring her down without Baron. She's the lynchpin in all of this, the connection between Conklin and the D.A. and the preacher and the campaign. It's all one. I don't know whether Jennifer actually lit any fires, but she was there with the marshmallows when it happened."

Mike turned off the player. "What are you going to do with this shoe bomb?"

"Copy to Jennifer, copy to Hector, one for the Bar Association, put it in the *Big Film*. Guido and I have a beautiful one-hour package almost ready for Lana, lays out the chain of conspiracy from the shooting of Wyatt up to this afternoon. We still need to work on the hearing this afternoon and the resignation of Baron, but we're close. The network's legal people are going to have fits, but I think we're okay until we get to Jennifer at the fire's point of origin."

The cop came back to me, deep furrows between his white brows. "What are you going to say about Jennifer and the fire?"

I glanced at Guido before I answered, because we had argued this one out. "We'll run the lab reports on the shoe found at the scene, highlight where they say traces of gasoline and paraffin were present. If we were doing a dramatization, I would have an actress run across the gravel lot, take off her shoes because they got full of rocks, slowed her down. And she was in a hurry. When that fire started, to quote the expert, 'Kaboom.' She's lucky all she lost was a shoe."

"That's all wild supposition," he said.

"I don't think so. When she ran away from Kelsey's, she just kept right on running. Like a jackrabbit, found some cover. She had the weekend to think things through, to talk with the other players. By Sunday night, she was still shaken, but resolved to gut it out to the end. To shut me up."

The telephone rang. Guido answered, said, "She is," and handed the receiver to me. But I heard only a dead line.

"Who was it?" I asked.

"Man." He shrugged a shoulder. "Asked for you."

"How did he sound?"

"Nervous, maybe. How much can you get from, 'Is Maggie there?' "

We all went back to work. The call, or Mike's reaction to it, unsettled me. Mike didn't say anything, but he pulled out his shirttail and tucked it back in behind the automatic holstered at his side. After a while, maybe half an hour, Casey, stretching her back, asked, "Can I take Michael up and show him around the studio?"

Mike scowled, so I said, "Later. We'll all go up and see what's happening."

"I'm bored," she said, and yawned. She stretched out on the old sofa and turned on a TV sitcom.

It was about five minutes later that there was a knock on the door. Everyone froze, except Mike. He unholstered his gun.

"Who is it?" he asked through the closed door.

"Ben, security. Courier delivered a letter for Maggie."

Mike opened the door enough to make sure that it was Ben, then enough to accept the envelope. He said thanks, then shut and bolted the door again. He held the envelope to the light, smelled it, bent it a couple of times before he handed it over to me.

The return address on the envelope was the district attorney's office. My name was handwritten on the front, and the notation that it was personal. I took out a sheet similar to the one on which he had written his resignation.

Over my shoulder, Mike read the single line on the page. He asked, "Do you get it?"

"I think so. You better call someone to go check on Marovich. Some of the things he said earlier—this feels bad."

Casey said, "Mom?" in a quavering voice.

She was sitting bolt upright, her eyes wide as she pointed to the television screen. There was a news break interrupting her program.

"The condition of the district attorney has not been confirmed. Paramedics are still in his offices. Earlier reports that gunfire was involved in his injury also cannot be confirmed. Members of Mr. Marovich's staff have reported that the district attorney, who resigned from the re-election campaign only hours ago, was alone in his office when they heard what sounded like a single gunshot."

Mike took the note from me, the single, handwritten line over Marovich's signature: *"Mea culpa. Mea culpa. Mea maxima culpa."*

CHAPTER
35

The Saturday night housewarming smelled like a house fire—Mike was barbecuing range-fed chickens and air-lifted Louisiana catfish. It was a good thing the weather held so that we could entertain outside, not only because of the volume of smoke, but because it seemed that many of our guests felt comfortable about bringing guests of their own. I floated from group to group, catching pieces of conversation, collecting hugs, before I moved on. Doing the lady of the house thing.

Hector brought his wife. She was beautiful. As she clung to him, she kept an eye on me, but didn't seem overly concerned I would steal him away in the tradition of Mike's women. Etta brought Baby Boy, both of them looking radiant when they announced their engagement.

Guido showed up with LaShonda and several of his film students and promptly disappeared with them into my new workroom.

James Shabazz had filled his car with the boys who worked in his store, and invited Mrs. Rhodes to ride shotgun. I remembered James saying once that he detested Mike. But after he collected a soda water with a lime slice, he walked straight for the barbecue. I walked after him, carrying a beer for Mike as an excuse to be nearby in case things turned ugly. Mike looked up and recognized Shabazz—Mike knew I had invited him—but he made no effort to seem welcoming.

"Messing up some pretty nice fish, officer," James said, offering his hand to Mike.

"You never did see things quite straight, Shabazz." Mike put a spatula in the offered hand. "Think you can do better, be my guest."

"That's your own mess. I can't help you at this point." James traded the spatula for the long-handled basting brush and slathered more barbecue sauce on the chickens at the far end of the grill. "Not that I could ever help you."

"I don't recall needing your help," Mike countered.

"That's a matter of opinion, officer. Perhaps you failed to see there can be more than one way to approach a problem. For instance, trying to keep young people on the straight and narrow: You used your stick, I preferred the reason of Allah."

"Yeah?" I saw a smile lift the corner of Mike's mustache. "You have an armed crackhead climbing through your window at night, tell me who you're going to call to save your sorry ass, me or Allah?"

Shabazz laughed. "At that point, it might be a toss-up."

Mike was getting ready with his next line when Bart Conklin walked up. "You two still at it? Some things never change."

Bart Conklin introduced his kids to James and Mike and me, said it was like an old neighborhood reunion. When I moved on, the three of them were debating, with about equal energy, how to tell when a chicken is well-cooked and how to keep the current generation of youth from murdering itself into oblivion. No one seemed to be changing any minds, but it appeared they were enjoying sparring.

There was a full contingency of dancers. Mischa brought his lover, a costume designer. Casey had her weekend guests from San Francisco, Stacy and Lisa, and some new friends from school to keep her entertained. The dance crowd took over a back corner of the garden, and were certainly more ornamental in their flowered dresses than the fading summer roses.

Lyle, my former housemate, was happy in the kitchen, making sure platters stayed full, rearranging all my drawers and cupboards.

Oscar appointed himself bartender and beer sampler. He presided over the keg, growing more voluble as the evening progressed. I heard him go into at least three versions of a CHP raid on his old body shop.

I knew Michael had invited his mother. I didn't know how I felt about her coming until he showed up instead with the girl from his Asian lit class, with little Sly, and with a box of cookies from Leslie. Surprised me how relieved I was that she had not come. Sly walked with new assurance in new sneakers, smaller models of the ones Michael wore.

Besides Leslie, there were other significant no-shows. Beth Johnson felt her new husband would be uncomfortable around people involved in any way with Wyatt. Linda Westman had to work. Jack Riley was away on assignment. Charlene sent a carniverous-looking orchid plant and her regrets, though we had not invited her.

Our work crew brought assorted family and significant others and showed off their handiwork in endless guided tours across the freshly varnished floors, through the stacks of unpacked boxes and furniture still draped in shipping pads. From the backyard, I waved up at an ever-changing audience leaning over my bedroom balcony.

Early helpers had found what was needed to furnish the living room and had arranged sofas and tables for those who wanted to escape the Cajun-sauce-scented pollution coming from Mike's cuisine in progress.

There were contingencies that tended to stick together: Mike's co-workers and my colleagues, though some were acquainted, ghettoized themselves from the beginning; news people and police have a natural aversion for each other. I think it was Ralph Faust, egged on by Lana Howard, who first breached the invisible barrier by bringing up the shooting of Baron Marovich.

"What's the official story?" Ralph asked Mike's lieutenant.

"Misadventure," was the lieutenant's sarcastic answer. "D.A. said he was packing up his desk, forgot the gun was in there, didn't know it was loaded. When he picked the damn thing up, it went off. Accidentally."

"Do you buy that?" Ralph asked. He reached out and drew me in, wrapped his arm around me. Trapped me.

Before he gave his answer, the lieutenant, a thirty-year man, looked around at the circle of friends, all senior detectives who had surely heard every possible lame excuse. What he got back from them was cynical head scratching, scowls, world-weary shrugs, snickers, and guffaws.

Grinning at his men like a fond papa, the lieutenant answered Ralph, "Do I believe that piece-of-shit accident story? Fuck no. Old B.M. sees his campaign go down the toilet so he gives out his sad little resignation letter. 'I'm such a Boy Scout,' he says, 'I can't fight dirty no more.'

"Then he takes his squeeze down to the Biltmore bar and gets blasted on high-dollar champagne—people saw them together, packing away champagne and caviar. Maybe she turns him down, too, 'cause when she leaves him alone, he goes up to his office—he's juiced, he's depressed, and his wife already told him she didn't want no more of what he has to offer—he gets out his old twenty-two and tries to eat it. Hell, he can't even do that right."

"Maybe he changed his mind," I said. "Maybe he just wanted to find out if anyone loved him."

The lieutenant looked at me as if I had just farted or something. Ralph pulled me closer, whispered in my ear, "If I'd known how much you liked high-dollar champagne, I would have taken a couple of cases with us to El Salvador."

I said to him, "Do you still fuck chickens?" Then I moved on, thinking about how variable truth truly is. How many thousand people were standing in Dealy Plaza the day Kennedy was shot? How many of them can tell you, with provable, incontrovertible certainty, what happened? Forget about why.

What do we ever know, anyway? Except what we want to believe, based on what someone wants us to hear.

What was Wyatt Johnson up to the night he was shot? I didn't know. Someday, Charles Conklin might come clean, maybe for a good book or movie deal, or to make a deal the next time he's picked up. If he does, whether his intentions are good or bad I would never trust what he has to say. I would never *know*. Not knowing is always the hard part for me.

In my own mind, I was fairly certain that both Hanna Rhodes and Jerry Kelsey had been eliminated to keep them from floating their own versions of events at an inconvenient time: fouling up a high-dollar wrongful imprisonment suit, injecting too much truth into a political campaign, messing up evangelical profiteering, impeding a fast climb up the career ladder.

Cheap motives for such costly results. Three dead, one I had killed myself. The surviving players weren't walking away un-

marked. The self-inflicted crease in Marovich's broad brow was
only the beginning of his problems. Jennifer was going up before the Bar Association, and the police were trying to put together a conspiracy charge against her.

The county fired George Schwartz for taking a job when he
was out on disability. There was a fraud charge against him,
and a lien to recoup the disability payments.

Charles Pinkerton Conklin? The D.A. decided not to retry
him for shooting Wyatt Johnson; he had already served more
time than most murderers draw. I knew it was only a matter of
time until he tripped himself up again, went back inside. I re-
gretted that he couldn't be hung with a big sign like a cigarette
warning label: Association with this man may be hazardous to
your health.

Mike rang a gong to announce that he had done all the damage to the food that he intended to do. Lyle had arranged the
remains on large serving trays, disguised the worst of it with
sprigs of parsley and lilies made out of turnip slices and carrot
sticks, and set it all out on paper-covered plank tables.

When Mike walked away from the smoke, I went over to
him. His face ran with sweat and he reeked like a fireman after
a slaughterhouse fire. While our guests queued up to the long
serving table, I took Mike by the hand and led him into the
house and up the stairs, hugging the wall so that the upstairs
tourers could become downstairs diners.

"Sure, I'll take a shower," he said, fondling my butt through
my skirt, "if you'll get in with me."

"You know I want to, baby," I said, helping him off with his
apron and shirt. "But if I do, you know what would follow and
all those poor people would be stuck in the backyard till the
sun came up waiting to say good-bye to us. It could get really
ugly down there. Just this once, I think you better solo."

"Okay," he said, taking off his pants without help—though it
broke my heart—while I ran the water warm. When he handed
me his pants, my eyes were not on his outstretched palm, or on
the little gold box he offered me. "Something for you," he said.

"I need to get back to our guests," I said, and fled without
going within two feet of that little box. I had to stop in the bedroom to wipe my own streaming eyes, to get some air.

At that moment, I loved Mike so much that I could barely
contain my passion for him. All evening I had hardly been able

to keep from jumping him—apron, spatula, smoke, and all—right there in the middle of things. But that damned gold box chilled me. For the second time.

I powdered my nose and fluffed my hair, got another breath of barbecue-scented air, and ran down to the backyard.

Lyle set down a bowl of fruit salad and intercepted me as I walked across the patio. He led me by the hand into the kitchen and handed me a wet towel.

"Aren't you having fun?" he demanded.

"Of course. It's a great party, Lyle."

"Then what are you crying about?"

I draped myself on him and buried my face in his neck. "God, I miss you."

"Not that much, you don't. You two fighting?"

"No." I wiped my face again. "Mike's pushing this marriage thing."

"So?"

"So, I'm not ready."

"The new tenants like the house," he said. "I told them I would talk to you about a lease. What do you want me to say?"

I stood up straight, blew my nose into a paper napkin. "I'll lease it for two years, four months, three weeks."

"You have to face things, Maggie," he said. "Don't put it off too long."

"Maybe I exaggerated about how much I miss you." I walked outside again.

As soon as the sun went down, the air grew chilly. I thought about going upstairs for a sweater, but hesitated when I saw that Mike was not down yet.

Michael was filling a plate for Sly when he called my name. "Where's Dad?"

"Cleaning up."

I followed Michael's gaze up to the balcony. Mike was standing there, leaning on the railing, looking down at me. I helped Sly butter a roll, then excused myself.

Mike was waiting for me at the top of the stairs. I walked into his arms.

"I'm sorry," he said, his breath hot against my ear. "I was teasing. I didn't mean to upset you like that."

His chest heaved under my cheek. I opened the top two buttons of his fresh shirt, ran my hand inside along his smooth, hard chest.

"What's in the box this time?" I asked.

He laughed, an embarrassed little laugh. But he handed me the damn gold box again. I opened it, like before. Found a gold key inside, like before.

"I don't get it," I said.

"Back door key this time."

I wrapped my arms around him. I think it was letdown that I felt. The only reality I knew at that moment was how I felt about Mike Flint.

"We should go down," I said.

When Mike said, "Why?" and began working on the zipper of my skirt, I couldn't think of a single reason.